STORM

In coelo et clarissimum solem nigra nubes

Płacz serdeczny y mey życzliwosci.

Płacz serdeczny y mey życzliwosci.

In coelo et clarissimum solem nigra nubes

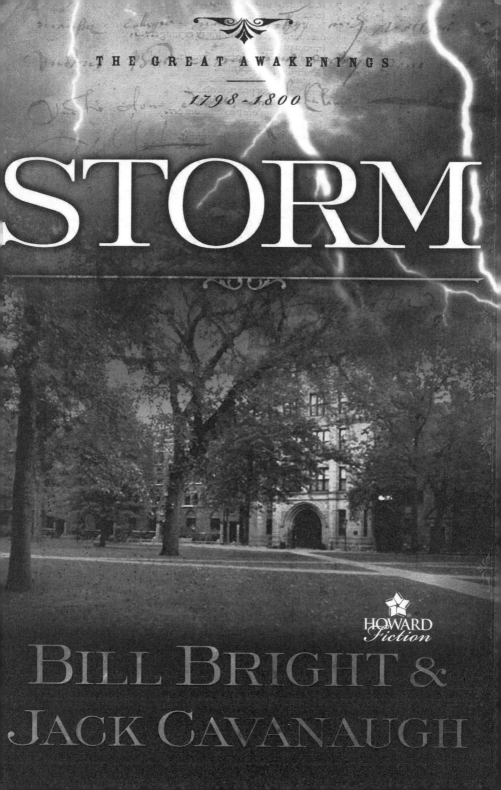

HOWARD
Fiction

THE GREAT AWAKENINGS
1798–1800

STORM

BILL BRIGHT &
JACK CAVANAUGH

Our purpose at Howard Publishing is to:

•*Increase faith* in the hearts of growing Christians

•*Inspire holiness* in the lives of believers

•*Instill hope* in the hearts of struggling people everywhere

Because He's coming again!

Storm © 2006 by Bright Media Foundation and Jack Cavanaugh
All rights reserved. Printed in the United States of America
Published by Howard Publishing Co., Inc.
3117 North Seventh Street, West Monroe, Louisiana 71291-2227
www.thegreatawakenings.org
www.howardpublishing.com

06 07 08 09 10 11 12 13 14 15   10 9 8 7 6 5 4 3 2 1

Edited by Ramona Cramer Tucker
Interior design by Tennille Paden
Cover design by Kirk DouPonce, www.DogEaredDesign.com

Library of Congress Cataloging-in-Publication Data
Bright, Bill.
  Storm / Bill Bright & Jack Cavanaugh.
    p. cm. — (The great awakenings, 1798-1800)
  ISBN 1-58229-493-3
    1. Yale College (1718-1887)—Fiction. 2. Secret societies—Fiction.
  I. Cavanaugh, Jack. II. Title.

PS3552.R4623S76 2006
813'.6—dc22
                                                          2005058940

DEDICATION

To Timothy Dwight, president of Yale College,

and all Christian educators, past and present,

who promote revival in the classroom.

egregius Vir Dominus Nicolas Cetner ...

... collegii ... ...

... ... et ... ...

... ...

... ...

Płyt ... y mey ... ...

In caelo et clarissimam solem nigra nubes par...

egregius Vir Dominus Nicolas Cetner ...

... collegii ... ...

... ... et ... ...

... ...

... ...

Płyt ... y mey ... ...

In caelo et clarissimam solem nigra nubes par...

FOREWORD
BY MRS. BILL BRIGHT (VONETTE)

In addition to our Lord Jesus Christ and his loving family, Bill Bright had two great passions in life: (1) helping to fulfill the Great Commission and (2) encouraging spiritual awakening and revival in America and in the world.

Bill fasted and prayed for many years that these two passions would see fulfillment. In each of his last nine years, he fasted for forty days, praying and yearning for the revival he believed to be coming.

The condition of the world and its need for repentance and faith in our Savior gripped his heart. He was burdened by the pervasive sin and people's hurts that he saw. Yet he believed in the power of fervent prayer and that God Himself does, indeed, long to send revival and grant mercy in response to the fervent pleadings of His people.

Beginning in 1994, Bill sponsored annual, nationwide fasting and prayer gatherings, bringing together thousands of Christian leaders and laypeople. In his 1995 book, *The Coming Revival*, Bill wrote, "I invite you to join me in praying that God will continue to use this fasting and prayer gathering as a spark to help set ablaze the Body of Christ in this most urgent and critical moment of history for our beloved nation and for the Church of our Lord Jesus Christ around the world." That would still be his plea today.

Bill promoted fasting and prayer for spiritual awakening and revival for many years. In fact, he immediately donated every dollar of the one-million-dollar prize he received with the 1996 Templeton Award in order to promote the movement worldwide. He once remarked that he was "the briefest millionaire in history."

With declining health due to pulmonary fibrosis, which finally took his life in 2003, and knowing that his time was short, Bill teamed up with Jack Cavanaugh to create a series of novels that would be set in American history during times of revival. He knew the books would probably not be published while he was alive.

These novels portray Christians "who were great believers, great hopers, great doers, and great sufferers," using his own words. Those attributes characterized his own life, and he recognized and admired the qualities in others.

Bill prayed every day that revival would sweep across our land, and I choose to believe he intercedes for our nation still. I like to think that his passion for America has not been diminished simply because he now resides in heaven.

It was Bill's fervent desire that this series of novels create a hunger for revival in the hearts of Americans; that the people would call out to God; and that God would hear their prayers and once again bless our great nation with a tremendous outpouring of His grace and power.

ACKNOWLEDGMENTS

Our heartfelt thanks go to—

Helmut Teichert, for recognizing our mutual passion for national revival and our belief in the power of fiction. If not for Helmut, this book would not have been written, for he brought us together.

Freelance editor Ramona Cramer Tucker, managing editor Philis Boultinghouse, and the other staff at Howard Publishing for their continual encouragement.

And Steve Laube, loyal friend and agent.

Iżali sie dziewek y mey życzliwości.

In cœlo et clarissimam solem nigra nubes par

Iżali sie dziewek y mey życzliwości.

In cœlo et clarissimam solem nigra nubes par

Agunt

PROLOGUE

"I smell revolution in the air."

A match flared. Light splashed on a face browned and weathered by a lifetime in the sun. The tobacco in the bowl of the man's pipe took hold of the flame and burned orange. Beside him a short, plump figure, little more than a silhouette in the night, took a pinch of snuff.

The two men, dressed for a formal dinner, stood beneath a strip of stars in a Philadelphia alley. Bright light and the sounds of a banquet spilled out a door left open a crack.

"What do you make of Minister Genet?" asked the shorter man. "He's an interesting individual, isn't he?"

"The man's got the pulse of the nation racing, that's for sure," said the captain. "Just look at what's happened since he arrived twenty-eight days ago. Artillery salvos. Jacobin clubs springing up all across the nation. His journey here from Charleston was one long string of toasts, ovations, and fraternal hugs. I tell you, rebellion's in the wind."

A roar of applause erupted from the banquet room. A second later a heavily accented French voice sang:

Liberty! Liberty, be thy name adored forever,
Tyrants beware! Your tott'ring thrones must fall;
Our int'rest links the free together,
And Freedom's sons are Frenchmen all.

1

A second round of applause, twice as loud as the first, erupted from the hall, followed by a drunken shout for a toast to Madame Guillotine.

"To Madame Guillotine!" the guests shouted.

The captain motioned to the door as evidence of his point. "See what I mean?"

"I recognize that glint in your eye. You have something in mind, don't you?"

The captain's pipe had gone out. He relit it. "A new government."

The matter-of-fact way in which he said it made the statement all the more shocking.

The squat man's mouth hung open. "You're not serious."

From his coat pocket the captain drew a folded sheet of paper. "Found this on the street." He handed it over. "They're all over Philadelphia."

The shorter man unfolded the paper. He let loose a low chuckle.

The handbill had a drawing, a woodcut of George Washington being led to a guillotine.

"I understand Jefferson himself would pull the rope," said the short man.

"To applause louder than anything we've heard tonight."

"You're serious about this?"

"To quote Mr. Jefferson, 'The tree of liberty must be refreshed from time to time with the blood of patriots and tyrants. It is its natural manure.'"

From the street came huzzahs and applause.

"Sounds like the party is breaking up," said the captain.

As the two men entered the street from the alley, they saw that a surprising number of people were gathered in front of the banquet hall to wait for Citizen Genet of France to make an appearance.

The street exploded with more cheers and huzzahs as Genet appeared. The steps to the hall formed a natural platform with a wrought-iron railing.

Genet raised his arms to quiet the crowd. *"Merci! Merci! Merci!"*

The assembly hushed.

"It warms my 'eart to see that Americans love liberty az much az zee French love liberty!"

People cheered and waved French and American flags.

"I only wish your President Washington could be counted among us. But, alas, I fear 'e cannot."

Catcalls and boos replaced the cheers.

Genet nodded his agreement. "It saddens my 'eart that your Prezeedent Washington eez not zee crusader of freedom that 'istory 'as painted 'im. For I spoke with 'im this afternoon, and what did I find? An old man and an enemy to liberty!"

More boos.

"I expected I would meet a man of zee people. Instead, I met a man who would make 'imself king!"

The crowd erupted into a frenzy.

"You do not want this?" Genet shouted.

"Nooooooo!" they shouted with one voice.

"Then what do you want?"

"Liberty! Liberty! Liberty! Liberty!"

"Don't tell me!" Genet cried. "Tell your prezeedent!"

The crowd moved with a single mind. It was an amazing and terrifying sight.

The two men followed the raucous mob past Independence Hall to High Street and a three-story structure that was considered the grandest house in Philadelphia. It was now the working residence of the president of the United States.

The mood of the crowd grew angrier as it reached the front of Washington's house. Bottles were thrown at windows. Men took turns running up to the front door and banging on it. One man shouted that they should storm the house and drag the president into the street. While there was plenty of verbal agreement to the plan, for the moment the people seemed content just to make noise.

Not even a curtain in the house rustled in response.

The captain observed from a safe distance. "They still have a taste for revolution in their mouths."

"What do you propose?" His compatriot had to shout to be heard over the crowd.

"All they need is a little encouragement, and streets will run with blood. Then after a time, when they've had their fill, they'll be ready for a new government. Only this time it won't favor the Boston merchants."

The short man agreed. "Are you certain you want to do this? It would mean coming out of retirement."

The captain shrugged. "Greenfield is too quiet and too far from the sea. Do you think the others will join us?"

While the short man mulled over his answer, he dipped a second helping of snuff. "They'd grab their muskets and march on Boston themselves if it meant wrestling control from Hamilton and his friends."

The captain smiled. "We'll assemble in New Haven."

His friend nodded. "When I contact them, what'll I tell them?"

The captain studied the mob that clamored for George Washington's head. "Tell them we're going to start a second American revolution. Only this time we're going to do it right."

CHAPTER 1

"Citizen Rush."

Asa gulped at the sound of his name, his prayers having gone unanswered.

He'd prayed that this moment would never come—that the two fellows preceding him would jabber the class away and there wouldn't be time for a second disputation. He'd prayed that the administrators would conclude that class disputations were inhumane and strike them from the Yale curriculum, giving him a last-minute reprieve. He'd even prayed that the Lord would return and time would be no more.

"Rush? Is there a problem?" Jacob Benson, the tutor, asked.

"No sir. I'm . . ."

Hugh Backhouse and William Park took their seats, grateful to relinquish the front of the classroom to someone else. On the topic "Was Samson a Self-Murderer?" their give-and-take had been far from spirited. Asa had been more entertained watching wood warp. Even so, he'd pretended to be interested, even offering a comment—something about Samson maybe believing he might survive the crush of the massive temple columns. But it was nothing more than a thinly disguised attempt to prolong the proceedings in hopes there would be insufficient time for a second disputation today.

"We're waiting, Rush."

Benson was a lean fellow. Thin as a rail stretched between two posts. Only instead of posts, he was stretched between two chairs. Amiable, friendly, and brilliant, Benson had graduated from Yale two years previous. He spoke with a French accent, even though his family hailed from Westerly, Rhode Island.

Under the tutor's gaze Asa slid out of his chair, uncertain whether his trembling knees would buckle under his weight. This was his first disputation at Yale, and he wanted to make a good impression. But the odds were against him. He had so little natural talent at his disposal.

Look up the word *average* in the dictionary, and it would say, "Synonym: Asa Rush." Every time he saw his reflection, he was reminded of how unremarkable he was. Short brown hair. A round face. Common nose. Not thin. Not fat. Not short, but not tall either. There was nothing remarkable about him. He did not have the regal bearing of a George Washington, the brilliant mind of a John Adams, or the poetic nature of a Thomas Jefferson—the men who most inspired him. Instead, he figured that by the age of forty, he would be potbellied and bald like Benjamin Franklin . . . without the wit.

What chance did average have in an academic setting that produced the likes of Jonathan Edwards and Timothy Dwight, who had been Asa's mentor while he was at Greenfield in Connecticut? Dwight had known enough Latin at eight years of age to pass the Yale College entrance examination and had been admitted into the college when he was thirteen. He was the current president of the school.

Four other Yale graduates who had disputed where Asa was scheduled to dispute had gone on to sign the Declaration of Independence. So what were the administrators thinking, letting someone as average as he into the college anyway? It had taken him three attempts to pass the Latin requirement for entrance. If he had any sense, he'd turn toward the back of the room, walk out the door, and keep walking until he was back at Greenfield.

The front of the classroom beckoned, needing a body to fill the void.

This morning, when he'd pictured himself standing in front of his peers, he was confident, eloquent. He marshaled his facts, lined them up in strategic fashion, and drilled them until they responded at the speed of thought. He'd been impressive, even witty.

But somewhere between Connecticut Hall and class, his well-drilled facts had scattered in every direction, and his wit had deserted him. Consequently, his goal changed. No longer did he hope to impress. Now he hoped to survive.

The plan was simplicity itself.

Get up.

Say what you have to say.

Sit down and live to see another day.

But now that Asa's time had come, his lesser goal seemed lofty and unattainable. He would have sold his birthright just to be able to take a deep breath.

"Courage, Citizen Rush," said the tutor from the back of the room. "This is a disputation, not an execution. You have the appearance of a man mounting a scaffold to Madame Guillotine!"

The class laughed. Asa laughed with them. Not a real laugh, mind you, but some alien sound he didn't recognize that gurgled in his throat.

"Cooper, get up there with him," the tutor said. "Show him how it's done."

His opponent in this dispute, Eli Cooper, slipped out of his seat and strode to the front of the class with smooth, easy strides, his second-year camblet gown rustling with each step. A native of Kentucky, Eli Cooper was tall and broad-shouldered. His cheeks creased handsomely when he smiled, which was often. Asa, a robeless first-year student, had seen Cooper on campus. They had not been introduced yet, but the Kentuckian appeared to be someone Asa would like to have as a friend.

In his science class Asa learned that physical bodies attract one another. That fact came to mind at this moment because it was the sole way to explain how he found himself in front of the class. The body of Eli Cooper must have pulled him there.

From the back of the room, tutor Jacob Benson addressed the class. "The question for dispute is this: Were the religious revivals of this century of God or of men? Asa Rush has been assigned to defend the position they were of God. Eli Cooper, the position they were of men. As usual, each man will make a statement, after which the dispute will begin. Rush will go first."

Asa tugged at his shirt as though it didn't fit. He licked his lips, which had become parched. He summoned his opening thoughts to present themselves for duty but, cowards that they were, they remained in hiding in some dark corner of his mind.

He had to say something.

His training came into play. *Restate the question of the dispute.* That would give him extra time to coax his thoughts out into the open.

Just as Asa opened his mouth to utter his first sound, a student he didn't know leaned over to another student sitting next to him and said in a voice too loud, "Poor devil. Whose mother did he murder to draw such an awful position to defend?"

The class laughed.

"Whittier, wait your turn," said the tutor. But his grin revealed that he appreciated the humor as much as anyone.

The attitude behind the comment did not surprise Asa. He had known his Christian beliefs would be challenged. Although founded by ministers, Yale had forsaken its spiritual roots. Asa was one of four men on campus who held to traditional Christian beliefs.

"Like Daniel walking into the lions' den," someone at church had warned him.

"Not so," Dr. Timothy Dwight had countered. "It's much worse than that. Lions are brute beasts. Asa will be facing an adversary far more crafty but just as deadly. A better analogy would be Jannes and Jambres, the magicians in Pharaoh's court who could charm snakes and win the Pharaoh's ear and enslave a nation."

Dr. Dwight, the new college president, was the reason Asa had applied to Yale. A conservative preacher, Dr. Dwight made no secret of the fact he was looking to recapture the spiritual ground that had been lost at the institution. To do so, he needed soldiers.

Asa had enlisted. Contrary to what the classroom wag had just said, Asa welcomed the challenge to defend the acts of God in colonial history. What they didn't know was that he had a secret weapon for this dispute.

If only he didn't have to stand in front of so many eyes when he used it.

He cleared his throat. "Events of . . . the decades . . . no, wait."

He squeezed his eyes shut. Why did the same mind that hummed like a well-oiled machine alone in his room chug and start fitfully under public scrutiny?

"T-take . . . taking up the subject on general grounds, I—I mean, we—ask whether the religious revivals of this present century were of God or . . . of m-man. It is clear, once all the facts are assembled, that . . . it is not only reasonable, but . . . um, p-prudent, to conclude that the revivals were from God."

Asa's opening statement was painful for both speaker and listener, he knew. Yet somehow he managed to assemble the facts of his argument—that in response to the influence of the declining morals of England, God had raised up men of courage to call the Colonies back to God. Men like Cotton Mather, Solomon Stoddard, Jonathan Edwards, George Whitefield, and Gilbert Tennent. And God blessed their efforts with the unmistakable outpouring of the Holy Spirit.

"So while human agency played a part—for that, um, is how God chooses to w-work in both the written record and verbal accounts that have been passed down to us, without blush or shame—the events in question are uniquiv—unquivic—" Asa paused, searching for another word. "Undeniably, from God." Taking a half step back, he exhaled, letting his knotted shoulders slump.

Silence followed.

He looked at the other students. Many of them were occupied by their own thoughts. Some scribbled on paper or in the margins of their books. A few watched him, as if expecting him to continue.

"Uh . . . that's all."

Eli Cooper stood to Asa's left, facing him, arms folded. Saying nothing, he stared at Asa. He didn't move. He didn't even blink.

Asa nodded to indicate he was finished.

Eli stared.

Asa motioned with a hand.

Eli continued to stare.

So Asa said, "I'm . . . done. Your turn."

Eli Cooper turned to address his peers. "Do not be swayed by my opponent's eloquence. God had little, if anything, to do with the events of the so-called revivals of the 1730s and 1740s."

The classroom came apart at the seams with laughter. Asa's face burned.

With a strong voice Cooper continued: "The events of those decades are a shameful smudge on our nation's colonial history, the calculated invention of a band of unscrupulous New England ministers in an attempt to revive, not the people, but a dying Puritan religion that had been their bread and butter for almost a century.

"Facts? My worthy opponent dares to call his offering *facts*? I'll give you facts:

"Fact. Upon careful scrutiny the so-called Great Awakening was not that great, and it failed to awaken much of New England. The geography of recorded revival events is checkered at best. While enthusiasm ran high in the Connecticut Valley, it was barely visible along the Hudson River Valley. In fact, one minister wrote, following the preaching of George Whitefield, that he could observe no further influence upon his people than a general thoughtfulness about religion. Had God shunned them?

"Fact. The so-called fires of revival spread where promoters of revival set them. The celebrated Mr. Whitefield followed a planned preach-and-print strategy. He employed a man by the name of Seward, who was a skilled and aggressive publicist, a stockjobber in London whose advertisements bore the same hyperbolic stamp as those he later placed for Whitefield. New England was papered with Mr. Whitefield's sermons. I suppose Mr. Rush would have us believe that the very printing presses Mr. Whitefield used were possessed by the Holy Spirit!"

Laughter.

"Fact. In a popular handbook on how to promote revival through preaching, Isaac Watts stresses style and substance while using the art of oratory. Watts encourages would-be revival preachers to exert power over men's fancies and imagination. He urges them to practice his prescribed methods until they can rouse and awaken the cold, the stupid, and the sleepy race of sinners. I ask you, why would an all-powerful God need to stoop to rhetorical tricks to spark the fires of revival, when in the Bible He managed to communicate well enough through the mouth of an ass? Or is it possible that, during the time in question, God used the same method as He did with Balaam?"

More laughter.

"Fact. While the revivalist historians are fond of portraying the revivals as unifying in nature, they were nothing of the kind, as the battle between Old Lights and New Lights attests. Indeed, the revival drove a wedge between churches, and between members and clergy within churches. Moreover, in that day, anyone who dared call attention to the harmful side of the revivals was singled out, harassed, humiliated, and vilified. This by so-called 'renewed and refreshed souls' within the revival movement.

"No, gentlemen. The revival was not of God. Generated by men, its fruit resembles nothing Mr. Rush and others would have you believe. Every aspect of the so-called fire from God can be explained away in natural and economic terms. It was nothing more than a combination of events, such as the increasing population of the Colonies, the growing number of printing presses, the increasing circulation of newspapers, and the rhetorical theatrics of a handful of men who were attempting to breathe new life into a dead religion. That, gentlemen, is the true history of the 1730s and 1740s.

"As for the Holy Spirit? All I can say is that there was little holy and nothing spiritual about those days."

Eli Cooper stepped back and folded his hands behind him, signifying he was finished.

The other students in the room stared with slack jaws. Not a one of them was dozing or staring out the window. No one was scribbling mindlessly in the margins of their books. To the man, they leaned forward, eager to hear more.

Which was fine with Asa. He intended on giving them more. He, too, had been impressed with Eli Cooper's rendition. The rendition, but not the facts. Cooper's interpretation of events had goaded Asa to action. It was time to bring out his secret weapon.

The tutor cued him. "Citizen Rush, care to respond?"

But Benson didn't mean it. The half grin on his face warned Asa that he'd be a fool to take this any further. The tutor—probably because this was Asa's first disputation—was being generous, providing a way of escape.

With a nod and a sigh, Asa returned to his chair, the same chair that had been his secure island of anonymity moments before. Only he didn't sit down. Reaching under the chair, he pulled an old leather-bound volume from his haversack.

Returning to the front, where a grinning Eli Cooper awaited him, Asa said, "I . . . have in my possession a journal. A firsthand account of revival events on the dates in question."

He opened the journal to reveal page after page of elegant old-school penmanship. At that moment something happened. Just holding the book seemed to calm him. Seeing the words on the pages gave him courage. It was as though the spirit of the journal's author had come to his aid, and Asa was not alone.

"This journal describes in detail the spiritual condition of the town of Havenhill, before and after revival." To his amazement, he spoke without stuttering. "The author of the account, Josiah Rush, my grandfather, describes the town as once happy and productive. However, having become infected with a spiritual malady that he termed *soul sickness*, the people became unhappy and unproductive. They lost the joy of living, the joy of relationships. Josiah Rush prayed for them, and after much prayer he recorded how the Great Physician cured the entire town. He relates that the change in them was so swift, so remarkable, that there could be no other explanation than that God did it. God, gentlemen. For no man can in a single meeting transform the hearts of an entire town so dramatically and so completely."

"Nonsense," Eli Cooper said. "It's an old preacher's trick, perfected by Solomon Stoddard and passed down to his grandson, Jonathan Edwards, who freely published it among the Colonies. It's a simple method. First you prepare the people by telling them the signs of revival so they will recognize the visitation of God when it comes. According to Stoddard, these signs are threefold: the quickening of the saints, sinners converted in an extraordinary way, and the unconverted growing more religious. Notice how general these signs are, gentlemen.

"Then, having set the stage, you warn the people to be vigilant for these signs and to alert others if you should happen to see them, for no one should miss out on proclaiming the Acceptable Year of the Lord! Now, what do you suppose happens after that? The dear saints, eager for a visitation of God, primed and vigilant, will see signs of revival everywhere! And if they don't see them, they'll fabricate them! I daresay a people so primed and eager could look under their beds and see revival among the dust balls!"

Laughter ripped through the room.

"You weren't there!" Asa shouted at Eli Cooper. "You couldn't know. How easy it is to malign something you neither saw nor could comprehend!" He held up the journal. "This is the faithful record of an eyewitness to history!"

"Voltaire," Eli said.

"What?" *What did a French philosopher have to do with anything?* Asa wondered. "My grandfather . . ."

"Voltaire."

Asa waited for Eli to continue.

Eli just looked at him.

So Asa continued. "This record of revival is penned by an educated man. A man without guile. A man who . . ."

"Voltaire."

Asa waited for more.

All he got from Eli Cooper was a grin.

"My grandfather, Reverend Josiah . . ."

"Voltaire."

Asa stared.

Eli stared back.

Asa narrowed his eyes. "If you have something to say, say it!"

Eli bowed. "Thank you for asking." Turning to the assembled students, he said, "Let me tell you about Reverend Josiah Rush. Something that his grandson would not want you to know. He was an arsonist. Preaching by day, setting fires by night."

Asa recoiled as though slapped. "He was not! Those charges . . ."

"There used to be a saying in Havenhill: where there's smoke, there's Josiah Rush."

Laughter.

Asa was beside himself. The dispute was now personal. His family honor was at stake. "My grandfather . . ."

"Voltaire!"

Hands on hips, Asa cried, "My grandfather . . ."

"Voltaire!"

Asa had had enough. "Would you be so kind as to . . ."

"I put it to you, citizens!" Eli Cooper boomed. "Given two testimonies, who would you believe? That of a preaching arsonist, or the great Voltaire, who said: 'Indeed, history is nothing more than a tableau of crimes and misfortunes.' Gentlemen, if ever there was a history of crimes and misfortunes, it is the history that we have been led to believe was a Great Awakening!"

Asa opened his mouth to reply, but he was outvoiced by a roomful of students who were on their feet:

"Voltaire!"

"Voltaire!"

"Voltaire!"

The dispute was over, and there was no doubt who the popular winner was. Some of the students were standing on their chairs. Even tutor Jacob Benson had unfolded his long legs and was on his feet, caught up in the chaos, his fist pumping the air, his voice one with the masses.

Asa stood alone.

Then, as if his victory was not yet complete, Eli shouted over the din, "And what do we do to those who perpetuate the evils of our past?"

"Off with their heads!" someone shouted.

Everyone took up the chant.

"Off with their heads!"

"Off with their heads!"

"Off with their heads!"

Asa knew they didn't mean him. They were just giving voice to the popular sentiment of the day to all things French. At least, that's what he hoped they were doing.

But as the chanting continued, the faces of the men in the room changed, as though a dark cloud overshadowed them. Their voices sharpened to an edge, the kind that turns a crowd into a mob. It was as though evil was egging them on, looking for the slightest excuse to let loose the dogs of destruction.

At that moment Asa Rush knew his days at Yale College would be more perilous than he'd ever dreamed.

CHAPTER 2

For the remainder of the week, Asa suffered the jibes and pranks of his fellow classmates. The most common was, in passing, a slicing motion with the flat of the hand to simulate the fall of a guillotine blade. The most bothersome was a pounding on his dormitory door after midnight with shouts that they were storming the Bastille. Then there were the little death ditties sung behind his back.

One wag, to the amusement of all who witnessed it, pantomimed losing his head. Every time the mime attempted to pick it up, he kicked it out of reach.

The weekend couldn't arrive fast enough. Asa figured that the distractions of two days' reprieve from books and classes and recitations would wipe clean the memory of his humiliating disputation. At least that was his hope.

Saturday showed promise. The flood of abuses slowed to a trickle. Sunday was even better. Following church services, he received only a single Madame Guillotine chop as students found other ways to amuse themselves. Some went hiking in the woods across the salt marshes at the base of East Rock, with a few venturous souls hiking as far as Judges' Cave at West Rock.

For those less inclined to sore muscles, there was the green situated across the street from the campus. Here college students and eligible women from the town participated in a decades-old precourting ritual that had all the trappings of an elaborate folk dance. Ever since the school had moved to New Haven, the village green had served as the mating ground for young romantics. The standing joke in the town was that more than half of the population of New Haven had been conceived—at least in thought—on this patch of grass.

Disdaining strenuous outdoor activities, and having no money, Asa opted for a chance at romance. He figured his prospects were slim. That didn't matter. He wouldn't have known what to do with a prospect if one presented itself to him. Until last week.

Last week a prospect had not only presented itself, it waylaid him. Up to that time he'd been content to be an anonymous participant in the courting ritual, though his scientific mind preferred to view it in different terms. Still a dance, of sorts, but grander. For him, Sunday was like a cosmic ballet.

He imagined the village green as a universe unto itself, upon which bodies moved in predictable patterns. The town women were suns around which male students orbited. Some orbited closer than others. Asa himself preferred a distant orbit. In fact, if he were to compare himself to a planet in the solar system, he couldn't. The scale of his orbit far exceeded that of Mr. Hershel's newly discovered planet, Uranus.

On Sunday afternoons the suns took their positions like clockwork in the green cosmos, and soon after, the planets took up orbit. The gravitational attraction between the bodies gave the afternoon its excitement when a planet would inexplicably alter its course and take up a new orbit. Given the time structure of the universe, such dramatic occurrences were rare. Yet when it did occur, the entire universe felt it.

The most spectacular of universe events was a rogue comet. In the year since Asa had been orbiting, he only saw it once. The phenomenon occurred when a planet succumbed to the extraordinary pull of a sun and broke orbit. No longer traveling on a sane elliptical path, the planet-turned-comet streaked across the universe in a bold, straight line, picking up speed as it went.

The universe gasped at the sight.

Asa's own orbit slowed, and his heart accelerated as he watched the streaking comet approach the sun. As the distance between the two bodies closed, Asa couldn't help but calculate the possibilities of an encounter. That close to the sun the comet could flame out and incinerate. Or the two bodies could collide, sending one or both of them spinning crazily. Asa guessed there was the possibility that the comet would somehow adjust at the last moment and enter a close, intimate orbit around the sun. But odds of that happening were astronomical.

He found himself holding his breath as the moment of encounter arrived. At the last possible moment, like a rock skipping off a watery surface, the speeding comet brushed past the sun and streaked across the universe and out of sight. As far as Asa knew, it was never to be heard from again.

Sometimes late at night Asa remembered that day. He wondered what it would feel like to be a comet. But on Sundays he felt no such wonder—only contentment to keep his distant orbit.

Until last Sunday, that is, when the universe changed with the appearance of a new sun. One with greater gravitational pull than Asa had imagined possible. A pull too great for him to ignore. A pull so great, it made him think crazy thoughts. Comet thoughts.

In the shade of a sturdy white oak, Eli Cooper crossed his arms. "Look at him!" he scoffed. "You'd think he never saw a woman before."

Phineas Phelps let loose with a toady laugh. "Yeah, look at 'im! The dunce!"

The radiance of the new sun was blinding. On Asa's fourth orbit it dawned on him that he'd seen her before. She had been but a girl, yet he was certain the woman sitting under the tree, with her yellow dress splayed in a glorious arc, was the same girl he'd met at Greenfield.

He whispered her name. "Annabelle."

Hearing it seemed to confirm his theory, and during this instant of inattention, his orbit decayed. It wasn't enough for anyone to notice but enough to make his next pass a few feet closer to his sun.

Appropriately, she did not sit alone. Next to her sat a straight-backed matron in black with an open book on her lap. The woman's head was bent low, and her jowls jiggled as she read aloud words Asa couldn't hear.

Then, to his horror, Asa noticed his altered orbit. It terrified and thrilled him all at once.

"This is madness!" He half-chuckled to himself, making no effort to correct his course. "Lunacy!"

Passing closer to his sun's radiant splendor than he ever thought he would dare was a heady experience. Even though his pace quickened and didn't slow to normal until he reached his apogee along the edge of the green.

Skirting the grass, he circled back into the heart of the green. *I'm going to do it*, he told himself as he wrestled with thoughts of madness and anarchy. He repeated the words because he hadn't yet convinced himself he was going to go through with it.

"I'm going to do it." This time his voice was husky with resolve. "A plan. A plan. I need a plan."

He was heady, not insane. Enough rational thought remained within to demand a strategy.

First off, he needed to change his trajectory. His present orbit, though wickedly thrilling, would not take him close enough. But he didn't want to be obvious about it. He wanted to enter a close orbit, not become a comet . . . though that now held a certain attraction.

I am mad! He laughed feverishly.

Clenching his fists, he fought off the madness long enough to think of a natural, believable way to alter his course enough to take him within close proximity of the woman in the yellow dress.

Think! Think!

An idea came to him. He tested it. *Yes. Natural. Believable.* It would do.

Blood rushed in his head when he realized he'd just removed one more obstacle from this mad, mad course.

A book. That's the key to believability.

Because he lived in the dorms across the street, a book could make his change in course believable. Now he needed a story to go with it.

A friend needs it. Good . . . oh! Better . . . a friend asked to borrow it, and I just now remember agreeing to loan it to him. Good . . . good . . . it's simple, believable, and would account for a sudden change of direction.

Having settled on a plan, he turned to the next phase: implementation. His physics studies came to his aid.

"The shortest distance between two points is a straight line," he murmured, as though he was the first man ever to conceive its profound truth. "Two points determine a line. Three points prove it."

Asa took a deep breath. He had his three points: himself, the tree under which Annabelle sat, and the dormitory. All he had to do was stay on his present heading and wait for the three points to align.

A shiver trilled his spine. He was going to do this. He could feel the resolve building within him. All he needed now was a visible sign, an indication that his change of course was no impulse, but rational, explainable.

He thought on this as, out of the corner of his eye, he charted the alignment of his three points. He was coming up on it quickly.

The idea for a visible sign came to him. He nodded with approval. The last piece had fallen into place. Now all he had to do was implement it.

This is madness . . .

Overhead the central orb of the astronomer's solar system burned brightly on the patch of green adjacent to Yale Universe, seemingly unaware of the wild anarchy in Asa Rush's mind.

"Not yet . . . not yet . . ." Asa neared the position of alignment. "Not yet . . . not yet . . . not yet . . . *now!*"

With a snap of his fingers and a roll of his eyes that would have made a theatrical director proud, Asa pretended he'd just remembered something. Pivoting at a right angle, he set himself on a course that would take him back to his dormitory and, not so coincidentally, on a headlong course in the direction of Annabelle.

Asa's heart raced faster. He told himself that while his orbit had altered, he was still a planet. Yet as his speed increased and as he grew hotter with every step, he couldn't help but think, *This must be how a comet feels.*

"Look at dat!" Phineas pointed at Asa. "What's he doin'?"

"Smooth," Eli mocked.

"Why'd he snap his fingers like dat?"

"To pretend he's forgotten something at the dormitory."

"What'd he forget?"

"Nothing, you thickwit. He's setting himself up for a chance encounter with that lovely creature under the tree."

"Hey! Dat's da girl you came to meet, ain't it?"

"Let's go." Eli set off toward the center of the green.

"Where we goin'?"

"To have some fun."

Asa wiped perspiration from the corners of his eyes. Like a flaming ball of fire, he was streaking across the green, caught in the gravity of his brilliant sun.

His course had been set and was sure, his feet plunging ever forward. The closer he came to her, the stronger her gravity. Asa couldn't have turned to one side or the other if he tried. He was close enough now to hear the deep, sonorous voice of the woman in black. On some level—certainly not a conscious one, for by this time all conscious thought had melted in the intense heat—he recognized the text the woman was reading. At present, though, it belonged to a different universe. One alien to the one in which Asa had embarked on this reckless adventure.

As he drew ever closer, he kept his eyes forward. No matter what the universe, it was always dangerous to look directly at the sun.

Just then a familiar haze fell over Asa's eyes. He groaned. "Not now! Please, not now!"

He tried to slow his steps.

Couldn't.

For most people, moments of anxiety sharpen their senses. For some, anxiety even increases their strength. Not so with Asa. It dampened his senses, dulled his intellect, and sapped his strength. The last time he'd faced it had been seconds before his first disputation.

From Asa's side of things it was as though he'd been engulfed by a large soap bubble. Sounds were muted. His vision blurred and curved curiously. He felt isolated from the world. The sounds most clear were his own breathing and the *thump-thump-thump* of his heart.

His stomach knotted. A bitter, herbal taste took up residence on his tongue.

He was doomed.

Doomed to streak by the sun called Annabelle.

Doomed to live the fate of a comet. To exit the universe, never to return.

With Annabelle only a dozen steps distant, Asa resolved himself to his destiny. He would streak silently by. Of course she wouldn't notice. She would never know anything had happened, while he would relive the horror over the course of a thousand nights.

He was almost upon her now. There was nothing left to do except . . .

An unseen force gripped him, ripping him free from the gravity of

Annabelle's sun, pulling him out of his trajectory and nearly out of his shoes, unceremoniously dragging him across the grass.

Asa's vision cleared. The first thing he saw was the hem of a yellow skirt growing increasingly distant. Looking up to see what force could be strong enough to knock a comet off its course, Asa spotted the twisted grin of Eli Cooper.

"You're going about this all wrong, sport," Eli said.

CHAPTER 3

"Let go of me!"

Asa yanked free from Eli's grip and in doing so stumbled. His feet clunked together like two wooden casks and down he went.

"Don't get yourself all in a huff." Eli peered at him. "I'm only trying to protect you from yourself, sport."

Asa scrambled to his feet, conscious of the fact that they were under the gaze of the entire universe. "Don't call me sport."

"He calls me thickwit," Phineas said, almost with pride.

"Well, I don't like people calling me names," Asa replied. "And I don't like them waylaying me in public, either!"

"I'm just trying to prevent a major blunder, sport. You should be thanking me. Had I not intercepted you, right now you'd be hightailing it to Connecticut Hall like a whupped dog."

"I would not! And . . . besides, you don't even know what I was doing. I was returning to my room to get a book for a friend."

"Ah!" Eli cried, as though he'd solved a puzzle. "You forgot it, didn't you, sport?" He turned to Phineas. "That's why the snap of the fingers! He was pretending to forget something."

"I wasn't pretending," Asa lied—and regretted it instantly. He wasn't even sure why he'd lied. Eli Cooper just affected him that way.

24

"Sure, sport," Eli said. "Anything you say."

"Are you calling me a liar?"

Eli raised his hands. "There's no need to." Then a crafty smile came over his face. "All right. Quick. What was the name of the book?"

"I-it was," Asa stuttered.

"That's what I thought. And the name of the friend. Come on. These aren't hard questions."

"I was—um—getting it for—"

"When did he ask you for it? Where were you? In the hallway? The chapel? Your dorm room?"

"We were . . . I was . . ." Sweat trickled down the back of Asa's neck, and he swiped at it. "I don't have to stand here and take this from you."

Eli placed his hands on his hips. "I know what you were doing, sport. It was obvious. So obvious even Phineas here could see right through you."

"Yeah!" Phineas said. "You was tryin' to get the attention of the same—"

Eli shoved Phineas in the chest. To Asa, he said, "You've been circling that girl in the yellow dress for the past hour. Then something inside of you cracked. Some little vial of courage or desire. And you thought, 'Why not? Why not try to get close to her? Who knows? Maybe she'll notice me. Say something to encourage me?' So you wrote this little play for yourself. Rehearsed it a hundred times in your mind until you got it just right—how you would walk right in front of her. Then, in passing, you'd risk glancing at her. Maybe make eye contact. She'd smile. You'd smile. Then, if you didn't do something stupid like trip over your own feet—"

Phineas guffawed.

"—you thought maybe you'd risk saying something. I don't know. Something wild and reckless, something witty, maybe even something provocative, like—'Nice day, isn't it?'"

Another guffaw from Phineas. This one earned him a glower from Asa.

Eli continued, "She'd look up at you, her eyes two limpid pools, and the way you figure, by this time next year, you're balancing little Asa Jr. on your knee."

"I don't write little plays in my head," Asa retorted. "And I don't have time for this nonsense." He turned to leave.

Eli grabbed his arm and swung him back around. "So what clever words had you planned on regaling her with if she happened to notice you?"

"I hadn't planned on being clever," Asa snapped.

"And I'm certain you would have succeeded." Eli laughed.

"What I meant was," Asa said, "that a lady of worth will not succumb to witty phrases that are designed to appeal to her vanity."

"Don't be so sure."

"A lot you know." Asa turned and walked away.

Eli rolled his eyes skyward. "The young! How pitiable. How naive. Where did we go wrong with them?" With Phineas trailing, he ran to catch up with Asa. "I did what I did because I want to help you." He matched Asa's stride.

"Mock me, you mean."

"You wound me! Whatever gave you that impression?"

Asa turned on him. "Possibly the scars I bear from our disputation. And the endless taunts that keep them fresh!"

Eli threw his arms wide in protest. "You bear me ill will for that? It was an assignment, sport! Nothing more. Is not the purpose of a disputation to dispute? Did I get to choose which side I would defend? Did you?"

"That much is true," Asa admitted. "But you took delight in attacking me."

"I was passionate! As were you, sp—" Eli bit off the last word. "As were you. It was simply my good fortune to be handed the popular position. Are you going to fault me for the current craze over all things French? I merely spied an element that I used to my advantage. You would have done the same."

Asa started to object.

Eli cut him off. "Correct me if I'm wrong, but is not the purpose of a dispute to martial the facts in such a way as to win over the hearers to a certain point of view? In truth, my passion was academic, not personal." Having presented his case, he awaited Asa's reply.

A creeping sensation that he'd played the immature fool spread over Asa. Had he made a cardinal error? Had he, in the heat of battle, succumbed to his emotions? Timothy Dwight, his tutor at Greenfield, was fond of saying, "Emotions make lousy generals." Had Asa allowed his emotions to outrank his reason? To his shame, it wouldn't have been the first time that had happened.

"You're saying it was only a grade to you."

"Nothing more," Eli insisted.

Asa stared at the ground. "Then I apologize for misinterpreting your intentions."

"Now you're talking, sport!"

Phineas grinned crookedly.

"We need a plan." Eli rubbed his hands together.

"I don't know," Asa hedged.

Patching up a difference was one thing. Turning matters of the heart into a group discussion was another thing altogether.

Eli put a hand on his shoulder. "Let's be honest. You need a plan. I've seen you attempt to be spontaneous. It isn't pretty."

Asa felt the keen jab.

"All I'm saying is that your chances of success will improve greatly if you have a strategy based on something other than wishes and dreams. And who better to help you maximize your strengths and minimize your weaknesses than a friend? Am I right?"

"Sounds reasonable," Asa said reluctantly.

"Of course it does. Tell me, what do you know about her, other than the obvious?"

"I think I've met her before," Asa said, uneasy in the way Eli set his eyes on the subject of their discussion.

"You have?" Eli pulled back. Dark suspicion flitted across his face, but only for an instant.

"If it's the same girl—I mean, woman."

"But you're not certain?"

"Fairly certain. Eighty percent. No, closer to ninety percent. Maybe ninety-three percent."

Eli lifted an eyebrow in amusement, as if waiting for Asa to settle on a number.

"Ninety-three percent," Asa said with finality.

"You're sure?"

"Aya. I'm sure. I think."

"So you're fairly certain you've met her before. That can work to our advantage."

"Ninety-four percent," Asa added.

Eli cocked his head.

"Ninety-four percent sure. I'm certain."

"How certain?" Eli asked.

Asa began calculating the odds.

"Do you know her name?" Eli asked.

"Annabelle. Annabelle Byrd."

Eli nodded.

"Why'd you ask tha—" A fist in Phineas's chest cut short the question.

Eli glowered at him. "It's important to gather all relevant information." To Asa he said, "Where do you think you met her before?"

"At Greenfield. That's where I grew up. My sister and I attended Dr. Dwight's school there."

Eli's eyebrows raised. "Girls attended this school?"

"Aya. Unusual, I know. Dr. Dwight took no small amount of criticism for it."

Eli's gaze wandered to the tree and the girl again. He was nodding. "Did Mistress Byrd attend this school?"

"For a short time. She began attending shortly after her family moved to Greenfield. Created quite a stir. The town was real proud that Captain Byrd chose Greenfield."

"What do you know of Captain Byrd?"

"Not much. Only that he's wealthy, and that he made his fortune at sea."

"How old were you at the time?"

"Twelve. No, thirteen. I remember because that summer Horace Watkins painted the exterior of his store. My father made an agreement with him that, in exchange for my services, he would—"

"Interesting," Eli said. "So you attended school with her. Did you get to know her?"

"She and my sister became friends. She wasn't there but a couple of weeks before Captain Byrd picked up and moved on. It was real sudden, a mystery to the town."

Eli cradled his chin between his thumb and forefinger. "So when she showed up here—"

"Two weeks ago," Phineas said, earning him another punch in the chest.

"—you recognized her. Is that when you began circling her?"

Asa felt the color rise in his face. "You seem to know a lot about her yourself."

"General observations. You hear things."

"What sort of things?"

Eli squared his shoulders and addressed Asa. "Things that can help you out. Here's the plan. Try to keep up." Turning his back on the tree and the girl, he began walking.

Asa fell in step beside him.

"First, stay away from politics. Whatever you do, don't say anything about Jefferson and the Republicans. Her entire family is staunch Federalists. Captain Byrd knows Washington and Adams personally. He's intensely loyal to them."

"Wait," Asa said. "Politics? I'd never talk to a woman about politics."

Eli turned to him. "We're talking man to man, right?"

"Aya. I-I guess so."

"Then you know from experience that in the presence of a beautiful woman, men turn into blathering idiots and say all manner of things they shouldn't say. No one knows why. It's just a fact of nature. All I'm doing is attempting to warn you that no matter what you say in your delirium, don't say anything kind about Jefferson. It'll scuttle everything."

Asa took a deep breath as the impact of what they were discussing hit him. They were talking about him standing in front of Annabelle Byrd and carrying on a conversation. His palms and neck began to sweat at the thought. "I still don't think I'd talk politics."

"Great. Keep the conversation general. How lovely the day is. The sky so blue, the grass so green. And try to work everything around to her."

"What do you mean?"

"The sky is so blue, but not as blue as your eyes. That sort of thing."

"Women like that?"

"Women love that."

Asa shrugged. His experience with talking to women had been restricted to relatives.

"Now, what's your sister's name?" Eli asked.

"Why do you want to know that?"

"Trust me, it's important."

Asa still had yet to warm up to a conversation involving his personal life. But he'd gone this far. "Maggy. Well, Margaret, actually. She prefers Margaret now that she's older."

"What did Mistress Byrd know her as?"

"Maggy."

"Then Maggy it is. Here's what you do. You walk right in front of her, and just as you pass her—"

"Wait a minute! That's what I was doing when you waylaid me."

"It's totally different. You were almost running past her like some kind of . . ."

"Comet," Asa said.

Eli grinned. "Comet? Oh! Then before when you were"—he made a large circular motion with his finger—"you were a planet. A planet in orbit!" He laughed.

Phineas joined him.

Asa winced. "Aya, it's hilarious."

"But wait." Eli grabbed Phineas by the arm. "If you were a planet, then that would make Mistress Byrd . . ."

"I got it! I got it!" Phineas cried. "She's the sun! Right? The sun!"

Eli laughed.

Asa cringed. Somehow it had sounded more profound in his head. "Have your laugh."

"Oh, don't become all defensive," Eli countered. "We understand. Really. We're laughing because all guys do that sort of thing."

"Really?"

Eli's lips twitched, as if he was trying to keep a straight face. "No!" he blurted, which set him and Phineas to laughing again.

There was nothing Asa could do but wait for them to laugh themselves out.

Wiping away a tear of mirth, Eli said, "In all seriousness . . ." But serious had yet to return, and he succumbed again to convulsive laughter.

Asa's eyes narrowed. "I'm leaving."

Eli's hand on his shoulder stopped him. "All right, all right, I'm done." He cleared his throat. "So when you streak by her—"

Asa turned to walk away.

Eli pulled him back. "I mean it this time," he promised. Another throat clearing. "When you pass in front of Mistress Byrd, your su—no, all kidding aside. When you pass in front of Mistress Byrd, casually glance over at her, stop, turn to her, and say, 'Annabelle? Annabelle Byrd? Why, Maggy and I were just talking about you!'"

Asa liked the sound of it. More importantly, he could see it playing out in his head. "I like it. What then?"

"That's it. At least, that's the hard part. Let her take it from there. If the conversation begins to lag, remember to say something about the sky or the grass."

"And apply them to her."

"Exactly. But not politics. Never politics. Whatever you do, don't—I repeat, don't—say anything kind about Thomas Jefferson."

Asa frowned. Had Eli not brought it up again, he would have forgotten all about that.

"All set?" Eli turned Asa back toward the tree.

"I-I think so."

Eli gave him a little shove. "I want a full report later tonight."

Eli and Phineas watched as Asa walked toward the tree and Annabelle Byrd.

When Asa was out of earshot, Eli said, "Let the comedy begin."

CHAPTER 4

The closer Asa came to the tree, the deeper the realization that he was actually going to do this. How different this was from the comet approach. Armed with scripted words on his tongue, he felt bolder, more confident. Perhaps because his goal this time was greater—an attempt at conversation instead of a wordless flyby—and greater resources had rushed to his aid.

Then, all of a sudden, his tongue drained of moisture. The walls of his mouth became equally parched, and each pass of his tongue—that restless slab of flesh—stuck and struggled like a fly caught in tar. How was he going to say his line without his tongue?

He didn't seem to be walking with any pace, yet the object of his desire, resplendent in yellow, was fast approaching. His thoughts roamed from a tongue too dry to a neck, palms, and underarms that were too wet, and he nearly altered his intercept course right then and there.

Instead he forced his mind elsewhere, to his opening line. He wanted it to be perfect in both inflection and gesture.

The entire approach rested on a glance, followed by a double take and an expression of surprise. The look of surprise was his cue to say, "Annabelle Byrd? Is that really you? Why, Maggy and I were just talking about you!"

Asa rehearsed the line several times until it didn't sound rehearsed. Then he mentally rehearsed the gestures. *Glance. Double take. Surprise. Line*, he repeated to himself.

He was so close to the tree that sheltered the radiance of his affections that he could hear the matron next to her reading aloud. The woman's voice sounded tired, yet she continued reading.

"Glance. Double take. Surprise. Line," Asa muttered.

Then, to his horror, he realized he was on a heading that took him straight to the tree! Anyone looking at him might get the impression he was brazenly approaching the young woman to talk to her! What had come over him? He altered his course slightly.

"Glance. Double take. Surprise. Line," he said again.

Line. My line! What's my line?

Asa panicked. He heard Eli's voice in his head. *"Whatever you do, don't—I repeat, don't—say anything kind about Thomas Jefferson.*

I won't! Asa argued. *But what's my line?*

He was almost to the tree.

"Greetings, Annabelle. I'm Thomas Jefferson's brother. Remember me?"

Asa groaned.

Why did Eli have to tell him not to mention Jefferson? It never would have entered his head otherwise!

Asa was twenty feet away from his sun and closing fast.

Glance. Double take. Surprise. Line . . . line . . . what's my line?

The cue is surprise. What follows the expression of surprise? Annabelle Byrd. That's it! "Why, Maggy and I were just talking about you!"

That's it! He repeated it, lest it slip his mind again.

Ten feet.

Just don't say anything about Thomas Jefferson.

Seven feet.

I won't! Leave me alone!

Five feet.

Keep your eyes distant, as though you're preoccupied. Don't look at her too soon.

Four feet. Or is it three and a half feet?

Glance. Double take. Surprise. Line.

Two feet.

Maybe it was the motion, or maybe it was the rustling of the grass, but the matron in black became aware of him. She stopped reading. Out of the corner of his eye, Asa saw her look up.

He licked his lips. It was time. He was ready.

He glanced, then looked away.

It was a masterful glance. The glance of all glances! During its execution Asa was certain—94 percent certain—that his facial features had remained impassive, as though at first he didn't recognize her.

Glance. Double take.

Asa did a double take. Well, in his exuberance, it might have been a triple take, but it didn't matter. It was effective. Now both the matron and Annabelle were looking at him.

Which was almost Asa's undoing.

Annabelle, his sun, his radiance, his glory, was resplendent. Alluring. Enchanting. The features he remembered were the same—only more. Much more than they had been when she was younger. Her skin was silkier. Her lips fuller. Her eyes deeper. *Much* deeper. So deep Asa almost fell in.

It took Herculean effort to corral his thoughts that had grown limp with awe and wonder. He berated them back into service.

Glance. Double take . . . double take. What comes after double take? Please, God, help me remember! What comes after . . . surprise! Quick! Act surprised!

Asa gasped and his hand flew to his chest. His eyes lit with the fires of memory as his mouth opened in astonishment. He was so taken by the drama of the moment that he forgot what came next.

Line. Line! What's my line?

Time ticked cruelly and silently. Long enough for a pitiless smirk to form on the matron's lips. The solar sun sizzled the back of his neck and steamed the grass upon which he stood. Waves of humid air engulfed him while Annabelle and the matron sat comfortably in the shade.

Asa held his dramatic pose, standing as still as a statue of a Shakespearean actor and just as dumb, while his mind ransacked every nook and cranny for the missing line.

Unable to find the line, he managed to uncover a clue.

The cue suggests the line. You're acting surprised . . . surprised at what?

Then mercifully—*thank You, Lord, thank You*—he found it, cowering in the back of his mind. At least he thought he'd found it. In his haste to say something, *anything*, he shoved it onstage. "Aha! Thomas Jefferson! Is it really you? Annabelle and I were just talking about you!"

"Why's he standin' like dat?" Lifting a hand to his chest and striking a pose, Phineas mirrored Asa's stance. "I don't remember talkin' 'bout that. Seems sorta silly, don't it?"

"Silly? It's hilarious!" Eli bent over, slapped his knee, and guffawed.

Phineas held the pose, as though by doing so, a revelation of sorts would come to him.

Eli shoved him out of the pose. "He's doing it because he's a chowderhead, just like you."

Phineas frowned.

"You should have seen him the other day during the disputation," Eli said. "Mentally, the thickwit has two left feet. Under pressure, he not only stumbles over them but manages somehow to get his tongue tangled up with them too."

"So when you told him about Thomas Jefferson . . ."

Eli howled. "A master stroke! A seed planted in fertile ground! I knew if I told him not to say something, somehow he'd manage to blurt it out for sure. At least, I'm ninety-three percent—no, make that ninety-four percent—sure he'd blurt it out."

"And Captain Byrd. He don't really like the Federalists and President Adams, does he?"

"Don't you see?" Eli smirked. "No, of course you wouldn't. That's the beauty of the whole scheme, my pumpkin-headed friend. The Byrds are dyed-in-the-wool Jefferson supporters. They hate, despise, loathe Washington, Adams, Hamilton, and anyone who remotely smells like a Federalist. And right about now, unless I've misjudged our love-struck simpleton, he's singing Federalist praises to the wrong woman."

"Wait," Asa stammered.

He wasn't certain what he'd said, but from the lingering sound of it, he knew it wasn't right.

"Wait. What I meant to say was—well, you can be sure it had nothing to do with Thomas Jefferson! At least, nothing good. I'm a Federalist through and through. My whole family is."

He was babbling, but he couldn't stop himself.

"Did you know I once met George Washington? In New York. My father was there on business. Not government business, just regular business. There was this parade, and my father put me on his shoulders so I could see. Of course, I was little at the time. Not like it was yesterday, or anything." He chuckled. "I don't remember it, but my father repeats the story often enough . . . which, of course, has nothing to do with now. But I did meet him. But if you were to happen upon George Washington and ask him if he remembered it, he probably wouldn't. Him being so presidential. Well, ex-presidential now."

The matron stared at him as though he were a loon.

Annabelle cocked her head, and raven curls dangled against milky skin. With a slightly disdainful tone, she said, "You would speak politics to a lady?"

"No! Oh no! Oh goodness, no! I would never . . . I mean, I was . . . but I certainly didn't mean to. What I meant was . . ."

"Then you're one of those men who are of the opinion that ladies have insufficient brains with which to talk politics."

"Yes!"

Annabelle's eyebrow raised in disapproval.

"I mean, no! I mean, I wouldn't . . . what did you say again?"

The matron snorted something under her breath.

By now Asa was thoroughly confused. However, enough brain cells were still functioning for him to know that any hope of recovering his dignity was lost. His sole recourse was to resume the path of the comet and exit this grassy universe forever.

With shoulders slumped and a disheartened voice, he said, "I think it best if I leave now." He turned to go.

Then the most curious thing happened. Annabelle Byrd sat up straight and began clapping. With enthusiasm she smiled and clapped.

Asa didn't know what to make of it. Was she mocking him? Her face showed no derision.

"Wonderful! Wonderful!" she cried.

Asa managed a crooked smile.

"A delightful and amusing performance, Master Rush!"

Asa blinked. "You . . . you remember me?"

"Of course I remember you! And I'm dying to hear how dear Maggy is doing. But first, this little performance of yours . . . how long have you and your friends been cooking up this little scene? It was masterful! And you played the part of the bumbling bumpkin to perfection, Asa! I didn't know you had actor's blood in you!"

"Well . . ." Asa shrugged and blushed.

"What's she doin'?" Phineas demanded. "Why's she clappin'?"

No longer laughing, Eli said, "I don't know."

"Lookee there! He's sittin' down with 'em! They're makin' room for 'im, and he's sittin' down with 'em! Well, if that don't beat all!"

Eli scowled. "That little toad." With determined strides he bolted toward the tree. "Come on. We're going in."

With a lilt in her voice, Annabelle said, "I remember Greenfield with great fondness. Maggy, is she well?"

"She's a beautiful young woman now," Asa replied. "And still as smart as a whip."

He squirmed with delight. He couldn't believe his good fortune. He was sitting under the tree at the center of the universe, having a conversation with the sun. Two thoughts came to mind, and neither of them had anything to do with Thomas Jefferson.

Thought one: *don't stare.*

No easy task, that. He'd never known his eyes to be so ravenous. But then, never before had they been in the presence of such a bounteous display of beauty.

Thought two: *try to sound intelligent.*

Once already she'd mistaken his bumbling as an act. She wouldn't make that mistake again.

"Married?" Annabelle asked.

Asa blushed. "No. I guess I haven't attracted the right woman yet."

Annabelle giggled. "I was still speaking of Maggy. Is she married?"

"Oh! I thought . . . but you didn't . . . Maggy? No, she's not married yet."

Annabelle playfully touched his arm. "You do that bumbling act effortlessly. Your timing is impeccable!"

If you only knew how natural it is for me. Asa wondered how long it would take her to realize that his oafishness was no act.

An uncharacteristic movement in the universe caught his eye. Eli Cooper was headed toward them, straight as a comet, with his gangly sidekick riding on his tail.

Asa's heart lurched. This wasn't the plan. What were they doing? Eli walked with head down, eyes forward, jaw set. Clearly, whatever he had in mind was not in Asa's best interests. He had the appearance of a man determined to pull back the curtain and expose the fraud.

"Look! Here come your friends!" Annabelle said.

"All part of the act," Asa quipped.

"There's more? How delightful!"

The quip appeared magically, as though from thin air. The words were not fashioned by any rational thought of which Asa was aware. It was as though he became aware of them as they were spoken, just as Annabelle had.

Eli reached the edge of the shade and stopped. "Madam"—he nodded toward the lesser beauty first. Then, with the bow of a gentleman, he said to Annabelle, "Miss, is this brutish bore, this silly simpleton, annoying you? Say the word, and we will escort him from the green."

"Are you a comedian?" Annabelle asked him.

Eli appeared confused. "Comedian?"

"What is your text? Is it poetical?"

"Poetical? Uh . . . if your lady wishes, I suppose," Eli stammered.

With a disappointed frown Annabelle touched her matron's arm. "He began rudely."

"Most rudely," the matron agreed.

Turning again to Eli, Annabelle asked, "Now, sir, what is your text?"

Asa grinned happily at Eli's discomfort. More so because he recognized what Annabelle was doing.

Eli pointed a rigid finger at Asa. "Look," he told Annabelle angrily, "I don't know what he's been telling you, but—"

Asa interrupted. "Good madam, he came to see your face."

Annabelle giggled at Asa. A silent communication passed between them. It was clear she knew he knew what she was playing at.

To Eli, she said, "Have you any commission from your lord to negotiate with my face? You are now most certainly out of your text, sir."

"What text?" Eli cried.

"It matters not." Annabelle's tone was sweet. "I will draw the curtain and show you the picture." With an elegant wave of her hand in front of her face, she struck a pose.

"Most excellently done," Asa said.

Though he was quoting text, it was the easiest line he'd ever delivered in his life.

Eli stood with his hands at his sides, mouth open.

"Lady, you are the cruell'st she alive," Asa declared, "if you will lead these graces to the grave and leave the world no copy."

A hand flew to Annabelle's bosom. "O, sir, I will not be so hard-hearted. I will give you divers schedules of my beauty: it shall be inventoried, and every particle and utensil labeled to my will. As item, two lips, indifferent red; item, two . . ." She glanced at Asa. Another secret passed between them. ". . . *green* eyes with lids to them . . ."

Asa nodded that he'd understood.

". . . item, one neck, one chin, and so forth. Were you sent hither to praise me?" She looked to Eli for a response.

"Phineas and I, we were just standing over there," Eli said, "when we saw this fellow accosting you."

"You mistake the gentleman," Asa said to Annabelle. "This is not Orsino's man. Sadly, he is Malvolio."

"That's a lie!" Phineas insisted. "His name's Eli Cooper!"

Annabelle turned to Asa. "Malvolio? That pompous, priggish man-servant?"

"In the flesh, I'm sad to say," Asa replied.

Eli was nodding now. "I get it. A play. Right?" To Asa, "You set this whole thing up just to embarrass me."

"On the contrary," Asa said, "it was not I who deviated from the text, but you. As for the embarrassment, I'm afraid you've done that all on your own. I was merely following this good lady's lead."

Annabelle smiled coquettishly.

Asa added, "I daresay, had you spent less time reading French philosophers and more time reading the poets, you might have picked up on the dialogue from *Twelfth Night*."

"Do you not know Shakespeare, Mr. Cooper?" Annabelle asked.

"Of course I know Shakespeare. I've read lots of his stuff. And I mean lots. I've read so much Shakespeare I speak blank verse in my sleep. In fact, they're still talking about my rendition of . . ."

But Annabelle stopped listening and turned to Asa. "Are you familiar with Mr. Sterne's novel?"

"*Tristram Shandy*?" Asa glanced at the matron, who lifted the book in her lap and rolled her eyes. He concluded that the matron rolled her eyes a lot.

"Martha has been such a dear to read it to me, but I fear both of us are having difficulty understanding it."

Asa sat forward. With enthusiasm he said, "You have to understand that the author delights in oddities. Not only with his material, but also in his methods. He takes the utmost pleasure in tricking the reader. You must expect the unexpected."

Annabelle was hanging on his every word, while Eli slouched and shoved his hands in his pockets.

Asa reached for the book that matron Martha handed to him. He flipped the pages with his thumb, searching for a particular text. "You see, Mr. Shandy is a fountain of obscure and useless information! For example, he's of the impassioned belief that everything in the world has two handles."

"That's exactly what I'm speaking of. Two handles? What do handles have to do with anything? It makes no sense."

Asa howled. "Nothing! That's the point. It's totally ridiculous. The fact that it makes no sense is what makes it funny."

Annabelle attempted to comprehend his meaning, but the furrow on her brow indicated she still didn't quite understand. She reached for the book and turned to the front. "Here, for example. Tristram Shandy believes that all of his problems in life stem from the fact that his mother asked his father if he remembered to wind the clock. Does that make sense to you?"

Asa laughed. "Do you really want to know?"

"Of course."

Asa signaled for her to lean close to him. Cupping his hand over her ear, he whispered to her.

Annabelle Byrd's hand flew to her mouth. She pulled back, laughing, her face crimson. "Master Rush! It doesn't say that, does it?"

Asa laughed with her. "You said you wanted to know!"

She handed him the book. "Show me!"

While turning to the appropriate passage, Asa couldn't help himself. He glanced up to see what Eli was doing. All he saw was Eli's back as he and Phineas walked away.

"Is he still watching?" Annabelle kept her eyes forward as she asked.

While continuing to walk beside Annabelle, Martha glanced over her shoulder. "Still watching."

Annabelle allowed herself a smile. So Asa was standing under the tree exactly where they'd left him after more than an hour of Sunday afternoon diversion.

"You're shameless," Martha said. "You know that, don't you? Pretending you didn't understand that vulgar novel."

"I know," Annabelle replied, still smiling.

"And that was no act when he first arrived. All that bumbling and stammering and hemming and hawing. No act. That was all him."

"I know," Annabelle said again, her smile widening.

CHAPTER 5

As Asa hoped, the weekend diversions had made the other fellows on campus forget about his disastrous disputation debut. And even if they hadn't, it wouldn't have mattered. From that one hour on the green with Annabelle, Asa had enough good feelings stored up inside to keep him happy through a crusade of jests.

And, not by coincidence, the word *crusade* accurately described the fury of Eli Cooper's vengeance. He was always careful to stay within the rules. But then, with him being a sophomore and Asa a freshman, the rules favored Eli.

From the first week of school, freshmen are taught the rules under which they will suffer for a year.

Whenever they approach a gate or door, they have to look around to see if there are any superiors—everyone on campus except fellow freshmen—within three rods of them. If a superior is nearby, they can not enter the door or gate until given permission by the superior to do so.

In passing up or down the stairs, or going through a narrow passage, freshmen are to step aside and make way for their superiors.

Freshmen are not permitted to run in the college yard.

When entering the room of a superior, a freshman must first knock on the door and always leave the door as he found it, whether open or shut.

Upon entering the room of a superior, a freshman is not permitted to speak until spoken to. He is to reply modestly to all questions and perform all instructions decently and respectfully.

Freshmen are not permitted to tarry in the room of a superior after they are dismissed.

Freshmen must always rise when a superior enters or leaves a room, and are never to sit in the presence of a superior unless expressly permitted to do so.

Above all else, freshmen are to obey general order number one: "To perform all reasonable errands for any superior, always returning an account of the same to the person who sent them."

Superiors have no trouble identifying errand-ready freshmen. They are the only men on campus not wearing robes. Professors wear black robes. Sophomores, juniors, and seniors wear camblet gowns. Freshmen are not permitted to wear either gowns or caps.

Infractions of the rules are dealt with quickly and with enthusiasm by a group of superiors, usually sophomores who are eager to give as they had been given the previous year. The attic is the usual disciplinary site, a part of the college Asa became very familiar with.

"You again!" A sophomore, with a long face that resembled that of a mule, leaned into Asa until their noses were almost touching.

Flecks of spittle hit Asa's face every time the sophomore yelled. Asa didn't know the fellow's name, only that he was a sophomore and that he enjoyed disciplining freshmen.

"I've seen slow-witted freshmen before, boy, but none as slow as you," Mule-face shouted. "Or are you just stubborn, boy? Is that it? Are you stubborn? Mule stubborn?"

Asa stood where they'd placed him when he entered the attic, with his toe cozied up to a crack between floorboards. It was dark, with only a half-dozen candles providing illumination. Black shadows stretched and slid along the floor and ceiling in constant motion, so that it seemed like there were twice as many accusers in the room—one flat, shadowy, and silent accuser for every human one.

"Answer me, boy. Are you stubborn or stupid?"

"Neither, sir!" Asa said.

"Neither? Well, you have to be one or the other to be summoned to the attic as often as you are."

Eli Cooper, the real reason Asa was summoned to the attic frequently, stood back, his arms folded, unsmiling but obviously approving of the trimming. That's what they called it. A *trimming*, a thrashing.

"So which is it, boy? Stupid or stubborn?"

Sweat rolled down the sides of Asa's forehead and into his eyes. He blinked. The sweat stung. "Stubborn, sir."

It was useless to put up too much of a fight. It only encouraged them. The harassing would continue until Asa completed the four parts to a confession: to confess, to be sorry, to ask forgiveness, and to promise reformation.

"Now that wasn't so hard, was it?" Mule-face chided. Playing to the room, he said, "We got ourselves a stubborn mule, men. He admits to it. Do you think that satisfies the first part of his confession?"

"I confess to violating the three-rod rule, sir," Asa added.

The sophomore rounded on him.

"Did I ask you a question, mule? Did you hear me ask you a question?"

"Sir, you asked if my admission to being stubborn satisfied the first part of confession. I was merely clarifying."

Asa knew it was a long shot. And he knew it was probably a mistake to offer the confession as he did. He took the chance in hopes of speeding things up.

"Now I'm confused," Mule-face said. "You said you were stubborn, but it seems to me that was a pretty stupid thing to do. Maybe you're more stupid than stubborn. Do you wish to change your answer?"

"No, sir."

"You want to stick with stubborn?"

"Yes, sir."

"Mule stubborn."

"Yes, sir."

Mule-face considered this. "All right. Then, maybe it is time to hear your confession."

"Sir, I confess to violating the three-rod rule, sir."

In truth, Asa hadn't violated the rule. As he approached the door to the chapel, he performed the required surveillance. No one was in sight. Then, just as he opened the door, one of Eli's friends popped up from behind a bush well within the offending distance. A whole group of them did this for sport.

It did no good to complain. They were smart enough to choose times and locations when there were no witnesses. It reduced an objection to a freshman's word against a sophomore's word, and freshmen never won that contest.

Mule-face was waving off Asa's confession even as he was speaking it. "Not good enough. Not good enough by half. We want to hear it in mule-ese."

"Sir?"

"The language of donkeys and mules, Mr. Rush. In other words, your native language." And if Asa still didn't understand, Mule-face said, "Bray, Mr. Rush. Bray."

Laughter encircled Asa.

Mule-face stood back, arms folded, and waited for Asa to bray.

Asa examined the figures in the shadows. There would be no reprieve coming from this bunch. He cleared his throat and let loose with what he thought was a pretty good imitation of a donkey.

"Louder, freshman!"

Asa gave it more effort.

A chant was taken up all around him. "Louder! Louder! Louder! Louder!"

Asa gave it everything he had.

"No, no, no!" Mule-face cried. "Not good enough by half! Like this—"

With the chant settling into a pounding rhythm, Mule-face leaned within inches of Asa's nose and let loose with a horrifyingly accurate donkey bray. His ears were pinned back, his teeth jutted forward, and even his breath had a barnyard smell to it. Mule-face had obviously done this before.

It was so well done, in fact, that Asa pulled back in astonishment. The room fell silent. Everyone stared at Mule-face.

In a small, hoarse voice, Mule-face said, "Like that, Mr. Rush."

Now that Mule-face had made a perfect donkey of himself, common sense argued that Asa should welcome the shifting of focus away from himself as a gift from God. However, whenever a group of men gather in a room, the roar of testosterone is so loud, common sense is rarely observed.

Asa couldn't keep his mouth shut. "A fine demonstration, Mr. Bottom. One that I could never hope to match."

Mule-face didn't get it. Asa wasn't surprised. Had fortune been shining on him, his comment would have gone unnoticed. However, fortune rarely favors the foolish.

Laughter rippled through the shadows.

"What's so funny?" Mule-face edged to the shadows, where someone enlightened him. Asa didn't hear it all, but he heard enough. Shakespeare and *A Midsummer Night's Dream*.

Asa's inquisitor returned enraged. "Very funny, Mr. Literary Scholar! Let's see how funny you think this is."

For thirty minutes Asa was trimmed by superiors. They spun him around. Blew tobacco smoke in his face. Made him bow to his shadow. And cuffed him repeatedly around the ears and cheeks.

Asa took it. He had no choice. The story of one freshman who had bolted from the attic was legendary. He had run, swearing contempt on his accusers, vowing that he would not stay and suffer their abuse a moment longer. He had taken his case to the Faculty Judgments committee. The faculty had ruled against him, noting that the freshman's actions were contrary to the laws of God and this college. He had been suspended until he made a full public confession.

STORM

So with little recourse Asa cringed and took everything that was dished out to him. He focused instead on revenge. His mind was a boiling cauldron of imagined reprisals. Bitterly rancid now, how sweet would be the taste when he spooned out a dose to each of these fools.

A hard cuff to the face and Asa tasted blood.

He grinned because it infuriated them.

He didn't know how or when, but he'd give back to them everything he got—pressed down and shaken together and running over—with the largest measure reserved for Mr. Eli Cooper.

CHAPTER 6

Some men command attention by entering a room. When Dr. Timothy Dwight entered a room, he commanded the attention of the men who command attention.

An intellectual giant, a preacher, and a poet, Dwight hoisted the burden of Yale upon his shoulders with the intent of rebuilding a ruined college. It had a reputation for coarse language, pranks, scuffles, and a notorious brawl with local sailors that had made national headlines. Within a year of taking the presidential oath of office, Dwight had instituted needed reforms, including mandatory chapel services, during which he preached daily to the student body. Prayer and praise became part of the college's curriculum.

Dwight's detractors accused him of turning the campus into a little temple. The president of Yale took their accusations as a compliment.

It was Dwight's dynamic spiritual leadership that had attracted Asa to Yale. In church circles there was an air of expectation that God's Spirit had been pent up too long in America's academic hallways, and that something exciting was soon going to happen. If it did, it would most certainly happen at Yale.

Asa hunched over a small desk in President Dwight's office. The late-afternoon sun streamed through the windows, stretching shadows across the wooden floor and up several shelves of books.

Dwight was pacing and dictating. "It is the negligent ship's captain who ignores signs in the heavens of an approaching squall. And make no mistake, gentlemen, storm clouds are roiling on the horizon, a storm far more foreboding than a bunch of rowdy students and dilapidated buildings."

While printing dilapidated, Asa's hand cramped. He freed it of the pen, shook out the cramp, and quickly finished the sentence lest he get too far behind. He needn't have hurried. Dwight stood in the center of the study. His head back, he rubbed tired eyes. Asa took advantage of the pause to flex his hand.

His head still back, as though he was reading from the ceiling, Dwight continued. "It threatens our colleges, our churches, our homes, our future. In size and force, it is unlike anything our nation has faced in its young history. Already its winds are testing the strength of our structures. Its thunder is echoing down the halls of our institutions." He dropped his arms to his side. "Your opinion, Mr. Rush. What do you think of it so far?"

Asa became rigid. He didn't mind reciting lines. He was good at that. But whenever one of his teachers or tutors asked him to formulate an opinion, his mind seized.

Who was he to pass judgment on someone smart enough to write a book that was required reading in colleges? Or a college president's sermon? What was he supposed to say? "Dr. Dwight, I think your introduction is weak and your analogy trite. Maybe you'd better rethink it"?

"Mr. Rush? Are you still with me?"

Without lowering his pen—he was still hoping it would not remain inactive for long—Asa said, "I-I . . . like it."

Dwight lowered his head and leveled one of his infamous glares at Asa. "Thank you for that vote of confidence, Mr. Rush. Now, do you mind telling me *specifically* what you like about it?"

Asa gulped. Hope kept his pen poised. "The storm analogy, sir. I think it's effective. Descriptive. Emotional. Roiling dark clouds and all."

"Is it?" Dwight asked.

The question sounded rhetorical to Asa. At least that's how he chose to interpret it. He hunched over the parchment, hoping the image would inspire Dr. Dwight to continue his dictation.

"Analogous to what, Master Rush?" Dwight asked. "The wind and thunder. To what are they analogous?"

Asa squirmed.

His was a privileged seat, reserved in past years for seniors. Far brighter students than he had squirmed in this seat. And as far as Asa knew, he was the only freshman ever to occupy it. At the moment, however, that privilege was an ill-fitting suit.

He'd heard Dwight describe his approach to discipline as governing by eye and tongue. Every student at Yale at one time or another withered under Dr. Dwight's blistering glance or felt outmatched and overwhelmed by his force of argument.

Asa took a deep breath. He cleared his throat. He sat up straight in his chair.

The silent shadow of the six-foot-tall president fell across Asa's desk.

Having run out of stalling tactics, Asa said, "Um . . . I would assume the storm is the French Revolution? Or . . . or more specifically, if not the Revolution itself, the popular theories that fuel it." He risked a glance at Dwight to see if his guess was correct.

"Go on," Dwight urged.

Asa would have loved to oblige Dr. Dwight, but he'd just blurted out every thought in his head regarding the subject. He could check again, but it would do no good. The cupboards were bare.

"What might the insubstantial winds of a revolution signify?" Dwight prompted.

Winds. Winds. Revolutionary winds. Insubstantial.

That was a clue. A definite clue.

Insubstantial revolutionary winds.

Asa squeezed shut his eyes in much the same way hands wring a wet rag to force out the last drop of water. "A theory . . . um, a postulate . . . an idea."

"Very good, Master Rush. I was aiming for idea. And the thunder?"

Some fellows feed off success. Not Asa. The rag was wrung. This was pure torture. There was nothing left in . . .

"Rhetoric!" he shouted. "Thundering rhetoric!"

"Excellent, Master Rush!"

Asa had no idea where that came from. A gift from God most certainly. It just popped into his head, and he said it.

"Are you ready to continue?" Dwight asked him.

That was the first question Dr. Dwight asked him for which Asa knew the answer with certainty. He was more than ready to continue. Ready didn't begin to describe how ready he was. He was itching to start. Desirous to start. Aching to start. Cramp in his hand? What cramp? It wasn't nearly as painful as the cramp in his brain from all the questions.

Yet he didn't want to show how utterly intimidated he felt. So, with a calmness he did not feel, he said simply, "Yes, sir. I'm ready."

Dwight braced himself with a breath and began. "Some observers scoff at those of us who are sounding the alarm," he said, falling into his public speaking cadence. "Are we children that we should cower every time the wind howls, or hide at the sound of thunder? I would answer, 'It is the wise man who protects his children from winds of hurricane force. It is the wise man who scurries his children to shelter at the sound of thunder, which is a harbinger of fatal lightning.'"

Asa scratched the words furiously.

Dwight took note and paused long enough for him to catch up. "Make no mistake, gentlemen," he continued, "the winds of deism are gathering force. The thunder of French skepticism is rattling the very foundation of our country. If we do not sound the warning now, within a generation it will be too late. The streets of our towns will be littered with barricades. Our colleges will become shrines to the pagan philosophers Hume and Voltaire. And our churches will be turned into museums.

"Did not the apostle warn us in his letter to the churches of Colossae: 'Beware lest any man spoil you through philosophy and vain deceit, after the tradition of men, after the rudiments of the world, and not after Christ.'

"Gentlemen, I have set out to accomplish three tasks. I shall endeavor, in the first place, to prove to you that this philosophy is vain and deceitful; secondly, to show you that you are in danger of becoming prey to it; and thirdly, to dissuade you by several arguments from thus yielding yourselves a prey."

Dr. Dwight had wandered to the far side of his desk and pulled out the chair with his eyes closed. Slumping into it, his head fell back. He breathed steadily.

Asa recognized the signs. They were done for the day. He set down the pen.

"Do you realize how great is the threat we face, Master Rush?" It was more of an opening line than a question.

Asa made no attempt to answer.

"The heart of virtue lies in an acknowledgment of the authority of God's laws and in the obedience to its precepts, Master Rush. Those who deny the authority of the Bible reject the only legitimate system of morality." His eyes still closed, he sighed. "I fear for our country. I fear that the fascination with the French Revolution and the fires that are fueling it—namely, deism and skepticism—are leading Americans toward a series of inevitable transformations." Dwight's tone was somber.

Asa leaned forward to better hear the concerns of the man he respected more than any other man in the world.

"If Americans become partakers in this national sin, our churches will become temples of reason, ordered worship will become a Jacobin frenzy, and virtuous young men and women will be polluted and debauched. Bibles will be cast into bonfires. Nationally we are already seeing the strain it is taking on our country with the approaching presidential election. The emerging party spirit is fraught with evils. The rise of Democratic clubs is akin to anarchy. Of this evil I have the most painful apprehension. While the steady and well-disposed inhabitants are sufficiently numerous and well inclined, they are so supine that our enemies generally prevail.

"I loathe the Jeffersonian tactics. Yet they will most certainly continue because they are effective. I have long been aware that the Democratic gentlemen intend to make a grand effort against President Adams. Their industry is immense and committed. Organized. Systematic. Everywhere visible. And they boast of certain, or nearly certain, victory. The introduction of Mr. Jefferson opposing a sitting president will ruin the Republic."

"What is your impression of the candidates, Dr. Dwight?" Asa surprised himself with the question. But how often did one get to ask such a question from such a learned man?

"I am doubtful about the election. Mr. Burr is a dangerous man, and all the unpopularity of his measures will fall on the Federalists. I have been informed that Burr has said that if he should be president, he will not leave one Federalist bone upon another."

"And Mr. Jefferson?"

"There is not, I presume, an Englishman who regards the character and politics of Mr. Jefferson and Mr. Madison with less approbation than myself. The former I consider as a cunning, the latter as a weak, man."

"You support President Adams."

Dwight smiled. "I am a Federalist, a New Englander, and a Yankee. And so is President Adams. There is no better man, in my opinion, to lead our country for another four years."

"And the Illuminati?" Asa asked.

A fearful expression came across Dwight's face, even more fearful than when he was talking about Jefferson.

"What do you know of the Illuminati?" Dwight asked.

"Only that they're a secret society of powerful and wealthy men."

"Evil, godless men," Dwight said with the same tone he might use to describe Satan himself. "Men who worship profit above all else. Men without morals or ethics except those shared among cutthroat pirates. Pray to God you never have anything to do with them."

"Is it really that bad, sir?"

Asa hoped his tone communicated that he wasn't questioning Dr. Dwight's assessment or judgment. It was just that the severity of the learned man's tone scared him. Asa read the newspapers. He heard the rhetoric. The threats. Like the one the Democrats were making that if Jefferson won the election and Adams refused to relinquish the presidency, they would take up arms and march on Washington.

Would it really come to that?

Would Adams and the Federalists defy the vote and attempt to maintain control of the presidency? There had never been an election like this one before. Who knew what men would do?

Asa needed to hear words of consolation.

Dr. Dwight turned and stared out his window. "I fear the mood of the country is much worse than the papers present it. Unless God intervenes, I fear these United States will be ripped apart by the dissension. Our fledgling country stands at a crossroads. This election will most surely put our Constitution and Christian faith to the test."

Asa had come to assume that the stability of the last twelve years of Washington's and Adams's administrations would continue forever. As it appeared now, his assumption had been naive.

"But enough of this!" Dwight said cheerfully. "Pull your chair closer and let's talk."

The invitation took Asa by surprise. He'd only been Dwight's assistant a couple of months, and this was the first time the president of the college set aside his office so openly. His grin was infectious.

"What do you hear from Greenfield?" Dwight clasped his hands eagerly. "Tell me everything. How's Maggy? Your parents? Does Old Man Garrett still have his headstone propped beside the front door of the general store? How long has he had it sitting there now?"

Asa thought a moment. "Going on thirty years."

Dwight laughed. "What does he say? 'I 'spect I'll be goin' ta meet my maker any day now.'"

Asa laughed at the memory. For the last three decades, every time anyone walked into Old Man Garrett's store in Greenfield, they heard the same prediction.

For a quarter of an hour, Asa caught Dr. Dwight up on the news from home. Maggy's letters were always upbeat, despite the fact that their father was dead and their mother had a weak heart. The school at Greenfield had been Maggy's salvation, one of the few in New England that allowed females to attend. Asa wondered if Dwight would attempt to open Yale to females, but he didn't ask.

"And your studies?" Dwight asked.

"It's harder here than at Greenfield. But then, I pretty much expected it would be."

Asa didn't say anything about his first disputation. He didn't know if Dr. Dwight had heard about it or not. He hoped he hadn't.

"You're eating? Getting plenty of rest?" Dwight asked.

It was no casual question. Asa knew there was a history behind it. When Timothy Dwight was a student at Yale, he had come to the conclusion, in his youthful zeal to succeed, that overeating was causing an annoying sluggishness that interfered with his studies. So he had restricted his intake of food to twelve mouthfuls of vegetables per meal. He had risen earlier every morning than the other students and parsed one hundred lines of Homer before breakfast.

It didn't take long before his health broke, and he was forced to cease his academic endeavors for a time. And while he managed to recoup his vigor, his eyesight was permanently damaged. He could not read for any length of time before being overtaken by severe headaches. He had to rely upon a succession of student assistants to fulfill his role as president and professor.

"Thank you for asking, sir," Asa replied. "I'm eating regularly and getting plenty of sleep."

"Cards? Are you staying away from cards?"

Asa suppressed a smile. It was the easiest question he'd been asked all day. "No card games for me, sir. No drinking either. I'm all too familiar with the negative effects they can have on a life and family."

On my father, he thought more specifically.

Asa concluded, "I find it best not to associate with those who drink and play cards. They're not the sort with whom I wish to mingle."

"You know I was quite a card player when I was a student here," Dwight said, his expression serious.

Asa's eyes grew wide. Was Dr. Dwight pulling his leg?

"It's true," Dwight insisted.

"Sir, I didn't mean to imply . . ."

"It was almost my undoing," Dwight admitted. "My grades suffered for it. Addictive, cards are. A vice. Nothing good can come from the hours wasted at a card table."

Asa breathed easier.

"Look at the shadows!" Dwight slapped the arms of his chair and stood. "It's getting late."

Asa stood also and half-turned to retrieve his writing tools.

Dr. Dwight called him back. "I'm wondering if I might ask a favor."

"All you have to do is name it." Excitement surged through Asa at the mere thought that Dr. Dwight would ask a favor of him.

"Do you recall John Hillhouse?"

Asa nodded. "We exchange occasional letters. He's married now and has a son."

When John's father had perished at sea, John had moved to Greenfield from Boston to live with his aunt. He'd had trouble fitting in at first. He was crude and arrogant. One day Dwight pulled Asa aside and asked him to befriend Hillhouse. Asa agreed, though reluctantly. He didn't like Hillhouse any more than the others did. Nevertheless, Asa agreed to try. The first couple of weeks were rough, but eventually Hillhouse came around, and Asa learned he wasn't such a bad fellow after all.

"I have a similar assignment for you," Dwight said. "A young man with potential. However, I fear he's falling in with the wrong sort. What he needs is a good friend."

"I'll do my best, sir."

A somber weight seemed to descend on the president's shoulders. His face registered it. "I don't believe he's a Christian, though he comes from a good family. What I'm asking of you goes beyond offering him your friendship. I want you to show him what God can do in a life committed to the cause of Christ."

Asa matched Dwight's mood. "Yes sir."

"You understand, don't you, that what I'm asking of you is more than just a personal favor? This is how we will lead America back to God—one life at a time. I am commissioning you to do everything within your power to enlist him in Christ's army."

Now Asa felt Dwight's burden. "I understand, sir."

"Get down on your knees."

Asa blinked at the somber tone. The seriousness in Dwight's eyes. The man's bearing. Everything about Dr. Dwight squelched any desire Asa had to ask him to repeat what he'd just said.

Asa knelt.

Dwight placed his hands on the boy's head. "In the name of Christ, the Lord, who is the image of the invisible God, the firstborn over all creation, in whom the fullness of God dwells to reconcile to himself all things, by making peace through his blood, shed on the cross.

"As a servant of Christ Jesus, by the will of God, I commission you into the army of the blessed, to live and to speak in such a way that all men may know without question that you are a man of God, a soldier of the king.

"In such capacity I commission you to demonstrate the undying love of Christ to one Eli Cooper, that he may turn from error to truth and life."

Dr. Dwight continued praying.

However, Asa heard nothing that was said following *"Eli Cooper."*

CHAPTER 7

Why did it have to be Eli Cooper? Of all people, why him? There were more devils on campus than had been cast out of Mary Magdalene, so why this particular one?

Asa took the stairs two at a time, his lungs burning from the effort, his wrist aching as he attempted to keep the spillage of water from the pitcher to a minimum.

How much did Dr. Dwight know about him and Eli Cooper? he wondered. Did he know about the disputation? About the events on the green? How could he? Did he know about the four trimming episodes? Or was it five now? Asa had lost count.

Turning a corner, Asa eyed the second flight of stairs. Catching his breath, he attacked them as he lamented having to scrap his plans for vengeance.

Whether he knew it or not, Dwight's commissioning had put an end to Asa's plans. Was this Dwight's goal all along? Asa felt at a loss. He had developed something of a sweet tooth for vengeful thoughts. They fed him during times of hazing. Consoled him at night. Gave him pleasure. In effect, Dr. Dwight confiscated all such thoughts from Asa while he was on his knees. How could Asa savor sweet revenge now, after the most godly man he knew had prayed prayers atop his head?

With a final gasp Asa reached the crest of the stairs. Sweat trickled down the sides of his face. He urged weary legs down a dormitory hallway that smelled of soiled clothes, an odor that would forevermore remind Asa of his college days. In his haste, water sloshed over the sides of the pitcher and onto his hand, spilling on the hallway floor.

Asa stumbled to Eli Cooper's door. He knocked. No one answered. He didn't expect anyone would.

Opening the door, he stumbled inside. The shades were drawn. In the dim light he could make out two beds and two desks. One bed was neatly made, but the bedclothes of the other were bunched up from a restless night. One desk was orderly—books stacked, pen and inkwell carefully aligned. A chair rested against it, its straight back as prim and proper as a schoolboy dutifully, if not eagerly, awaiting a new school day. The other desk was piled high with all manner of items, most of them having no proper place on a desk—a rumpled pair of breeches, one shoe, a hairbrush, an overturned basin, the stub of a cigar, and a stale half loaf of bread.

Asa had been inside the room only once before, a few minutes ago to get the pitcher for the water. He'd found it partially under the bed. Now he stood in the center of the room at attention, holding the pitcher of water, and waited.

The better part of an hour passed before Asa heard sounds in the hallway followed by the opening of the door. Two robed figures entered. From the expression on Eli's face, he'd forgotten that Asa would be waiting for him.

With him was Mule-face, the sophomore who had presided over Asa's most recent trimming. Until now Asa had no idea that the fellow who could bray with the best of them was Eli Cooper's roommate.

"Well, look what we have here." Eli grinned.

"As ordered, sir," Asa replied. "With your pitcher of water, fresh from the well."

"That's not my pitcher." Eli looked over at the basin and pitcher on the commode on the orderly side of the room. "*That's* my pitcher."

Asa didn't believe him. It probably showed on his face.

Sophomore Mule-face let out a whoop and collapsed onto the unmade bed. "Hey, what do you know! The frosh found my pitcher. Where'd you find it, boy? I've been looking for it for over a week."

"Word for word, Mr. Rush, repeat my instructions to you," Eli demanded.

Asa's arm, weary from holding the pitcher of water, wavered. "Sir, you instructed me to go to your room, get your pitcher, fill it with water, then return to your room and wait for you."

"That's correct. A task at which you have failed, Mr. Rush."

Asa closed his eyes. His arm felt like it was going to fall off. "I did as you requested, sir. I fetched you a pitcher of water."

"Correction," Eli said. "You fetched Tappan a pitcher of water. My pitcher is still empty."

"Much obliged," mule-faced Tappan said with a toothy grin. "You can just set it anywhere."

Asa eyed the cabinet with the washbasin on Tappan's side of the room. Like the desk, it was piled high with clothes and shoes and papers.

Asa approached it from several angles, attempting to find enough surface upon which to place the pitcher. As he pushed to make room, he started an avalanche, resulting in a book and a pair of underclothes falling to the floor.

"Watch it!" Tappan shouted. "That there's a carefully designed system. You mess with it, and I'll never be able to find anything!"

Asa retrieved the fallen items—picking up the underclothes by pinching the very edges of them—and placed them back on the pile. He had to pat them down to get them to stay.

"Now, Mr. Rush," Eli said. "My pitcher of water. Already, due to your extreme ineptness, you have kept me waiting an unreasonable amount of time for no good reason. Unless you have a valid reason you'd like to offer now?"

Asa knew what Eli was hinting at. Another trimming.

"An honest mistake, sir. Nothing more. You sent me to your room to fetch a pitcher and draw you water. I did as you requested."

"I sent you to fill *my* pitcher. And *my* pitcher is not filled," Eli argued. "A punishable offense."

"Your instructions were inadequate," Asa replied. "You failed to identify which pitcher was yours. Never having been in your room before, how was I to know?"

Asa's chest swelled with fury. Dr. Dwight had commissioned him to witness to Eli Cooper, but that didn't mean he had to lie down and let the fellow use him as a doormat.

"Of course, you may file a complaint with a faculty member," Asa said, "but I'm confident your effort will fail."

Eli stared at him.

Asa stared back.

"My pitcher of water, Mr. Rush?" Eli said. "I'm still waiting."

"Yes, sir," Asa replied.

Flush with victory—a small one, but it felt good—Asa grabbed the pitcher from the commode.

"I'm waiting, Mr. Rush!"

Asa bolted out the door and down the hallway.

"Mr. Rush! Stop!" Eli Cooper's reverberating voice overtook him.

Cringing, Asa stopped.

"Get back here."

The moment Asa reentered the room, he knew they'd gotten him. Their grins told him.

"What are the rules for freshmen regarding running?"

Asa sighed.

"Mr. Rush?"

"Running on campus is forbidden," Asa said.

"I smell a trimming!" Tappan cried. "And none too soon. I thought tonight was a lost cause. That I was going to be so bored I might even be forced to crack open a book or two just to maintain my sanity—perish the thought."

"My water, Mr. Rush," Eli said with a satisfied smile.

Asa turned to leave.

"And we'll expect you tonight," Eli said to his back. "You know the place."

As Asa descended the stairs, he thought of kneeling in Dr. Dwight's study and how that moment, which he'd thought at the time was so noble, had snatched from him forever his just revenge.

Shifting a book nervously from hand to hand, Asa turned onto Crown Street. His steps slowed. His mouth hung open. Never before had he seen such an array of wealthy houses.

He pulled a piece of paper from his pocket and compared the address written on it with the address of the corner house. He had a ways to go.

The sky disappeared as he sauntered down the canopied street. Impressive two-story mansions appeared and disappeared between the trees until he reached the address he was looking for.

For some reason he wasn't surprised it was the largest mansion on the block. Huge hedges set it off from the street. A rose-lined walkway led to the front door. As Asa approached, the house seemed to grow in size until he felt dwarfed before it.

There was a moment of indecision as he stuffed the address into a pocket. He looked at the door, then at the book in his hand. Opening the cover, he read the inscription. Second thoughts plagued him.

He turned to leave.

With a grunt, he turned back.

A burst of resolve propelled him toward the door. He knocked.

Matron Martha must have been passing behind the door even as he knocked, for it opened instantly.

Amusement spread across the woman's face. "Four weeks. Impressive. I figured it would have taken you at least five weeks to find the house. That is, if you ever worked up enough nerve."

"I've come calling on Miss Byrd," Asa said. "Is it too early for her to have visitors?"

Martha stepped aside, inviting him in. "Follow me."

Asa stepped into a world of wealth—the extent of which he had never thought possible, short of royalty. As the matron led him into the bowels of the mansion, his head swiveled, attempting to take in everything. Making himself dizzy, he fell like a drunk against an oil painting of a frowning Puritan minister.

Martha scowled at his clumsiness and straightened the painting.

Next they passed double doors opening into a library of such size that it boggled Asa's mind. It was easily double or triple the size of Yale's library. Had someone told him such a library could be found in America, he would have argued the point.

"Don't dawdle," Martha scolded.

The end of the hallway emptied into a cavernous kitchen. Half a dozen servants busied themselves with meal preparations. Loaves of bread were lifted from an oven. Sweet potatoes were peeled. Ducks were plucked.

The woman plucking the ducks glanced up to see who was trespassing in her kitchen, but her hands continued to move so quickly, they were a blur.

Martha opened a door leading outside.

Before he saw Annabelle, he heard her laughter. Although he'd only heard her laugh that one afternoon, he knew he'd recognize it anywhere. To him, Annabelle Byrd's laughter was invisible candy. The more he heard it, the more he wanted.

As Martha and Asa stepped into a spacious garden, his smile was harpooned by the sight that awaited him.

Annabelle swung happily on a garden swing, her hair and petticoat rustling backward and forward. She was a heavenly sight.

Behind her stood the devil. Eli Cooper, smiling, pushed Annabelle in the swing.

Asa muttered to Martha, "You could have warned me."

"What? And miss seeing the expression on your face? You would deprive me of that?"

Eli was finishing an anecdote. "So I said to him: 'Only if you're a codfish!'"

Annabelle laughed. "You didn't! Tell me you didn't!"

"God's honest truth!" Eli said.

Asa was standing on the edge of hell, peering into paradise. Now every laugh from Annabelle was an arrow to his heart. Every laugh from Eli was salt in the wound. Asa didn't know what to do with himself—with his hands, his feet, his eyes. He wanted to stop looking, but he couldn't.

Finally he found it within himself to turn to leave.

"Miss Annabelle!" Martha called. "You have a male caller! Another one!" She looked at Asa and shrugged. "Just doing my job."

"Asa!" Annabelle squealed. "What a delightful surprise! Come join us!"

If Asa found any pleasure in the moment, it was from the look on Eli's face just then.

With a gentle shove from Martha, Asa ambled toward the swing. His thoughts tumbled. Swinging was really a two-person activity, wasn't it? What was he going to do? Push her from the front? Alternate pushes with Eli? It didn't look like Eli was about to give ground anytime soon.

Not knowing what to do, Asa stood off to one side and watched.

After several minutes a movement caught his eye. He hadn't seen her until now, but sitting nearby, on a cast-iron chair, was an elderly woman. Her back was ramrod straight, her hands were folded in her lap. She observed Annabelle swinging without the slightest expression, amused or otherwise. From the motionless wrinkles on her face, this looked to be her natural state. Never once did her eyes blink.

For a while Asa shifted from one foot to the other. After a time he got tired and spied a rock. When he sat down, though, his knees nearly hit him in the chin.

Unable to watch Annabelle's merriment—or, more to the point, her

Eli-induced merriment—Asa thumbed through the book he'd brought with him. Again he read the inscription. He fingered the page with thoughts of ripping it out.

"Asa!" Annabelle called. "Push me! Eli is leaving."

With enthusiasm, Asa rocked forward to get up. His first effort failed. A second effort was no better. He felt like a turtle trying to right itself. He dared not look to see if Annabelle was watching his struggle. A third effort, with the assistance of a hand, was successful.

Brushing the grass from his hand, Asa approached the swing.

Having bid Annabelle farewell, Eli put a shoulder into him in passing. "Don't get any ideas, sport."

"Don't call me sport," Asa replied.

Annabelle said cheerfully in Eli's direction, "Tuesday. You won't forget?"

Eli turned and promised he would not forget. Then he was gone.

Their words passed in front of Asa with all the subtlety of messages borne by carrier pigeons. Would that they were. Asa would have shot them out of the sky.

"Hurry, Asa!" Annabelle cried. "My feet are dragging."

Dropping the book on the grass, Asa took up Eli's position, and in seconds Annabelle was giggling. Asa pushed dutifully, but there was no joy in the activity for him.

"What a pleasant surprise that you came calling on me! It's very thoughtful."

Asa mumbled something about being in the neighborhood.

Annabelle didn't seem to notice his lack of excitement. "Two handsome suitors in a single afternoon? It's enough to turn a lady's head."

Asa merely pushed the swing and didn't comment.

"Is anyone back there?" Annabelle laughed.

"I'm still here."

For several minutes Annabelle Byrd swung in silence. Then, "Stop the swing, Asa," she said. "I've had enough."

Asa stepped back and let the swing's arc die a natural death.

Climbing out of the swing, Annabelle turned to Asa. "Is something wrong?" she asked, concern on her face.

Asa couldn't look at her. "Nothing's wrong." He bent to pick up the book.

"Asa?"

"It's my fault," Asa said. "I should have scheduled an appointment."

Annabelle approached him. "You're angry."

Asa turned toward her but still was unable to meet her eyes.

But Annabelle Byrd was not to be put off easily. Taking him by the arm, she led him to a cozy bench set among the roses.

The old woman seated on the cast-iron chair followed them with her gaze.

Seated beside him on the bench, with their knees almost touching, Annabelle Byrd was agonizingly close. But instead of sending his spirit soaring to the heavens, as he would have expected, it was a slow flame that simmered his emotions.

"Eli was here to see my father," Annabelle explained. "He's one of Father's boys."

Eli was stumped. "One of your father's boys?"

"I really shouldn't be telling you this, but . . . every year my father takes applications from college students who cannot afford an education. He chooses two or three of the most promising and sponsors them. He requires regular progress reports. That's why Eli was here."

"And do all of your father's boys push you on the swing following their reports?"

Annabelle laughed as she placed a hand on Asa's cheek. "You are so adorable when you're jealous!"

The hand on the cheek earned a grunt from the iron-chair chaperon. Annabelle returned her hand to her lap.

"And Tuesday?"

"Father has something he wants to discuss with Eli but didn't have time today. It was wrong of me to call Eli a suitor. I apologize. The wicked side of me wanted to make you jealous. Had I known you'd take it this hard, I never would have done it. In truth, you are the only suitor I have had today."

Her smile was apologetic. Her green eyes glistened. Her femininity was overwhelming. Asa couldn't bring himself to believe that someone so breathtaking had a wicked side. He felt the fool for acting so petty.

"I brought you something." He handed her the book.

Holding it so she could read the spine, she said, "*Tristam Shandy!*"

"It's the next installment."

Annabelle wriggled with excitement. It was the best thank-you Asa could have received.

"How timely!" she declared. "Martha and I just finished the first book. I didn't know there would be another. It's quite hilarious, you know. Now that you've opened our eyes to the intricacies of the humor."

Asa felt like he was glowing as Annabelle opened the book, which is what he was waiting for her to do. She noticed the inscription and read it aloud.

> *A book unopened is a path not taken,*
> *A world unexplored, an uncharted sea.*
> *It would be my honor to walk this path with you.*
> *Asa Rush*

"Oh, Asa! What a lovely sentiment! This inscription. Where is it from?"

"From?"

"Who wrote it?"

"I did."

Annabelle laughed. "I mean, who composed it?"

Asa grinned. "I did."

"Why, Asa Rush! There's a poet inside of you! You composed it for me? How sweet!" She clutched the book to her bosom. "I will cherish the book and the inscription all the days of my life."

Again her hand found his cheek, prompting a similar response from the prune-faced chaperon. Only this time Annabelle let her hand linger.

In that moment Asa tasted heaven. He watched with unbridled joy as she read the inscription again, tracing a sensual finger over the words as she read.

"What's that?" Martha asked.

Annabelle and Martha stood side by side as Asa disappeared down the street. Annabelle handed Martha the book.

Martha read the spine and made a face. "Another copy?"

"A sequel."

"Wasn't one bad enough?"

"Look at the inscription."

Martha opened the cover. She chuckled. "Sappy."

Annabelle grinned and walked inside.

Martha followed her. "When he showed up the same time as Eli, I thought there would be trouble. You played them masterfully."

"It's too easy."

"We're not really going to have to read this, are we?" Martha complained as she shut the door.

CHAPTER 8

The light of a single candle danced with a shadow on the page. Asa watched the performance distractedly. He'd stopped concentrating on the words a long time ago. A mistake, since he had one final recitation from Jedidiah Morse's *American Geography* to complete before break.

He forced himself to concentrate, reading the first paragraph of chapter 12 for the third time. Reaching the end of the page, he turned it. Practiced eyes fell on the first words of the top paragraph: "From this data, we can reach but one conclusion . . ."

From what data? Asa wondered.

He'd done it again.

Angrily he turned back to the start of the chapter and began again. A minute later he slammed shut the book with a scream. He shoved the book forward and his chair back with such force that the chair toppled onto its side.

The clamor prompted the pounding of a fist on the adjoining wall. "Keep it down, Rush! Some of us are trying to study!"

Asa stood in the center of his dormitory room. His roommate's bunk was empty. Sam Gurdon had received special permission to take holiday early for his sister's wedding in Boston.

He and Gurdon got along well enough. Their schedules were so dissimilar that they rarely saw each other except at night.

Asa was glad he had the room to himself tonight. He took advantage of it by pacing.

"We have to settle this," he said aloud.

The only other movement in the room was that of the candle, and it didn't seem to know what he was talking about.

"I despise him. I loathe him," Asa continued. "And it's not likely my feelings are going to change anytime soon. I know what You're going to say. 'Turn the other cheek.' Well, I've done that, haven't I? And what do I have to show for it? Two bruised cheeks. Am I going to have to sport two black eyes and a gap-toothed smile before You're convinced that this just isn't going to work?"

Asa continued pacing. Erratic arm movements punctuated his disputation.

"Besides, it's mutual. He has no more regard for me than I have for him. He's had it in for me since the day we squared off against each other in class. He publicly attacked me! Without provocation, I might add. Every time we're in the same room, on the same green, in the same garden, I want to rip into him. I know that's not a commendable Christian attitude, but that's how he makes me feel."

With the dim lighting in the room, Asa didn't see the chair on the floor. His foot kicked it, and he managed to catch himself just before he tumbled head over heels.

Frustrated, he snatched the chair and set it upright. Then, as another thought struck him, he punctuated it by shoving the chair, and it clattered to the floor a second time.

Bam! Bam! Bam!

"Come on, Rush! We only have a few minutes until lights out!"

"Sorry!" Asa shouted at the wall.

Rolling his eyes toward the ceiling, Asa gave voice to the new thought.

"And he may have gone to Crown Street to see Captain Byrd, but when I got there, he had his hands on Annabelle's . . . swing. And if anybody's going to put his hands on Annabelle's . . . swing, it's going to be me!"

He bent over and righted the chair again.

"And where does he get off calling me 'sport'?"

He shoved the chair into the desk. Missing the well, it hit the drawer side and clamored to the floor a third time.

Bam! Bam! Bam!

"RUSH!" came the angry voice through the wall.

"Sorry!" Asa called.

He picked up the chair. His hands gripped the back so fiercely, his knuckles turned white.

"I just can't do it," he cried. "It's as simple as that. Dr. Dwight is going to have to find someone else to be Eli Cooper's moral guide, or Christian inspiration, or whatever it is I'm supposed to be. Besides, had Dr. Dwight known of our relationship beforehand, he would be the first to agree I'm the last man for this job."

His hands worked the back of the chair.

The thought of telling Dr. Dwight was not a pleasant one. Asa would do almost anything to keep from seeing disappointment in Dr. Dwight's eyes. But anything didn't include buddying up to Eli Cooper.

"I'll go to his office and tell him in the morning. No, wait. I'll tell him after the break, when I get back from Greenfield. I can bring him news from home and then ease my way into asking him to withdraw his commission."

A thought struck him. He wondered what kind of home life produced someone like Eli. What kind of parents . . .

"No!" he shouted at the ceiling. "I know where You're going with this! And the answer is no! I've already written to my family, telling them I'd be home during the break. No!"

He released the chair and swung around.

"No!"

Pacing again, his head rolled side to side, as though he were in agony.

"No! I haven't seen Maggy in months!"

He put his hands on his hips defiantly.

"It's asking too much! I've never traveled farther than Philadelphia! It would consume my entire break! I'm not going to do it!"

In the hallway Asa could hear the distant voice and footfalls of the resident steward in what had come to be a nightly ritual.

"Lights out!"

Step. Step.

"Lights out."

"I'm not going to do it!" Asa hissed.

The steward was right outside Asa's door. "Lights out, Mr. Rush!"

Asa walked over to the desk, cupped the flame, and extinguished it.

"I'm not going to do it!" he told the dark.

With Philadelphia to his back, Asa Rush headed toward the western frontier, keeping Eli Cooper and his two traveling companions in sight. The trio was approaching a sharp turn in the road. Asa slowed his horse. His mount, more suited to the field than travel, was a loan from his roommate, Gurdon, another first-year student who was more than eager for Asa to borrow it. No payback terms were stipulated, which bothered Asa the longer he rode. He didn't know Gurdon well enough to know what he'd gotten himself into.

As the three men took the curve, Eli glanced over his shoulder, then continued riding.

When the coast was clear, Asa pulled out from behind a cluster of trees. After a couple of days on the road, he'd become experienced at anticipating potential trouble spots. While he had a map's knowledge of where he was going, following someone who was familiar with the trail gave him a sense of added assurance. And while he didn't like to think of it, in the back of his mind, he figured that if he happened upon any sudden danger, Eli would come through in a pinch. They had their differences, but he didn't think they were so great that Eli would wish him dead.

Now that the decision to head west on his break had been made, Asa had to admit to enjoying the sense of adventure that accompanied the journey. Everyone he'd known who had traveled west returned with lots of stories to tell. Now he would be one of the storytellers.

At the moment, he was still waiting for a story to present itself. So far the trip had been rather monotonous. The only tale he had to tell was of a sore backside, road grit between his teeth, and sunburned skin.

<hr />

Asa fought back an onslaught of panic. He blinked dust from his eyes. It had been two days since he'd lost sight of Eli, and now he feared he'd lost the town of Huntington as well.

He'd traveled all morning on a dirt strip not wide enough to call a road and had yet to encounter a person or any kind of structure that suggested civilization. All he knew was that he was heading west, and that—gratefully—from the sun.

Two days ago he lost Eli in a downpour. The sky turned black, the heavens let loose, and Asa was unable to see anything farther than ten feet. This morning, when the weather broke, he assumed he was on the road to Huntington. But he found himself riding into the rising sun when he was supposed to be heading west. That correction made, he should have reached Huntington hours ago, according to his calculations.

Just then he heard something. He cocked his head and smiled. If it was what he thought it was . . .

On the right side of the road, a wall of bushes blocked his way. He rode on until he found an opening. A short descent, and he was over-looking the Ohio River.

Finally, a landmark he recognized.

Now to find Eli.

Whistling, Asa followed the ancient river downstream.

CHAPTER 9

While he still hadn't managed to catch sight of Eli, Asa knew this much: he was in Kentucky. Earlier in the day he passed through Salt Lick and Sharpsburg. Eli's home—Millersburgh—would be coming up soon. None too soon for Asa, though. He'd come to one conclusion so far on this journey. He had the backside of a student, not an explorer—one that was better suited to a classroom chair than a horse's saddle.

Asa didn't anticipate having any trouble locating Eli come morning. Millersburgh wasn't New York or Boston. Which meant that tomorrow morning would be the day of reckoning. What were the chances of convincing Eli that he just happened to be riding through Millersburgh? Every scenario Asa imagined ended with Eli throwing a punch at him, or worse.

Maybe he should wait until Sunday. Eli would think twice about killing him in church on Sunday, wouldn't he?

Asa rode into a thick patch of air. He smelled the river before he saw the bridge. To the familiar *clop, clop, clop* of his horse's hooves Asa crested the bridge. As he did, he saw a glow of light just beyond a forest of trees. And he heard something too. It was faint, but it sounded like music.

The music of a thousand voices.

STORM

The encampment was woven into the trees and terrain. Asa estimated there were about forty wagons in all with an equal number of buggies or carriages, a greater number of horses, and thousands of people. The glow Asa saw from a distance was that of hundreds of candles, lamps hanging from branches, and torches bobbing along, lighting the way for campers.

Asa saw a trio of young men on the outskirts, laughing and shoving one another in play.

"Excuse me," Asa called to them.

They stopped and studied him, but not out of fear or suspicion.

Asa motioned to the broader activity. "What's going on here?"

They looked at him strangely. "You must be the only person this side of the Mississippi who doesn't know!"

Asa couldn't dispute that.

"Revival. A real Holy Ghost barnburner! Can't you feel it?"

Asa looked around him. At present he felt road weary and hungry. However, his interest was piqued. He rode on. The closer he got, he did begin to feel something, as all around him people were humming or singing or walking hand in hand or hugging or crying until it seemed the very trees trembled with excitement.

He dismounted and secured the reins to a bush, then allowed himself to be swept along with the general flow of foot traffic. They appeared to be drawn to the ridge beyond which Asa could see only stars.

A hand clamped down on his shoulder from behind.

Startled, Asa turned to see the heavily bearded face of a stranger.

"This your first night, son?" The man's eyes sparkled clear blue. His smile revealed overlapping teeth.

"Does it show?" Asa asked.

The man let out a laugh that drew stares. "You look a tad bewildered, that's all. Don't worry. You're among friends. God's people. Whatever you're looking for, you'll find here. And more."

"I'm looking for Eli Cooper," Asa said.

"He owe you money?"

Asa grinned. "A friend from college."

The man turned to two other men and three women he appeared to be traveling with and asked them if they knew Eli. "Sorry." The man turned back. "Is he from around here?"

"Millersburgh."

"We're from Paris," one of the women told him.

Odd. They don't look or sound French.

The woman smiled, as though she'd read his mind. "Paris, Kentucky. Just a few miles from here."

By now they had crested the hill, and a huge field opened up to them, populated by a restless sea of heads.

The bearded man and his companions wished Asa well as they split off and strode purposefully through the crowd. Asa stood for a moment on the crest, taking in the sight before him.

People everywhere were clapping, stamping, trembling, singing, laughing, dancing, raising their hands into the night air, and some had fallen onto the ground and were motionless. No one seemed alarmed at those on the ground, though to Asa they looked unconscious. The rest of the people stepped around them.

Venturing in among the masses, Asa passed a woman, her face turned heavenward in ecstasy, her hands raised in praise, her cheeks wet with tears. A man on his knees was doubled over in agony, rocking back and forth, wailing for God to forgive him. Two young ladies were hugging and laughing and crying all at the same time. It was a valley charged with emotion.

There were four preachers in four different sections of the field preaching simultaneously. One stood atop a wagon bed, and another on a wooden box. One was on a cider barrel, and one on a small platform erected for this sort of thing. A few feet away a fifth preacher jumped up on a tree stump and began expounding with a deep voice that rolled like thunder.

Each preacher seemed to have his own congregation of listeners with the fringes overlapping. Contrary to what one would think, there was no confusion. While one group was singing, another was praying, and yet another was shouting encouragements to the preacher. Each group seemed to be part of a grand symphony of worship and praise.

As Asa moved among them, he knew now what the boy who initially greeted him was talking about. There was an energy here. He could feel it invigorating him. He no longer could feel the effects of his journey. He wanted to sing. To shout. To join his voice with others in praise. He couldn't imagine anyone's standing here and not feeling what he was feeling. It would be like jumping into the ocean and not getting wet.

Asa gravitated toward one lanky preacher with hollow cheeks who was instructing his congregation to back away from his makeshift wooden-box pulpit.

"Form a pen. Form a pen," he said repeatedly, and he backed them away from an area about twenty feet square.

Once the area was cleared, the preacher stood in the center of the pen. Someone started singing, and the others in the congregation joined in.

"If you need God, join me in this pen," the preacher said, his eyes framed by earnest eyebrows. "You know who you are. God knows who you are. And He knows your need. You can't hide it from Him, no matter how hard you try. Join me. Join me in this pen."

The congregation sang and waited.

"Your sin, your sin, your sin. Black sin. Deadly sin. As deadly as a serpent's bite and twice as painful. Your sin will do you in. Why carry it any longer? Why embrace an adder? Join me. Join me here."

A middle-aged man, hunched over, stepped into the pen. Then a woman wringing her hands. The preacher went to each of them in turn. Greeting them. Praying for them.

Another man stepped into the pen.

Then another.

As the preacher prayed with the woman, all of a sudden she shrieked and fell to her knees. She buried her head in her hands and wept. The preacher stood over her, praying and praying and praying.

The congregation sang harder. Louder. With greater emotion.

Another man came. Then another woman. The preacher moved among them and prayed for them. They prayed for themselves. As one by one they dropped to their knees, from the congregation came shouts of encouragement and prayers. The singing and praying fell into a rhythm.

After a time Asa moved to a different part of the field, where he saw something similar to the pen. Only this time there was no preacher. A group of people had formed a ring by joining hands. A call went out to anyone who needed prayer to step into the ring.

Several people accepted the invitation. Those in the ring prayed for them with cries of such anguish that Asa was moved to tears. One woman in the circle had a child with an illness that had confounded the doctors. She held her little girl, who looked to be about three years old, in her arms. Her tears dampened the little girl's head. The circle prayed for them.

Another preacher caught Asa's attention, his voice cutting through the night air with authority. "Do we adopt the Holy Scriptures as the only rule of faith and practice?"

All those gathered around him replied, "Amen! Preach it, brother! Hallelujah!"

"Do we adopt the Holy Scriptures as the only standard of doctrine and discipline?"

"Amen! Hallelujah! Preach it!"

"Do we pledge to the world that the Holy Scriptures is the Book of books? That God is its author? And that we will not cotton to any other teaching that is not in accord with God's Holy Word?"

The response was louder still. "Amen! Preach it! Hallelujah!"

The preacher held up a Bible. "The world, the devil, and Tom Paine have tried their force but all in vain!"

The congregation cheered and praised God.

Asa grinned. He remembered one line in particular from Thomas

Paine's *The Age of Reason* that had startled him. Paine had written, "My own mind is my own church."

Such words were the stuff of the Enlightenment, the new French philosophy that New England minds were embracing.

Not here, though, near Millersburgh, Kentucky. Not if these people were any indication of the general populace, and it sure appeared to Asa that's exactly what they were. After the stuffiness of Yale academics, Asa found their emotion and enthusiasm refreshing.

What time was it?

Asa didn't know. All he knew was that he was dead tired. He could barely keep his eyes open.

He stumbled to his horse and untied the reins. With his hands reaching for his saddle, he rested his head against the side of the horse and fell asleep.

"Some pillow you got there, son," a voice said.

It startled Asa awake. He made a face. His mouth tasted of horse and leather.

"How far'd you ride?" asked the voice.

Asa turned and focused half-asleep eyes on a man in his forties, round of face and body.

"Connecticut," Asa replied.

The man let out a low whistle. "I didn't take you for a local, but Connecticut? That's a long way."

Asa didn't disagree with him.

"But then, I guess you do look like a Yankee at that."

"That bad?"

The man laughed. "You're all right, Yankee."

Asa tried to muster enough energy to mount his horse.

"Got a place to stay, Yankee?" the man asked. Then he answered his own question. "If you had a place to stay, you wouldn't be sleepin' against your horse, would you? Follow me, Yankee. Let's see if we can find you a bed."

Asa didn't know the man, so he should have been cautious. But a tired man is easily led, especially if there is the promise of a bed, and Asa followed dutifully. He was too sleepy to be polite and refuse.

"Name's McGee. Willie McGee of Lexington."

Asa offered his hand. He had forgotten he was still holding the horse's reins and that he had to transfer the reins to his other hand before he could shake hands with his host. But finally he figured it out.

"My brother Luke's a local," McGee explained. "He's here with a whole passel from his church. Maybe one of them has an extra bed. We can ask anyway."

McGee led Asa down a trail and past several campsites. In the distance Asa could see the wooden bridge he'd crossed when he first arrived.

They came upon a blazing campfire, around which five men sat talking with the ease of men who have known each other for years. The mood of the men was in contrast to other campfires he'd happened upon during his journey. None of these men started as he approached or reached for their guns or looked him over as though he were some kind of snake.

"Evenin' Pastor Campbell. Luke. Found this here Yankee propped against his horse asleep. Thought we might be able to find him a place to lay his head."

The man called Luke said, "Mildred Swanger may have a space in the back of her wagon. Her son didn't come with her. Had some fence mendin' to do."

"I have a bedroll," Asa offered. "A wagon under which I could unroll it would suit me fine."

"Are you a Catholic, son?" Pastor Campbell asked.

"No sir. Why do you ask?"

"Don't know of too many men when offered heaven would settle for purgatory."

The men around the campfire laughed.

Asa grinned.

"Luke, why don't you and your brother wander over to Mildred's wagon and see if she's up to company?" Pastor Campbell suggested.

The two men nodded and left.

"Have a seat, son," Pastor Campbell said.

Asa didn't feel like socializing. All he wanted to do was go to sleep. Nevertheless, he tied up his horse to the wagon wheel and took a seat. He looked up and found himself the center of attention.

"What's your name, son? Or should we just call you Yankee?" Pastor Campbell was a friendly sort. Short gray hair. Square face. Ready smile. He spoke with the clipped tones of a man who was accustomed to being in charge.

"My name's Asa. Asa Rush."

"And you hail from?"

"Greenfield, Connecticut."

"And your father? What does he do?"

To the man, everyone around the campfire had settled back and was content for Asa to entertain them with his life's story. He couldn't help but think if they knew how dull his life's story was, they wouldn't be so interested.

When Pastor Campbell asked about his father, Asa cringed. He wasn't keen on talking about his life, and he certainly didn't want to talk about his father, especially to a minister. But before he could respond, Pastor Campbell said, "Wait a minute! Rush . . . Rush . . . but not Greenfield. Havenhill. Right? You wouldn't be a relative of that preacher in Havenhill, the one during the Great Awakening?"

Weary, Asa nodded. "Josiah Rush. My grandfather."

Campbell sat up, looking impressed. "Men, we are in the presence of revival history. Josiah Rush was an extraordinary man. He prayed for his town, even though they'd falsely accused him of setting a fire that killed three people. Despite their anger, he never ceased to pray for them." He turned to Asa. "Did you know your grandfather?"

"A few faint memories. He died when I was young. I know him mostly through his journal."

"You read his journal?" Campbell said excitedly.

"I have his journal."

"With you?"

Asa laughed. "No, I didn't bring it with me. It's back in my room at school."

"Guess it was too much to hope for," Campbell replied, "but you never know. But you have read it. And now you've come to witness revival firsthand?"

Until Pastor Campbell said this, Asa hadn't realized exactly who it was he was sitting with, and who he had spent the evening with. At Greenfield and Yale, churches were praying for revival. But these people *knew* revival. They knew what it was like to feel the power of the Holy Spirit as He moved among a large gathering.

They were different. Even the men sitting around the fire with him were different. They weren't drunk. They didn't talk in crude language. There didn't appear to be a mean soul among them, which was very unusual. It had been Asa's experience that in any group of men there was always one who was spoiling for a fight, who picked on the weaker man, who was never happy unless he was ridiculing someone or pounding him with his fists. There was no such man here.

When Asa looked up from his ruminations, he realized they were expecting him to say something. He grimaced. He was so tired that he'd forgotten the question.

"And so you've come to witness revival firsthand?" Campbell prompted him with a smile.

"Actually, no. I didn't even know revival was going on here. I came . . ." He blinked in thought. How could he explain his reason for coming without sounding like he was stalking a man? "I came with a friend. We got separated."

"What do you do for a living, son?" Campbell asked.

"I'm a student at Yale."

"Yale?" one of the men exclaimed. "Isn't that where your boy goes, Pastor? Maybe they know each other."

A screw turned in Asa's gut. It was too much of a coincidence for him to just stumble upon Eli's father, wasn't it? Still, in the deepest regions of his mind, Asa just knew that the next word out of the preacher's mouth was going to be Eli. But he had to ask. He had to.

"Really?" Asa said nervously. "What's your son's name?"

"Walker," Pastor Campbell replied.

Asa breathed easier. *Walker. Not Eli. Walker.* What was he thinking, anyway? The preacher's name was Campbell, not Cooper.

He shook his head. "I don't know anybody named Walker, but I can ask around when I return."

Just then McGee and Luke returned.

"Mildred said she's got a spare bed and would be glad to share it," McGee reported.

"She wasn't too keen on him being a Yankee, though," Luke added.

"She said she hopes you don't mind there being two other bodies in the wagon. She's got two young 'uns."

Asa stood. "Right now any bed sounds like heaven to me."

Pastor Campbell laughed and slapped him on the back.

The next morning, after having spent a luxurious night on a mattress, Asa rode into Millersburgh in search of Eli. The town was smaller than he'd expected, consisting of a single street of shops.

It appeared to be deserted. He rode the length of the street and back again without seeing anyone. Signs in windows indicated that the owners of the shops were at the revival.

Asa dismounted in front of what appeared to be the general store—Miller's Drygoods—according to one window. The other window displayed two dresses: one that would fit a woman, the other a girl. Asa peered through the front-door window past the sign that read:

GONE TO REVIVAL
HERE AT MILLER'S DRYGOODS
ADVICE AND SALVATION ARE FREE;
THE ONE IS WORTHLESS, THE OTHER PRICELESS.
AS FOR ME AND MINE,
WE'VE GONE TO STOCK UP ON GOD'S GRACE.
COME JOIN US.
TAKE THE ROAD SOUTH TO HINKSTON CREEK.

There was a handwritten note at the bottom of the sign—

If you need anything, help yourself.
Leave a note on the counter, and I'll add it to your bill.
Arthur Miller

Asa tried the door. It was unlocked. A bell jingled, announcing to no one his presence.

Closing the door behind him, Asa wandered inside. A chill shook him. Being alone in the store without the owner present felt wrong.

He shoved his hands in his pockets and wandered the store between barrels of meal and bolts of cloth, shovels and picks propped in a corner, and dried meats hanging from the rafters.

On the counter was a pile of scraps of paper, each listing an item and a family name. A few scraps of paper had coins of payment anchoring them in place.

The bell rang, startling Asa. He turned to see a boy of eight or nine standing in the doorway.

The boy seemed just as startled as Asa.

Asa smiled.

The boy ventured into the store but kept his distance. He worked his way behind the counter and stared at a row of tins on the shelf. He worked his way down the shelf, fidgeting as he did.

"Can I help you with something?" Asa asked.

The boy, fear in his eyes, glanced up at Asa, as if he were afraid to take him up on his offer, but also afraid not to.

"What were you sent to get?" Asa asked kindly.

The boy stared at the tins.

"Did you forget?" Asa prompted.

The boy began to cry.

Asa lowered himself to the level of the boy. "Maybe I can help you. Tell me as much as you remember."

"Poppa," said the boy.

"Your father sent you. All right. Did he tell you to look behind the counter?"

Hope shined from behind glassy eyes. The boy nodded.

Asa scanned the shelves. "All right, that narrows it down. What else did he tell you? Did he describe what it was you should look for?"

The boy pointed to the tins.

"All right. Can you remember anything else?"

The boy tried hard to remember. He squinted so hard he appeared to be in pain. "Class . . . class . . . classy . . . barko."

"Classy barko," Asa repeated as his eyes moved from tin to tin. Most of them were herbs and potions and dried medicines. He reached for a tin. "Calcium carbonate?" Asa asked, holding it in front of the boy.

The boy stared at the tin. He wasn't eager to take it.

"Does your father's stomach hurt?" Asa asked.

The boy's eyes opened wide with wonder and delight.

"He sent you to get something for his stomachache?"

The boy nodded.

Asa handed him the tin. "Then this is probably the right stuff."

The boy snatched it from Asa's hand and ran for the door. The bell sounded again.

An instant later the boy returned, slapped a piece of paper on the counter, and hurried back out the door.

Asa studied the crumpled paper.

One tin
Calcium carbonate
Frank Stillman

He chuckled. "Well, that would have made things easier."

With a sigh, Asa left the drygoods store. The street looked exactly like he'd left it. Not a soul in sight. He wasn't going to find Eli this way.

Mounting his horse, he rode back to the encampment.

CHAPTER 10

There was something about standing under a celestial canopy of stars that fueled the frontier revival. Once the sun set and the stars and candles came out, the preaching improved and the Spirit went into high gear.

"I do believe, without a doubt, the Christian has a right to shout!" one preacher proclaimed.

The response from the crowd was enthusiastic.

Asa felt a tug on his hand. He looked down to see wide blue eyes staring up at him.

"Are you a preacher?"

The blond-haired girl couldn't have been more than seven years old. She was barefoot.

"I'm sorry, no. Can I—"

But she wasn't listening. She'd already gone on to the next nearest man. "Are you a preacher?"

For the next several minutes Asa followed her, observing her hunt. With each tug of the hand, she appeared more and more desperate.

Asa scanned the encampment, hoping to find Pastor Campbell, or maybe one of the men he saw preaching last night.

He saw only strangers.

The little girl was growing frantic.

Asa knelt down in front of her. Her eyes flashed hope, then faded when she realized she'd already asked him. Now she was looking past him, still looking for a preacher.

"Maybe I can help you," Asa said. "What's wrong?"

"It's my daddy." Tears threatened in the little girl's eyes.

"Is he sick?"

The girl nodded.

The memory of earlier today in the drygoods store was fresh. At least Asa knew where to find calcium carbonate if needed.

"If your daddy's sick, he needs a doctor. Maybe we can find a doctor."

The girl looked disgusted. She yanked herself away and tugged on the nearest man's hand. "Are you a preacher?"

"Sorry, dear," the man replied.

Asa grabbed her by the arm. "Take me to your father."

"You're not a preacher."

"No, I'm not, but I go to a school that makes preachers."

It was the best he could offer, and it was good enough. She took him by the hand and led him through the crowd.

She pulled him out of the revival field, past the last row of wagons, across the bridge, and into the woods. She pulled him with determination, seeming to know where she was headed. But the deeper they went into the woods, the more Asa's concern grew. Where was she taking him?

The dark woods didn't seem to bother the girl, but they bothered him. They conjured up all sorts of images, most of them violent. Nearly every one of them ended with him lying dead in the forest with a group of men standing over him, shaking their heads and saying how foolish it was for anyone to wander into the woods without some kind of weapon.

After minutes that seemed like hours, Asa caught sight of a flickering in the distance. A campfire. As he was pulled closer, he saw a wagon. A woman leaned against it, her arms folded. Her attention was riveted on a man seated at the fire.

All of a sudden Asa saw that a gun was pointed at him.

"Just turn around and go right back to where you come from," the gunman ordered. His words were heavy, as though he was drunk.

"He's a preacher, Daddy! He can help."

Asa didn't know why the girl chose to lie, but now didn't seem the time to correct her. At least not until he discerned whether the man with the gun thought his being a preacher was a good thing or a bad thing. He did wish, at this instant, that he was a preacher, though. Didn't schools of theology teach preachers how to talk drunken men into surrendering their firearms?

"I've come a long way to see you," Asa said quietly.

"Then you have a long way back," the man retorted, "and the sooner you start, the sooner you'll get there."

The little girl had a grip on Asa that anchored him to the spot. The woman was looking to him as though he were some kind of a savior. All of a sudden he had an overwhelming feeling of inadequacy.

They wanted him to stay.

The man wanted him to leave. He wanted to leave.

Two to two. A tie.

Bracing himself with a deep breath, Asa prayed for courage and took a step forward.

"You ain't too smart, are you?" the man challenged. "I'm gonna give you one more chance to walk away."

"I can't believe you'd shoot a man with your wife and daughter looking on," Asa said.

The man shrugged.

There was a sharp crack. The woman screamed. A cloud of smoke rose from the pistol.

Asa shuddered. The bullet had whizzed past his head.

"Still think I won't shoot?" The man reached into his pocket and pulled out another bullet. Searching another pocket, he found a piece of cloth wadding. With shaking hands he attempted to reload the pistol.

An idea came to Asa. With a kindly wink Asa convinced the girl to release his hand. He walked over to the girl's father, sat next to him, and watched him botch several efforts to load the gun.

"Here, let me help you." Asa grabbed the gun from the man before he could object. "Powder?"

The man pointed to a powder horn at the base of the rock upon which he sat.

Asa reached for the horn, poured a measure down the barrel, added bullet and wadding, and began ramming them down.

The man frowned. "You think you're real clever, don't you?"

"Name's Asa."

"Henderson."

Asa tapped the bullet down with vigor, replaced the rod, and handed the loaded weapon back to Henderson, who didn't seem to know what to do with it now.

While a puzzled Henderson eyeballed him, Asa said to the girl, "So, are you enjoying the revival? Have you met any children your own age?"

"You know I'm gonna blow my brains out," Henderson said.

"Figured as much," Asa replied. He turned to the woman. "Is that coffee in that pot? I sure could use a cup."

The request spurred the woman into dutiful action. She produced a tin cup from the back of the wagon and served Asa. For a time while Asa sipped the coffee, the two men stared at the fire.

"You know," Asa said, "a pistol might not be the best way to take your life."

"Yeah? What would you use?"

"Oh, I don't know . . . something less messy, that's for sure. Think about it. You're going to leave your wife an awful mess—your brains scattered all over the ground and wagon. But then, what do you care that the last thing your daughter will remember about her father is his brains on a rag?"

Henderson glanced at his daughter. "You got a better idea?" he asked Asa.

"Something sharp. Something that can cut to the heart. Quick. Efficient. I have just the thing in my saddlebag. Unfortunately, my horse is all the way back at the encampment."

Henderson smirked. "You're not gettin' me to go back there with you. I ain't that dumb."

Asa took a sip of coffee. "I'm not trying to get you to go back there."

"Sure you are."

"You think I want all those people to watch you kill yourself? It would ruin their good time." Asa lifted a finger in thought. "You know, your wife might have what we need here." Setting aside his coffee cup, he stood. "Don't go anywhere," he told Henderson.

While Asa disappeared behind the wagon with Henderson's wife, Henderson called out, "There's a rifle under the bunk on the right side. But it's not loaded, so don't waste your time."

Asa popped his head around the wagon. "Think, man. That would be just as messy as a pistol now, wouldn't it?"

"I thought you were goin' to try to get me to put down my pistol."

"If I wanted to do that, why would I have handed it back to you?"

"You got a point there." Henderson appeared to reflect for a moment. Then he yelled, "My huntin' knife is back there somewhere. Cleaned some rabbit with it last night. But the wife's kitchen knives might be sharper. You know, thinner. They're in a wooden box on the left."

Asa reappeared. "Need something sharper than kitchen knives. And I found it. Just what I need."

Henderson's expression took on the sardonic exasperation of a man who has been tricked. "The Good Book? Shoulda known you were pullin' a fast one. All you preachers are the same."

"I'm deadly serious," Asa insisted, taking his seat. "If you really want to kill yourself, there's no better way than to do it with this."

"A book?"

"Sharper than any two-edged sword."

"Get outta here." Henderson raised the pistol.

"Look, I can prove it." Asa opened the book and began flipping pages until he found what he was looking for. He held it to one side so Henderson could see it.

"Can you read?"

"'Course I can read," Henderson said.

"He's real smart," his wife added.

"Then see for yourself." Asa pointed to the words as he read them. "'For the word of God is quick, and powerful, and sharper than any two-edged sword, piercing even to the dividing asunder of soul and spirit, and of the joints and marrow, and is a discerner of the thoughts and intents of the heart.'" He lowered the book. "A pistol can't do that."

Henderson sat back. His eyes remained fixed on the open book. The barrel of the pistol slumped in his lap.

Asa said, "If you want to kill yourself, this is the way to do it. This book has killed thousands of men. Hundreds of thousands. Men much bigger and stronger than you."

Henderson's wife let out a whimper.

Henderson himself furrowed his brow in thought. His tongue worked side to side, sliding between his teeth and gums. He appeared skeptical.

"Do you know why it's so good at killing men?" Asa added. "Because God wants them dead."

Henderson frowned. "You're makin' that up."

Asa plunged back into the book, furiously turning pages. "Look for yourself."

Henderson read aloud. "'For ye are dead, and your life is hid with Christ in God. When Christ, who is our life, shall appear, then shall ye also appear with him in glory. Mortify therefore your members which are upon the earth; fornication, uncleanness, inordinate affection, evil concupiscence, and covetousness, which is idolatry.'" He looked up. "Mortify. What does that mean?"

"Put to death. Kill."

Henderson stared at the word.

"Didn't I tell you?" Asa cried. "It's a command from God. You're no good to Him the way you are. You're no good to anyone. Not your wife. Not your little girl. It's time for Henderson to die."

Tears came to Henderson's eyes. "I'm no good. I know that. I hate who I am."

"So does God. He wants to kill you as much as you want to kill yourself. Maybe more."

"All right, then. Let's do it."

Asa stood. "You have to be serious about this. I'm not going to waste my time helping a man kill himself who's not serious."

Henderson's wife, a fist to her mouth, was weeping, but she didn't move to interfere.

Henderson stood. "I'm serious."

The pistol dropped to the ground.

"Over here," Asa commanded. He led Henderson to a clear space.

His head hanging, Henderson followed.

"Get on your knees," Asa said.

A spark of suspicion flared in Henderson's eyes. "I'm not gonna pray."

"Haven't you been listening? God doesn't want to hear your whining excuses. He wants you dead! Now get down on your knees!" He pushed Henderson to the ground.

"God wants me dead," Henderson muttered. "First thing God and I ever agreed on. All right, I'm ready."

Asa circled the man kneeling on the ground. Henderson's wife and daughter looked on in wide-eyed horror. When Henderson couldn't see him, Asa shot a reassuring glance to them. Slipping the Bible under his arm, he pressed his hands together.

The woman nodded and pulled her daughter to the ground. Once on their knees, they began praying.

"What's taking so long?" Henderson groused.

"Shut up and state your name."

"Why should I—"

"The accused will state his name!"

"Amos. Amos Henderson."

"Amos Henderson, you are a drunk, and a liar, a man of anger and of filthy speech. You are a cheat—"

"I ain't never cheated any man!" Henderson objected.

"The condemned man will remain silent!"

"I just don't want to die for somethin' I didn't do."

"Fair enough. But you do admit that you are a man with a wicked heart, a reprobate and a sinner, who has broken God's laws."

"I don't know what reprobate means, but I done all them other things."

"A man who has tried to do the right thing but can't. A pitiful wretch."

"I tried to be a good husband and father, but I can't." Henderson began to weep. "It's like there's a devil inside me."

"You deserve to die."

"That's true. I deserve to die."

Asa continued circling Henderson. He'd come this far but was uncertain what to do next. He was hoping that, by now, Henderson would be crying out to God for mercy.

Lord help me, he prayed silently. *Help me to help this man.*

A thought came to him.

"And so, Amos Henderson . . . ," he cried, "prepare to die."

"I'm ready."

"Prepare to meet God."

"I'm prepared."

"Your judge, who casts sinners into hell, a lake of fire, a realm of eternal torment."

"I deserve it."

Asa circled. What now? He had a man on his knees before God in the middle of a forest. What should he do now?

He looked at the Bible in his hands. "Sharper than any two-edged sword," he muttered. "Piercing even to the dividing asunder of soul and spirit." He circled Henderson one more time.

Several feet away the man's wife and daughter, both in tears, prayed.

"Amos Henderson, I deliver you to your judge and executioner to carry out the sentence of death." Then, almost as an afterthought, Asa said, "And may God have mercy on your soul."

Rounding Henderson one last time, Asa slapped the Bible against the man's chest.

Henderson clutched the book, staring with the horror of a man who had just been skewered by a sword. His eyes rolled back into his head. He fell forward in a heap, motionless.

"What did you do?" Henderson's wife exclaimed as she and her daughter came running.

Asa pantomimed slapping the book against Henderson's chest. His arm did an imitation of a falling tree.

Henderson's wife bent over him with her daughter beside her. She put a hand on his back, then an ear. "He's still breathing."

"He's in God's hands," Asa replied. "I witnessed much the same thing at the revival. People lying on the ground as though dead. That's where I got the idea. For a while there, I didn't know if it was going to work. I could only take him so far. After that it was up to the Spirit."

"God did this to him?"

Asa nodded.

Henderson's wife started to turn him over.

"I think it's best you leave him as he is," Asa said.

"Are we just supposed to sit here and do nothing?"

Asa sat on the ground. "We wait. And we pray."

CHAPTER 11

The stars overhead moved in their preordained course. Shadows stretched. Asa's backside complained loudly enough for him to get up and stretch. He brushed the dirt from his pants.

"I think he stopped breathing." Henderson's wife raised up on her knees.

"Are you sure?" Asa asked.

"Sarah, honey, go climb in the wagon," she said.

"I can run get a doctor!" Sarah insisted.

"No! I told you to get in the wagon!"

The little girl took several halting steps backward. Clearly she didn't want to leave.

Asa bent over, placing his hands above his knees. The words, "Do you want me to run and get a doctor?" were on the tip of his tongue. He wanted to say it but didn't want to say it.

But before he could say anything, Henderson began to shake. At first like he had a chill, then uncontrollably.

His wife sat back, her hands hovering over him, not knowing what to do.

Sarah's hand flew to her mouth.

Then, as suddenly as the shakes started, they stopped.

A minute passed. Then another.

Henderson's wife had reached the breaking point. She looked at Asa. "Run get a doctor."

Henderson began to shake again. This time with noise. His face was in the dirt, but it sounded like he was weeping.

His wife grabbed his shoulder and turned him over.

Clutching the Bible to his chest, his shoulders shaking, Henderson's face was scrunched into wrinkles. But they weren't wrinkles of remorse. He was laughing.

"Dead men don't need a doctor," he proclaimed.

Asa, Sarah, and Henderson's wife stared down at the laughing man. He looked directly at Asa.

Thumping his own chest, Henderson said, "He's dead. The old wretch inside is dead! Dead as a doornail!"

"Dead as a doornail!" Sarah repeated, a smile on her face.

Henderson made no effort to get up. He seemed to be enjoying just lying on his back, looking up at the black sky and the faces of those gathered around him.

"The old Henderson is indeed dead," Asa agreed. "It's time for him to rise to a new life."

He held out a hand, and Henderson took it.

The man who arose looked taller. Healthier. Robust. His wife stared at him as though she didn't recognize him. He laughed and threw his arms around her with a bearlike grip. He did the same with Sarah, who beamed so hard Asa thought she would burst.

Asa's attention was distracted by the sight of three men running toward them. He recognized one of them.

"Is everything all right?" a winded Pastor Campbell asked. "We got word Sarah came into camp begging for a preacher."

Words weren't needed. A smiling Henderson, with one arm around his wife and one arm around his daughter, was explanation enough.

"Looks like we're too late." Campbell smiled too.

"No, Preacher, you're right on time," Henderson replied. "Ethel was just about to make a new batch of coffee. Come join us."

"Only on the provision you'll tell us what happened here."

Henderson laughed. "Well, things started getting interesting when I shot at the young preacher."

"And so Asa here has him get on his knees, execution style," Campbell said, clearly relishing telling the story. He scratched his beard. Flecks of gray and thinning hair showed his age. But sharp, twinkling eyes indicated the man inside to be very much alive; the kind of man who loved telling a good joke or story.

Asa scanned the men seated around the campfire. He recognized some of them from the night before, but a couple of faces were new to him.

"And here's Henderson, on his knees in the dirt, his head bowed, ready to die!"

The men were picturing the scene in their minds. Asa could see it in their eyes.

"What'd he do?" one of the men asked.

Campbell shrugged as if Asa's next action was obvious. "He pulled out his sword."

"Sword? He had a sword?" the man cried.

Campbell glanced at Asa. "Sharpest sword in the world. Isn't that right, boy?" He winked.

Asa grinned sheepishly. Having heard Campbell's rendition of the account several times now, he enjoyed it more each time.

The story concluded with the usual grins, guffaws, and congratulations.

Campbell clapped Asa on the back. "I'm not sure you realized what happened out there today, son. We've been praying for Amos Henderson for years."

A bearded man added, "We thought it an answer to prayer that he let his wife drag him within five miles of the revival."

"Amos has been one mean drunk," Campbell said. "Ain't that right, boys?"

Several men offered details.

"Beat his wife last Christmas."

"My wife teaches at the school. She sees bruises on poor little Sarah all the time."

"Been in more scrapes than a grizzly bear hunter."

"Darn near killed Billy Hoskins. Bit off his ear over a seat at a card table."

Asa's grin faded as he began to realize just who it was he'd come up against.

"God was watching over you, son," Campbell concluded. "No doubt about it."

"Yeah, no doubt," Asa said shakily.

"You didn't happen to drink any of Ethel's coffee while you were there, did you?" The bearded man who asked the question was a jovial sort. His cheeks and forehead were about the only skin you could see on his face, and they were jolly red.

"We have women at church socials whose job it is to keep Ethel away from the coffeepots," Campbell explained. "Sweet woman. None sweeter. But she makes the worst cup of coffee this side of the Appalachians."

A chorus of hoots and laughs from men who had tasted her coffee confirmed the preacher's account.

Asa liked these men. He liked being around them. "I did have to chew a little before swallowing," he admitted.

The campfire appeared to blaze higher with the laughter.

Campbell laughed loudest. "You gotta respect a man who can survive Ethel's coffee and then lead her husband to the Lord!"

"Not bad for a Yale man," the bearded man added.

A pall fell over the group. Men eyed Campbell nervously.

"It's all right, Jonas," Campbell said kindly.

"Sorry, Preacher." The bearded man hung his head.

Campbell turned toward Asa. "I'm afraid my son Walker's experience at Yale has soured us on the school. I let him talk me into it. Now I'm sorry I did."

"Don't give up on him or the school," Asa replied. "Dr. Dwight, the president, was my teacher at Greenfield and the reason I'm attending Yale. He's the finest Christian man I know."

"I appreciate your loyalty, son."

"There are a lot of fellows who have been swayed by French philosophers, but that's why Dr. Dwight came to Yale. To reclaim it for God. There's no better Bible scholar in the land. And he preaches every day in chapel. A powerful preacher. All the students are required to attend."

Tears came to Campbell's eyes. "I hope you and Walker can meet up. Maybe you could travel back together. He could use a friend like you."

"Well, if I don't meet up with him here, I'll look him up back on campus," Asa offered. "You never know."

He said it to comfort Pastor Campbell. It was the right thing to say.

And easy to say here, Asa admitted. Yet in the back of his mind, he had a disturbing image of getting back to Yale and discovering that Walker Campbell was none other than Mule-face the sadist.

A kind-looking woman poked her head into the circle long enough to tell the men their wives had supper ready. Nothing could break up the festivities around the fire quicker than a call to eat.

As Asa stood, Pastor Campbell gripped his arm and leaned close. "Miss Mildred pulled out earlier today. You'll be staying with the wife and me tonight."

Before Asa could open his mouth to object, the pastor added, "We insist."

Asa had never had so many people make a fuss over him. All evening they were slapping him on the back or shaking his hand or telling him they wanted to meet him. He even ran into Amos Henderson, who had cleaned up and was walking around the revival field. Ethel grasped one hand, and Sarah held the other. They were the very portrait of a happy family.

Amos nearly crushed Asa's ribs with a hug.

Pastor Campbell told the story of Amos Henderson's salvation four more times in Asa's hearing. The preacher was a natural-born storyteller. He couldn't have been prouder of Asa, had Asa been his son. And Asa drank in the fatherly attention. His father had never looked at him like Pastor Campbell looked at him.

"Esther Rogers needs a visit," Mabel Campbell said. "She and Earl are camped down by the bend in the creek."

It was late. The last time Asa had looked at his watch, it was ten minutes to two in the morning. It was just the three of them sitting around the fire now—Pastor Campbell, his wife, and Asa.

Mrs. Campbell moved from place to place, tidying up, gathering cups and discarded items. She embodied all the characteristics of a loving mother. While her body had seen slimmer days, her smile was friendly, her voice soft, and eyes warm. The couple talked about personal things. Asa felt a little uneasy listening in on a married couple's conversation, but since they hadn't yet shown him where he would bed down, there was nowhere else for him to go.

"I'll stop by and see her first thing," Campbell said. "Is Earl's rash any better?"

"Didn't ask. Esther didn't say. And the Klines would like you to stop by their tent. Mary said Patrick's been asking questions."

"How old is he now?"

Mabel straightened up to think. "Eleven, come fall."

"Eleven!" Campbell scrunched up his face as though he was in pain. "Seems like he was born just a couple of years ago."

"Walker was nine when he was born."

"That seems just a couple of years ago as well. Have you heard from him today?"

Mabel shot a glance at Asa. He didn't know why.

"Sent word with the Cabot boy. Said he'd be staying at the tavern tonight."

Campbell took the news in silence, but it obviously displeased him. To Asa he said, "The boy refuses to attend the revival. Says he'd sooner go to a sacrifice to Zeus." Campbell scoffed. "Thinks he's being clever."

Mabel Campbell smoothed the hair on the top of her husband's head and bent over and kissed him good night. To Asa she said, "If you need anything, help yourself."

Campbell offered Asa a refill on coffee, but Asa declined. Campbell poured himself another cup and settled into his seat with a groan.

Asa's thoughts turned to sleep.

Campbell seemed to want to talk, but he stared at Asa long enough to make him wonder.

"Frank Stillman says a Yankee helped his boy in town this morning," Campbell said. "Frank came down with a first-class bellyache and sent Henry to town to get some medicine."

"Calcium carbonate," Asa said. "I thought I'd ride into the town to take a look around. Didn't expect it would be a ghost town."

It occurred to him that this would be a good time to ask Pastor Campbell if he knew Eli Cooper. He'd thought of asking him earlier, but the conversation had always veered another direction, so he just hadn't done it yet. Of course, that's what he told himself. In truth, he wasn't anxious to find Eli. What with the revival and Pastor Campbell and all, finding Eli Cooper right now would spoil everything.

"That's how revival works," Campbell said.

Asa returned from his mental diversion. "Calcium carbonate?"

Campbell laughed. "I was thinking more of one person at a time. You and young Henry. You and Amos Henderson. I don't want to discount all the preaching. After all, I'm a preacher. But revival is one person acting Christlike with another person. Let's say, for example, Henry Stillman grows up to be another Jonathan Edwards or George Whitefield. And he remembers back to that kind Yankee's example in

Miller's Drygoods as the first time he saw Christ in another man. Why, that's monumental."

"I never thought of it that way."

"That's the only way to think of it. Jesus called His disciples one by one. He touched their lives. They touched other lives."

Asa could see the possibilities.

"I say that because I get the impression you see this as our revival, but it's just as much your revival as it is ours. Now you can take it back with you to Yale. Just remember: while some revivals have been known for the great preaching, true revival is sparked by the simple acts. One person at a time."

A warm sensation in Asa's heart confirmed Pastor Campbell's teaching.

"So," Campbell said with an airy wave of his hand, "what do you think of all this? The crowds. Four preachers preaching at the same time. The shouting. The bodies on the ground."

Asa raised an eyebrow. "It's different from what I'm used to."

Campbell laughed. "You can say the same thing for pretty much all of us."

"Isn't this normal for out here?"

Campbell took a sip of coffee. "I don't think it's ever normal when the Holy Spirit starts to move. Pentecost wasn't a normal day."

Asa grinned.

The fire crackled.

"I've never seen anything like this before. I was trained in a denomination that is known for order. And these people here?" Pastor Campbell motioned all around him with his hand. "They're the salt-of-the-earth kind of folks. Practical as the day is long. No, what's happening out here is far from normal."

Asa liked listening to Campbell. And he'd been around the man enough to know that once the pump was primed, he didn't need questions to keep him going. So Asa just listened.

"At first I had my reservations," Campbell continued. "Frankly, some of what was happening disturbed me. But then I remembered that there were those who objected to Pentecost too. Then one of the leaders stood up and said something to this effect: 'Leave them alone. If what they are doing is of men, it will come to nought. But if it is of God, not only will we be unable to overthrow it, we may very well find ourselves fighting against God.' Well, for a man who's surrendered his life to serving God, the last thing I want to find out is that I'm fighting against Him."

Asa couldn't imagine Campbell ever being in a position opposite God.

"And I got to thinking," Campbell said. "In the long run, it's not what happens out here in the field, is it? Whether there's one preacher or twenty. Whether people are slain by the Spirit or get the shakes or bark like dogs. What matters is what happens to them when they go home. That's when we'll know if something significant has happened here. If lives are changed. For instance, if Amos Henderson goes home and takes to drinking and beating his wife and child again, then what has happened out here is of no account. A changed life, Asa. That's the proof of salvation. Not what a person says, or doesn't say, or how loud he says it. If he's no more like God afterward than he was before, He wasn't in it. He just wasn't in it."

Asa's heart was stirred further. The man had a point. Pastor Campbell seemed born to preach, even if it was to a congregation of one at the moment.

"Mind you, we've had our share of detractors," Campbell said. "Would it surprise you if I told you most of them are church people? Some of them have traveled all the way from the East coast to tell us that we're doing it all wrong. That God won't honor what's being done here. We've also had the Deists come and look down their long, thin noses at us and try to enlighten us frontier heathen." He chuckled. "But all you have to do is look them in the eye to see their hearts, and listen to what they have to say and how they say it to know that no earthly father would ever send one child to go and say such things to another child. And if an earthly father would never do such a thing, what makes them think our heavenly Father would do it?"

Asa watched Campbell carefully. The older preacher was getting riled.

Campbell frowned. "There was this one fellow who brought a walking stick with him. Only this walking stick had a nail protruding from the end. The man took it upon himself to walk among the people and stick anyone lying on the ground. He was convinced a good puncture would rouse them from their act."

Asa straightened, as if feeling the puncture himself. "What did you do?"

"Well, we couldn't just let someone roam freely about the field sticking people, could we? We sent a couple of deacons after him."

Asa leaned forward.

"But by the time they caught up with him, it was too late."

Campbell paused. Leaned back. Sipped his coffee.

Asa smiled. It was a blatant storyteller's tactic, and he recognized it. Campbell was milking the story for all it was worth. And it was working.

Finally, with a grin, Campbell went on. "The Holy Spirit beat us to him. By the time the deacons caught up with him, the man himself was flat out on the ground. With his stick beside him."

"What happened?"

"Well, it seems the man made a fatal mistake. He stopped to listen to one of the preachers. A relative of one of our punctured converts recognized him and summoned help. They formed a prayer circle around him, and the Holy Spirit did the rest."

Asa laughed.

In the distance he could hear a chorus of voices singing a hymn.

It was still dark when Asa stirred. He sat up and blinked. It took a moment for his eyes to focus, and a moment longer to comprehend where he was—in the back of the Campbells' wagon. He didn't know exactly where Pastor Campbell was sleeping, but he could hear him snoring. Or was that Mrs. Campbell?

Something had awakened Asa, though he didn't know what. Possibly the snoring. He wondered what time it was, but it was too dark to see his pocket watch, so he didn't even reach for it. He turned over to go back to sleep.

No sooner did his eyes close than he remembered he still hadn't asked Pastor Campbell about Eli Cooper. He told himself he wouldn't put it off any longer. He'd ask him in the morning.

The tilt of the wagon interrupted Asa's thoughts. It was the motion that resulted when someone climbed into the wagon. Asa stared at the wood grain of the sideboard. Perhaps Pastor or Mrs. Campbell needed something in the wagon?

Since they'd probably be upset if they knew they'd awakened him, Asa lay still, for their sake.

Whatever it was they were looking for, it was taking them a good while to find it. The wagon rocked as feet scuffled.

Asa was wide awake now, wondering what it was they needed. Wondering if he should turn over and tell them that he was awake. That it was all right to light a lamp so they could find what they were looking for.

Just then a hand clawed at his blanket. Pulled it down. Asa turned over, expecting to find a sleep-walking Pastor Campbell, trying to climb into his bed.

"You!" Eli Cooper shouted. "What are you doing in my bed?"

His breath reeked of alcohol.

Pastor Campbell and Mabel appeared instantly at the back of the wagon.

"Oh, Walker!" Mabel said when she saw Eli's condition.

"*Walker?*" Asa cried.

CHAPTER 12

Asa had never seen a bluer sky. The air was crisp. Invigorating. Everything about the day made it good to be alive . . . until he stepped around the wagon and saw Eli hunched over the campfire. He looked like he'd been dragged behind a team of horses all night.

Mabel Campbell was doing a balancing act with a frying pan, eggs, bacon, and toast that would make a circus juggler envious. There was something about the smell of fried eggs and bacon in the woods that rubbed Asa's stomach pleasurably.

"Good morning, Asa!" Mabel announced.

The woman was like this every morning. That much was evident.

"Help yourself to some coffee," she added. "Eggs will be ready soon."

As Asa poured himself some coffee, he risked a glance at Eli. All he saw was the top of Eli's head, bent over his own cup of coffee.

"It's so nice that you boys have finally met," Mabel said.

Asa hesitated before he answered. "Actually, our paths have already crossed."

Eli's head snapped up, and he shot Asa a murderous glare.

"You know each other?" Pastor Campbell's voice came from behind the wagon. The man appeared a moment later.

Eli's eyes were fixed on Asa in warning, but Asa saw the fear on his face. Eli was deathly afraid of what Asa would tell his parents.

Asa relished the moment before he opened his mouth. "Eli was my opponent during my first disputation. He clobbered me. Your son has a strong public presence. He's very charismatic."

Mabel smiled proudly. "Have you heard him sing?"

"Ma!" Eli complained.

Her attention on the eggs sizzling in a skillet, she said, "He has the voice of an angel. And that's not just a mother's opinion, either. Just ask any of the women in the church, and they'll tell you the same thing."

Campbell waved her away. "You're embarrassing the boy." But there was a twinkle in his eyes as he said it.

"What? It's a law now that a mother can't be proud of her son? I only wish Walker would use his voice for God instead of carrying on at the tavern."

"*Walker,*" Asa said. "That's why I didn't make the connection. I know him as Eli. And, of course, the last name is different." He sneaked a peek at Eli, who was still staring at him.

"Walker's adopted," Campbell explained. "His parents died in a fire when he was an infant. They were our two closest friends."

"His full name is Walker Eli Cooper. We've always called him Walker. Everyone knows him as Walker. I don't know why he changed his name to Eli when he went away to college," Mabel proclaimed.

Eli made no attempt to explain it to her.

"Well, you boys can get better acquainted on the trip back. When are you leaving?" Campbell asked.

Eli grunted. "Soon as we're done eating."

They all fell silent at Eli's curt words.

Mabel scooped the sizzling bacon out of the frying pan.

Campbell stirred. "I should probably let him tell you, help you pass the time on the road, but I want to hear it again myself." He winked at Asa and spoke to Eli. "Have you heard what Asa did yesterday? The whole camp's buzzing about it."

Eli looked suspiciously at Asa and shook his head.

"You remember Amos Henderson, don't you?" Campbell asked. "Lives out by Possum Wash?"

"I remember him," Eli said.

"Well, you know how mean he could get, especially when he was drunk. The other day, little Sarah came running into the camp looking for a preacher. She couldn't find one, but she found Asa . . ."

And once again Campbell beamed as he told of Asa's encounter with Amos Henderson.

Millersburgh was a silent hour behind them when Eli glanced over his shoulder. The road was deserted. He pulled his horse to a stop and dismounted.

"Get down," he ordered.

From the fury in Eli's eyes, it was clear this wasn't an invitation to pick flowers.

"Whatever you have to say to me can be said on horseback," Asa replied. "We have a long road ahead of us."

"I said, get off your horse! Get off or I'll pull you off!"

Asa paused long enough for Eli to come toward him. He held up a hand, and Eli backed off.

No sooner had Asa's foot hit the ground than Eli was on top of him, spinning him around, shoving him against his own horse, pinning him with fists clenched full of Asa's shirt.

"Hey!" Asa cried.

"Just what do you think you're doing?"

"What are you talking about?"

"You're spying on me!"

"I am not!"

"Then what are you doing in Kentucky?"

Asa's mind raced. "Um . . . revival. I'm here for the revival."

Eli's face loomed large since it was only inches away. "You want to humiliate me. That's it, isn't it? To humiliate me in front of my parents, and then when we get back to Yale . . ."

"I said only nice things about you to your parents! I could have told them about—"

"You're going to spread it around campus that Eli Cooper's old man is a hands-in-the-air, frontier-revival preacher, aren't you?" Eli tightened his grip on Asa's shirt.

"I don't know what you're—"

"That Eli Cooper's parents are Bible-thumping, Holy Ghost worshipping lunatics."

"Hey! I happen to like—"

"You're demented, Rush. Do you know that? Demented."

"Look, Eli, just give me a chance to—"

But Eli cut him off. "I'm warning you . . . if I hear the slightest rumor about my parents back at Yale . . . if I so much as see a freshman look at me and hide a snigger . . ."

"I'm telling you—"

"I'll find you and break your lips."

"My lips?"

Eli gave him a final shove. "And a few bones as a bonus."

Asa straightened his shirt. "Look, Eli, it's a long way back to New Haven. Just give me a chance to—"

But Eli wasn't listening. He launched into Asa with force, knocking him to the ground, kicking him in the ribs and the stomach and the legs. And all the while he shouted, "Just stay away from me. Stay away from my parents. And while we're at it, stay away from Annabelle. Do you get that, Rush? Or do I need to punctuate it with a few more exclamation points?"

Doubled over, Asa tasted dirt and blood. It took several moments for his senses to look past the pain of the assault to realize that Eli had climbed onto his horse and ridden away.

His pain expressed itself with groans as he managed to get to his feet and brush himself off.

Eli Cooper was but a speck on the horizon when Asa shouted, "Oh yeah? Well, you have lovely parents!" Then, as an afterthought, "And you're nothing like them!"

His clothes and throat coated with road dust, Asa slumped in the middle of a long wooden table, sipping his drink. A bowl of some kind of stew lay untouched in front of him. The tavern keeper called it "meat stew with fixin's."

The table at which he sat was packed. Elbows jostled him from both sides. Three or four fellows talked at once. Asa's attention wandered from conversation to conversation. Truth be told, after several days alone on the road, he enjoyed the sound of human voices, even if they were coarse and crude.

With a scraping of the bench opposite him, three of the louder men got up, paid their bill, and left. With the level of noise reduced, Asa picked up the conversation at a corner table behind him. When he had arrived, he'd considered joining the four men who sat there. There were two empty places at the time. But then a spot opened up at the long table, and he took it instead.

"We have to be ready," one of the voices at the corner table was saying. "Hamilton's broadside has handed the election to Jefferson on a silver platter."

"Why would he do that?" another voice asked. "Don't get me wrong. It's the best thing that could have happened for us. But why would Hamilton attack his own man like that?"

"Why else? He wants to be president."

"But he hates Jefferson! At least Adams is a Federalist."

"They're all a bunch of dogs, if you ask me. What do we care if one cur rips apart another cur? As long as the Federalists are out and Jefferson is in."

Asa took a bite of stew and wished he hadn't. He pushed his bowl away.

"But do you really think they'll give it up? The presidency, I mean? Even if Jefferson gets the votes?"

"What are you sayin'?"

"I'm sayin' we've never been here before. His Highness Washington was unopposed for two elections. Then he hands the throne to the heir apparent, Adams. This is the first time the office has been contested. What if the Federalist refuses to give it up?"

"Can he do that?"

"Why not? He has control of the army, doesn't he?"

A new voice said, "Jefferson has control of the people. If Adams refuses to relinquish his throne, we take it from him. We march on the White House."

"Do you think it will come to that?"

"All I can say is that some states loyal to Jefferson are mustering their militias. If King Adams refuses to relinquish control of the nation, we take it from him the French way."

There was a general murmur of agreement around the table.

A softer voice joined in. "In fact, there are certain parties, if you get my drift, who are makin' plans to ensure that that throne is empty even before the election. They call themselves the Illuminati."

This excited the table.

Asa couldn't believe what he was hearing. A plan to assassinate President Adams? He wanted to turn to see the faces of the men who were talking but didn't dare. He kept his head down and his ears open.

"You're goin' to meet two of them tonight."

"Tonight? Here?"

"There are powerful men in this country who have had their fill of the Federalists and His Highness Washington and King Adams who will do anything to ensure that Jefferson—and Jefferson alone—is the next man to sit in the president's chair."

"But the election. Hamilton's public diatribe against Adams virtually ensures his defeat."

"Elections are quirky things. Far too unpredictable where personal fortunes hang in the balance. Ah! Here they come now!"

Out of the corner of his eye, Asa observed two men coming into the tavern. They were hailed by the men at the corner table.

"Citizens, I do hope you haven't drained the ale barrel dry," one of the newcomers announced.

Asa froze. He knew that voice.

He kept his head down as two dark forms passed like specters in front of him. Asa prayed he wouldn't be recognized.

The greetings at the table commenced.

Only then, with their attention diverted, did Asa risk a glance.

His suspicions were confirmed.

Jacob Benson, his Yale tutor, hailed the tavern keeper and ordered two flasks of ale as he joined the men at the corner table.

Sitting down at the table with him, unaware that Asa was but a few feet away, was a grinning Eli Cooper.

CHAPTER 13

Asa hurried across the Yale campus. His head was stuffed full of memorized text from Gravesande's *Mathematical Elements of Natural Philosophy*, and he feared if he jostled it, some of the facts would spill out and he'd lose them.

He hated recitation. It seemed a waste of time. The procedure was always the same. The tutor slouched in a chair with the textbook open on his lap. He would ask questions about the required reading, and the student would regurgitate the text as best he could. The tutor would then hand the textbook back, and the whole procedure would repeat itself the next day. Today promised to be more of the same, with one exception. It was the first time Asa would see Jacob Benson, his tutor, since the tavern on the trip back from Kentucky.

Neither Benson nor Eli was aware he'd overheard them. Asa had managed to slip out of the tavern unnoticed, timing his departure with that of several other men. Since then he'd toyed with several comments he thought he might toss out casually to Benson. Test his reaction. But then he decided it was too risky. He had to assume that any friend of Eli Cooper's was no friend of his.

Asa brushed past a trio of students just as an argument erupted. One of the disputers punctuated his point with a shove that sent his opponent crashing into Asa, knocking the textbook from his hands and—Asa was sure of it—several key facts from his head.

No apologies were offered. After recovering, the one who was shoved, shoved back. Doing his best to avoid scuffling feet, Asa bent down, picked up his book, and continued on his way.

He missed Kentucky. The revival atmosphere he'd experienced there was absent from Yale. In fact, it was just the opposite. In Kentucky he'd felt an acceptance, warmth, love, and fellowship, such as he'd never known before. He liked it. Here, campus life centered on bawdy talk about weekend wenching, excursions to the local tavern, cursing, dares, and drinking. Everyone was in competition with everyone else. They were quick to take offense.

Asa hadn't realized it until Kentucky, but constant exposure to this kind of competitive atmosphere had a wearing effect on his emotions and attitude. Now that he knew life didn't have to be this way, he longed for the kind relationships he'd experienced during the revival.

He rounded a corner of the Union Hall and nearly plowed into the back of Eli Cooper, who was standing with several other students. Putting his head down, Asa made a mad dash around them.

He could hear Eli telling the others, "It's unbelievably uncivilized on the frontier. The people are crude. The way of life barbaric. Absolutely no amenities to speak of, and the intellectual level of the townspeople? They're Neanderthals. Give me Boston or New York or Philadelphia any day."

"What did you expect to find?" one of the students asked.

"His parents live out there," another reported.

"My parents are dead!" Eli spat.

"Then why'd you go out there?"

"The urge to explore. Now that I've seen it, you couldn't drag me back out there."

"Interesting. What's the political climate out there? Is it Adams or Jefferson country?"

Asa turned another corner and didn't hear the answer.

Seated on the sofa a discreet distance from Annabelle Byrd, the recitation that had so concerned Asa earlier was forgotten, as were many of the facts he'd memorized for it. In the short course of the day, he'd gone from sitting opposite a bored Jacob Benson to sitting next to the saintly Annabelle Byrd. From gazing upon the grizzled visage of his lanky tutor to stealing glances at the smoothest skin he'd ever seen. From spewing forth geographical facts, dully and dutifully, to making every effort to keep from stammering because his heart was galloping faster than a racehorse.

The Byrds' sitting room was lavishly decorated with an eight-foot-wide fireplace and mantel, several oil paintings of persons and scenes united by a nautical theme, and a huge tapestry dominating one wall that depicted what appeared to be an ancient Norman battle. In the corner of the room, seated in a stuffed armchair, sat plump Martha, looking as bored as Jacob Benson during recitation.

In contrast, Annabelle was very much alive. Her green eyes danced merrily. He knew this from occasional glimpses. Most of the time she kept her eyes appropriately downcast, as befitting a lady of her breeding. Asa contented himself with the curve of her smile and lived for the moments she permitted him a view of her eyes.

Annabelle Byrd was the perfect woman. Easy to talk to. She laughed at all the right times. And she seemed to enjoy Asa's company.

"Of course, I'll have to make it up to my mother and sister," he said.

He'd been describing his trip to Kentucky.

"They were expecting to see me. But the trip to Kentucky was worth it, just to be part of the revival. I'd go back in a heartbeat."

"It sounds so heavenly!" Annabelle reached for the tea service. "More tea?"

Asa lifted his cup and let her serve him.

"So unlike here," Annabelle said. She didn't pour herself more tea.

"My thoughts exactly!" Asa exclaimed.

"We can only pray that God will see fit to bless New Haven with revival."

Asa nodded his agreement, then berated himself inwardly. He should have timed it better. He had nodded as he was sipping tea and spilled some on his trousers. As casually as he could, he moved his cloth napkin over the spill. Annabelle didn't seem to notice.

"I'll visit Greenfield during our next scheduled break in a couple of weeks. Of course, I won't be able to stay as long as I would have, had I not gone to Kentucky, but then how often does an opportunity like that present itself?"

"If only my father weren't so ill," Annabelle replied. "I'd love to see Greenfield again. And Maggy."

"She has become an exceptional woman," Asa said of his sister. "I don't know how much you remember of our family, but since my father's death, Maggy has had her hands full, caring for Mother. Mrs. Adams has been a constant source of encouragement to her. Maggy speaks of her in every letter."

Annabelle tilted her head in thought. "I don't recall a Mrs. Adams in Greenfield."

"Oh, she's never lived in Greenfield. Like her husband, she hails from Braintree, where she still lives."

"And her husband?"

Asa laughed. "This is amusing. You haven't made the connection?"

Annabelle's lower lip protruded in a pout. "I'm glad my ignorance is a source of amusement to you."

"No! No, that's not it!"

Setting his teacup down, his hand reached out to her, stopping short of touching her. A glance at the chaperon indicated he'd done right by stopping. Otherwise, he would have heaped error upon error.

"Please forgive me," he cried. "It's just that I thought you knew. Her husband lives in the White House. Abigail Adams's husband is president of the United States."

Annabelle touched her fingers to her lips. "Silly me! Of course! I should have put two and two together."

"No, it's my fault. I assumed you knew. Believe me, the last thing I would ever want to do would be to embarrass you, or intimate in any way that you are ignorant. I misled you. It's my fault entirely. I thought everyone in Greenfield knew that Abigail Adams was a friend of the family. And since you used to live there . . ."

"You're very sweet, Asa. And you're forgiven. Maybe it's the hour." Her hand covered a yawn. "Oh! Now I am embarrassed!"

"My fault again, for keeping you up." He stood. "I should leave."

"So soon?"

"It's late."

Annabelle reached over and touched his hand. "Before you leave?"

"Yes?"

"Would you be so kind as to do something for me?"

A throat clearing sounded in the corner. Martha was shaking her head.

Annabelle scowled at her. "It's not naughty, and I'm going to ask!" Ignoring Martha's scowl, she told Asa, "I know this is an imposition, and if you think it's too personal"—a conciliatory glance at Martha—"please feel free to decline."

Asa's interest was piqued, but even before hearing the request, he knew he'd agree to do it, if for no other reason than Martha didn't want him to.

"It's just that it's been so long now." Annabelle paused, appearing to struggle briefly with her emotions. "You see, my father did this for me every night for as long as I remember. And, well, since he's been sick . . . Martha and I . . . but it's just not been the same."

She walked a short distance to a small stand and opened a drawer. She returned carrying a black book, which she held out to Asa.

"Every night before bed, Father read to me from the family Bible. And while I love Martha dearly for filling in for Father, there's just no substitute to hearing the Bible read in a strong male voice, don't you agree?"

STORM

With a warm smile Asa took the book from her. "It would be my honor."

Annabelle took her seat on the sofa, nestling into the corner with anticipation. "We've been reading the proverbs. Chapter twenty-nine, I believe."

From the corner, Martha said, "We completed chapter thirty last night."

Asa nodded. He turned straight to Proverbs, the thirty-first chapter. Annabelle leaned close to him to see the page. She pointed to where they had left off. Asa almost didn't see it. He closed his eyes when the fragrance of her perfume hit him. It took a minute to rally his senses enough to read.

"'Who can find a virtuous woman?'" he read. "'For her price is far above rubies. The heart of her husband doth safely trust in her, so that he shall have no need of spoil. She will do him good and not evil all the days of her life.'"

Annabelle let out a sigh. It was almost a whimper.

Asa glanced over at her.

She appeared deep in thought.

He skipped over some verses and continued. "'Strength and honour are her clothing; and she shall rejoice in time to come. She openeth her mouth with wisdom; and in her tongue is the law of kindness.'"

Annabelle grew increasingly restless as Asa read.

He eyed her again before returning his gaze to the book. "'Her children arise up, and call her blessed; her husband also, and he praiseth her. Many daughters have done virtuously, but thou excellest them all. Favour is deceitful, and beauty is vain: but a woman that feareth the LORD, she shall be praised.'"

"Enough!" Annabelle cried.

"But there's only one verse remaining in the chapter," Asa said, startled.

"Please, have mercy and stop!"

Asa set the Bible down on the tea set. "Did I not read it right?"

Annabelle's head was in her hands. Black ringlets dangled against her fingers. "It's nothing you did. Please forgive me, it's just . . ."

"Just what?" Asa couldn't imagine what he'd done to affect her this way.

"I'm being silly."

"Please tell me."

"It's just that . . ." Her voice came out choked. "That passage of Scripture . . . well, it reminds me of my mother. And I fear . . . I fear that . . ."

Asa didn't know what more he could do to let her know that she could tell him anything. He hovered without touching. He searched for a different word or phrase that might convince her of his sincerity.

Annabelle dabbed her eyes with a handkerchief. "She was such a model Christian woman and mother. And I'm such a wicked person at heart that I fear I will never be like her, much less like the woman described in the Scriptures."

"Nonsense!" Asa said, shocked. "I find it difficult to believe that you harbor any wickedness, and I have no doubt at all that you will make a wonderful wife and mother."

Annabelle attempted a smile. "You're very kind. But you don't know me."

"I know enough to recognize a truly humble Christian woman when I see one. And while, I admit, I have not known you long, I can say with certainty that I have witnessed in you many of the elements listed in Proverbs 31. And those qualities cannot be faked."

Vivid green eyes and a brilliant smile dazzled him. "Do you really think so?"

"I do."

Annabelle touched his cheek lovingly with her hand, earning a verbal rebuke from Martha. While Annabelle appeared annoyed by the warning, she obeyed and lowered her hand.

"You're sweet, Asa Rush. The sweetest man I know. And I don't know what I did that God would send such a kind man my direction, but I thank Him for it every night. Just being around you makes me a better woman."

Asa beamed.

"May I ask one other request of you?"

"Anything."

"Will you pray for me daily? Just knowing that you're praying for me will give me strength."

Asa was so taken by her request, he didn't know what to say, what to do.

A moment passed between them. Then another.

A shadow of disappointment passed over Annabelle's features.

Honored and humbled, Asa dropped to his knees before her. He grabbed her hands in his and bowed his head.

Annabelle started but didn't pull away.

"Almighty God," Asa prayed, "I present to You Annabelle Byrd, Your precious child. Fill her with Your grace to overflowing, with wisdom sufficient for this age, with love enough to sustain a family. In everything she does, may she be a reflection of her God. And to the extent to which she honors You with a heart of worship, may her husband and children someday rise up and call her blessed. Amen."

He lingered but an instant, then looked up.

Annabelle gazed down on him with tenderness. Tears glistened in her eyes. "Thank you," she murmured. "That was lovely."

Asa stood.

"I'll tell you who will be blessed," Annabelle said to him. "The woman who gets you for a husband."

Until that moment, Asa hadn't realized they were still holding hands. A grunt from the corner called their attention to it.

Annabelle blushed and stepped back.

Asa felt the need to explain. "During the revival in Kentucky, people formed prayer circles to great effect. And I thought, We may only be two, but the principle is the same, isn't it?"

"It might have been even more effective if the circle had three, don't you think?" Martha said sarcastically from the corner.

It was Asa's turn to blush. He didn't say it, but for some reason, had there been three people in the circle, it just wouldn't have been the same. Especially if it had been Martha, who had given every indication that she disapproved of him.

"It was a spontaneous act, Martha," Annabelle said, coming to Asa's rescue. "Had invitations been sent out, it wouldn't have been as sweet."

It was clear Martha wasn't buying the explanation, but she held her tongue.

Annabelle walked Asa to the door with their chaperon trailing them. "I had a lovely time, Asa."

"I guess this is good night, then."

Beyond the far end of the hallway, someone was knocking rather boisterously on a door. The women exchanged glances. The knocking persisted. Martha appeared to be in a quandary.

"Answer the door, Martha. I'm perfectly safe here with Asa."

They watched in silence as she traveled the length of the hallway, then disappeared.

"It's late for someone to be calling," Asa said, concerned. "Should I wait?"

"I'm sure it's nothing. Probably Joseph, my father's manservant. He locks himself out regularly."

With another glance down the hallway, Asa nodded. "Then I'll say good night."

But he didn't move. It was as though a gravitational force held them close. Only with effort would Asa be able to break it. And he didn't want to, so he made no attempt.

Neither did Annabelle.

Instead, giving in to it, she leaned toward him and kissed him on the cheek. Her lips were warm and soft. Her scent intoxicating. Asa's head swirled with the most delicious sensation.

Annabelle touched the stubble on his cheek.

Then she turned suddenly away and hid her face in her hands. "I shouldn't have done that! Now do you see what a truly wicked woman I am?"

"You're nothing of the kind!" he insisted.

He attempted to turn her back to him, but she resisted.

One moment.

Then another.

Finally she gave in to him.

"The moment Martha is gone," she wailed, "I lose all inhibition. You must think me horrible!"

He could feel the mist in his eyes. "Not at all! It has been a wonderful night with a wonderful ending. Truly memorable."

"It has been a memorable night, hasn't it?" She hesitated.

Asa was within inches of her. He was aching to kiss her, but should he? Did he dare? He leaned forward, then caught himself and stepped back.

Instead, he asked simply, "May I call on you tomorrow?"

"I'll be disappointed if you don't."

"Good night, then. I'll be praying for you."

"You don't know what that means to me."

"Good night."

He turned to go, opened the door, then turned back. "Good night, sweet, sweet Annabelle." The door closed.

As soon as the door closed behind Asa Rush, Martha appeared in the hallway.

Annabelle sighed. "I thought he would never leave! Where did you put the other one?"

"In the library."

"How do I look?"

Martha fussed over her mistress's dress and hair. "A prayer circle of two?"

Annabelle laughed. "When he dropped to his knees like that, I thought he was going to ask me to send him on some sort of quest to prove his love to me."

"Somehow I have a hard time seeing you in a tower pining for his return. There—you look presentable."

"We may have a problem." Annabelle tapped one finger on her chin in thought. "What if God answers Asa's prayers and makes me a righteous woman?"

"I don't think even God could do that, m' lady." Martha's expression of disbelief was almost comical.

Annabelle grinned. "I'll take that as a compliment."

"As you should."

"Onward, Sancho?"

"Onward, m' lady."

They proceeded down the hallway, toward the library doors.

Before opening them, Annabelle turned to Martha. "Act two!"

CHAPTER 14

"I hope I haven't kept you waiting too long," Annabelle said as she swept into the library.

Her dour-faced chaperon came in behind her and closed the doors.

Eli stood facing a bookshelf with an open book in his hand. When he saw Annabelle, his jaw dropped momentarily. Then it snapped shut at the same time as the book.

"It was worth the wait," Eli murmured.

From the way his eyes roamed her hair, her face, and her body, he was obviously pleased with what he saw.

And she was pleased he was pleased.

"Let the trumpet of the day of judgment sound when it will," Eli said with conviction later that night.

He sat beside Annabelle on a sofa in much the same way Asa had done earlier in the evening.

"I shall appear with this book in my hand before the Sovereign Judge," he continued, "and cry with a loud voice, 'This is my work! There are my thoughts! And thus was I! I have freely told both the good and bad, hid nothing wicked, added nothing good.'" He settled back against the couch and eyed Annabelle, as if anticipating her response.

127

"Did you write that?"

He gave a wry smile. "Rousseau."

"Is he a fellow student?"

Eli laughed. Annabelle thought he looked particularly attractive when he laughed.

"Jean-Jacques Rousseau," he explained. "A French philosopher and a political theorist."

"I thought for certain you had written it. It sounds just like you."

Eli sat up a little straighter. She could tell he liked her praise. She knew he would. It urged him on.

"According to Rousseau, the problem with education is basically a problem of motivation. Teachers rush into things too quickly. They talk of geography before the child knows the way around his own backyard. They teach history before the child understands anything about adult motivation. It would be far better to let questions arise naturally. When a child is self-motivated, the teacher cannot keep him from learning."

Annabelle wasn't listening. She was thinking how much men loved to hear themselves talk, how hearing the sound of their own voices convinced them that what they were saying was true. She would wait for him to finish, then give him another healthy dose of praise.

He sat back, his eyebrows raised, signaling he awaited a response.

"That is so true!" Annabelle gushed. "I never thought of it that way!"

Eli grinned like a lap dog having his ears scratched.

Annabelle leaned forward. "Do you know how attractive you are when you get passionate?"

Eli's doggy grin turned wolfish.

"My father has gone to bed for the night," she added. "Do we dare?"

His eyes signaled his eagerness.

She stood, took him by the hand, and led him across the room.

Eli glanced nervously at Martha. Annabelle knew the chaperon would make no objection. She would follow their script down to the letter and would even give him smirking approval.

"Uh . . . what about her?" Eli whispered to Annabelle.

Annabelle released his hand to open a cabinet door. Inside, the shelves were stocked with a wide assortment of liquor bottles.

"Don't mind Martha," Annabelle murmured. "She enjoys a little wine on occasion." She pulled back and pretended to be shocked. "Unless that's not what you meant!" A hand to her mouth for effect. "Eli Cooper! What did you think we were going to do?"

She enjoyed watching him turn a delightful shade of red. Stammering would surely follow, she reasoned.

"I-I . . . when y-you . . . I-I naturally . . . but I would never . . ."

I was right. Men are so easily led.

Annabelle laughed wickedly and stroked his arm. "Really, Eli! With Martha in the room?"

She smiled to reassure him, to let him know she was not offended. She allowed her gaze to meet his and linger seductively, indicating that, given different circumstances, she might be receptive to whatever it was he was thinking.

Then she let him off the hook by turning her attention to the selection of drinks in the cabinet.

As the alcohol took effect, laughing came more frequently and their voices grew louder. Even Martha joined in with an occasional comment that set them howling.

At last Annabelle jumped up. "Let's do something fun!"

Eli's grin indicated his willingness.

"It's sort of like a party game," she said.

"I like games."

"Do you like role-playing?"

Eli shrugged. "Can't say I've done any role-playing. Like actors on a stage?"

"Something like that. I only have the one book, so we'll have to share."

She went to a bureau drawer and pulled out a book. Returning, she settled eagerly on the sofa.

Eli's eyes settled on the book, and his smile faded. "The Bible?"

"It'll be fun!" she insisted. "But you have to sit closer."

He scooted toward her.

"I won't bite! Closer!"

He moved until their shoulders were pressed against each other. She felt him shiver when his body touched hers, and she knew he liked the closeness.

"All right," he said. "But you're going to have to convince me. Believe me, I've spent hundreds of hours in front of an open Bible, and I can't recall a single good time."

She paid no attention to him as she opened the Bible and searched for the text she had in mind. When she found it, she pointed to a verse. "I'll start." With a wiggle of her shoulders, she began. "'Let him kiss me with the kisses of his mouth: for thy love is better than wine. Because of the savour of thy good ointments thy name is as ointment poured forth, therefore do the virgins love thee. Draw me, we will run after thee: the king hath brought me into his chambers: we will be glad and rejoice in thee, we will remember thy love more than wine: the upright love thee.'" She paused. "Now you."

She pointed to the sentence she wanted him to begin reading.

He had to lean over in front of her to read it. He shivered slightly as she breathed on his neck. "Uh, right. 'As the lily among thorns, so is my love among the daughters,'" he read.

"Very good! You're a natural at this!" Annabelle squealed. "Now, me again."

Eli's expression showed that he was enjoying her little game. She hadn't doubted for a moment that he would.

"'The voice of my beloved!'" she read. "'Behold, he cometh leaping upon the mountains, skipping upon the hills. My beloved is like a roe or a young hart: behold, he standeth behind our wall, he looketh forth at the windows, shewing himself through the lattice.'"

She leaned back and pointed at the next verse. His turn.

Eli read, "'Rise up, my love, my fair one, and come away. For, lo, the winter is past, the rain is over and gone; The flowers appear on the earth;

the time of the singing of birds is come, and the voice of the turtle is heard in our land; The fig tree putteth forth her green figs, and the vines with the tender grape give a good smell. Arise, my love, my fair one, and come away.'"

"'By night on my bed,'" Annabelle read, "'I sought him whom my soul loveth: I sought him, but I found him not. I will rise now, and go about the city in the streets, and in the broad ways I will seek him whom my soul loveth: I sought him, but I found him not. The watchmen that go about the city found me: to whom I said, Saw ye him whom my soul loveth? It was but a little that I passed from them, but I found him whom my soul loveth: I held him, and would not let him go, until I had brought him into my mother's house, and into the chamber of her that conceived me.'"

She pointed to Eli's part. As he leaned in front of her to read his part, Annabelle ever so slowly moved the book so he had to lean even farther. With his neck stretched in front of her face, she bent forward and kissed it softly and repeatedly.

With each kiss Eli's voice trembled as he read.

After a lengthy good-bye that was highlighted by three kisses—Annabelle would allow only three, enough to encourage him without giving him the wrong idea—she closed the door.

Turning to Martha, who had left them alone just as she had with Asa, Annabelle asked, "They're here?"

"Eleven of them," Martha replied. "Perkins sent his servant with a note informing us he'd be thirty minutes late."

Annabelle rolled her eyes. "Mark my words, Samuel Perkins will show up late on Judgment Day. How do I look?"

For the third time that night, Martha fussed over her.

"Do you have my notes?" Annabelle asked.

Martha handed her a sheaf of handwritten papers. Annabelle marched determinedly to another wing of the house. She paused outside the closed doors of the conference room to compose herself.

Stern.

Businesslike.

A woman who could not be trifled with.

Annabelle felt Martha's admiring eyes upon her as she opened the doors.

"Act three," Annabelle said under her breath in passing.

She strode into a room dominated by a huge, polished wooden table. Seeing her, the eleven men, all in their fifties and sixties, stood. *As they should*, she thought and smiled inwardly. They were all men of wealth and power and very much aware of their importance, yet they stood in deference to her.

"Gentlemen," Annabelle greeted them. "Welcome to my father's house."

"And how is Captain Byrd tonight?" The man at the head of the table spoke for all of them. He was the shortest fellow in the room and appeared to be frail, with a full head of gray hair precisely parted and combed.

"Not well enough to attend tonight's meeting," Annabelle said, "but well enough to attend to business. I have recorded his thoughts regarding the items on tonight's agenda."

The chairman nodded courteously. "If you will hand them to Mr. Chapman, he will see to it that they are entered into the minutes."

Annabelle made no effort to relinquish the papers. "I'm afraid that is unacceptable, gentlemen."

"Unacceptable?" The chairman's tone was clipped.

"It is Captain Byrd's wish that I represent him at the meeting tonight."

A wave of response—universal and negative—circled the table.

"Miss Byrd, I'm afraid—"

"Mr. Chairman," Annabelle interrupted, "it is my father's express wish that I give voice to his thoughts, and that I be his eyes and ears for the duration of this and subsequent meetings until he himself is able to attend."

Another wave of protest began to swell.

She addressed it before it could gather momentum. "I'm certain you can appreciate my father's position. A personal accounting is far more enlightening than a reading of the minutes."

"With all due respect to your father, Miss Byrd," the chairman muttered, "the actions of this committee—"

"Are the actions of a gaggle of old geese," Annabelle finished.

It was all she could do to suppress a laugh. To her dying day she would relive this moment in her mind whenever she needed an amusement.

"See here, Miss Byrd!" The chairman glowered.

"I have never in my life been so appalled at the weak-sister bleating as recorded in the minutes of the previous meetings," Annabelle announced. "For the last year I have served as my father's secretary and confidante in the matters set before this committee, and to me, gentlemen, your conversations sound more like the cacklings of old women at a quilting bee or afternoon tea than men of vision and purpose! Gentlemen, is there not a backbone among you?"

While they were still stunned by her outburst, she pulled out a chair for herself and sat down. The message was clear. If they wanted her removed from the room, they were going to have to do it physically.

After several moments of uneasy silence, the chairman said, "Very well, then. I call this meeting of the Illuminati together."

The late-night meeting went about as Annabelle thought it would. A lot of ranting about the Federalists acting like royalty. One report quoted President John Adams as saying it was his belief that his son should succeed him as president in the same way a prince succeeds a king.

Reports were heard of organizations forming in cities for the sole purpose of convincing people to vote for Jefferson. Aaron Burr was leading the way in New York with promising results, though it was difficult to say whether or not this tactic would work since it had never been tried before. Several of the men argued that the traditional battle of newspaper articles, not local politicking, was the key to winning the election.

Speaking on behalf of her father, Annabelle favored the local organizations. Should it become necessary, these organizations could be armed quickly—like political minutemen to take the presidency by force.

"You were masterful!" Martha told Annabelle as the last of the Illuminati departed.

"You were listening at the door?"

"Heard every word."

Annabelle sighed. It had been a full evening. "I was masterful, wasn't I?"

"You could teach a chameleon colors."

"Imagine what I could do if I wasn't shackled by these." Annabelle swished her petticoats. With every passing day she was more dissatisfied with the conventions of society that trapped her, as well as so many other women, in lesser roles in the world's view.

"All in all, a successful evening, I'd say," said Martha.

"There's one thing that concerns me."

"Oh?"

"Asa."

"That groveling puppy?"

"You forget that he's praying for me."

Martha laughed. "As I said earlier, there are some things even God can't do."

Annabelle laughed with her. "True."

"I've readied your bed, m' lady. Get a good night's sleep. You deserve it."

"In a while. I still have work to do. I must report to Father."

"Can't it wait until morning?"

Annabelle started up the stairs. "You know how he hates being kept in the dark."

CHAPTER 15

Night's cloak covered the campus. Eli slipped away from Annabelle Byrd's house and moved from shadow to shadow, pausing only long enough to listen for human sounds. It was a good hour and a half past the time candles were extinguished in the dorms. Should he get caught outside his room, he could be expelled.

It would be worth it, though.

For the third night in a row, he'd let time slip away while courting Annabelle Byrd. First there was the night they took turns reading from the Bible. That had turned out to be a lot more fun than Eli thought it would be.

Then last night he and Annabelle had spent the evening amusing themselves with an old-fashioned courting stick, a hollow tube about an inch in diameter and about six feet long. It was designed to allow couples to whisper endearments back and forth while other family members were in the room. Eli found it wickedly fun to hear Annabelle's breathy advances with her chaperon sitting just a few feet away.

Tonight she had read French poetry to him. While he wasn't fluent in French, he had known enough to be aroused. And even if he didn't understand a word, he could sit all night just watching her mouth as she read.

Annabelle Byrd had the most incredible mouth . . .

"*Bonsoir*, Citizen."

Eli started at the voice.

From the depths of the shadows stepped tutor Jacob Benson.

Eli saw his academic life pass before his eyes. He was doomed. "You startled me."

"A night of carousing?" Benson asked.

Eli kept his confession to a grin. "Are you going to turn me in?"

"Was she worth it?"

Eli's grin widened. "Had I known I'd get caught, I would do it again."

In the distance someone coughed. Footsteps echoed against the brick walls.

Benson grabbed Eli and yanked him deeper into the shadows. Together they watched as a night watchman made his rounds.

Eli's academic career breathed new life. Benson didn't want to be seen tonight any more than he did.

"You have a rendezvous of your own," Eli said once the watchman was gone.

"What can I say? The night, she is young. I am on my way to see my love now." Even in the dark there was a glint in the tutor's eye.

"Do I know her?"

"I'm certain you have heard of her," Benson replied, "but I doubt you have met her. She is new to this country."

"French?"

"But of course!"

Eli grinned. "I had a taste of French romance myself tonight. There's nothing sweeter." He glanced around. "But now, if you'll excuse me, it's time to—"

Benson stopped him with a hand to his chest. "*Un moment, sil vous plait.* I've been waiting here for you. A bit of unfinished tavern business. After all, these are the times that try men's souls."

The hand.

The phrase.

Both turned Eli serious. Benson had used the same phrase the night he'd recruited Eli to sit in on a meeting of revolutionaries during his return trip from Kentucky. At the time Eli had thought it was a chance encounter. Now he wondered if Benson had been lying in wait for him then as well.

"It is the consensus of liberty-minded citizens," Benson said, "that the reports regarding a Federalist coup should be taken seriously. From all indications, that rogue Adams has all but conceded defeat in the upcoming elections, and he has signaled that he has no intention of handing the presidency over to Jefferson."

Eli frowned. "I thought that was just rumor."

"Credible sources have convinced us otherwise. The Federalists will attempt to maintain their grip on the presidency at all costs."

"By what means?"

"Adams is commander of the army, is he not?"

"But the army won't follow him if he loses the election, will they?"

"Who is to say? Several months separate Election Day and Inauguration. During that time, Adams will still be president. I wouldn't put it past the Federalists to pressure him to order Jefferson arrested on some charge or another, possibly treason."

"The people won't let him get away with it."

Benson shrugged. "All they have to do is link Jefferson with French revolutionaries. They don't have to prove anything. Just make the accusation."

"The president may control the army, but he doesn't control the state militias," Eli said.

"Exactly. And we have cells of followers in every state ready to march on Washington if necessary."

"A second revolution."

"Only this time we'll do it right. Believe me, there are plenty of men who are aching to do to the Federalists what the French did to King Louis."

"Execution? Do you really think it will come to that?"

"We can only hope." Benson flashed a smile.

Eli didn't tell his tutor that he didn't share that hope. Nor did he share the tutor's desire for blood. But Benson must have sensed it, for he regarded Eli with disappointment.

"So what do you want from me?" Eli asked.

"You, *mon ami*, are in a unique position to force Adams to relinquish the presidency."

"Me? I fail to see how."

"Do you play chess, Cooper?"

Eli scratched his chin. "You want me to challenge the president to a game of chess?"

"You know how important it is to keep one's opponent on the defensive, forcing him to make moves to protect himself, moves he wouldn't make otherwise."

"I'm listening."

Benson revealed an evil grin. "We're going to capture his queen."

Eli couldn't believe it. Had he heard Benson correctly? "You want me to kill the president's wife?"

"I said *capture*. Just long enough to persuade Adams to vacate the White House."

"Why me?" Eli asked.

"Because you are in a unique position to get the information we need to pull it off."

Eli had his doubts. But once Jacob Benson explained the plan to him, not only was he convinced he could do it, he was eager to do it.

⚜

The air coming off the harbor was heavy and wet, coating everything it touched with a slick sheen, but it didn't dampen Jacob Benson's sense of anticipation. Tonight he would meet the woman of his dreams.

The street emptied onto the docks where only a single ship showed any activity as large wooden crates were hoisted from its hold.

"Where do ya think you're goin'?"

Two men with clubs blocked his passage. They were both wide in the shoulders and—from the dull look in their eyes—thick in the head. Compared to Benson, who could have been mistaken for a flagpole on a dark night, the two men were so muscled, they outnumbered him four to one.

From the way they kept slapping the clubs in their open hands, Benson concluded they'd just been given new clubs tonight and had yet had a chance to beat anyone with them. He didn't plan on being the first.

He had but a single word for them. "Robespierre."

Their reply was to step aside and let him pass.

"Sorry to ruin your fun, boys," Benson called back as he strolled toward the ship. The fog gave the off-loading activity a dreamlike appearance, which was perfect. For Benson, tonight was a dream come true.

"Are you Benson?" A stocky man approached him. He moved with authority.

Benson identified himself.

"Name's Foster," the other man said. But he didn't offer Benson his hand.

They stood in silence, watching as one crate after another was deposited on the docks.

"Seems like a waste if you ask me." Foster's voice was thick and husky, as though he'd swallowed too much of the thick air.

"Why do you say that?" Benson asked.

"Why import something you can build yourself?"

"Just wouldn't be the same," Benson said. "There's something poetic about French death."

"Well, don't know nothin' 'bout that," Foster fired back. "Would you like to see one?"

"You have one built?"

"As ordered."

A pleasurable chill caressed Benson's flesh as Foster led him to the far side of a warehouse. *This must be how other men feel when their future fathers-in-law introduce them to their brides,* he thought as they rounded the corner.

What Benson saw next took his breath away.

Twin wooden beams rose parallel into the night sky. Between them, running on tracks the length of the beams, was a shiny metal blade.

"She's more beautiful than I imagined," Benson said.

"She?"

"Is your soul completely devoid of poetry, Foster? This is the mistress of all true revolutionaries—Madame Guillotine."

"'Course it is," Foster said flatly. "You ready to test it? I had one of my men purchase a hefty cabbage."

"Cabbage?" Benson cried. "*Mais, non!* That will never do! Does this look like a tool for making salad to you? God forbid!"

Foster, looking uneasy, studied him. "What did you have in mind?"

"I have arranged for a more suitable test."

Even as Benson was speaking, a carriage arrived bearing three men—a driver and two men in the back passenger seat. One of the men was drunk. So drunk he couldn't keep his head from flopping from one side to the other with the movement of the carriage. He was singing.

"Now wait a minute!" Foster insisted.

The carriage stopped, and the two men assisted the drunk from the backseat. Jacob reached into his coat pocket and pulled out a black executioner's hood.

Foster renewed his objection. "You're not really going to—"

"Really, Foster," Benson said. "What did you, think we were going to do with these things? Would it help if I told you the man is a staunch Federalist? That he voted twice for Washington?" He leaned confidentially toward Foster. "That—even a man like you, with no poetry in his soul, will appreciate this—his last name is Adams?"

"No one told me you'd be killing a man tonight," Foster cried.

"My dear Monsieur Foster, if all goes well, he will be but the first of thousands. We're going to teach the French a thing or two about how to implement a reign of terror."

Benson pulled the black hood over his head just as the drunken man caught sight of the guillotine. Then he came face to face with Benson. Sobriety fell suddenly upon the drunk. His eyes widened with terror. He began to sob.

Benson waved in annoyance. "Stick something in his mouth. He's putting a damper on the festivities."

The man was bound and dragged to the guillotine. There was no scaffold. The instrument of death rested on the docks.

While the victim struggled and had to be forced onto his knees, Jacob Benson took his place beside the guillotine. He stroked the wooden beam with a tender hand, then raised the blade.

The victim was shoved into place, his head secured with the sliding of a wooden yoke.

Shouts announced what was about to happen. A crowd gathered. But no one did anything to stop the execution. In fact, they seemed eager to see the guillotine in action. Until now they'd only heard or read about it.

Jacob Benson fingered the rope, enjoying the moment.

Then, without ceremony, he yanked it.

There was a *whoosh* and a *thud* and, just like that, it was over. A man lay dead at his feet. It was as though a door had scraped against the floor and slammed, shutting Mr. Adams out of this world. He now stood on the other side, awaiting his eternal destiny.

A cheer went up from the dockworkers.

Benson removed the executioner's hood. With tears in his eyes, he kissed his wooden consort. "Welcome to America, Madame Guillotine."

CHAPTER 16

It took two kicks to get his horse to pick up the pace. The horse was tired. Asa was eager to get home. It had been the better part of a year since he'd seen Maggy, and he was eager to enjoy the carefree atmosphere she was so good at creating. Some women were good cooks. Maggy was good company.

A chill had settled in the Connecticut River Valley, announcing winter's approach. It was still a couple of weeks away, but even now the wind had teeth.

Asa's journey had been uneventful. There was no chance of his getting lost. Follow the Connecticut River north. That's all a person needed to know to travel from New Haven to Greenfield.

His stay would be brief. He felt bad about it, having deserted Maggy during the long summer break for the trip to Kentucky. In her letters she said she understood and was looking forward to hearing about the revival. He hadn't told her about following Eli, just that he had gone to the frontier to witness revival firsthand.

And he was anxious to tell her about Annabelle. He'd mentioned nothing of Annabelle in his letters home. He wanted to see the expression on his sister's face when she learned he was courting the wealthy Miss Byrd.

He spurred the horse again.

With every mile from campus, the concerns of study and recitations and disputations weighed less and less. It wasn't as though he was running away from them. They'd still be there when he returned, and he'd be ready to take them up again, though the weight of university study was much greater than he thought it would be.

And the burden of Eli Cooper would also be there when he returned. Hours before Asa had departed on break, Dr. Dwight had summoned him, wanting a report on "The Cooper Project." Asa attempted to fashion a favorable progress report, but it was all smoke. He knew Dr. Dwight recognized it as such, though he was too much of a gentleman to say anything. For the second time he prayed over Asa, renewing Asa's commission.

If that wasn't bad enough, Asa received a letter from Kentucky. Eli's father. Mostly it recalled the good times they had together. He told Asa everyone was still talking about him and Amos Henderson. And while Pastor Campbell never mentioned Eli directly, the inquiry was invisibly wedged between every line. Was there any encouraging news about his adopted son?

As Asa approached Greenfield, he once again shrugged off all concerns of school and Eli Cooper. Within the hour he'd be home.

At last.

Seated at the table, eating, drinking, laughing, and exchanging news with Maggy.

He could think of nothing better.

Asa could hear Maggy's laughter through the door. No tonic had the effect on him as did his sister's laughter. It felt good to be home.

Just as he put his hand to the door latch, he heard male laughter. Asa's eyebrows raised.

Maggy entertaining a *male* visitor?

Well, well, well! he said under his breath.

Could it be that he wasn't the only one who'd been less than forthcoming in their exchange of correspondence regarding matters of the heart? A surge of big-brother protectiveness welled inside him. He would be interested in meeting this man, to find out what his intentions were toward his sister.

Asa already knew one thing about him. He could make Maggy laugh. He had a sense of humor.

That was a good start. But Asa wanted to know more. He hitched up the haversack that was slung over his shoulder and opened the door.

A pair of grins greeted him.

"You!" Asa shouted

At the table, opposite Maggy, sat a boisterous Eli Cooper, clutching a mug.

"Asa! It's about time you showed up. Where'd you wander off to in Northampton? I looked for you for over an hour before continuing on."

"What are you—"

Maggy pushed away from the table and ran to Asa, throwing her arms around his neck, giving him a fierce hug.

Over her shoulder Asa watched with horror as Eli lifted the mug in a silent cheer.

Maggy took a step back. "You look thinner."

Asa thought the same thing of her. A year younger than he, Maggy had always been wiry but strong. When they were children, Asa could outwrestle his sister, but first he had to catch her, and she was faster than he. Looking at her now, his heart beat proudly. She appeared every inch a lady, which made walking in and seeing her sitting across the table from Eli Cooper that much more painful.

"I'd be willing to bet Asa used to wander off as a child," Eli said, picking up the conversation from before. "Am I right?"

Linking her arm in his, Maggy led her gap-mouthed brother to the table. "On the contrary," she replied. "He was never the adventuresome type. Used to hang on to Mother's apron all the time."

Eli laughed. A little too heartily for Asa's comfort.

Still holding on to Asa's arm, Maggy turned to him. "Why didn't you tell me you were bringing a friend? Look at this place! I just thought it would be you, so I didn't bother to clean."

Eli answered for him. "He told me you'd make too much of a fuss if you knew I was coming. So I insisted he keep it a surprise. I'm just a frontier boy. Don't like people making a fuss over me."

"Nonsense! You don't strike me as the kind of man who would be any trouble."

"You'd be surprised," Asa said.

While Maggy removed biscuits from the oven, Asa glared at Eli and dumped his haversack in the corner. It landed against another haversack, which he recognized as belonging to Eli.

"You men wash up. You're both covered with road dust. And I'll put the food on the table. Rabbit stew, Asa. Your favorite."

Asa couldn't believe he hadn't smelled it until now, which showed how upset he was. Normally the aroma of Maggy's stew would have prompted his stomach to perform happy backflips. But at present, anger as heavy as bricks weighed it down.

"I think I'll say hello to Mother first," Asa said.

"She just lay down a short time ago," Maggy reported. "Would you mind doing that later? She's so restless lately that when I manage to get her down, it's best if . . ."

Asa nodded and followed Eli out the door.

"I don't know about you, old friend," Eli said, loud enough for Maggy to hear, "but I'm hungry as a bear coming out of hibernation. And if that stew tastes a fraction as good as it smells—"

"Don't dawdle, you two," Maggy ordered. "It's nearly ready!"

Asa began to shut the door behind him.

"Oh, and Asa?" Maggy added.

He paused in the doorway.

Gaiety sparkled in her eyes. Using a wooden spoon as a pointer, she gestured at Eli and whispered, "I like him!"

Asa hurt himself biting his tongue. He closed the door.

Eli's face and hands were dripping with water when Asa caught up with him.

"What are *you* doing here?" Asa challenged.

"How come you never told me you have a sister? Younger, right?"

"Answer me! What are you doing here?"

"It's obvious she got all the good looks." Eli dried himself on a nearby towel. "And talking with her, it's apparent she got more than her fair share of the family's brains. Which means you really got the short end of the stick all the way around, doesn't it?"

Asa grabbed Eli by the shirt. "WHAT ARE YOU DOING HERE?"

With a thrust of his arm, Eli broke Asa's grip. He hovered menacingly over Asa, patting him on the cheek. "What kind of a thing is that to say to an old school buddy? Relax. We don't have much time before we have to head back. Don't ruin it."

And with that he pushed past Asa and entered the house once again.

Bowls scraped clean of rabbit stew and biscuit crumbs littered the table.

"And so your brother," Eli said with storyteller tones, his hands motioning expressively, "tells Amos Henderson to get down on his knees, with poor Amos's wife and daughter looking on. And there stands Asa with the Bible in his hand, holding it like it was some kind of executioner's sword."

Asa briefly looked up to catch her glance of admiration, then continued to sit beside her glumly, his head propped on his hand.

This was Asa's story, and he had wanted to tell it. Especially to Maggy. Why did everyone get to tell it but him?

"Well?" Maggy pleaded. "What did he do?"

She asked it of Eli, Asa noted. She didn't ask him, her brother, who was sitting right next to her. She asked *Eli*.

Eli laughed. "Well, Asa raises the Bible over his head . . ." Eli raised a flat hand in demonstration.

"That's not how it happened," Asa muttered. But no one was listening to him.

". . . and he brings it down, slapping it hard against Amos's chest."

With a swoop, Eli brought his hand down, slapping his own chest with a *thud*. "And old Amos . . ." Now Eli's arm was a tree—teetering, then falling, complete with whistling sound effects. "Face to the ground! Lying there in the dust as though dead!"

Maggy clapped her hands.

"Naturally, his wife and daughter are horror-stricken. They come running over. His wife falls to her knees. His daughter cries out, 'Poppa!' And Asa stands over the man, his hands folded, looking down on him like a mortician. And then . . ."

Asa groaned.

". . . the next thing you know, to everyone's astonishment, Amos Henderson rolls over, clutching the Bible to his chest, and he's laughing!"

"Laughing?" Maggy asked.

"Laughing like a loon! His wife and daughter don't know what to make of it, but Asa . . . he knows exactly what happened, but he lets Amos tell it himself. Amos sits up, looks his wife in the eyes, and says, 'The old Amos is dead!' Then he gets up, hugs his wife, and says, 'This is the new Amos. Jesus raised me from the dead!'"

Maggy clapped again. She turned to Asa. "How exciting! Is that really what happened?"

"Something like that," Asa grumbled.

"Oh, I wish I could have been there. The whole revival atmosphere. I wish I could have seen it!"

"He didn't just roll over like that," Asa groused.

"Did you say something, Asa?" Maggy asked.

"I said, he didn't just roll over like that. It took awhile. It was more dramatic. Having to wait. Built up the tension."

He was being pathetic. He knew it, but he couldn't stop himself.

Pushing away from the table, Asa stood. "I'm going to see Mother."

His mother's bedroom door was cracked open. Asa knocked softly.

When there was no answer, he stepped inside, closing the door partway behind him.

Early evening twilight lit the room. His mother lay on the bed, fully clothed on top of the covers. She looked peaceful but drawn and sickly.

Asa lifted a chair and set it down beside her bed. For an instant he cocked his head toward the sound of Maggy's laughter.

"Who are you?" his mother asked.

His mother was gazing up at him.

"Hello, Mother." He reached for her hand.

She pulled it away. Fear filled her eyes.

"Mother, it's—"

"Maggy!" Her voice was raspy. Strained. She cried louder. "Maggy!"

The door swung open.

"I'm here, Mother." Maggy went to the bedside and clasped her mother's hand.

"Why did you let this man into my room?" The voice was peevish.

"Mother, it's Asa," Maggy murmured.

"It's not right for you to let one of your male friends into my room when I'm sleeping."

"It's Asa, Mother. Your son."

"I don't have a son. Now please ask him to leave."

"Mother . . . ," Asa tried again, attempting to stroke her hand.

Asa's mother shrank from his touch.

"I'll wait outside," Asa said, his heart pained.

He listened just outside the doorway as his sister spoke in calm tones. She didn't attempt to convince their mother she had a son. All Maggy did was calm her down.

After a while she came out.

Asa and Maggy exchanged glances.

"I didn't want to tell you in a letter," Maggy said.

"How long?"

"She's been like this for a couple of months. I was hoping that when she saw you, she'd . . ."

Asa nodded. Maggy didn't say it. She didn't have to. Nor did she have to remind him that if he'd come home during the summer break, it would have been different. Back when Mother still knew she had a son.

Asa needed to be alone. He walked back to the kitchen . . . and then straight out the door.

The scene in the bedroom haunted him. He knew he would replay it for years to come. Nobody had to tell him that—he just knew it.

It was unnatural for a son to see fear in his mother's eyes. Worse still to be the source of her fear.

As Asa walked, he mourned. The woman lying on that bed may have looked like his mother, but she was no more his mother than if she was stretched out in a coffin. The body was there, but his mother was gone.

CHAPTER 17

Eli knew something was wrong when Asa had emerged from the back room and brushed past him without so much as a sneer. A moment later a subdued Maggy appeared and began clearing the table.

"Should I leave?" Eli asked.

Maggy gave him the briefest of glances and a weak smile. "No," she said, stacking the bowls. "Mother's health is failing. Her mind. Asa didn't know. You know how he is. He just needs some time alone."

Eli didn't know how Asa was, but he didn't correct her. She thought they were friends.

"And you?" Eli asked.

Maggy managed a brave smile. "I've had time to adjust."

Eli began helping her clear the table.

"No! Sit!" she insisted. "You shouldn't be doing that. You're our guest."

"I don't mind." Eli picked up the stack of bowls.

She intercepted him. Tried to take the bowls from him. "But I do."

He didn't let go. She tugged. He held tight.

Tears came to her eyes. *She wasn't as adjusted to her mother's health as she claimed to be*, Eli thought. His feelings surprised him. Under different circumstances he would welcome the chance to get to know Maggy better.

"Don't make me get violent," she threatened.

Eli released the bowls.

For the next several minutes the clatter of dishes and the swish of Maggy's dress were the only sounds in the room.

Eli wandered to a window ledge that doubled as a bookshelf for five volumes. His finger passed over the titles as he read them silently. He pulled one book from the shelf. "Your brother shouldn't leave trash like this lying about." Eli leafed the pages.

Maggy cocked her head to see the title of the book. "Why do you assume that's Asa's book?"

"It's not?"

"Actually, I'm borrowing it."

"You shouldn't be filling your mind with this bibble-babble."

Maggy faced him with a hand on her hip. "Bibble-babble? That's some vocabulary for a Yale man."

"A few other words come to mind, but they're not the sort of words one uses in mixed company."

"Actually, I find Mr. Burke's conclusions very insightful."

Eli snapped the book shut and faced her. "Mr. Burke's denunciation of the French Revolution is nothing more than a flagrant misrepresentation of the facts!"

Maggy's blue eyes sparked with fire, indicating an intelligence that Eli found quite attractive and shocking, considering this was Asa Rush's sister.

"On the contrary," she said, "Mr. Burke gives a reasoned appraisal of the French Revolution from the perspective of a man who cherishes law and order over the glorification of murder and injustice masquerading as democracy."

Eli hefted the book. "Reasoned appraisal? Did I hear you right? Did you say reasoned appraisal? This is nothing more than an unprovoked attack filled with English rancor and prejudice. What right does Edmund Burke have troubling himself with the affairs of another country? And for your information, the French Revolution is a heroic struggle for liberty by a people who have been oppressed for centuries!"

Maggy didn't back down. "It may have started out that way, but it quickly degenerated into government by a committee of monsters whose thirst for blood has proved to be insatiable!"

"Typical female logic," Eli crowed. "You read one book and take it for gospel truth. Do you want to know what this book is? I'll tell you. It's darkness attempting to illuminate light."

"Typical male logic," Maggy threw right back at him. "Too lazy to think for yourself, you stand there, parroting another man's words, and think yourself wise."

Eli grinned. Frankly, he was shocked she recognized the quote.

Maggy frowned. "What are you smiling about? You think I haven't read Thomas Paine's *The Rights of Man*?"

"Just because you've read a book doesn't mean you know what you're talking about," Eli argued.

"I know enough not to swallow the rhetoric of starry-eyed Jeffersonian anarchists just because it's fashionable."

"No harder to swallow than the mush Federalists spoon-feed to closet royalists! Are you really willing to toss aside so quickly the inherent rights of man just because Their Highnesses Washington and Adams tell you it's in your best interests to kowtow to them?"

"For one thing," Maggy insisted, her face turning red, "I don't kowtow to anyone. For another thing, I happen to know President Adams—actually, I know his wife, and I've met him on a couple of occasions—but I know enough to know that he's a wise and godly man who has this nation's best interests at heart."

"And Jefferson doesn't? As for Adams, his only interest is how history will portray him."

"And Jefferson's only interest is seeing his own words in print. He seems to think that putting them on paper magically makes them true."

Eli stepped back. He crossed his arms. "You know, you're a lot quicker than your brother. And much better at disputation."

"Do you always do that?" Maggy asked.

"Do what?"

"Change the subject when you're losing an argument?"

This was how it was supposed to be.

Asa swung the ax. With a *crack*, a piece of wood split in two. He tossed the two pieces onto a growing pile. A few feet away Maggy moved up and down the rows of a garden in death throes. With winter a few weeks away, she harvested the last of the squash.

Eli was nowhere to be seen.

Asa broke into a grin at the thought.

This was how he'd envisioned the trip. Just family. Maggy tending the garden. He chopping wood and bursting at the seams to tell her about Annabelle.

When Eli left that morning, he hadn't said where he was going or when he'd be back. Asa didn't care. Eli was gone, and life was good again.

"Do you remember Annabelle Byrd?" Asa asked, placing another log on the stump.

Maggy straightened up, one arm cradling several squash. "Now there's a name I haven't heard in years. What a specimen she was!"

Surprised by Maggy's answer, Asa paused. He had set his feet to swing the ax but didn't. He wasn't sure what to think of her curt words or what to say, so he said nothing. Just waited for more.

Maggy bent down and lifted a large leaf. "What made you think of Annabelle?"

"She lives in New Haven now. Not far from the college." He decided to play it safe for now.

"Did you see her?"

Maggy wasn't making this easy for him.

"I . . . um . . . happened upon her one Sunday at the village green just opposite the school. That's where everyone goes to be seen and socialize."

Maggy grinned. "Is that why you went there? To be seen?"

Asa felt that no answer was the safest answer to that question. He swung the ax. Another log split in two.

"Did you speak to her?" Maggy prodded.

"Briefly. She remembers you."

Maggy laughed. "I'm sure she does."

Asa didn't know what that meant. "Weren't the two of you close?"

"I was the only person who would put up with her insults and innuendos," Maggie fired back. "She had a sharp tongue and enjoyed using it."

Asa frowned. "I don't remember that about her."

"Of course you don't. The only thing boys see about Annabelle Byrd is that she's pretty. When you spoke to her the other day, what was she like?"

Asa sniffed. "Pleasant enough. Like I said, she remembered you fondly."

Maggie stood there, with dirt smudges on her dress and hands, still cradling the squash. "A word of advice? Stay as far away from her as you can. She's trouble."

All the invigorating strength had left Asa's arms. Now they were just tired. All the brace had gone from the brisk air. Now it was just cold.

"I thought the two of you were old friends," he said.

"Annabelle Byrd has no friends. Just victims."

Asa could feel himself growing defensive. "People can change."

"Some people never change."

Asa cocked his head. He was puzzled. This wasn't like Maggy. Not like her at all.

"And don't look at me like that!" Maggy cried.

"Like what?"

"You don't know what she was like. Annabelle Byrd is a cruel and vicious person, just like her father. I think she enjoys hurting people. Do you remember Captain Byrd?"

"Barely."

Now Maggy appeared perplexed. "Boys aren't aware of anything that goes on around them, are they? If it's not on the top of Rocky Mountain, or something to be explored on the Mohawk Trail, it doesn't exist for them, does it? Do you have any idea what was going on in town when you were growing up?"

Asa scratched his head. Maggy had already discarded the mountain and the trail, which probably ruled out all the river activities he remembered from boyhood. Those things and school and an abusive father were all the memories he had of Greenfield.

"I remember that Captain Byrd was wealthy," he said lamely.

"Do you know how he got his wealth?"

Asa shook his head.

"That's the point. Nobody else knows either. However, what *is* well known are his connections to the Illuminati. You have heard of the Illuminati, haven't you?" Her tone was pedantic and insulting.

He didn't like it when she was like this. "Yes, I've heard of them. Dr. Dwight speaks against them often."

"Thank God for Dr. Dwight! Are you aware that they are spreading disillusionment all over the country through what they call Democratic Clubs? That there is a club right here in Greenfield and they've been holding regular hunting trips, which are thinly disguised drills in preparation for a second revolution?"

"I've heard rumors about them. Didn't know one was here in Greenfield."

"Courtesy of Captain Byrd," Maggy proclaimed. "Though he didn't live here long, he made enough connections to organize a cell. One of the club's handbills happened to come into my possession. It said that the Constitution was a leaky vessel that was hastily put together and should be scrapped in favor of a more enlightened document. They advocate overthrowing the government through a reign of terror similar to what is going on in France."

"But Annabelle wouldn't . . ."

"*Annabelle*, is it?" Maggy said in a frosty tone.

He attempted to explain. "She seemed sweet when I spoke with her."

Maggy stepped over several rows of garden to get to him. "Is there something you're not telling me?"

Anger and concern swirled in her gaze and tinged her voice, both vying for dominance.

Her anger angered him.

Her concern concerned him.

Enough that he decided to take a cautious route. "That Sunday on the green?"

"Yes?"

"Eli was there too. I think he's attracted to Annabelle."

Maggy pursed her lips as though to hold back an explosive response. It was a losing effort. "How can men . . . all they see is a face and a figure . . . all they hear is flattery! How can they be so . . . so . . . You have to warn him, Asa. Promise me you'll warn him!"

"But I—"

Warning Eli Cooper about any danger was the last thing on Asa's mind.

"If you value your friendship with Eli, you'll warn him," she retorted. "Annabelle Byrd is not what she appears to be. If he were to wander into a swamp that you KNEW was inhabited by an alligator, you'd warn him, wouldn't you?"

"Now that you put it that way." Asa suppressed a smirk.

"Promise me!"

It was Asa's turn to glare at her. "All of this concern over a man you've just met?"

"He's your friend. I'm concerned for him."

"You appear to have taken a personal interest in him."

Maggy looked away. "I just don't like the idea of Annabelle Byrd getting her clutches in anyone. You'll warn him, won't you?"

"Speaking of warning people, there are a few things you need to know about—"

The snort of a horse announced an arrival. Asa and Maggy turned and stared as Eli rode around the corner of the house.

"Am I interrupting something?" he asked, evidently sensing the tension. "A family matter, perhaps?"

Maggy became flustered.

Odd, Asa thought. *Nothing ever flusters her.*

"Asa was just . . . chopping wood." She pointed to the pile of wood as proof. "And I was . . ." She hefted the squash in her arms.

One squash escaped and fell to the ground. She bent to pick it up, and two more fell.

Again, Asa thought, *very unlike Maggy*. He glanced toward Eli.

From atop his horse Eli looked on with amusement.

At last Maggy corralled the errant squash. She leaned close to Asa. "Warn him!" she whispered, then hurried toward the house. "Supper will be in thirty minutes," she called back. "Finish up here, then wash up."

Eli dismounted with a grin. Asa watched him watching Maggy until she disappeared around the side of the house. When Eli turned back, Asa hefted the ax and tossed it toward the unwelcome guest.

"I still don't know exactly what you hope to accomplish here," he told Eli, "but if you're going to eat my family's food, you're going to earn it."

Asa scooped up an armload of wood and left Eli standing beside the woodpile with an ax in one hand and his horse's reins in the other.

A vision of Eli wandering into an alligator-infested swamp came to Asa's mind, and he grinned to himself.

CHAPTER 18

With their backs to Greenfield, Asa and Eli rode south in silence, the picture of two friends on horses heading back to school. Maggy had stood beside the house, waving, until they could no longer see her.

Asa had never had the chance to warn Maggy about Eli. He'd have to do it by letter.

"I like your sister," Eli said.

Asa glanced at him warily.

"Intelligent, though her politics are dangerously archaic. Fun. Great figure."

"Just forget about Maggy."

"Might just wander up this way again," Eli mused. "She gave me permission to write to her."

Asa ground his teeth. He'd heard his sister tell Eli she'd welcome his letters and another visit. Didn't she realize she was inviting a snake into the house?

"You've had your fun," Asa retorted. "You got your revenge. Now stay away from Maggy."

Eli lifted an eyebrow. "Revenge? You think that's why I came up here?"

"Isn't it? You came here to get back at me for going to Millersburgh. Well, you got your revenge. We're even."

158

Eli grinned. "More than even, I'd say."

"What do you mean?"

Eli's eyes flashed wickedly. "My father may be a backwoods religious eccentric, but he wasn't the town drunk. And my mother isn't crazier than a loon."

Asa was midair before he realized he'd launched himself from his saddle. He caught Eli by surprise too. The force of the attack sent both men toppling over the side of Eli's horse and onto the ground.

The force of the impact stunned them both, but only for a moment. Now that Asa had Eli on the ground, he didn't exactly know what he wanted to do with him. His anger demanded an outlet, but he wasn't the punching kind. Never had been.

Eli, on the other hand, seemed to be on familiar ground. While Asa angrily grabbed fistfuls of shirt, Eli scrambled for position. Straddling Asa, he landed two quick blows and was about to throw a third when he must have realized Asa wasn't fighting back.

His chest heaving, Eli glared at Asa. "What did you do that for?"

Asa was too busy inventorying his pain to reply.

With a final shove Eli climbed off him. "You're as crazy as your mother. Do you know that?"

Asa remained on his back while Eli dusted himself off.

"Just stay clear," Eli added. "If I hear one word around campus about my father, the whole world will know about your drunk father and crazy mother, got it?"

Asa glared back at him. "Just stay away from my sister."

"Are you kidding? Considering the stock from which she came? I'd have to be crazy. But wait—then I'd fit right in with your family, wouldn't I?" Eli mounted his horse.

Asa started to get up.

"Stay down there! Don't get up until I'm well out of sight."

And he rode off.

Asa stayed on the ground. Not because Eli had told him to, but because every movement meant pain. The similarity between this parting of the ways and the one in Kentucky was not lost on him.

"We've got to find another way to say good-bye," he muttered.

A grimace and several groans later, he was back on his horse. All in all, the trip home was a nightmare.

Finding his sister consorting with the enemy.

His mother not knowing him.

Maggy's hostility toward Annabelle.

Maggy was wrong, of course. It was difficult for him to imagine Annabelle Byrd was ever the person Maggy described her as being. But if Annabelle had been, Asa was convinced she had changed. The girl Maggy had described and the woman Asa knew were two different people.

Yet it was so uncharacteristic of Maggy to react as she did to his mention of Annabelle. Generally his sister was a good judge of character, as well as compassionate and quick to give people the benefit of the doubt. What was it about Annabelle that—

Asa sat back in his saddle, struck by a realization.

Annabelle was to Maggy what Eli was to him.

Eli was flint; Asa was steel. Every time they came together, there were sparks. Some people were like that. There was no explaining it, other than that was the nature of things.

Was Annabelle Byrd flint to Maggy's steel? And if she was, what could Asa do to make them compatible? It was a puzzle all right, but one worth solving.

With something to occupy his mind, Asa settled in for the long ride home.

Eli Cooper sat on the edge of his bed, wondering when his roommate would return. After the ride back from Greenfield alone, he was eager for company. As he stripped off boots that were coated with road dust, he considered his options.

There were the usual congregating places on campus, the taverns, and Annabelle. He smiled. Was there really a choice?

He'd head over to Crown Street and surprise her. If she wasn't available there was always the tavern. And if she was available . . . His smile widened.

There was a knock at his door. It began to open before he responded to it. A violation of campus rules. Someone was going to get a trimming. Eli would make sure of that.

"Oh, it's you," Eli said.

Tutor Jacob Benson strode with lanky legs into the room. "Good trip?"

"I got what we need."

"Did you have fun getting it?"

Eli smiled at the thought of Maggy. "Aya."

Benson settled on the edge of the bed opposite Eli and listened as Eli relayed the information he'd gleaned about Abigail Adams in Greenfield.

"Will that do it?" Eli asked when he was finished.

Benson smiled. "Checkmate."

Asa didn't find Maggy's note until he was back in his room. She'd apparently stuffed it into his haversack as he was packing to leave.

Asa,

Forgive the haste with which this note is penned. I wanted to speak of this to you before you left, but we were never alone.

"Don't I know it," Asa complained.

When Eli and I were alone, he asked me a lot of questions about my relationship with Abigail Adams. More questions than one would consider normal for general conversation.

When I told him she was staying at Quincy rather than the president's mansion due to her health, he began asking questions about the residence. He asked me to describe the interior, how many servants they had, their closest neighbors, and her daily routine. When I commented on his interest, he said something to the effect that he'd heard President Washington has insisted on being treated like a king and he was curious if the Adams had similar royal tastes.

I fear Eli may be involved with something dangerous. While he's too good of a man to do something violent . . .

Asa winced from the bruises of his most recent beating and reflected back on all of his trimmings at Yale—most of which were a direct result of Eli Cooper. "My dear sister, you don't know him very well, do you?"

. . . given his trusting nature and political naiveté . . .

"Bah!" Asa scoffed so hard it hurt his throat.

. . . I fear someone may be using him as a pawn for wicked purposes. Consequently, I have sent an urgent message to Abigail, informing her of my suspicions.

Warn him, will you?

And you will also warn him about Annabelle? Her seductive powers are considerable, and men are so weak.

I know you'll do the right thing. You always do. Eli is fortunate to have a friend like you, and you him. Your strengths complement each other.

I pray for you both.

Maggy

P.S. I really like him, Asa.

Crumpling the note, Asa threw it across the room with such force it aggravated his ribs and set his head to throbbing.

What had come over Maggy? How could she be so blind when it came to Eli and Annabelle?

However, he shared her suspicions about Eli's motives regarding Abigail Adams. The Eli he knew could easily be part of some dastardly plan involving the First Lady. Which meant that now that the First

Lady had been warned, there would certainly be some kind of armed detachment protecting her. Which also meant that anyone involved in a plot against the First Lady would be walking into a trap.

For the first time since his arrival in Greenfield, Asa felt happy. Eli's arrest for crimes against the president would certainly convince Maggy about his true nature.

"Beware of false prophets, which come to you in sheep's clothing, but inwardly they are ravening wolves," he said. "Ye shall know them by their fruits."

CHAPTER 19

Asa's eyes teared with admiration.

President Dwight stood tall on the chapel platform. Confronting those on campus who openly ridiculed Christian conviction, he'd challenged them to take him on in public disputation.

One by one he listened respectfully as they stated their cases against the Bible. One by one he tore their positions to shreds. Then, in brilliant fashion, he constructed a rock-solid argument for the Christian faith.

"In the final analysis, any philosophy that denies the existence of a sovereign God is nonsense masquerading as sublime thought," he preached, his voice bold, his stature imposing.

Asa was fascinated. Dr. Dwight had shifted the debate from one of a mere intellectual problem to an issue of far greater consequence—the moral implications of skepticism. He based his argument on Psalm 14:1: "The fool hath said in his heart, There is no God. They are corrupt, they have done abominable works, there is none that doeth good."

Then Dwight envisioned what an infidel world must inevitably look like. "For what end shall we be connected with infidels?" he thundered. "Is it that we may assume the same character and pursue the same conduct? Is it that our churches may become temples of reason, our psalms of praise Marseillois hymns? Is it that we may change our holy worship into a dance of Jacobin frenzy? Is it that we may see the Bible cast into a bonfire? Is it that we may see our wives and daughters the victims of legal prostitution; soberly dishonored; speciously polluted; the outcasts of delicacy, of virtue, and the loathing of God and man? Shall we, my brethren, become partakers of these sins? Shall we introduce them into our government, our schools, our families? Shall our sons become disciples of Voltaire, and the dragoons of Marat; our daughters the concubines of the Illuminati?"

Asa scanned the chapel pews for Eli, to see his reaction to Dr. Dwight's overpowering presentation. If anybody could reach Eli, it would be Dr. Dwight.

Asa craned his neck this way and that but still didn't see Eli. *Odd*, Asa thought, *since chapel attendance is required*. Finally, Asa spotted him. He and Jacob Benson, slouched down on the back row, were in animated conversation.

They weren't even listening to Dwight.

The Yale president continued by describing the radical conversion Americans would see in their cities once they returned to God. "Civic leaders will rule justly and in the fear of God. They will cease to be a terror, because none will do evil. The brothel will no more hang out the sign of pollution. The dram shop will no longer solicit the surrender of reason, duty, and salvation to drunkenness and brutality. Night will no more draw her great curtain over those felonious sins. In the family also, no drunken, cruel husband; no false, abandoned wife; no rebellious, graceless, debauched children."

While Asa was staring at Eli, Eli glanced up. Asa was tempted to look away, as though he'd been caught doing something wrong. But some inner sense told him not to.

Their gazes locked. Now Asa couldn't look away even if he wanted to. The two men faced off across rows of pews.

Then Benson said something to Eli, who turned to him to listen.

Asa felt a sense of satisfaction. Eli had looked away first.

"Salvation is the one thing needful," Preacher Dwight was saying. "Seek this above all things and seek it always. Pray to God every morning and evening, with all thy heart, to sanctify, to preserve, to bless, and to save you. Never lose an opportunity to be present at the worship of God. Read the Bible every day and two chapters at least. Devote the Sabbath to religion only. Possess yourself by loan or otherwise of religious books, and read them carefully. In a word, let religion and salvation be always uppermost in your mind."

Dwight paused. He stepped to the side of the lectern. "Let me ask you. And let each individual answer solemnly in his own mind. Do you love God? Do you desire to please Him? Do you cheerfully obey His commandments?"

The very air seemed charged with energy when Dwight invited those who wished to stay and pray to join him at the front of the chapel.

Six men went forward.

The others were free to leave.

Out of the corner of his eye, Asa saw Eli and Jacob Benson walk out.

They were the exception. Most of the men stayed—not going forward, not leaving. Their eternal futures hung between heaven and hell.

They were curious.

Attracted.

Afraid.

They watched and waited, anticipating that something mysterious, something amazing was about to happen, and not wanting to miss it if it did.

A few more men went forward.

Then a few more.

Then the dam broke. It was as though the whole world suddenly turned holy. Everywhere Asa looked, men were on their knees praying. The scene sent a warm chill through him. He laughed with joy.

Was this really happening at Yale? The bastion of skepticism? When Asa had first come here, only three other men admitted to being Christians.

Now look at the place, he thought, astonished. Everywhere men were praying, crying, laughing, and even hugging! It wasn't Kentucky, but it was no less holy.

At the sight of Dr. Dwight on his knees surrounded by praying students, a surge of emotion swept over Asa. The kind that comes with the realization of a long-awaited dream.

When Dwight had accepted the position as president of Yale, he told everyone his goal would be to reclaim the institution for God. Nobody had believed it could be done. Yet here he was, surrounded by a praying student body.

Asa went to join them.

Dr. Timothy Dwight looked exhausted. He perched on the edge of his desk, rubbing his eyes.

Hunched over the small secretary, pen poised, Asa anticipated a rewarding session. Still basking in the glow of this morning's chapel service, he had looked forward to this afternoon alone with Dr. Dwight.

A soft light filtered through the room. Hazily holy. As befitting the sanctuary of a godly man.

A thought struck Asa. He liked it. In the margin of the paper, he wrote, *I, Tertius.*

The two words signified a role he could accept with pride—an amanuensis to a great man of God. The apostle Paul had Tertius. Dr. Dwight had Asa Rush.

Dwight broke the silence. "You were in chapel this morning?"

"A memorable morning, sir."

"A humbling experience," Dwight replied.

The admission surprised Asa. He would have thought an experience of such magnitude would be exhilarating. "It has to feel good, though, doesn't it?" he asked. "Your command of facts, the rush of preaching, knowing that you're God's chosen prophet delivering His message?"

"Is that how you viewed this morning's events?"

"It was obvious, wasn't it? You demolished every argument, then built an unshakable case for the claims of Christ with personal conviction. Dr. Dwight, there are men who dream of doing what you did this morning."

"Are you among them?" All six feet of presidential frame unfolded as Dwight turned his complete attention to Asa.

"I would never presume to do it as well as you, sir," Asa replied.

"I would think not, Mr. Rush. You'd be fooling yourself to think you could ever preach as well as I."

Asa blinked, unsure what to do with such an uncharacteristically arrogant statement.

"I heard of your disputation. You faced off against Eli Cooper with less-than-stellar results."

Asa felt the sting of that day afresh. "It was my first disputation. And Eli Cooper is a second-year student."

"Is that how you rationalize the outcome?"

Asa squirmed. Why was Dr. Dwight attacking him like this? "With practice, I hope to get better."

"And on what do you base your hope?"

"Well, sir . . ." Asa's mind cramped and ached under the keen gaze of his mentor. How was he supposed to know the basis of his hopes? "Well, sir, I suppose . . . No, I don't suppose. I'm *certain* that my oratory skills will improve, because I'm determined to do better. I will practice hard, and I won't give up. I won't. You'll see. By the time I graduate, I'll be just as good as Eli Cooper, if not better."

"Not likely."

"Sir?"

Dwight sighed and rubbed his eyes again.

Asa felt like doing the same, only he was in such a state of shock over the course of this conversation that all he could manage was a shake of his head.

When Dwight spoke again, his voice was tired and husky. "Tell me, Mr. Rush, what happened this morning in chapel?"

Completely off balance now, Asa said, "I'm not sure what you're asking."

He wasn't ready to change topics. He wanted another chance to convince Dr. Dwight of his sincerity to excel as a speaker.

"Your impression of the revival," Dwight prompted. "Tell me what happened and what it meant."

"Well, sir . . . I saw a bunch of cocky students cut down to size by a truly great man of—"

"After the preaching, Mr. Rush."

"Oh, after the preaching." Asa scratched his head "Well, sir, after the preaching, men felt convicted. A good number of them went forward to join you in prayer, while others formed prayer clusters and prayed on their own. And, if I might add, what happened today was a long time in coming. Now that God has a foothold on this campus, I'm certain we're going to see a whole new atmosphere around here. And once news of today's events gets out, I wouldn't be surprised if revival spreads throughout New England, to other churches and cities, just like it did in the days of Jonathan Edwards and George Whitefield."

"I agree with you, Mr. Rush."

Relief surged through Asa.

"It *will* be different around here. For how can a man encounter the living God and not come away changed?" From the look in Dr. Dwight's eyes, the thought that had been in his mind had chosen now to express itself.

Asa didn't mind listening. It sure beat fielding questions.

Dwight cleared his throat. "Change, Mr. Rush—continuing, inevitable change—is the mainspring of the world. The natural direction of this change is downward. Destruction, disorder, decay; such is the way of this world. Physically, our bodies grow old and die; buildings falter over time and collapse; societies grow corrupt and self-destruct. Civil laws and codes may slow their destruction, much the same way a healthy diet and exercise may postpone a man's death. But like the physical body, nations conform to the natural cycle. They're born, they grow old, and they die. Change in a downward direction is simply the way of things in this world, Mr. Rush.

"Christianity is the world's hope. Change, Mr. Rush, is the essence of Christianity. It recognizes that life is not static, that all things change. But instead of bowing to life's inevitable decline, Christianity offers the hope of regeneration. Second Corinthians 5:17: 'Therefore if any man be in Christ, he is a new creature: old things are passed away; behold, all things are become new.' Do you understand what this means, Mr. Rush?"

"I think so, sir."

From the way Dr. Dwight stared at him, he didn't appear to be convinced.

"If any man be in Christ, he is a new creature!" declared Dr. Dwight. "His life changes, and this in direct contradiction to the decline of the natural order. Ask a man to describe his Christian conversion, and what does he do? He begins by describing what his life was like before Christ changed him. Then he describes what his life is like following his conversion—the new creature!"

Asa felt the charge of Dwight's spiritual fervor. It exhilarated him— and scared him—all at once. It scared him because he was a congregation of one. He knew that this discourse had something to do with him.

"It is this hope of change that fuels our prayers for revival, Mr. Rush. We see the way things are and see the way they can be in Christ. The contrast in the two visions drives us to our knees. How we desperately want to halt the downward direction in our nation, our towns, and colleges, our families, and in our own lives. And in our desperation, we cry out to God, knowing that He and He alone is the Author of life. That He alone can reverse the natural downward trend and give us new life! Do you believe this, Mr. Rush?"

Asa grinned. Finally, an easy question. "With all my heart, sir. That's why I'm so happy to witness what occurred on campus today."

"Yes, so you have said." Dwight appeared less enthused. "You agree that change is needed?"

Haunted by images of abuse from several trimmings, Asa was able to say, "Yes, sir!" with conviction.

Dwight nodded solemnly. He turned his back as he continued speaking. "I noticed in your report of this morning's events that you were quite enthused about the change that is taking place in your fellow classmates' lives."

"Yes, sir," Asa said cautiously.

"Yet you failed to mention any change in your own life."

A slap wouldn't have startled Asa more. Was Dr. Dwight questioning his salvation? "Sir, are you . . . I assure you, sir, I am a Christian."

Dwight swiveled to face him. "Salvation is a process, Mr. Rush. While it begins in an instant"—he snapped his fingers—"growth toward maturity occurs over a person's lifetime. This, too, is salvation."

Sweat beaded on Asa's brow, even in the somewhat chilly room. "Sir, if I—"

"The very nature of the word *revive* suggests a rekindling of an already established condition, which means, for believers, revival is not so much about *them* as it is about *us*."

"Yes, sir. I—"

"So naturally, while I share your excitement over the changes we can expect to see on campus as a result of revival, you can understand my concern that when I asked you to describe this morning's events, you failed to mention experiencing any *personal* change. Either you are acting incredibly humble, or . . ."

Dr. Dwight left the sentence hanging, so Asa could finish it himself. As he did so, Asa felt the sting of conviction.

Like the other students, he had attended the chapel services. Unlike them, he had come out of the chapel the same as when he went in. Unchanged.

His gaze fell, landing on the two words he'd penned earlier.

I, Tertius.

He wondered if Tertius ever felt personally convicted while recording the apostle Paul's epistles.

"I've acted the arrogant fool," Asa said.

"So you have."

Asa's mind turned inward, sorting through thoughts and actions and feelings, taking inventory.

"It's a matter of surrendering your will to God," Dwight murmured.

Asa nodded humbly. "I'm willing."

"Are you?" Dwight's discerning eyes focused on Asa's, as if trying to peer right into his soul.

Again with the jab, Asa thought. Why was Dr. Dwight being so hard on him?

"You must ask yourself if you're willing to do what *God* wants of you . . . not what *you* want to do for God."

The fog of confusion lifted. "Oratory."

Dr. Dwight's reply was blunt. "It is not your gift."

Dreams die hard. How many hours had Asa imagined himself addressing great congregations, expounding with power the great truths of God? Even now he clutched the dream with ferocity, not wanting to give it up. It made him feel good.

Asa closed his eyes.

That's why I'm holding on to it, isn't it? It makes me feel good. Not because it's God's will for my life. Not because it would be a benefit to others. But for the praise and attention of people looking up to me, admiring me, speaking well of me.

"Worshipping me," he muttered. "Me. Not God."

The ache in his gut intensified. A part of him rationalized that hundreds of people could be helped by his oratory. That now he was aware of the temptations that came with oratory, he could avoid them. What would it hurt? He could still do what he wanted and serve God.

"It's not your gift," Dwight said.

Asa looked up. "Is it Eli Cooper's gift?"

Dwight didn't answer, but his silence confirmed Asa's suspicions. "Are you ready to do what God has called you to do?"

A cold dread washed over Asa as he realized all that the question meant. "This is about Eli, isn't it?"

"It's your gift."

Asa snorted. "Eli Cooper is my gift? Pardon me, Dr. Dwight, but I find it difficult to believe that I was put on this earth for Eli Cooper." His tone had an edge to it. Sharper than he'd intended.

Dwight did not seem to notice. He stared off toward the window, as if envisioning another time, another place. "Eli is but the first of many."

Asa turned his head.

"Listen to me," Dwight insisted. "God has blessed you with an incredible gift. You demonstrated it early on, at Greenfield. Asa, you have an incredible gift for personal evangelism. God has put it within you to empathize with people. You feel what they feel. Do you know what a great and powerful gift that is? You can connect with them in ways I can't. Do you realize how blessed you are?

"The Bible records that Jesus preached, but his greatest encounters, the encounters that changed lives most dramatically, were personal. Nicodemus who came to him under the cloak of night. The woman he met at the well. A social outcast, she drew water when none of the other women were there. Mary and Martha and Lazarus, who became close friends. And his disciples! Every one of them chosen individually, not as a result of a sermon.

"Asa, the real work of revival occurs before and after the preaching, by men and women like you who, by your example, by your words, lay the foundation and then lead inquirers to Christ. While this is every Christian's duty, you have a unique God-given gift for it."

Amos Henderson came to Asa's mind. So did Henry Stillman, the boy at Miller's Drygoods store.

"One person at a time," Asa said.

"Exactly."

"That's what Eli's father told me."

"You've met Pastor Campbell?"

"During summer break I rode out to Kentucky."

"Then you witnessed the revival that's going on out there?"

Asa nodded.

Dr. Dwight's eyes lit up. "I want to hear about it sometime. As for Davis Campbell, I've only had the privilege of corresponding with him by post. In his letters he comes across as a godly man."

"He is." Asa retreated to his thoughts.

Dwight evidently did, too, since he was also silent.

"John Hillhouse," Asa said, referring back to their Greenfield days.

"I suspected then that God had gifted you. The way you befriended John confirmed it. God changed the course of his life through you."

Again the room fell silent.

There remained one final transaction. Both men knew it. Apparently Dwight had said all he intended saying.

It was left to Asa to make his decision. "You and Pastor Campbell don't know what you're asking!" he blurted.

"We're not the ones doing the asking. We're merely the messengers."

"Do you realize how difficult this is for me?"

"God would never ask you to do something unless He knew that you could indeed, by faith, do it."

"But we're talking about Eli Cooper!"

"God has great plans for Mr. Cooper."

Dwight's words were meant to help, but they only made things harder. What if Asa was successful and Eli turned his life over to God? And what if Eli became a great preacher? That had been Asa's dream! Did God really expect Asa to sit in a pew and watch Eli Cooper living *his* dream?

Asa looked down.

Two words looked up at him.

I, Tertius.

It was one thing to be Tertius to Dr. Timothy Dwight. But if God asked, would Asa Rush be willing to be Tertius to Eli Cooper?

Asa's head fell into his hands. "I can't do this."

Dwight draped an arm over Asa's shoulders. "Jesus, give him strength," he prayed.

Asa knew what he had to do.

He laid down the dream.

The sun had set when Asa left Dr. Timothy Dwight's office on the day of the great Yale revival. The man who left the office was not the same man who entered.

He'd changed.

CHAPTER 20

His hands in his pockets, Asa wandered aimlessly, pondering the change that had come over him. He felt good. At peace. With God, himself, and his decision.

He even felt good about Eli Cooper. He no longer thought of Eli as a threat, but as someone who needed to find what he himself had found.

Arrogance had nothing to do with it. Asa knew he was in no way superior to Eli. Having experienced afresh redeeming grace, the possibilities of a redeemed Eli Cooper captivated him. His feelings were more akin to a doctor administering a lifesaving elixir. Only in Eli's case, a better analogy might be one man warning another man of a cliff ahead—one that is obscured by fog. Or an alligator.

Asa chuckled at the remembrance of Maggy's analogy. Somehow he had to figure out a way to stop Eli Cooper without getting himself seriously hurt in the process.

Coming out of his reverie, he found himself at the end of Crown Street. He didn't know if God had led him here, or if it was his own doing, but since he was here, it seemed only logical to pay a call on Annabelle.

Of course there was a chance she wasn't home or was not prepared to take visitors. That didn't deter him. He was ready to talk about what had happened to him today, and who better to listen than Annabelle?

Maggy was wrong about her. Someday she'd realize how wrong, and they'd laugh about it. The old Annabelle Byrd may have been mean and devious, but people change.

Asa strode down Crown Street with eager steps. Out of the corner of his eye he caught a movement. With the movement came whistling.

Asa turned. He'd recognize that jaunty step anywhere.

Eli.

What's he doing here?

Asa's first thought was that Eli had followed him. The assumption had a history to it, given the way Eli had showed up at Greenfield. However, as Asa darted behind a tree, Eli gave no indication that he was aware of Asa's presence.

Retreating two more trees from the road, Asa figured to let him pass. The suddenness of Eli's appearing unsettled him. He couldn't dismiss the thought that God had arranged it. Was it a test to see if he really had changed?

Asa hammered the tree with his fist. He wasn't ready. He needed more time.

Then an even more disturbing thought hit him. Not a puzzler, but a blow to the gut. Was Eli coming this direction to go to Annabelle's house? Possibly to report to Captain Byrd, his sponsor? Or possibly to . . . ?

The idea so repulsed Asa, he didn't want to think it.

Either way, Eli's visit would ruin everything. How could Asa call on Annabelle, knowing that Eli was in the house? That he could walk in on them at any moment?

Asa swallowed a draft of air to calm himself. He told himself not to be hasty. For all he knew, Eli would pass Crown Street without so much as a glance. Asa simply had to be patient, wait, and see what happened . . . and then he could shoot himself.

A clatter of horse hooves interrupted Asa's reverie.

A tall rider hailed Eli by name and Eli turned.

Asa positioned himself to get a better look.

Jacob Benson.

The rider pulled up beside Eli. "Where you headed?" Before Eli could answer, Benson added, "Doesn't matter. Change of plans. It's on for tonight."

"Tonight?" Eli sounded startled.

Benson scanned the surrounding area. Evidently, he didn't see anyone within hearing distance, so he continued. "Our man just arrived with news. She's putting up at Middletown tonight."

A shiver ran down Asa's spine. Benson could be referring to anyone. Then again, could Maggy have been right about Eli being caught up in some kind of plot involving Abigail Adams? If she was right, then Jacob Benson was in on it too. He and Eli had been as thick as thieves lately.

From behind the tree, Asa strained to hear everything that was said. He needed to know for sure who they were talking about. He'd barged into Eli's personal affairs before with painful consequences.

"The plans were for Quincy," Eli said.

"Plans change. She's on her way to the new house. Can you get a horse?"

"I think so."

"Hop on. I'll give you a ride back."

Eli grabbed Benson's hand and swung up behind him. With a jerk of the reins, Benson turned the horse back toward campus, spurring the animal into a gallop.

Not until they were at a good distance did Asa step from behind the tree. His heart and mind were in a footrace. His feet set out to catch up with them.

He'd heard enough to know he had to do something to warn the First Lady and to save Eli from doing something incredibly stupid.

The eastern horizon grew hazy white in front of Asa as he approached Middletown from the west. A low fog crept up from the river, blanketing the road and making it difficult to see. His back and neck and tailbone ached from riding all night.

Asa grunted out of frustration. He hadn't seen Benson and Eli since catching a glimpse of them riding away from campus nearly twelve hours earlier accompanied by two men. This little excursion had all the earmarks of disaster: four to one odds, he didn't know where they were, and he didn't have a plan. And to think he'd had to hustle to get to this hopeless position.

His attempts to borrow a horse from his usual sources at the dorm had come up empty, forcing him to pay an exorbitant sum for a questionable mount at the Minuteman Tavern. Hanns Tinker, the owner, was notorious for making a comfortable living by gouging Yale College students for products of questionable value and shoddy services.

Just as he was leaving, Tinker shoved a pistol flat against his chest.

"What's this for?" Asa cried, not certain what to do with it.

Tinker grunted. "What do you think it's for? You would travel un-armed at night? What are you, crazy?"

Tinker overcharged him for the pistol.

Asa had no time to argue. He set out at a gallop, hoping to catch sight of Eli and the others before reaching Middletown. But the road was deserted the entire journey. Even now, in the predawn hours, the streets of the city were deserted.

With no clue as to where to go from here, Asa's mind turned on him. Had he heard correctly? Did Benson say Middlefield or Middlebury? Or Thomastown?

The harder Asa tried to grab hold of the memory, the more slippery it became. Had he ridden the better part of the night in the wrong direction?

He halted the horse on a main street that paralleled the river. He looked north, then south. It was a coin toss.

Where would the First Lady lodge? At an ordinary tavern? At the home of a friend or one of her husband's political supporters? She could be anywhere.

Asa's sigh turned frosty and curled in front of him. One thing was certain. He was nearly frozen. His fingers were stiff, his cheeks chapped, and his nose could easily be mistaken for an icicle. In his haste to catch Eli, he'd not taken the time to get his heavy jacket and gloves, and now he regretted it.

With a pull on the reins, Asa turned south. He wished he could say he had a gut feeling, but all his gut was telling him was that it wanted some fried eggs, a hefty slab of bacon, and a piping hot cup of coffee.

He came to a small stone bridge that arched over a creek. Halfway across he thought he heard conspiratorial whispering. For all he knew, the whispers were harmless enough, but at this hour of the day, on a deserted road, all whispers would sound conspiratorial. Pulling his horse to a halt midspan, Asa cocked his head to locate the whispers, at the same time placing an icy hand on the butt of the pistol. Had he needed to, he doubted his frozen finger could pull the trigger.

All was silent.

He dismounted. Standing in the middle of the bridge, he looked around. Several yards distant, just inside a patch of trees, he saw two horses. He saw no sign of their owners.

"Shh! Shh!"

The sound came from beneath the bridge.

Drawing the pistol from his waistband, Asa took two silent steps to the edge of the bridge and peered over the stony edge.

In the dark, at first they looked like rocks. Then two faces took shape, squinting up at him. Something waved. It looked like a stick, but intuition told him it was a gun.

"What you lookin' at?" called one of the men. "Be on with you now, if you know what's good for you."

"Ya heard 'im," said the other face. "Nuttin' here for you. Get along wid ya!"

Asa held out both hands to indicate he meant them no harm, realized one held a pistol, and pulled it behind his back. "Sorry. I—"

He could tell, by the way they looked up at him, they didn't appear to be interested in his departure any more than his apology.

Asa backed away from the edge. He didn't turn his back for fear one of the bridge trolls would make a sudden appearance. He knew he should wonder what two grown men were doing under a bridge at this time of morning, but wondering took time. And Asa had the distinct feeling he was running short.

He glanced down the road. A few more dwellings, then nothing but trees. His fifty-fifty hunch had been wrong. Mounting up, he turned back toward town.

After he'd put some distance between him and the bridge, he chanced a look over his shoulder. All he saw was a quaint, unassuming stone bridge with a ribbon of fog where the water should be. Anybody approaching it would be unaware that it was inhabited.

The thought occurred to him that these were the same two men who rode out of New Haven with Eli and Benson. He couldn't be certain, though. All he saw of them in New Haven were their backs, and the faces he'd just seen under the bridge were shrouded in shadow. Were he to bump into them later today, in broad daylight, he doubted if he would be able to recognize them as the bridge trolls.

A short time later he passed the road that had delivered him to Middletown, and soon came upon the Boar's Head Tavern. Doors and windows were shuttered tight. It appeared as quiet as a catacomb. It was like no other tavern he had seen. There was no activity. No sound. No horses. He assumed there was a stable in the rear.

To stop or not to stop, that was the question. But even if he did knock on the door and wake the innkeeper, what would he say? Everything that came to mind sounded suspicious.

"Excuse me. Might you have the First Lady staying with you tonight? If so, could I possibly have a word with her?"

"Look, here's my dilemma. You see, my sister and the First Lady are close friends, and Maggy sent me to warn her that two fellows I attend college with . . ."

"Hello. You know how college students can be, don't you? Well, some Yale students are planning to kidnap the president's wife. Might you know where I could find her?"

"Quick! I've got to see the president's wife! Her life might be in danger!"

His eyes fastened on the tavern's front door as he rode past it. Somehow he had to locate Eli and Benson and let them lead him to the First Lady.

Male voices and the clatter of a carriage caught his attention. In the alley next to the tavern, a black carriage appeared, pulled by two handsome horses and led by a stocky man with a mustache. He was talking to another man who walked beside the carriage. Taller with beefy arms and an old-fashioned tricorne hat.

The moment they saw him, the two men stopped talking and appeared to slow their step. Asa touched his hat in way of salute and continued on his way. They were still eying him when Asa turned away. The man with the mustache had polished black stones for eyes.

Asa rode a short distance before spying another alley. He turned down it, dismounted, and peered around the corner of a milliner's shop. In the window of a shop was a black velvet bonnet that he thought would look striking on Annabelle. He only thought fleetingly of cost. It would make the perfect gift for her.

The black carriage was now in front of the tavern. Asa could see only the one man, the one without the hat. He had climbed up to the driver's seat. The other man may have gone inside the tavern, or he may have boarded the carriage.

The tavern door opened. Out stepped the man in the tricorne hat. He opened the carriage door. The edge of a dark blue dress appeared, then the woman. The edges of her matching bonnet concealed her face.

Was it, or was it not, Abigail Adams?

STORM

Asa had to know. But how?

"Careful there, Mrs. Adams," said the man.

Asa's heart gave a start.

A second start stopped his heart cold.

Jacob Benson.

CHAPTER 21

The Yale tutor was concealed from the men in the carriage, but not from Asa.

And then Eli moved into position, also concealed, his back to Asa.

Both men were mounted, ready to go after the carriage.

While Abigail Adams climbed inside, Benson turned to check on Eli and saw Asa. Apparently Eli saw the surprise register on Benson's face, because he swung around and spotted Asa too.

Asa's heart chilled under their gaze.

Before Asa could call out a warning, the man in the tricorne hat shut the carriage door and clambered up beside the driver. A snap of the reins and the carriage jolted forward.

Eli's head bounced from Asa to the carriage and back to Asa again.

"I can't believe you!" Eli hissed at Asa. "Stay out of this! You hear me? Stay out!"

The carriage was still within shouting range. Asa opened his mouth, then closed it. Eli's eyes were narrowed to slits, his pistol leveled at Asa. The combination was an efficient cork.

Eli gave a final warning. "I said stay out of this!" Then he spurred his horse after the carriage.

With one last murderous glance at Asa, Benson also spurred his horse in pursuit. Asa could only watch. The carriage was now too far distant.

Just then two more riders appeared. Benson's men, from the looks of them.

Four to one. What chance did Asa have against four of them? But he had to try, didn't he? The president's wife was in that carriage.

He started to mount his horse. The horse backed away from him. He ordered it to stay, then tried again. Again the horse resisted, this time with a toss of its head. As far as it was concerned, they'd reached their destination.

"Don't do this to me," Asa pleaded. He patted the horse reassuringly. "Your country needs you. That's the president's wife in that carriage, and some bad men are after her. It's up to us to save her."

The horse eyed him with one eye.

Asa tried mounting again. This time the horse didn't resist.

"Good boy!" Asa cried. "Now let's go save Mrs. Adams."

He kicked the horse's sides, leaning forward in anticipation of forward movement . . . which never came.

"Let's go boy! Let's go!" Asa shouted, his heels jabbing.

The horse turned and looked at him.

"You're a Jeffersonian, aren't you?" Asa said.

He never knew what it was that got the horse moving, but something he said did the trick; for the next thing he knew, he was galloping after Eli, trying to stop him from doing something stupid.

The scene spread out before him. The carriage was bounding out of town toward the bridge. Benson, then Eli, trailed it. Their two cohorts approached from opposite sides. The drivers had not yet noticed they were being followed.

Asa was too far away to do anything.

Or was he?

The bridge.

The men beneath it. If they weren't with Benson and Eli . . .

"Of course!"

Asa drew the pistol from his waistband.

He readied it.

And fired into the air.

The heads of the two men on the carriage snapped around. The driver pumped his arms, urging the horses into a gallop. The other man bent low. When he straightened up, he held a rifle.

Benson glanced back and muttered a few things Asa didn't hear, didn't want to hear. Eli didn't bother to look back.

The two men flanking the carriage shot at it and yelled for the driver to pull up. Neither their shots nor their shouts had any effect.

The guard seated next to the driver returned fire with no apparent damage.

Having fired his only shot, Asa shoved his pistol into his waistband. Even if he could reload, who would he shoot?

The guard next to the driver repositioned himself to fire. He seemed unconcerned about the two riders flanking the carriage. Just then Asa saw why.

Rifle barrels appeared out of both sides of the carriage. Asa blinked. Both sides? The only person he had seen climb into the carriage was Abigail Adams. Someone else had to have been waiting for her inside. Two other people, in fact, to account for the two rifles.

A bullet whistled past Asa. He felt a rush of blood to his head. Only once before had a bullet been fired at him. He didn't like it. But then, the guards didn't know he wasn't one of the abductors, did they?

The carriage reached the bridge.

Now Asa would see if his hunch had been accurate.

Benson fired at the coach. The guard beside the driver slumped. His rifle fell overboard and clattered against the stone walkway.

Eli had his gun drawn but didn't fire.

At the crest of the bridge, the carriage fairly leaped to the other side. Asa caught a glimpse of an arm protruding from the right side. Blue cloth with lace trim. The hand raised the rifle and fired.

"I was right." Asa spurred his horse. "It's a trap! Eli! It's a trap!"

No sooner had he said that than the two men from beneath the bridge appeared, rifles drawn. They fired at the would-be kidnappers.

On the far side of the bridge, the carriage pulled to a stop. Two men, one wearing a blue dress, jumped out and fired at their pursuers. The driver grabbed a rifle and joined the fight.

Benson took a hit but managed to stay on his horse. One of the other abductors wasn't so lucky. Hit square in the chest, he somersaulted backward off his horse and hit the ground with a *thud*.

Eli continued toward the carriage. His jaw was set, his eyes fixed with determination. It was as though he hadn't comprehended that Abigail Adams had never been in the carriage. He rode straight toward the bridge and guns. He showed no more awareness of the danger than a moth shows to a flame.

"Eli! It's a trap!"

He was close enough to hear Asa's warning. He wasn't listening.

Digging his heels into the side of his horse, Asa pulled up next to Eli and shouted.

Eli ignored the shouts.

Asa reached out and tried to grab the reins of Eli's horse.

But there were no reins to grab. No horse either.

It went down with a horrible, grunting sound, and Eli with it.

The horse and Eli dropped so quickly, Asa lost sight of them momentarily. He pulled back on the reins and glanced in the direction of the others. Benson was slumped over his saddle. His horse trotted toward the river. Both unidentified kidnappers were on the ground, which meant that Asa was the only rider left.

Make that the only target left.

The two men from under the bridge were crossing the bridge now to get a better shot at him. The man in the dress took aim.

There was a puff of smoke. Asa ducked. A bullet whistled by.

With a yank of the reins, he turned his horse around. Eli lay sprawled out. He managed to prop himself up on his elbows. Beside him, his horse lay prone, breathing heavily, with a red wound on its chest.

"Get up!" Asa demanded.

Eli looked at him. Then looked past him at the gunmen. This time his eyes registered the danger.

Asa closed the distance between them. Like Benson had done the night before, he extended his arm.

Eli understood.

Bullets creased the air. Some exploded in the dirt.

Asa slowed. Eli grabbed his arm, swinging up behind him.

With a kick of his heels, Asa prayed that this time his horse would not object to one more gallop.

The horse needed no encouragement. With Eli holding on from behind, they were soon out of range of the guns.

A glance over the shoulder revealed no pursuit. The carriage remained on the far side of the bridge. The man with the tricorne hat, the one Benson had shot, was stirring as his partner checked on him.

Heading east on the same road he'd taken into Middletown earlier, Asa didn't halt until they were well out of town.

With farmland stretching as far as the eye could see, they came to a patch of trees beside the road that appeared to be a wayside rest area.

Neither man had spoken.

No sooner had the horse stopped when Eli climbed down. As he did, he grabbed Asa by the coat and yanked him off the horse.

The attack took Asa by surprise. His feet flew into the air, and he landed on his back. The impact forced the air from his lungs with such suddenness that he found it difficult to catch his breath.

He stared up at an angry Eli, who stood over him. Eli's hands were clenched. His chest heaved.

"What did you do that for?" Asa asked. For lack of breath his protest was more of a wheeze.

"Just what do you think you're doing here?" Eli shouted at him.

Asa tried to get up.

Eli's foot landed in his chest and shoved him back down. "I want to know why you think it's your mission to ruin my life!"

Asa was on his back, but he found enough breath to shout back. "Ruin your life? Ruin it? I just saved it!"

"You did nothing of the kind! Everything was going fine until you alerted the guards."

Asa couldn't believe what he was hearing. "Fine? You call that fine? Maybe for them. In case you didn't notice, that was a trap! Had I not intervened, right now you would either be dead or captured."

"How do you know it was a trap? You don't even know what we were doing."

"Oh yeah? That man in the blue dress? You thought it was Abigail Adams. You and Benson were trying to kidnap the president's wife."

Eli glared down at him. "You couldn't have known that," he said uneasily.

"It's lucky for you I did."

Asa tried again to get up. Again Eli put a boot in his chest and shoved him back down.

"Let me up!"

Eli stared into the distance, as though Asa was an afterthought. "I want you on the ground, where I can keep an eye on you."

While Eli paced, never more than a step or two away, Asa watched his feet. He figured he could launch himself at Eli, wrap his arms around both legs, and drive him to the ground. But then what? Eli was stronger. He could pummel Asa into the dust without breaking a sweat.

"Maggy figured it out, didn't she?" Eli said to the air. "It had to be Maggy. Asa isn't smart enough."

"Hey! I'm not deaf, you know!" Asa insisted.

Eli paced awhile longer before he bent over Asa, pointing a finger at his face. "My patience with you has run out. I'm tired of you and your family putting your noses in places they don't belong. You're in over your head. Stick to your recitations and studies. The next time you meddle in my affairs, I'll bury you in a hole so deep, it'll take you a year to climb out."

With a boot in Asa's stomach, Eli used him as a step.

When Asa's eyes opened, Eli was atop his horse, looking down at him.

"I mean it, Asa. Don't cross me again."

He rode off, leaving Asa lying on his back on the side of the road.

"Wait! Where are you going? That's my horse!"

With a groan, Asa sat up. He managed to roll over onto his knees, then got to his feet. The dirt road before him stretched to the horizon. As Eli rode away, he grew smaller and smaller, and as he did, Asa's anger grew greater and greater at the realization that he was going to have to walk back to New Haven.

"That's gratitude for you!" he yelled at Eli's back, even though it hurt his ribs to do so. "That's the last time I'll save your life! Do you hear me? Never again!"

He glanced around him. The morning sun edged over the horizon, signaling another day. The fields and houses in the distance looked peaceful, seemingly unaware of the drama that had just unfolded or the swirling storm of emotions that raged inside Asa.

He kicked the dirt.

If he thought it would do something to dissipate his rage, he was wrong. It was like tossing aside a cup of hurricane.

With nothing else to do, he set out for New Haven. Three steps and he stopped. There was something else for him to do.

Reversing his direction, he headed back toward Middletown. There was a bonnet in the window of the milliner's shop that was perfect for Annabelle.

Why waste the trip?

The thought that he might run into the men who had nearly trapped Eli and Benson in their ill-conceived plan occurred to him. Asa figured he could slip in and out of town without being noticed.

After all, they wouldn't be looking for him, would they? Who would be dumb enough to escape an attempt to kidnap the president's wife and then come back to buy a hat?

CHAPTER 22

December 3, Election Day

The entire campus buzzed with excitement as students anticipated the outcome of the hard-fought and often bitter contest between John Adams and Thomas Jefferson. Once good friends, now the two men and their respective parties had nothing good to say about the other. Politically, the nation was divided. It was this very partisan spirit that the recently deceased George Washington had hoped the country could avoid.

During the campaign, his opposition portrayed John Adams as more British than American, old, addled, and toothless—a querulous and vain Yankee. Jefferson, on the other hand, was decried as a radical visionary, more French than American, a weakling, a swindler, and a howling atheist and infidel. It was said that if Jefferson were elected, family Bibles would have to be hidden away to keep them from the fires of Jeffersonian atheists.

Both sides predicted that if the other party won the election, the United States would come to an end.

Today, with the political parades and rallies and threats and dire predictions over, by order of Congress, presidential electors from each state were gathering in their respective capitals, casting their votes either for the addled scold or the atheist visionary.

By law each elector would cast two votes for president. The man with a majority of votes would become president. The man with the second-highest number of votes would become vice president, regardless of party.

The New England states were each expected to cast their two votes for Federalist President John Adams and C. C. Pinckney, a respectable South Carolina lawyer who had served as minister to France. The frontier and southern states were expected to cast their votes for Democrat-Republicans Thomas Jefferson and Aaron Burr.

As election day approached, it didn't look good for the Federalists. An unofficial count of electors indicated that Jefferson would emerge the victor, the final blow against Adams coming from South Carolina. But it was generally conceded that Alexander Hamilton's earlier vitriolic public attack on his own president had been the broadside that had sunk Adams's ship of state.

Now the Federalists feared that Adams would garner the second-most number of votes and end up as Jefferson's vice president, a nightmare for both parties.

"What's to keep the Federalists from killing Jefferson?"

A handful of students who gathered on the walkway nodded thoughtfully to the big-eared student's harangue. As Asa hurried past, late for his afternoon recitation, he caught part of the students' supposition.

"Adams would then be president again, wouldn't he?" thundered the passionate speaker. "All I can say is that Jefferson had better keep his guard up. I wouldn't put it past some of those Federalists to go after him. They're ruthless, I tell you. Ruthless."

"What happens if either Jefferson or Adams were to die before the ballots were even counted?" another student asked. "Who would get their votes? All I'm saying is that a lot can happen in ten weeks."

By law the electoral-college ballots would not be opened officially and counted until February 11. However, nobody in his right mind thought that the outcome of the election would be kept secret for ten weeks. Word of how the electors voted was bound to leak.

Had he the time, Asa would have preferred to stay and take part in the discussion. But at present, his mind was full, trying to hold on to a rather slippery epistemology theory from Enfield's *Natural Philosophy*.

The new tutor wasn't as easygoing as Jacob Benson had been. Newly appointed and eager to show off his advanced status, tutor Erwin Ruggles took criticism to a whole new level. "It's important not only to know the author's words, Mr. Rush, but his *intent*. Not only to know *what* the author said, but *why* he said it."

None of the students liked Ruggles. With Benson all they had to do to get a passing mark was demonstrate they'd read the material. But Benson had mysteriously disappeared. Rumors around campus were that he had grown disgusted over the election and had boarded a ship for France.

The last time Asa saw him, Jacob Benson was slumped over his horse, heading toward the Connecticut River on the road just outside Middletown.

Asa hadn't told anyone about that night. The newspapers were equally silent. For several days Asa had scoured every page, thinking there would be some explanation for the exchange of gunfire at the Middletown bridge. He found nothing. It was as though the incident never happened, even though two men were dead. Possibly three, if Benson's wound was fatal.

Of course, Eli Cooper knew what happened that night, but he wasn't talking either. He refused even to look at Asa in passing. He acted as though Asa didn't exist.

Asa didn't care. He'd tried his best, hadn't he? Eli should be thanking him. He'd saved Eli's life, hadn't he? What more could he do? His conscience was clear.

If Eli didn't want to talk to him, it was Eli's problem.

If Eli didn't want to look at him, that was Eli's choice.

There are some things you just can't do, Asa told himself. *You can't make a person like you. And you can't make a person get his life right with God.*

No matter how highly the president of the college and the man's father think of him. Or Maggy.

Asa sighed. Maggy didn't know Eli like he knew Eli. And nobody could accuse Asa of not trying his hardest. Every time he tried, Eli beat him up.

Now it was up to Eli. If Eli wanted help, he knew where to find Asa.

A fist came out of nowhere. It grabbed Asa by the shirt, yanked him behind a bush, and slammed him against the brick exterior of Union Hall. When the swirling white stars cleared from his vision, Asa found himself face to face with Jacob Benson.

With one arm, Benson pinned him against the wall. With the other, he pressed the tip of a knife blade under Asa's chin. "Surprised to see me?"

Streaks of mud covered the man's face. His cheeks and chin were grizzled even more than usual from several days' growth of a heavy black beard. His eyes were bloodshot, his breath rancid.

"You're alive," Asa said.

"It'll take a better man than you to kill Jacob Benson."

"That's not what I was trying to do . . . sir." Asa added the formality at the end with uncertainty. When Benson was a tutor, it was required. But what was the protocol for a tutor you thought might be dead but wasn't and now held a knife to your throat?

"What were you doing in Middletown?" Benson seethed.

His forearm pressed hard against Asa's chest, making it difficult not only to talk but to breathe.

"Trying to stop you," Asa admitted.

"Stop us from what?"

"From kidnapping the First Lady."

"How did you know about that?"

"I figured it out."

Apparently, Benson didn't like that answer. He pressed the tip of the blade harder against the bottom of Asa's chin.

Asa felt his skin pop. "It's the truth," he insisted.

"You couldn't have known."

"Think about it. It was obvious. Why else would Eli ask my sister so many questions about Abigail Adams?"

Benson mulled this.

Even if he rammed the knife into Asa's skull, Asa wouldn't have told him that Maggy was the one who'd figured it out.

"I heard you shouting that it was a trap," Benson hissed. "Why did you shoot at us, then warn us?"

"I didn't shoot at you. My shot was a warning. Earlier I'd crossed that bridge and saw two men hiding under it. Not until the carriage took the south road did I realize it was a trap."

"You still took a shot at Eli."

"You're wrong. I shot into the air. I had to do something to precipitate the guards' response. Don't you see? They wanted you to cross the bridge. That way they could cut you down in a cross fire. Had I not warned you when I did, you'd all be dead."

"I don't buy it," Benson spat.

"Whether you buy it or not, it's the truth."

"All right, then answer me this. How did you know we would make the attempt that night? I just learned of it that night myself."

Asa didn't want to answer that question.

"Think of it this way, Rush. This is the most important recitation you'll ever make. Pass, fail. Get my drift? If I like your answer, you live. If I don't, you die."

Asa took a deep breath. He never had liked recitations. "I overheard you tell Eli."

Benson's eyes squinted.

Asa had seen the look before. The tutor wanted more; otherwise, he'd fail.

"At the end of Crown Street, I was out for a walk. I heard you ride up and didn't want to be seen, so I hid behind a tree. You told Eli it was on for that night."

"Aha! But I didn't tell him WHAT was on for that night!"

"Eli said he thought you were going to do it at Quincy. I put two and two together. Then you offered him your hand, he climbed onto the back of your horse, and you rode off together."

The pressure of the knifepoint eased, but not the arm against his chest. Asa interpreted that as a passing grade.

"You were following Eli, just like you did to Kentucky."

Asa was surprised Eli would have told him about that. "No. I told you. I was out for a walk. Eli was behind me. If anything, he was following me."

Benson studied Asa. "I still don't like it. I blame you for what happened at Middletown."

"Blame me? How can you blame me?" Asa cried.

It was an instinctive reaction. Had he thought about it, he probably would have kept his mouth shut. But now that he'd started it, he had to finish it.

"Did you see what was wearing that blue dress? Either Abigail Adams has sprouted a forest of black hair on her forearms, or that wasn't Abigail Adams! How can you kidnap someone who isn't even there?"

Benson took exception to his tone. The forearm shut off his air. The knifepoint popped a second hole in his chin.

"You're in no position to give an opinion, Rush!" he seethed. "You may have talked yourself out of having your throat slit here in the bushes, but only because there's someone I want you to meet. A real lady, don't you know. Tall. Slim. Razor-sharp wit. A real femme fatale, if you get my drift."

"Hey! What's going on here?"

Over Benson's shoulder Asa saw the student with the big ears and a couple of his buddies.

Benson kept his back to the other students. Speaking into Asa's chest, he told them, "Keep walking. This doesn't concern you."

"All right, then. That's one vote," said Big-ears. "Now let's hear from the other side before me and my pals cast the final vote."

But Jacob Benson apparently didn't think the vote was going to go his way. With a final shove that knocked the remaining wind from Asa's lungs, he turned, lowered his head, and pressed past Big-ears and his friends.

With a forearm against his chest and a knife to his chin, Asa had not seen that Benson had a crutch. The former tutor leaned on it heavily as he hobbled away.

"What did that bloke want from you?" Big-ears asked. "You owe him money?"

"That was Jacob Benson, wasn't it?" one of his buddies declared. "Did any of the rest of you get a good look? I could swear that was Jacob Benson."

"Nah, look at him!" another said. "Couldn't be Benson."

"That's not Benson," Big-ears said with authority. "Benson sailed to France."

Asa touched his chin, then looked at his finger. He saw blood. Taking a deep breath, he watched his old tutor hobble away. He wondered if Eli had put him up to this.

He also wondered how much trouble he'd be in if he missed his recitation. He was already late. Worse, when Jacob Benson bounced him against Union Hall, all of the philosophical facts had fallen out of his head.

CHAPTER 23

Saturday came none too soon for Asa. Once he made it past the morning, the day held nothing but promise.

He spent early Saturday making up the philosophy recitation he missed on Wednesday when Jacob Benson pinned him against the wall and threatened to slit his throat. Sticking with the throat theme, Asa had sent word to Ruggles that his was sore and asked to reschedule.

From the way Ruggles grilled him Saturday morning, it became apparent that either the tutor felt it necessary to impress on Asa the importance of attending regularly scheduled recitations, or the poor bloke had no social life and decided to entertain himself ad infinitum at Asa's expense. From what Asa knew of Ruggles, he thought the latter reason was the more likely one. Ruggles questioned Asa not only about the author's theory of epistemology and his *intent*, but also about the publisher's choice regarding serial commas and semicolons during the editing of the book.

Asa didn't escape until afternoon, and then only after promising to go with Ruggles to the tavern for a mug and a chat at a later date. The tutor was eager to talk about the election. He said he read in the *National Intelligencer* that neither Adams nor Pinckney received a single electoral vote in South Carolina. That the editors of the paper declared Jefferson and Burr had triumphed.

When Asa did manage to break away, it took another hour before his head cleared and he was able to think straight.

He spent the rest of the day preparing for the evening. He had arranged to call on Annabelle. She was expecting him.

Not wanting to leave anything to chance, he'd sent her a letter, asking permission to call upon her this evening. She replied that she could receive him at eight o'clock, not before. In the last line of her letter, she wrote that she looked forward to his visit with great anticipation.

Asa must have read that line fifty times.

Standing in the snow outside the Byrd mansion with a hatbox under his arm, Asa pulled out his watch. He was an hour and fifteen minutes early. Slipping the watch back into his pocket, he did his best to shrug off the night and the cold.

He fully intended to wait until eight o'clock to present himself at the front door. It was a rude guest who presented himself earlier than the agreed-upon time, especially where a lady was concerned. And while Asa didn't have an abundance of experience in these matters, tales of suitors being kept waiting by ladies long past the agreed-upon time were legendary.

Asa didn't mind waiting. Inside, after the agreed-upon hour, or outside in the snow. The anticipation itself was intoxicating. Yet it paled compared to being in Annabelle's presence. It had been weeks since he'd seen her, and he didn't want to miss a minute.

So he paced in front of the mansion to keep warm, imagining what he would say to her when he first saw her again and how she would respond with delight when she opened the box and saw the hat he bought at Middletown.

The interior lights of the mansion painted elongated yellow squares on the snow. The warm red brick exterior framed by trees, flocked with snow made for a picturesque winter scene. It put Asa in a Christmas mood.

He considered waiting until Christmas to give Annabelle the hat, but only briefly. He didn't want to wait that long to hear her squeal of delight when she opened it.

As though on cue, a squeal came from the house. Distinctly feminine, followed by laughter. A door slammed, followed by a flash of lavender streaking across the window of the downstairs corner room.

There was only one person Asa knew whose squeal sent shivers of delight up his arms.

He grinned. Something had put Annabelle in a playful mood. The thought excited him. His evening prospects were looking brighter and brighter.

Asa was drawn to the window. He knew better than to go around peeking inside people's windows, but the thought of seeing Annabelle in a happy, unguarded moment was too much of a temptation to resist.

Walking at an angle to the window, from tree to tree to keep from being seen, Asa approached the house.

Just as he reached the window, Annabelle squealed again, passing for a second time in front of the window.

Asa drew back as she passed, then inched forward and peered through the window. He'd not been in this room before. It was some sort of sitting room. Possibly a sewing room, because he saw an embroidery frame and spools of thread on a table.

His view was hazy. The windowpane was clouded by the winter air. But he could see clearly enough.

Annabelle stood a few feet in front of a closed door. Her face was alight with excitement. Her chest rose and fell from running. Her eyes darted about the room. It looked as though she was searching for a place to hide.

A voice—indistinct—came from the other side of the door. Asa could barely hear it. But Annabelle evidently heard it.

The door opened a crack.

She threw herself against it, slamming it shut. Laughing.

A muffled sound came from the other side.

"I am hiding!" she called gaily. "I'm hiding behind this door!"

Another muffled sound.

"No!" Annabelle cried. "Go around!"

The door pushed open a crack. Alarmed, Annabelle squealed. Placing her back against the door, she pushed with her feet, slamming the door shut.

Asa couldn't take his eyes off Annabelle's face. He'd never seen her giddy like this. Her eyes sparkled. Her cheeks were red. Her smile carefree. A wayward curl dangled against her temple. Just looking at her, his heart seemed to grow larger inside his chest.

Inside the room, the door opened a crack. With a renewed effort, Annabelle shoved it closed.

It opened again. This time wider, steadily wider. Annabelle's feet slipped on the floor. She was powerless to stop it.

Whoever was pushing on the other side had an obvious advantage. Captain Byrd? That would be fun, wouldn't it? Asa didn't know Captain Byrd, but the prospect of a father having a close enough relationship with his grown daughter to play games brought a smile to Asa's face.

More likely, it was Martha or one of the other servants. Possibly Martha *and* another servant. But Martha could force the door open alone. She was big enough.

Annabelle's feet slipped on the hardwood floor, despite her efforts. It made it appear like she was walking backward.

"I'm coming in!" The mumble was no longer a mumble.

Asa's heart froze. It had nothing to do with the winter temperature. That voice was familiar to him. Too familiar.

Fingers appeared around the edge of the door.

Annabelle saw them. She laughed and hammered them with a closed fist. They retreated to the other side.

The opening continued.

Annabelle gave one last thrust and stopped it. Then she stepped quickly away.

The door flew open.

Eli Cooper spilled into the room onto the floor.

Annabelle shrieked with delight.

Grinning, sweating, his hair looking like bird plumage, a laughing Eli shook a warning finger at her, then slowly maneuvered his legs beneath him to get up.

"No, no . . . you stay down there!" Annabelle laughed.

A wolfish grin on Eli's face signaled his rejection of her order.

Her arms outstretched, Annabelle backed away. She didn't turn and run.

Why doesn't she turn and run? Asa wondered. *Unless . . .*

Eli grabbed her by the wrists.

Annabelle struggled, but not too hard.

He shoved her into the corner of a sofa, landing next to her. The struggle continued. Annabelle shook her head no, but her eyes said yes.

Asa backed away. He didn't want to see any more. He couldn't watch any more.

Annabelle squealed again.

Asa didn't look. He didn't want to know.

His heart, which had been warm and large moments ago, shriveled and ached. Apparently a fist had punched him in the gut, then disappeared. He hadn't felt the initial blow, but he could feel its aftereffects.

Retreating a few steps from the window, he retraced his path to the road, then slumped against a tree, the hatbox under his arm, shielding himself from the house lest anyone happen to glance out a window.

His whole world went dark. All his recent thoughts had Annabelle in his future. Now he had no future. And the present didn't look so good to him, either.

He was slumped against a tree on Crown Street. He didn't know why.

Nor did he know why he wondered what Maggy would think if she knew he was here.

He pulled his watch from his pocket. Again he didn't know why. What difference did time make? What difference did it make knowing that in forty-five minutes Annabelle was expecting him to call on her? It wasn't as though he was going to keep his appointment now.

He had a hatbox under his arm. He didn't know why. He had no one to give it to.

He held the hatbox in front of him and stared at it absent-mindedly. A flash of inspiration hit. The box and its contents had a purpose after all, and Asa was eager for it to fulfill its destiny.

Ripping the top from the box, with a roar, he flung it as far as he could. The round top sailed past several trees before hitting a trunk dead on and plummeting to the ground.

Next to sail was the empty box itself. It crashed and rolled in a circle before dying.

Now the hat. Asa started with the ribbon. He ripped it off and threw it. Then he tried tearing the hat in two. But when it proved to be more than a match for his strength, he slammed it against the side of a tree.

It hit with a splat and slid to the ground.

Asa picked it up and threw it again. Then again. And when that seemed to be too laborious without inflicting enough damage, he held on to the brim and whacked it repeatedly against the tree with all his might, until he was sweating and gulping air.

With one final heave, he threw the battered and crumpled hat into a bush.

He stared at the hat with the blazing eyes of a victorious gladiator, his chest rising and falling from the exertion.

He felt better.

But only for a moment.

Then the rush of vanquishing a hat dissipated, and the empty ache of reality ate at his chest until it was hollow.

Asa sunk to his knees in the snow.

CHAPTER 24

Only one emotion is strong enough to rally a brokenhearted man in a short period of time. Revenge.

Asa hoped he wasn't too late.

After self-pity had turned to rage, he circled the house and hid in some bushes in the back. At fifteen minutes before the hour, Annabelle would expect him to approach from the front. So it made sense that she would have Eli leave by way of the back door.

Asa's plan was to catch Eli in the act. This was a necessary first step. If he waited and asked Annabelle about Eli, she could simply deny it. And he would respond how? By confessing to standing in the bushes and spying on them? He needed a better strategy.

Maggy had been right about Annabelle all along, hadn't she?

However, if he caught Eli leaving, he would have evidence to prove his allegation.

But what if Eli claimed he merely had one of his meetings with Captain Byrd?

Asa thought a moment. He needed to catch Eli inside with Annabelle. He could go to the front and show up early. He could say that he was so anxious to see her again, he couldn't help himself. He could say that convincingly.

But what if Martha opened the door? She could ask him to wait and place him in another room while Eli slipped out the back. And what if Eli slipped out the back while he was circling around to the front?

Asa stared at the back door. Everything pointed to it as the key to catching Eli and Annabelle together.

But he couldn't just knock. He had been inside before when someone knocked at the back door. Martha answered it. And being loyal to Annabelle, she would keep him waiting outside while Eli slipped away out the front door.

Which left only one course of action, if he was man enough to take it.

"Strike that," Asa muttered. "Angry enough. Betrayed enough. Hurt enough. Crushed enough."

Apparently he was, because he came from behind the bush and strode with purpose toward the back door.

What if it's locked? he asked himself. *If it's locked, the plan dies a stillborn death.*

"Only one way to find out." Asa placed his hand on the latch. It clicked. The door opened. Asa stepped inside.

He found himself inside a deserted kitchen. He'd passed through here once before, going the other direction. On the other side of the room, there was an open door that led to a hallway, the main artery of the house. Several rooms lay off it. The front door at the far end. If he commanded the hallway, he commanded all exits to the house.

Asa crossed the kitchen on cat's paws, listening. He thought he could hear Annabelle's laugh. It sounded distant. He hoped it was a good sign that Eli had not yet left.

But what if he had? What if Eli had left the house while he was out front beating up a hat? If that was the case, instead of appearing righteously justified for breaking into the house, he would look . . .

"Foolish," Asa muttered.

The sound of a door opening echoed down the hallway.

Stay? Or go?

To his right was a narrow stairway. A servant's access to the second-floor rooms.

But if he was going to catch Eli, he had to hold his position.

At the far end of the hallway Martha backed out of the room, closing the door behind her.

She didn't see him.

Asa jumped sideways onto the stairs and out of sight.

He could hear Martha's regimented footfalls. They were getting louder. Too loud.

Grimacing, as though a facial expression could make his feet hit the steps more softly, Asa ran up the stairs. Pausing on the top step, he listened.

Martha's footfalls grew louder still until she appeared at the foot of the stairs. Her head was down as she grabbed the guardrail and started climbing. The way she filled the stairway reminded Asa how large she was.

Asa backed around the corner and looked for a place to hide. He was in another hallway, and it was dark. Closed doors marked its length like a ruler.

The footfalls on the stairway grew nearer.

Asa skittered to his right, searching for an alcove or passageway or something he could step into without opening a door. He found nothing but walls and doors the entire length of the hall.

With no place else to run and with no going back, he stood with his hand on the latch of the last door, hoping that Martha would turn the other way and he could double back behind her, sneak back down the stairs and outside. Standing uninvited in the upstairs hallway of another man's house had taken all the revenge out of him and replaced it with fear.

He waited to see which way Martha would turn.

She appeared, shoulders first, then grew to daunting size, preoccupied by something as she rose full height onto the landing.

Then the worst that could happen, happened.

She turned his direction.

Without knowing what or who lay behind the door, he worked the latch, stepped inside, and closed the door behind him. A glance had shown him he was standing with his back against the room's *only* door. He prayed with all his heart that Martha wasn't headed for this room.

His ear close to the door, his fate in the sound of footfalls, he listened.

A door opened and closed. Then . . . silence.

Asa closed his eyes and dared to breathe again.

When he opened them, he took in the room. Dark wood and sparse furnishings indicated it was a man's room. A framed cutlass hung on one wall, a picture of a merchant ship on another. An old captain's hat sat atop the bureau. Asa's gaze fell on the bed. His heard jumped. It was occupied.

He'd only seen Captain Byrd two times when he was younger, and then from a distance. However, the man's profile was distinct enough that Asa knew immediately he was in the captain's bedroom. A large forehead, strong nose, and pointed chin were tilted slightly his direction.

Asa's eyes had adjusted to the dark enough to see that the man's eyes were open. He was looking directly at Asa.

"Sir, I can explain," Asa said.

He expected outrage. None came. Just a steady, unnerving glare.

"I've come to call on your daughter, and . . ."

There was something about the man's gaze that was off. Unnatural. Asa stepped closer. That's when he noticed an odd medicinal odor and he realized that the captain had not moved since he came into the room. There had been no rustle of sheets, no cough, no living sound.

Asa stepped closer still.

The captain's eyes were fixed on eternity. His skin looked leathery. Not only was he dead, he had been dead for some time, and someone obviously had gone to great measures to preserve his body.

Standing beside the bed, Asa pondered what this meant. Obviously the man had died. While it appeared to be from natural causes—there were no obvious signs of abuse or struggle—without lifting the covers, he couldn't tell for certain. And lifting the covers was not an option in his mind.

So why had he not been buried? For what purpose would some-one preserve a dead man and keep him in his bed? Was keeping the captain's death a secret advantageous in some way? And if so, to whom? And what was Annabelle's role in all this? Surely she was aware of her father's death, but was she keeping his death a secret under duress, or of her own accord? And what kind of woman could be so carefree and even flirtatious downstairs, knowing that upstairs . . .

"Martha!"

Asa's head snapped in the direction of the door. Annabelle's voice had come from the hallway.

"Martha!"

She was headed this way. Hopefully Martha would answer her and that would be that. But Asa wasn't taking any chances.

On the far side of the room was a window. He ran to it and looked out. Then down. There was no ledge to block his view from the second story, and consequently, nothing to break his fall.

Now there were two voices in the hallway.

Asa crouched behind the far side of the bed, just in case. Perhaps the two women could conduct their business in the hallway without—

The door opened.

Asa dropped to the floor. Looking under the bed, he could see two pair of feet illuminated by the dancing light of a candle.

"Where is he?" Annabelle approached the bed. The light continued around the foot of the bed. Asa slid under the bed so that the dead Captain Byrd's body was directly over him.

"It's not like Asa to be late," Annabelle continued.

She walked where Asa had crouched seconds earlier. Asa heard a drawer slide, then the sound of rummaging.

"Should I be concerned?" Annabelle said.

The drawer slid shut.

"His tardiness is a blessing," Martha replied. "For a while there I thought you would never get Eli to leave. I thought there were going to be fireworks for sure."

Annabelle's feet retraced their steps. "Oh, you worry too much."

"Do I? What would you have done had they run into each other?"

Annabelle laughed lightly. "You know me. I would have thought of something."

"No doubt." But Martha's tone suggested she wouldn't have wanted to put Annabelle's boast to the test.

"Besides, Asa has served his purpose. He's expendable. And after the other night I'm surprised Benson hasn't stuck a knife in him."

Martha smiled. "Is it just me, or does Benson look even more attractive with a crutch? Sort of like a pirate, don't you think?"

Without any regard to the dead man lying in the bed, the two women walked to the door.

"If you're finished with Asa, why are we wasting our time tonight?"

Annabelle sighed. "You don't throw away a perfectly good man, Martha. Who knows when you might need one? Asa would walk off a cliff if I asked him."

The door shut, and the voices faded down the hallway.

"Asa Rush! You put a fright in me!"

Annabelle didn't wait for him to step inside. She went to him, taking him by the arm and leading him into the house.

While still in the captain's bedroom, he had given the women time to get down the stairs. Then he sneaked out, walking along the edge of the hallway to avoid creaking floorboards. Tiptoeing down the stairs, he slipped through the dark kitchen and out the door.

Walking around to the front of the house, he fought the urge to return to his dormitory. His insides were such a muddled mix of ill feeling, he didn't want to look at Annabelle. But he had unfinished business with her. If he didn't take care of it tonight, he doubted he ever would.

"I apologize for being late." His voice was flat and hard. He didn't like the sound of it, but he doubted he could do anything to change it. He wasn't very practiced at deception.

"Is anything wrong?" Annabelle cooed. "You don't sound like yourself."

"It's been a hard day. I had to make up a recitation this morning, and my tutor did a good job of making me pay for ruining his Saturday."

"The brute!" Annabelle cried. She led him into the sitting room, hanging on his every word. Her brow was furrowed, and she looked genuinely concerned.

"He's a new tutor. Wants to prove himself. Our other tutor was easier on us. A guy by the name of Jacob Benson. Funny thing, he just up and disappeared. Nobody knows what happened to him."

Annabelle offered him a seat, then sat next to him. As Asa sat, he studied her face, hoping to catch some sign of recognition when he mentioned Benson's name. She showed none.

"Martha will be in shortly," Annabelle said. "I know how you insist on everything being proper and all. No matter how much a couple cares for one another, it's important that they give every evidence of propriety, don't you agree?"

Asa took a good, hard look at the woman next to him. He found it hard to believe this was the same woman he'd seen through the window playing hide-and-seek with Eli. Now she acted as though they were sitting in a pew on Sunday.

He ached to look at her. A part of him wanted to start the evening again. To pretend he never looked through the window. To pretend he hadn't seen what he saw upstairs. To go pick up the hat he bought at Middletown, straighten it until it looked new, and give it to her as a present.

"Maggy sends her love," Asa said.

"How sweet! She is such a dear."

"Funny thing." Asa forced a chuckle. "When I went to Greenfield—"

"And left me here all alone!" Annabelle pouted. "I still haven't forgiven you for that."

Before tonight Asa would have apologized all over himself until she said she forgave him. But that was before. Before he knew she kept her dead father in a bedroom upstairs.

"Well, guess who followed me up to Greenfield?" Asa said.

Annabelle shook her head, her expression blank.

"Eli Cooper!"

She shook her head again, her expression unchanged.

Martha walked into the room carrying the embroidery frame Asa had seen through the window. With a glance and without a word, she sat in the corner chair and started to work.

"You remember Eli," Asa said. "He was pushing you on the swing that one time I came to visit."

At the sound of Eli's name, Martha's head snapped up. Asa saw her out of the corner of his eye.

"One of my father's boys," Annabelle replied, as if pretending to remember. "Are the two of you friends?"

"It's hard to define the relationship I have with Eli," Asa said. "But let me tell you, he really took a shine to Maggy while he was up there. And she to him. I wouldn't be surprised if the two of them get together."

Annabelle's composure cracked. It was just for an instant, but anger flashed unmistakably across her face. "Really? I'm so happy for Maggy! Though I'm a bit surprised. That day he was here, I got the impression he was something of a rogue."

Asa laughed. "That's putting it mildly. But you know Maggy. She's never been a very good judge of character."

Annabelle hid a yawn with the back of her hand. "I'm sorry, Asa," she apologized. "But it has been a long day for Martha and me as well."

Asa stood. "Understandable. Considering the late hour, I figured our visit would be brief."

"Before you go, will you do something for me?" She had taken his hand and was hanging on to it, looking up at him. "Will you read from the Bible? You know how much comfort Martha and I derive from your voice and God's words."

Asa smiled, more inwardly to himself than to her. She'd given him the opening he needed. "Is your father still too ill to read to you?"

"Oh no! Haven't you heard?"

For an instant, Asa thought she was going to tell him the truth.

"Father sailed for the Caribbean two days ago."

"No, I hadn't heard," Asa returned. "How long will he be gone?"

Annabelle smiled bravely. "With Father you never know. But Martha and I are used to it. We've managed to carry on in his absence before, haven't we, Martha?"

From the corner, Martha barely looked up long enough to form a thin grin.

Annabelle retrieved a Bible from the drawer. The sliding sound was exactly the same one Asa had heard while hiding under the dead man's bed upstairs. He wondered if it was the Bible Annabelle had taken from the bedside drawer and if it belonged to the man in the bed.

"If it's all the same to you," Asa said, "I don't feel up to reading to-night. I hope you understand."

In the corner Martha gave a genuine smile.

"Really?" Annabelle exclaimed. "But we were so looking forward to it."

"My apologies." Asa made his way toward the front door without waiting for her.

She caught up with him and took his arm. "Asa? Are you angry with me?"

There were tears in her eyes. Even though he was staring at them, Asa couldn't believe it. Actual tears.

"Angry? I can't begin to describe how much I have looked forward to seeing you tonight."

CHAPTER 25

Asa was so angry, his hands shook.

It had been more than an hour since he left the Byrd mansion, and he still couldn't get the image of Annabelle's tearful expression out of his head.

"Oh, Asa! Are you angry with poor innocent me?"

How could she be so brazen? So calculating?

"Jezebel!" Asa fumed. "Daughter of Delilah! How can men be so blind when it comes to women?"

He sat at his desk in the dormitory room, balling and unballing his fist around a pen. A solitary candle cast flickering shadows against the walls. Gurdon lay asleep on his bed, his back to Asa.

Earlier, when Asa returned to the room from the Byrd mansion, he found a stack of papers on his bed with a note from Gurdon.

> *Payback for borrowing my horse.*
> *Copy my speech. Need it legible by morning.*
> *G.*

The draft from which Asa had to copy was a hodgepodge of paragraphs—some circled, some bracketed—with arrows and numbers filling the margins, suggesting he had some semblance of order in mind. The words themselves made as much sense as twigs tossed on the ground.

Asa's copy wasn't much better. With the stranglehold he had on his pen, his letters were arthritic, and there were a number of ink splotches. The fact that Gurdon waited until the last minute to ask him to copy the pages only added to his fury.

But then Asa thought he might as well do something to keep himself busy. It wasn't like he was going to be sleeping anytime soon, was it?

He crumpled up his first attempt and started again.

"Candles out, boys! Candles out!" The nightly cry echoed down the hallway.

Asa closed his eyes and sighed heavily. How was he going to get Gurdon's speech copied by morning?

"Rush! Gurdon! I said candles out. Don't make me come in there."

Gurdon stirred but didn't waken. Asa capped his inkwell and blew out the candle.

For a good fifteen minutes he sat in the dark, waiting for the dormitory to settle down for the night. Then, using his fingertips for sight, he gathered the papers and his writing kit. Making his way silently down the stairs, he slipped into the night.

He had two possibilities. Find an empty room and risk detection by the night watchman, or go to the tavern. If caught, the punishment would be greater for leaving campus, but then the risk of getting caught was less.

He decided on the tavern.

Avoiding large open spaces, Asa managed to make it across the street to the common without being seen. The open expanse of the common would be the riskiest part, where there were no buildings and trees were sparse.

He left six-inch-deep footprints in the snow as he hurried toward the cover of the first large tree.

Seeing the tree proved unfortunate. It tripped a latch on a closet door in the back of his mind. An avalanche of unwanted memories spilled out.

Under this tree Annabelle and Martha had sat reading *Tristram Shandy*.

Asa cringed with fresh pain at the memory of how eager Annabelle was for him to read to her. An act. Even then. It seemed so obvious now.

Eli had stood here. And the toady Phineas.

Asa remembered their expressions when Annabelle showed her preference for him over Eli. What a coup that was for him.

Eli was better looking.

More mature.

More charismatic.

Yet Annabelle had chosen him over Eli.

Asa stepped into the shadow of the tree. He turned and checked behind him. The campus spread in front of him. Dark. Asleep. Not so much as a bird or a ground squirrel moved.

"Why was that?" Asa said aloud. "Why did Annabelle choose me over Eli?"

He knew he should have asked this question weeks ago, but he hadn't. He knew why. There was always a part of him that knew it wasn't real. That his world with Annabelle was a bubble, and questions were sharp objects.

Now that the bubble had burst, he could ask the question. "Why me?"

He thought back to that day. How different everything was. It was sunny. The grass was green. His first glimpse of Annabelle prompted a double take. Even now an involuntary moan escaped his lips.

Then Eli and Phineas showed up and nearly ruined everything. But just when he was about to flee the common, Annabelle rescued him.

"Why?" he said again.

Having read *Tristram Shandy* was his salvation. He'd read it. Eli hadn't. Annabelle said she didn't understand it. What was there to understand? Crude humor. Ridiculous situations. There was nothing to understand. Yet, she made it an issue . . . Why?

They spoke of the past. Of Greenfield. And Maggy. Annabelle remembered her fondly.

"A fondness Maggy doesn't share," Asa told himself.

All of a sudden unrelated thoughts began pairing up.

Maggy and Annabelle.

Annabelle and Eli.

Eli and Maggy.

Asa began walking. He didn't go anywhere, but he couldn't stand still.

Eli's trip to Greenfield. Asa had thought Eli went for revenge and came away with a plan to kidnap Abigail Adams.

But what if he went with a plan? What if his sole purpose was not to aggravate Asa, but to interrogate Maggy?

The realization welled up inside Asa and came out in a loud, visceral grunt.

Annabelle Byrd played a part in the attempted abduction of Abigail Adams! But how much of a part? She provided a key piece, but who planned it? Jacob Benson?

Asa's face screwed up with disgust.

Now there was a revolting thought—Annabelle Byrd and Jacob Benson. There had to be some kind of buffer between them. Captain Byrd came to mind, but he was dead.

So where did Eli fit in all this? Was he part of the team, or was he being played just like Asa had been played?

Maggy said she feared Eli was in over his head. She could be right. She was right about Annabelle.

Asa walked to where he could see the dormitory. For a long time he stared at Eli Cooper's darkened window.

With a full head of steam, he retraced his steps toward campus.

"I'm not going to get any rest until I get some answers," he said, as though his words were rocks thrown at Eli's window. "And if I can't sleep, you're not going to sleep."

BAM! BAM! BAM! BAM!

The rap of knuckles on wood echoed loudly down the dormitory hallway. Much too loudly.

Asa didn't care. "Cooper!" he shouted at the door. "Cooper! Get out here!"

Other doors opened. Men in long johns and nightshirts stumbled into the hallway.

"Keep it down, will ya?"

"Some of us are trying to sleep!"

BAM! BAM! BAM! BAM!

"Cooper!" Asa shouted again. "If you're not out here by the time I count to—"

The latch sounded. The door began to open.

Asa launched himself forward. The door reversed direction, freely for a couple of inches, then . . .

BANG!

. . . against someone's nose and forehead. It sent him reeling, and he went down, hard.

Asa heard the crash. It was too dark to see.

"What . . . ?" Eli's voice cried.

A match flickered. Eli's roommate, Tappan, stretched groggily toward a candle, his hand wavering in search of the wick. "Whas goin' on?" he asked huskily.

With the initial flash of the match, Asa saw Eli's face. It was clear he had caught on quickly what all of this was about.

"I sure hope you're the ghost of Asa Rush, because if you're the real thing, I'm gonna . . ." Eli, hair tousled, started to get up.

Asa stood over him. With a foot to Eli's long-johns-covered chest, Asa shoved him back down. "I know about you and Annabelle Byrd!"

Eli's eyes flashed anger. Again he tried to get up. Again Asa shoved him back down, which only seemed to make Eli angrier.

"Don't try to deny it," Asa accused. "I saw you. You were over at her house tonight."

Murderous eyes glared up at him. "I'm not denying anything." Eli shoved Asa's boot off his chest. "I'm just getting up so I can beat you to a pulp."

"Well, do it outside!" someone standing in the doorway said. "We want to get some sleep."

"Yeah, take it outside," Tappan agreed.

Asa looked at all the guys standing around in their nightclothes. If the dormitory resident lived on the second floor, this little gathering would already be history.

"Put some clothes on." Asa made his way out of the room. "I'll be waiting for you outside."

The others parted to let him pass. One of those standing in the hallway was Gurdon.

As Asa passed him, he asked, "Did you get my speech copied?"

Shivering beneath an oak tree, on the south side of Connecticut Hall, Asa took his watch from his pocket. Angling the face toward the moonlight, he saw the minute hand closing in on midnight. He stamped his cold feet to get some feeling into them and wondered why people used words like *hot* to describe anger when his was doing absolutely nothing to keep him warm.

His patience waning, he turned toward the door when it opened.

Eli Cooper came out swinging.

Asa ducked but not far enough. The blow hit him in the temple and propelled him into the tree. The bark made an imprint on his cheek before he dropped to his knees.

"You're just aching to die. That's it, isn't it?" Eli yelled. He motioned for Asa to stand up so he could hit him again.

Asa stayed down. After the day he'd had, dying was not all that unattractive. He just didn't want to get hurt doing it.

"Who told you that Maggy was friends with Abigail Adams?" Asa insisted.

"Maggy?" Eli cried. "I thought this was about Annabelle."

"Just answer the question. You didn't go to Greenfield to pay me back.

You went to get information on Abigail Adams. Who told you about Maggy?"

If it was possible for Eli to be impressed with anything Asa did, he appeared to be impressed now. "Did you figure that out all by yourself?"

"Who?" Asa demanded.

"Benson told me."

Asa studied Eli's face to determine if he was telling the truth. He appeared to be. Which confirmed some kind of connection between Jacob Benson and Annabelle Byrd. It also suggested that Eli wasn't part of that team. That he, too, was being played by Annabelle.

"She's not what she appears to be," Asa said.

"Maggy?"

"Annabelle. I saw you with her tonight."

"You couldn't have."

"Don't try to deny being at the Byrd mansion. I saw you there."

"With Annabelle?"

"With Annabelle," Asa confirmed, rubbing the side of his head. The blow had knocked his eyeball out of whack. Everything in his left eye was blurry.

Eli folded his arms. "I'm surprised you'd admit something like that. I *was* with Annabelle tonight . . ."

"Then you admit it!"

". . . and we were inside the mansion the entire time. Which meant that if you saw us, you were peeking through the window. I always knew there was something strange about you, Rush, but I have to admit even *I* am surprised you turned out to be a pervert."

Asa grimaced. In his eagerness to get Eli to confess he'd been with Annabelle, Asa had overplayed his hand.

"I wonder what Dr. Dwight's reaction will be when he learns that his favorite first-year student spends his evenings peeking through windows of private residences."

"It's not like that," Asa said. With a groan he rolled to one side and sat with his back against the tree. The cold, damp ground seeped through his pants. He would have stood, but his head was still spinning.

"You deny it? Then how do you explain seeing me with Annabelle? Had you just been watching the entrances, you might have concluded I was there to meet with Captain Byrd."

He doesn't know, Asa thought. Another indicator that Annabelle was playing Eli.

"She's not who you think she is," Asa said.

"Beautiful? Vivacious? Fun? If you don't think she's any of those things, Rush, you're sicker than you look."

An unguarded memory of Annabelle sitting beside him on the sofa came to mind. The blow with which it struck Asa's heart was worse than Eli's blow to his head. It took him a moment to rally.

"I don't know what she's up to," he said softly, "but I have reason to believe that she has some sort of devious plan for you."

Eli laughed so loud that snow fell from the branches of the tree and landed on Asa's pants. He brushed it off. "Annabelle Byrd, devious? Ridiculous! That girl doesn't have an ounce of a brain in that gorgeous head of hers. She is pampered, spoiled, flighty, and flirtatious, but devious? The only devious thoughts in her head are how to get you to compliment her one more time."

"You're mistaken," Asa said flatly. "That's what she wants you to believe."

"Oh! Oh *now* I understand!" Eli raised a finger to signal a profound insight. "You went there tonight, hoping to woo her yourself. And then you saw her with me. What's the matter, Rush? Truth hurt?"

"Eli—"

"What's the great mystery here? That she would prefer me to you? That's obvious, isn't it?"

"It's true I went there to—"

"And not the first time, is it, Rush? What? Have you been making a nuisance of yourself? Did she finally tell you to your face that you were wasting your time?"

"I'm trying to help you."

Eli's tone turned threatening. "Well, I don't need your help. I got the girl, you're outside sitting in the snow, and all is right with the world." He turned to go inside. Swinging back around, he warned, "Stay away from Annabelle." Then, gritting his teeth, he leveled a stiff forefinger at Asa. "And for the last time, STAY . . . AWAY . . . FROM . . . ME!"

The door to the dormitory slammed shut.

For several minutes Asa didn't move.

"Well, at least I learned something tonight," he told himself. "I learned it's hard to win an argument when you're sitting in slush."

CHAPTER 26

His backside frozen, Asa trudged toward the tavern, retracing his earlier steps. He still had Gurdon's speech to copy.

He'd gone back to confront Eli with every intention of being a force to be reckoned with, yet once again had found himself on the ground, staring up. There was a definite pattern here, and Asa didn't like it.

Confront Eli.

Get licked.

Then get angry.

Oh, and one thing more—vow to wash your hands of him. Tell yourself that you've done all you can do. More than any sane person would do.

Asa sighed. Surely this pattern of events wasn't God's grand scheme for his life, was it?

At least the dormitory resident didn't wake up, though how he managed to sleep through the ruckus was a mystery. And, Asa reminded himself, he'd learned that Annabelle was using Eli. He didn't appear to be part of the cabal.

Crossing the common, his head down against the wind, Asa began shivering violently. No amount of garment adjusting did any good. He couldn't remember ever being this cold in his life. Thoughts of a roaring fire at the tavern drove him forward. He told himself that nothing short of an act of God would slow him in his pursuit of that fire.

Looking up, Asa slowed, then stopped.

He blinked.

Stared.

Then God spoke to him.

Before him stood a church. Asa had seen it a hundred times before, but never like this. Its white clapboard siding shone in the moonlight. His gaze lifted upward—from the front doors, to the steeple, to the cross. The cross, too, shimmered white against a black winter sky.

Asa stopped shivering. His eyes were transfixed on that cross.

"You're not going to let me off the hook, are You?" he said aloud.

Giving voice to the question was for his sake, not God's. Asa already knew the answer.

Dr. Dwight had commissioned him to reach Eli.

Reverend Campbell was praying for him to reach Eli.

Maggy was hoping he'd reach Eli.

And now God was telling him directly. *Bring Eli to me.*

The message couldn't have been more clear, had the words been spoken. *The task is hard. Do it anyway.*

What if Jesus had given up? Said the task was too hard? Said mankind was too stubborn? That they didn't want to be saved?

Eli threatened you, hit you.

Soldiers scourged Jesus.

Eli knocked you down.

Soldiers lifted Jesus up and nailed Him to a cross.

They killed Jesus. What if Eli kills you?

Asa's gaze fell to the graveyard beside the church.

You wouldn't be the first to die advancing the cause of Christ. Take another look.

Headstones littered a dark landscape.

Where are the saints?

Asa stepped toward the graveyard.

Show Me the saints.

Asa's gaze fell from one cold grave to the next.

Show Me the saints.

"They're not here."

They're not there.

"They're with You."

The door to the tavern banged open. Asa ran to the serving bar. Hanns Tinker stood hunched over a stack of bills. The wind rearranged his stacks.

"I have an idea . . . ," Asa began excitedly.

"Close that door!" Tinker bellowed.

Asa ran and closed the door, then hurried again to the bar. "I have an idea . . ."

"That would be a first," Tinker said.

"It's a really good idea."

"Not likely. There are no good ideas in the middle of the night. Only evil ideas. Good ideas wait until mornin'."

"And I need your help."

"It'll cost you."

"You don't know what I'm going to ask."

"Whatever it is, it'll cost you," the tavern owner replied.

"I need to borrow a book."

"What? Does this look like a circulatin' library? Drink, we got. Books? Not so much."

"I'm guessing you'll have this one," Asa said. "The *Code Duello*."

Tinker rose up. He had a big head on a big body, and right now the eyes in that big head were squinting at Asa. "I was right. Only evil ideas exist at this hour."

"Do you have it?" Asa asked.

Tinker turned and rummaged through a stack of papers he'd tossed into a wooden bucket. Pulling out a pamphlet, he tossed it onto the heavily scarred bar.

Asa grabbed at it eagerly.

A huge hand slapped it down, pinning it in place.

"Two and a half cents," Tinker declared.

"What?" Asa protested. "I want to borrow it, not buy it!"

"To buy is more. To borrow—two and a half cents."

Asa needed the book. Though it pained him to pay Tinker's price, he pulled three coins from his pocket and slapped them on the bar. One of the coins came up heads. Lady Liberty stared at him, as though she was questioning the wisdom of his plan.

Taking the booklet, Asa looked for a place where he could work. The rooms with the beds were in the back. The common area was a large room with two long tables and benches in the center. Against the walls were smaller tables.

Several students already occupied the smaller tables, their heads in a book or hunched over parchment. Asa recognized them. He needn't fear that any of them would turn him in. They were here just as illegally as he was. And they were here for the same reason. To finish their schoolwork.

Only Asa had something else to do first. He situated himself at the end of one of the long tables. It was an easy choice. Sitting on the bench meant his backside was closest to the fire.

Setting his parchment and writing tools aside, Asa opened the pamphlet and began to read. Over the top of the book, he could see Tinker watching him.

After a few minutes of reading, Asa's plan hit a snag. Nothing disastrous. But it did mean he'd have to wait until morning. He continued reading.

A half hour later, Asa set the book aside. He rubbed his eyes and pulled out a sheet of parchment. Slowly, deliberately, he drafted a letter. When he was finished writing the letter, he read it and decided it was satisfactory. Setting it aside, he placed Gurdon's speech in front of him and began copying.

A punch in the shoulder roused him. A second punch woke him. It took two good blinks before Tinker came into focus.

"You done with that?" the tavern keeper asked. A sausage finger pointed at the pamphlet.

"Um . . . yeah." Asa was still not awake. A fog had settled in his brain. He handed Tinker the book. "Is it morning?"

"It's gettin' light outside. You serious about this?" Tinker shook the book at him.

Asa stretched. "Aya."

"Hmm. Wouldn't have taken you for the type."

Tinker picked up an empty mug. Asa had ordered a cider to keep him awake while he copied Gurdon's speech. The completed pages lay in a neat stack on the table.

"I should charge you for a night's lodgin'," Tinker said before he ambled off.

Asa stretched. The smell of sausage spurred his stomach to suggest breakfast. He counted his coins. Had he not rented the pamphlet, he would have had enough.

He pushed away from the table. As he moved, his head cleared. He picked up the letter he'd written earlier and read it over. The fact that it still sounded like a good idea this morning proved Tinker wrong.

Asa put on his coat, gathered his things, and walked to the door.

"Nice knowin' ya," Tinker said as Asa left.

Hunching his shoulders against the cold, he crunched his way toward campus. He found it amazing how much better his mood was with dry pants and a warm coat.

He passed the church. The steeple looked majestic in the morning light. The graveyard appeared as foreboding as ever. What did it matter?

"They're not there," Asa muttered under his breath.

When he reached Connecticut Hall, he entered the same door he'd used when he went to confront Eli, with much the same determination he had then. As it turned out, his timing was impeccable. Asa took that as a good sign.

No sooner had he reached Eli Cooper's door, when it began to open. Asa helped it along forcefully as he stepped into the room.

The previous night's scene repeated itself, only this time there was light to see it. The door slammed into Eli, knocking him backward. He stumbled over the mess on the floor and crashed onto his back.

Tappan jumped up on the bed to get out of the way of the fight. As it did the night before, the doorway began to fill with onlookers attracted by the commotion.

Exactly as Asa had planned.

Asa didn't give Eli time to recover. He put a foot on his chest, pinning him to the floor. Had eyes the ability to shoot flames, Eli's would have fired a couple of pillars a foot high. His jaw clenched, then opened—no doubt to spit brimstone.

Asa cut Eli off before he had a chance. "I know, I know. You're going to kill me. Well, here's your chance."

Asa dropped the letter he'd written in the tavern onto Eli's face. "You've pushed me around long enough. You've punched me, harassed me, stolen my horse, and now you've stolen my girl. I want satisfaction."

Grabbing the letter, Eli held it up to read it. He grinned wickedly. "You're challenging me to a duel?"

"I want satisfaction." With that, Asa turned to leave.

The expressions of those standing in the doorway were ones of shock and delight. They parted, allowing Asa to leave.

As he did the night before, Gurdon stood in the hallway with the others.

As Asa passed his roommate, he handed him the copied speech. "We're even now."

CHAPTER 27

December of 1800 found the nation in a state of high anxiety. With the fever of politics still in the people's blood, they could do nothing but wait. If there was one thing both Federalists and Jeffersonians could agree upon, it was that the framers of the Constitution had created their own nightmare by separating voting day and the counting of the ballots by a full ten weeks.

On the Yale campus the week before break, talk of the election and Christmas took second place to rumors of the impending duel between Asa Rush and Eli Cooper. It took less than a week after the event for people to refer to the night of the challenge as "Asa's Raid."

"Is it true?" tutor Erwin Ruggles asked during a recitation.

"Dueling is illegal," Asa replied.

Ruggles sat back in his chair, his arms folded with Asa's textbook open on his lap.

As was customary, Asa stood in front of him. He had been standing there for a full ten minutes, and Ruggles had yet to ask him a question regarding philosophy.

"Are you familiar with the *Code Duello*?" Ruggles asked. "It covers the practice of dueling with special emphasis on points of honor."

"I'm familiar with it," Asa replied.

In fact, it had been Rule 15 of the *Code Duello* that had prompted Asa to wait until morning to deliver the letter of challenge to Eli. Challenges were never to be delivered at night, unless the party to be challenged intended leaving the place of offense before morning. The reason: "It is desirable to avoid all hotheaded proceedings."

"Were you aware that dueling used to be referred to as judicial combat? It was alleged that God judged the man in the right and let him win, while sending the loser to . . . well, you know."

"Really? I hadn't heard that," Asa said without enthusiasm.

"Who's your second?" Ruggles asked. "If you don't have one, I'd like to offer my services. My qualifications include a thorough knowledge of the code. I could be a tremendous asset to you."

"Thanks. I'll keep that in mind."

It had been this way ever since the morning Asa challenged Eli. Word had spread with lightning speed, with little regard to the facts. One version of the telling had Asa slapping Eli with a leather glove that had once belonged to the Marquis de Lafayette.

Consequently, Asa couldn't walk across campus now without people pointing at him and whispering about him. He noticed the same to be true of Eli. And whenever the two of them happened to be in the same vicinity, the air became electric, as though everyone expected Asa and Eli to brandish swords on the spot and have at it.

Following his recitation with tutor Ruggles—which turned out to be Ruggles reciting the *Code Duello*—Asa headed back to his dorm room. He found the constant scrutiny of the whole affair to be quite tiring and planned on taking a nap before his scheduled work time in Dr. Dwight's office.

Yet no sooner had Asa opened the door to his room than Gurdon was in his face.

"Let me be your second," Gurdon pleaded.

Closing the door, Asa pushed past him, tossed Enfield's *Natural Philosophy* onto his bed, and sat on the edge.

Gurdon stood in front of him, waiting for an answer. "You haven't chosen a second yet, have you? I wanted to ask sooner, but before I did, I wanted to send for these."

Gurdon pivoted to get something. When he turned back, he held a polished wooden box, exquisitely constructed and decorated with inlaid carving. Gurdon opened the lid for Asa to see.

Nestled against a dark blue velvet bottom were two dueling pistols. They pointed in opposite directions, as though they knew the purpose for which they were created.

"May I?" Asa asked.

With an eager grin, Gurdon hefted the box for Asa to take one.

The pistol proved to be heavier than Asa thought it would be.

"Large caliber, smoothbore flintlock," Gurdon said proudly.

"Where did you get these?" Asa asked.

"They belonged to my uncle."

Asa had never seen a more finely crafted weapon. "Have they ever been used?"

Gurdon nodded sheepishly. "You're holding the one that killed him."

Asa looked up, startled.

"It's all right. Nobody liked my uncle. He was a wealthy, pompous bore and a poor shot. We all knew he'd die in a duel sooner or later."

All of a sudden the pistol felt heavier, as Asa realized he could be holding the instrument of his own death. When he'd conceived this plan, he'd known it could possibly result in his death. But holding the dueling pistol somehow made death more of a reality than it had been when he was holding a pen.

"Well? Can I?" Gurdon asked.

Gurdon's brown hair had red highlights in it. Asa had never noticed that before. And he had freckles. Two faint spangles, one under each eye. Asa hadn't noticed them before either.

He placed the pistol in the box. "All right. You're my second."

Gurdon let out a *whoop* that bounced off the walls. The next instant he was back with another request. "Can I tell Emory Keller? He's my best friend in the world."

"Let's try to keep things quiet, shall we? You can tell Keller, but no one else. After all, this whole thing is illegal."

Gurdon was out the door in a flash.

Asa sighed. He knew that before nightfall everyone on campus would know Gurdon was Asa's second. After the initial way that news of the duel had spread, Asa knew there was no way to keep anything related to the duel quiet. At the same time, it seemed foolhardy not to make an effort.

Asa fell back onto the bed and stared at the ceiling.

Sleep didn't come. Thoughts of death did.

The text for Sunday's sermon provided an interesting diversion for Asa. He often heard the sermon twice. Once while taking notes for Dr. Dwight in his office, and a second time in chapel the following Sunday.

There were times when Asa, a congregation of one, found the office sermon to be exceptional, and he would think Dr. Dwight couldn't possibly preach it any better on Sunday. And he'd be wrong. While an office sermon could stir Asa's soul, Dwight's Sunday sermons came alive.

The title for this week's sermon was "Each Man's Life a Plan of God." The text was John 21:18–23, where Jesus commanded Peter to follow Him and Peter replied by inquiring what plans the Lord had in store for the apostle John.

Asa's spine tingled when Dr. Dwight addressed what he referred to as "the accidental allusion" to the future and the death of John, which the author chose to record at the end of the Gospel he wrote.

"How prominent the thought of the ending is as we look at the close of the chapter," Dwight said as he paced, his gaze lowered, his chin in his hand. "Is it not so with the ending of every life? In our ordinary thinking of this ending, it seems like the one great event, which gathers about itself all solemnity, and seems to include within itself the sum of all the past and all the future. But when we move forward in our thought from the beginning and through the life, it becomes an incidental thing, the natural ending of the life whatever it may be; the subordinate, not the principal event—subordinate to duty and service and character, which are the principal things; the passageway from a living in one sphere of activity to living in another.

"We enter upon the duties and struggles of our coming life—and the call from the Master is, 'Follow Me.' We know not the end, but it will be the end of service to Him here, and the opening of something higher and better than on earth."

"Amen!" Asa said before he knew he'd said it.

Dwight smiled and turned. "I'm glad you approve, Mr. Rush. But that's not the end. There's more."

Asa's face burned. "Yes sir. I didn't mean to imply that it was, only that I . . . found . . . the thought . . . particularly . . ."

Dwight was pacing again. "The one word: Follow me, fills the sphere of duty; and the one word: What is that to thee? Commits the future to His keeping, and thus may give to us, each and every one, a perfect peace." He paused, then added, "Now you may say amen, Mr. Rush."

"Amen," Asa said, though with not nearly the conviction as before.

After arranging the pages of the sermon on the assistant's desk, Asa stretched his aching back. He'd been hunched over for more than an hour. It would feel good to get outside and walk in the fresh air.

"There is one further matter to which we must attend before I let you go," Dwight said.

"Yes sir."

"Take a memo."

Asa had already capped his inkwell. Dr. Dwight was not known to wait for such trivial things, so Asa uncapped the inkwell and scrambled for a fresh sheet of paper. Dr. Dwight had already begun dictating. Asa had to scribble to catch up.

"A disturbing, yet persistent, rumor on campus has caught my attention." Dwight stood with his hands clasped behind his back, looking out his office window. A beatific afternoon light illuminated his face and chest. "While I trust it is just that—an insubstantial rumor and nothing more—nevertheless, I feel compelled to address it."

Asa's pen scratched loudly.

"To wit: The Illegality of Dueling in the state of Connecticut."

Asa nearly dropped his pen. He swallowed hard.

"Am I going too fast for you, Mr. Rush?"

Asa didn't dare look up. "No, sir."

"Not only is this practice illegal," Dwight continued, "it is immoral, and any student found participating in a duel will be summarily dismissed from Yale College."

". . . dismissed from Yale College," Asa mouthed silently as he wrote.

"Take that to the printer, Mr. Rush. Tell them to print fifty copies affixed with the seal of the president and post them throughout the campus. That will be all for today."

The president stood motionless at the window as Asa gathered his things, placed Sunday's sermon on Dwight's desk, and took the notice regarding dueling with him to deliver it to the print shop.

Two letters awaited Asa when he returned to his room.

My dearest Asa,

> *Have I done something to offend you? It seems an eternity since last I saw you. My heart is in tatters until the moment I once again behold your face. I implore you, relieve me of this wretched condition by calling on me at your earliest convenience.*
>
> *I know it is unbecoming a lady to admit it, but I worship you.*
>
> *Annabelle Byrd*

Surprised by the utter lack of emotion Annabelle's letter stirred in him, Asa opened the second letter.

My dear Brother,

Will you be coming home for Christmas? I wouldn't blame you if you don't come. Given Mother's condition, it's difficult to imagine it being festive. But it would do my heart good to see you. Please come if you can.

Maggy

P.S. If you're worried about what to get me this Christmas, persuading Mr. Cooper to come home with you would be present enough.

Flopping onto his bed, Asa decided to ask Gurdon if he could borrow the horse over Christmas. He made a mental note to ask before Dr. Dwight's dueling notice was posted. Once Gurdon saw the consequences of being his second, he might back out.

Asa really didn't want to make the journey to Greenfield during the winter. But it wasn't fair to leave Maggy alone for Christmas.

He chuckled at the thought of inviting Eli Cooper to join him. It might be worth it just to see his expression.

And then there was Annabelle. What was he going to do about Annabelle? He could ignore her and hope she would just go away. But he had a feeling it wouldn't be that easy.

Then again, the duel might take care of that problem too.

CHAPTER 28

Christmas morning proved to be quiet. So Maggy and Asa decided to risk taking their mother to church services, thinking familiar faces and the seasonal music might do her good.

When longtime friends greeted them, Mother stared at them blankly. The greeters seemed to think if they reminded her of enough events and relationship ties, she'd remember them.

She didn't.

After a while she began making rude remarks about people's appearances in a loud voice. Things like:

"Look how fat that fellow is!"

"Did you see the nose on that man? It's huge!"

"What is she doing bringing that child to church? She's a spawn of the devil, she is!"

For the most part, people forgave her. All except for Stanley Patrick. He really did have a huge nose.

Things went from bad to worse during the Christmas service. Following a song, some of the children stood in a line in front to read the Christmas narrative from the Gospel of Luke. Mother chose that time to sing an obscene tavern song. Neither Asa nor Maggy knew where she'd learned it, but she knew it well and sang it loud. Asa had to clamp his hand over her mouth.

Two of the boys standing in the front of the church were overcome with an onset of the giggles, and no amount of angry glares sobered them.

Asa and Maggy excused themselves to take her home. Mother wore herself out by singing the tavern song. By the time they got home, she was ready for a nap.

The word *well-intentioned* came to Asa's mind when describing Maggy's kitchen skills. While the goose was overcooked, and the gravy was thin as water, she scored a bull's-eye with her bread pudding.

While she cleared the dishes, Asa chopped wood and stoked the fire and lit the candles on the small tree in the corner. Brother and sister exchanged gifts. She got him a new writing kit with a sharkskin case. And he gave her the novel *Pamela* by Samuel Richardson.

"Are you trying to tell me something?" she asked, reading the subtitle— *Virtue Rewarded.*

Asa grinned. "It's the story of an exceptional young woman in exceptional circumstances. I thought it would inspire you to better yourself."

Maggy laughed and hit him with the book.

She hadn't said anything to him when he'd showed up on the doorstep alone, though she was obviously disappointed. At one point Asa made a comment about Eli having other plans for Christmas. Maggie pretended not to care. She said she only wanted to make sure he had somewhere to go for the holidays.

Asa said nothing about the duel. She wouldn't understand, and it would only worry her.

He lit the candles on the tree, and they spent the rest of the afternoon sitting on the floor talking about nothing and everything. Mother slept the remainder of the day.

In the morning Asa said his good-byes and set off for New Haven and Yale. The weather was foul, so there was no telling how long it would take him to get back.

Just as he was leaving, Maggy slipped him a letter, asking him to deliver it to Eli. It gave Asa something to brood about the entire journey back to campus.

—❤—

January arrived bitter and cold. The weather kept everyone inside, allowing plenty of time for conversation and introspection.

An article in the *National Intelligencer* concluded, "Mr. Jefferson may be considered our future president," reflecting popular sentiment based upon unofficial discussions with electors. Should next month's counting of the ballots result in any other outcome, cries of Federalist tampering would be louder than the proverbial "shot heard 'round the world."

For their part, the Federalists stirred the volatile political pot by charging voting irregularities and suggesting that a second national election be held. This raised the blood pressure of a few politicians but little real interest.

At Yale the other heated topic on campus was the impending duel between Asa and Eli. Since the posting of President Dwight's notice regarding dueling, discussions were guarded and hushed, but that only seemed to make them more exciting.

Following Christmas break, the seconds began performing their duties. Asa's second, roommate Sam Gurdon, was undaunted by the notices posted all over campus that threatened expulsion.

"Honor is at stake," he insisted when Asa asked if he still wished to be his second. "Any law, be it school or state, which diminishes honor ought to be ignored."

It sounded eloquent, but Asa had the impression Gurdon was in it more for the excitement than the honor.

As a result of choosing Gurdon as his second, Asa's academic life became harder. Tutor Erwin Ruggles took the selection of Gurdon as a personal slight and, as a result, grilled Asa mercilessly during recitations.

At one point the tutor became so heated that Asa wondered if he'd have a second duel on his hands.

For his second, Eli Cooper chose Rufus Tappan, his roommate. For some reason Asa thought Eli's second would be Jacob Benson, whose mysterious disappearance still haunted the campus. It would have given the whisperers something else with which to stir the breeze, and the intimidation factor would have unnerved Asa.

Gurdon pointed out Tappan to Asa. "A few of us call him 'Dr. Trimming.'"

While Asa didn't recognize the name, he recognized the face. Gurdon's nickname was fitting.

"I've always thought of him as Mule-face," Asa said.

Gurdon liked that. The resemblance was obvious.

According to the code of dueling, the role of the seconds was, above all, to reconcile the parties without violence. Given Gurdon's enthusiasm for the duel and Tappan's penchant for violence, it was doubtful either of the seconds would perform this part of their duties with any zeal.

As the offended party, Asa drafted a list of grievances, beginning with his public humiliation during their disputation when Eli had rallied the students of the class to execute him by guillotine.

Also on the list were several physical beatings, which in each case followed an attempt by Asa to do good to Eli; Eli's failed plan on the common to humiliate Asa in public before Annabelle Byrd; and an accusation that Eli secretly pursued Annabelle romantically while fully cognizant that Asa was courting her.

"Whew!" Gurdon said, reading over the list. "He really did all these things? Where I come from, nobody would have thought twice about taking him behind the barn and giving him a good old-fashioned horse-whipping."

Gurdon delivered the letter.

Asa waited and worried.

According to the code, if the recipient apologized, the matter ended.

Satisfaction demanded.

Satisfaction received.

And Asa's plan would go down the drain.

He was counting on Eli not backing down.

To his relief, Mule-face—*Tappan, his name's Tappan*, Asa reminded himself—delivered a response categorically refusing to apologize.

The duel was on.

The next item of business was the matter of weapons and the designation of time and place. These were at Eli's discretion.

"Sabers," Tappan said.

Asa watched the seconds do business. Tappan had come to their dorm room to deliver Eli's refusal to apologize and didn't seem to mind that Asa was there.

At the mention of sabers Asa's heart lurched. His only experience with sword fighting was dueling with tree branches as a boy.

Tappan turned to Gurdon. "Do you know where we could get dueling sabers?"

Gurdon scoffed. "Dueling sabers? Whose idea was that? That's old-world thinking. Nobody uses sabers anymore." He showed Tappan his uncle's dueling pistols.

Tappan fairly drooled on them. "These will be more than adequate."

"Then it's agreed?"

The two seconds shook hands.

Asa couldn't help but wonder how Eli would react to pistols over sabers. Asa had taken it as a good sign that Eli requested sabers. He had images in his mind of Eli being a crack shot, him being from the Kentucky frontier and all. But if Eli's first choice of weapons was a saber, maybe Asa had a chance.

"One shot," Tappan said.

"Three," Gurdon replied, as per Asa's instructions.

Tappan shook his head. "I don't know . . ."

"If after the first shot satisfaction is given, no other shots are necessary.

However, if satisfaction remains in question, why waste time going through the process all over again? Three shots ensures that the matter will be settled that same day."

Gurdon persuaded Tappan. He agreed to three shots.

"Time and place?" Gurdon asked. "We prefer Winter Harbor. Sea level. We don't anticipate the sand being a problem."

"But then, that's not your decision to make, is it?" Tappan replied. Having given in to Gurdon on the choice of weapons, he clearly wanted to dictate time and place.

"Well, you're not thinking East Rock, are you? We could never agree to that. Asa has a problem with high places."

Tappan squinted his eyes in an attempt to appear daunting. "Does it look like I care about your man's problems? He can always withdraw the challenge, couldn't he? I say East Rock. Ten o'clock in the morning."

"Unacceptable!" Gurdon cried.

"Them's our terms."

Gurdon swung around and paced angrily, to the obvious delight of Mule-face Tappan. The two men seemed to forget Asa was standing there.

"All right," Gurdon agreed, but only with great reluctance. "A Saturday?"

"February twenty-first."

Gurdon thought aloud. "Four weeks from now . . . I don't know if that'll give my man enough time."

Tappan shouted, "He should have thought about that before he challenged my man! February twenty-first. Those are the terms."

"All right! All right! Don't bite my head off!"

The two seconds shook hands. It was over. Tappan left the room with a jaunty stride.

To Asa the whole scene had seemed like something out of *Tristram Shandy*, the oddball novel.

The door closed, and Gurdon did a little dance.

"You tricked him," Asa said.

"He never saw it coming." Gurdon squealed with rapturous delight. "We got everything we wanted. Pistols. East Rock. And three weeks."

"You got us four weeks."

"Couldn't help myself. I was having too much fun. Will that be a problem?"

"I chose the right man for my second."

To himself, Asa added, *He got me one more week to live.*

CHAPTER 29

Days before the counting of the electoral ballots, tongues wagged, rumors flew, tempers flared. The small town of Washington was a hotbed of activity, not surprising since so many politicians—twenty-five to thirty at a time—lived cooped up together, taking their meals at the local boardinghouse.

Jeffersonians were convinced there was some kind of Federalist plot to prevent the inauguration of their candidates. Reports were rife of a conspiracy to assassinate Jefferson.

One Philadelphia politician said there had been "no time that I can remember since 1776 that so many people have concluded that opposition to the national government is a duty and obedience a crime. If the Federalists prevent the accession of our man to the presidency, that day is the first day of revolution and civil war!"

For their part, Federalists, fearing the worst, floated all manner of schemes to turn the election to their favor. And if that wasn't possible, to turn defeat to their advantage.

Some argued tying up the House proceedings to prevent either Jefferson or Burr from assuming office. Others sought to invalidate several key electoral votes on technical grounds and declare Adams the winner. Still others plotted to string out any proceedings in the hope of inducing either Jefferson or Burr to make a deal.

The day to count the ballots fell on a Wednesday. The Sunday before, pulpits favoring both sides predicted that the outcome would signal the end of America.

February 11, 1801

At Yale, students huddled in the common room, awaiting the election returns. While the matter was settled in Washington, the rest of the country had to agonize for the length of time it took for a dispatch rider to reach them.

Asa sat with Gurdon and several of his friends. Most of them, including Gurdon, were Jeffersonians, but not of the radical kind. The loudest corner of the room was reserved for the radical Jeffersonians. Among them was Eli Cooper.

The door burst open.

A figure dusted with snow ran into the center of the room and stood. He waited for silence, undoubtedly planning all the way from Washington exactly how he would relay the news.

He waited too long for one student.

"WELL?" the student shouted.

"A tie!" cried the rider.

The room erupted with voices. For a time it was pandemonium. Then after a while all must have realized that as long as they were shouting, they couldn't hear the actual vote count.

Chants of, "Give us the numbers," sprouted up all over the room until everyone had joined in the chorus. But the dispatch rider wasn't about to surrender his moment of fame too quickly. He waited until once again the room was silent.

With a voice clear and strong, he announced: "John Jay, one vote."

Some of the students threw things at him.

"Charles Pinckney, sixty-four votes."

"Get on with it!"

"John Adams, sixty-five votes."

The Jeffersonian corner erupted with cheers. Given the rider's opening statement and having calculated the possible vote counts, they didn't need to hear the rest.

With a disgruntled expression, the dispatch rider completed his report, though few people could hear him.

"Aaron Burr, seventy-three votes; and Thomas Jefferson, seventy-three votes."

Next to Asa, Gurdon and his friends celebrated. The Federalists in the room, including Asa, knew there was little hope Adams would win. They were, at least, hoping he'd finish second and become the vice president.

"Finally! Jefferson's president!" one of Gurdon's friends yelled.

"Not so fast," Asa said. "Jefferson hasn't been elected yet."

Gurdon's friend rounded on Asa, going from elation to anger in an instant. A sign of the times, it seemed. He was ready to fly into Asa with fists. Gurdon held him back.

"All I'm saying," Asa explained, "is that Jefferson and Burr tied. One will be president, the other vice president."

"He's right," Gurdon said of his roommate.

"Hogwash! Everyone knows that Jefferson ran as president and Burr as vice president."

"It's not for them to decide," Asa said. "According to the Constitution, in the event of a tie, the House of Representatives votes to break the tie. They may choose Aaron Burr as president."

"They wouldn't!" Gurdon's friend wailed.

Gurdon moaned. "They could. If for no other reason than spite. The House of Representatives is controlled by the Federalists."

Asa did a poor job concealing his smile over the horrified expression on Gurdon's friend's face. He knew he shouldn't take pleasure in the man's discomfort, but supporters of John Adams had so little to smile about nowadays.

Gurdon sat on his bed polishing one of the dueling pistols. Asa stared at his text of the collected works of the great Roman statesman and orator Cicero. It was a futile exercise. The closer he got to the day of the duel, the harder he found it to concentrate.

"I have procured a surgeon," Gurdon said.

It fell to the seconds to arrange to have a doctor available during the duel.

"He knows the situation?" Asa asked.

"Do you mean does he know it's an illegal duel? Yes. He's a man who values honor."

Asa nodded. An image flashed in his mind. In it he was lying on his back, mortally wounded, staring up into the face of Gurdon's honorable surgeon.

"He's the surgeon who attended my uncle," Gurdon said.

"That's . . . good," Asa said, not knowing exactly what was appropriate to say to such a statement. "To have an experienced surgeon, I mean."

Gurdon's attention was on cleaning the pistol. "You really ought to practice firing one of these. Smoothbores can be tricky."

Asa chose not to reply. Gurdon had been after him for weeks to practice firing the pistol.

A voice cried in the hallway. "News from Washington!"

Gurdon and Asa stopped what they were doing and listened as the disembodied voice announced the news.

"On the thirty-third ballot . . ."

The dispatcher paused. Asa wondered if all dispatchers were frustrated actors.

". . . Thomas Jefferson remains one vote shy of victory."

Groans erupted up and down the hallway. Several *thuds* were heard. Probably shoes thrown at doors in frustration. After three days of voting, the House of Representatives had yet to elect a president.

According to newspaper reports, no sooner had the electoral ballots been announced when the representatives gathered in their chamber. They agreed before the count that if there was a tie, they would assemble immediately and remain in session until the election was decided. Furthermore, they would entertain no other business until the election was decided.

As soon as they assembled, they voted. Jefferson emerged one vote shy of victory. Five hours and fifteen votes later—taken in rapid order—the results remained the same. The results of the last ballot—the nineteenth of the day—were announced at three o'clock in the morning with no change.

Now, after four days and hours of backroom deal making, the deadlock remained. The House would not meet on Sunday.

"I thought Jefferson and Burr had a deal," Asa said. "From what I read all the way back in December, Jefferson contacted Burr over the possibility of a tie. He supposedly offered Burr greater responsibility than the previous vice presidents had been given, and Burr spoke openly of 'Jefferson's administration.' What happened?"

Gurdon shook his head. "Maybe someone got to Burr. Told him he'd never have another chance like this one. Knowing that you're one or two votes away from becoming president of the United States might affect the way a man thinks."

"How do you think it's going to turn out?"

Again Gurdon indicated he didn't know. "All I know is that we're not going to have a Federalist as president."

Asa stared at his book a moment. "Were Washington and Adams really all that bad?"

"Are you kidding?" Gurdon sputtered.

From the fervency with which his roommate spoke, Asa decided not to say any more. After all, the man had a gun.

In a way, the election drama was a blessing. The men on campus seemed to have forgotten about the duel. Asa was able to walk to chapel and classrooms without everyone staring at him.

Occasionally someone would ask him if the duel was still on, or if he and Eli had already dueled. Asa's standard reply was, "What kind of a question is that? You know dueling is illegal."

Asa gave the seconds credit for keeping the date of the duel quiet. The initial all-campus buzz following the challenge had concerned them. With possible expulsion hanging over their heads, the seconds agreed it was in their best interests to keep quiet about the details.

Every once in a while Asa would wonder how Eli was faring. Did he have trouble sleeping at night too?

For the most part, their schedules kept them at opposite ends of the campus. Once, however, Asa found himself alone with Eli in a room.

It was afternoon, and Asa was scheduled to take dictation for Dr. Dwight. He stumbled upon Eli sitting in the small waiting room just outside the president's office.

The two exchanged glances.

"Dr. Dwight told me to tell you to wait," Eli said.

Asa peered in the direction of the office. The door was closed. There were three straight-backed chairs in the room against the wall. Asa took a seat at the end opposite Eli.

For several minutes neither of them spoke or looked at the other. Asa strained to hear beyond the president's door for some sign of a meeting. It was unusual for Dr. Dwight to meet with someone during this time. He was very protective of his study time.

"What are you doing here?" Asa asked.

"What's it to you?"

Asa shrugged. "Just asking."

Several more minutes passed in silence. Eli leaned forward, his forearms on his legs, his hands clasped. "I did some research for him. I dropped it off. He told me to wait here for him and to tell you to wait when you arrived. Now you know everything. Happy?"

Asa scoffed. "I really don't care . . ."

"I'm not going to apologize," Eli said abruptly, speaking to the floor. "You got what you deserved."

Taking a deep breath, Asa rested his back against the chair, folded his arms, and smiled. There was a tone in Eli's voice Asa had never heard before, and unless he was mistaken, it was fear.

Eli frowned. "What are you grinning at?"

Asa's smile grew. "The last thing I want from you is an apology."

The furrows on Eli's brow deepened. "You really want this duel? You're that angry? Angry enough to kill me?"

"I want satisfaction."

"I'm not going to apologize! And if you insist on putting a pistol in my hand, I will defend myself. I will kill you."

Asa acted as if he didn't care.

The room fell silent.

"Do you think he knows?" Asa nodded toward the president's office door.

"Of course he knows! Why else would we be sitting here?"

Asa lifted an eyebrow. "If he knows, why doesn't he do something about it?"

"What can he do? Lock us in our dorm rooms? We haven't done anything wrong, yet."

"And if he finds out after the duel?"

Eli's eyes met Asa's. If it was fear Asa had heard in his voice, there was none in his gaze. "Whoever is still alive, he'll expel."

The president's door latch sounded. Both Asa and Eli jumped.

Dr. Dwight stepped out. Behind him was an empty office. "Eli, you can go."

Eli jumped up so fast you would have thought he was sitting on a spring.

"Asa, we have work to do." Dr. Dwight turned and led the way into his office.

Not then nor during the hour Asa spent with him did Dwight give any indication he knew of a duel.

CHAPTER 30

Monday brought similar news from Washington. Two more votes in the House of Representatives—numbers thirty-four and thirty-five—with identical results. The nation was still in a deadlock.

"What happens if they don't break the deadlock by inauguration day?" Gurdon asked. "Will Adams still be president?"

The question came out of the dark. It wasn't unusual for the two roommates to talk before falling asleep.

"The way I understand it," Asa replied, "if that happens, we won't have a president or vice president. And if the newspaper I read is correct, the nation will be without a president for nine months."

"Nine months?"

"Congress will have adjourned."

"As unhappy as people are about this whole election, if that were to happen, I doubt if we'll have a government in nine months," Gurdon said.

"What have you heard?"

"Just a couple of fellows I know who work at the docks. There's insurrection in the wind. Wouldn't take much to whip up a French-style revolution."

Living on campus tended to shelter students from the thoughts of everyday people. Asa hadn't realized the restlessness was so widespread.

Tuesday, February 17, 1801

The bells of New Haven rang. There was fresh news from Washington. The deadlock was broken. Jefferson was president, and Burr was vice president. Reports out of Washington were murky as to what broke the deadlock.

Some said the Federalists soured on Burr once they got a good taste of his irascible nature. Others said Jefferson made a deal with the Federalists. None of the principal parties were talking openly. And while there was general relief that the election had finally been decided, nobody in Congress seemed very happy about it.

Asa had an unusual perspective on the election outcome. He wondered if he'd live long enough to see Jefferson inaugurated as president.

Saturday, February 21, 1801

Asa and Gurdon walked side by side down Orange Street, a straight shot to East Rock. The 350-foot summit rose up in front of them. Gurdon carried the wooden box with the two flintlocks under his arm. His expression was grim.

The sky stretched from horizon to horizon in dazzling, translucent blue. Asa couldn't help but muse that if this was to be his last day on earth, he couldn't have picked a better day to leave.

Like any young man, he'd daydreamed about what it would be like to go into battle. He imagined the eve of battle to be a blur, while the actual fighting unfolded with crystal clarity. This morning, however, the day he would face enemy fire, the clarity of meaningless detail surprised him.

Choosing which shirt to wear, as though it mattered.

Brushing his hair. He noticed it was thinning.

Experiencing everything for the last time. The last morning he'd spend in the dormitory room. The feel of his felt hat when he put it on, and the smoothness of the metal latch as he closed the door of his room. Stepping from snow to gravel as he left campus property for the last time.

And now, the harshness of the sun in the corner of his eye. The warm rays hitting his face. His last morning.

Every detail was razor sharp. Every sense keenly felt.

"Dr. Bayard will meet us at the summit," Gurdon said. "The surgeon," he added, in case Asa had forgotten.

"His services . . . ," Asa began, thinking he'd forgotten a detail. "I haven't made arrangements to pay him. If necessary, contact my sister in Greenfield. She will—"

"It's taken care of."

"Thank you, but you've done enough. I can't ask you to—"

Gurdon interrupted. "A family favor. No money is exchanging hands."

Glancing at his roommate, Asa felt a surge of emotion. "You're the best second a man could ask for. I'm recommending you to all my dueling friends."

The two men laughed.

They'd reached the foot of East Rock and began the climb.

***

Cresting the summit, Asa's heart beat wildly. At times it seemed to skip a beat. He felt nauseous and dizzy. He told himself it was the climb.

The view and the cold air combined in a powerful one-two punch to take Asa's breath away. He could see all of New Haven, the harbor, Long Island Sound, several surrounding towns . . . and tutor Erwin Ruggles walking toward him.

Pocket watch in hand, Ruggles asked, "Where is everyone? I was beginning to think you'd turned coward."

"You told him?" Asa glared at Gurdon.

"He threatened to give me failing scores on recitations if I didn't," Gurdon replied.

Asa turned to his tutor. "You're aware you could lose your position for being here?"

"Nonsense. Lose my position for taking a Saturday-morning walk on Eagle Rock? Is it my fault if I happened upon a duel in progress? Speaking of which, where's your opponent?"

A black single horse carriage clattered up the hill. A portly middle-aged man climbed out. Gurdon greeted him, then started the introductions. "Dr. Bayard, this is Asa Rush."

"Challenger or challenged?" the physician asked. He peered at Asa from beneath two white bushy eyebrows. Fleshy folds lined his face.

"Challenger." Asa extended his hand, wondering if the level of treatment depended upon his answer.

The doctor appeared to be impressed with him.

A couple of horses crested the hill. Eli and his second, Rufus Tappan, rode up.

As the two men dismounted, Gurdon approached them to introduce Dr. Bayard.

Eli brushed past him. "This is your show, Asa," he said curtly. "Let's get this over with."

Erwin Ruggles spoke up. "If I may . . . Rule Seven of the *Code Duello* states that no apology can be received in any case after the parties have actually taken ground without exchange of fires."

"What's he doing here?" Eli protested. "You're only allowed one second."

"He's out for a Saturday walk," Asa explained, "and just happens to know the rules for dueling by heart."

By the way Eli looked at Erwin Ruggles, it was clear the two hadn't met before.

Apparently feeling the need to explain himself under Eli's glare, Ruggles added, "I quoted Rule Seven just in case you wanted to get started by apologizing. It's too late for that."

"Right." Eli eyed Ruggles suspiciously. "Well . . . good. Because I wasn't planning on apologizing."

While Asa and Eli removed their coats and hats, the two seconds huddled over the open box and loaded the pistols.

Standing next to Asa, Ruggles leaned in and whispered, "They're doing it correctly. They must do it in the presence of each other. That is, unless they pledge their mutual honors—"

Dr. Bayard grabbed Ruggles by the collar and pulled him aside.

Once the guns were loaded, the seconds handed them to each of the disputants.

"The distance will be the standard ten paces," Tappan proclaimed.

"Actually . . ." Ruggles held up an intervening finger. "The *challenged* chooses the ground; the *challenger* chooses the distance; and together the seconds fix the time and terms of firing."

Eli shook his head in disbelief. "Seems like a lot of rules just to shoot at each other," he muttered.

Everyone turned toward Gurdon. "Um . . . the standard ten paces sounds fine to me. Asa?"

Asa took a deep breath, very much aware he was holding a loaded pistol in his hand. Somehow this plan had seemed so much better when he was thinking about it in Hanns Tinker's tavern. "Te—" His voice failed him. He cleared his throat. "Ten paces."

Ruggles hedged. "Now the terms of firing."

The seconds looked at each other, then at Ruggles.

"What are our choices?" Gurdon asked.

Ruggles grinned, delighted to be asked. "Your choices are three: by signal; by word of command; or, at pleasure."

"At pleasure," the seconds said together. From the expression in their eyes, it was clear neither of them wanted to give the command to fire.

"Can we just get on with it?" Eli was already stepping further into the open, away from the others.

Asa followed him.

At one point Eli stopped. "This is as good a spot as any." He turned his back to Asa.

Asa put his back to Eli. A cold wind whipped between them and around them. Asa's shirt-sleeves flapped. He gazed straight at the horizon, over the town and the bay. For some reason, his eyes wouldn't focus. He blinked several times, trying to force them. That helped a little.

He could feel the warmth of Eli's back through his shirt. Asa thought now would be a good time to say something. Nothing came to mind. He wished he'd thought of it sooner. He could have prepared something.

"Well, do we just start walking, or does someone count?" Eli yelled.

"I'll do it!" Ruggles shouted back. Before anyone could object, he said, "One . . ."

Asa took a step. His back grew cold.

"Two!"

"Three!"

"Four!"

"Five!"

Is it just me, Asa wondered, *or is Ruggles counting awfully fast?*

"Six!"

"Seven!"

A drop of sweat rolled into the corner of Asa's eye.

"Eight!"

With his free hand he reached up and brushed the sweat from his eye.

"Nine!"

All of a sudden everything stilled.

To this point, Asa's heart had been beating ten or more times for every count. Between the count of nine and ten, it calmed.

He calmed.

He figured God was preparing him for heaven.

CHAPTER 31

At any moment Asa expected to see angels coming for him.

"Ten!"

He turned.

The black hole of Eli's barrel stared at him, and a short distance behind it, Eli Cooper.

A fraction of a second separated the sound of the two pistols.

A puff of smoke rose over Eli.

Asa heard death rush past him with a fearful whistle. A second puff of smoke rose around him from the knees up. He'd never raised his arm. His pistol had discharged into the ground.

Eli lowered his weapon.

Asa took a breath, surprised he was still able to.

"A misfire is equivalent to a shot!" Ruggles was insisting. "How many shots have they agreed upon?"

"Three," Gurdon said unsteadily.

"No! That's it! No more!" Eli shouted. "This is crazy. I'm leaving."

"You can't."

Everyone stopped. There was shock on their faces.

Asa knew why. They'd expected Ruggles to say something like that, quoting some rule.

But it hadn't been Ruggles who had spoken.

It had been Asa. What had been so unusual about it, Asa knew, was the way he'd said it.

So calmly.

Recovering, Eli closed in on Asa, his eyes blazing, sweat streaming down both sides of his face, despite the cold wind. "You want an apology, is that it? All right. I apologize! There, I said it. It's over."

"It's not over," Asa said. "We agreed to three shots."

"Are you crazy? In case you hadn't noticed, I nearly killed you! And you nearly shot your own foot off!"

"You were the one to wrong me," Asa said evenly. "I demand satisfaction. Unless I'm mistaken, if the aggrieved party is not satisfied, a second shot is in order. Am I out of line, Ruggles?"

Erwin Ruggles stepped forward. "Was the offense verbal, or were there blows?"

"Both," Asa said.

"Then, actually, Rule Five comes into play. No verbal apology can be received for such an insult, unless the offender hands over a cane with which you would beat him."

Asa turned to Eli. "Either take the field or forever be branded as a coward."

He saw a flash of the old Eli in his eyes. The familiar Eli. The one who loathed Asa with a passion.

Eli shoved the pistol at Tappan. "Load it."

Asa handed his pistol to Gurdon, whose hands shook so badly as he was loading it that the doctor had to finish the job for him. Apparently Gurdon wasn't finding dueling to be nearly as romantic as it sounded.

In the field, their backs to each other for a second time, Eli and Asa stepped to Ruggles's count.

Asa had thought the second time would be easier. He was wrong.

"Eight."

"Nine."

Unlike before, time did not slow.

But Asa did. He heard the shot before turning. A fiery fist slammed into his side, spinning him to the ground.

The next thing he knew, the back of his head was on the cold ground and he was staring up at the cloudless sky, listening to his own labored breathing. He heard the sound of men running. Then the face of Dr. Bayard blotted out the sun.

Asa had dreamed this.

When Dr. Bayard touched him, Asa's side exploded with pain. It was worse than getting shot.

It eased.

Then it came again. Searing, mind-numbing pain.

Asa heard himself scream. He sounded distant.

Dr. Bayard pulled back. "Bad enough."

Behind the surgeon was a background of familiar faces, including Eli Cooper. His mouth was a thin line. Without saying anything he turned and walked away.

"Cooper!" Asa called.

Instantly he regretted his action. The pain was enough to bring tears to his eyes. But his business here wasn't done. "You agree to three shots."

Eli kept walking.

"Actually," Ruggles said, "you can't insist on a third shot when you haven't fired a second shot."

The doctor and Gurdon glared at Ruggles as though he was insane.

Ruggles defended himself. "I didn't make up these rules!"

Asa felt the ground for the pistol. It had fallen from his hand. "Gurdon, help me."

Gurdon didn't make a move. He simply stared, wide-eyed, at the doctor.

"You're my second!" Asa shouted. "Do your job!"

The doctor gave a slight nod.

With the pistol in his hand, Asa raised it to fire into the air.

"Ahem," Ruggles interrupted.

"What now?"

"Rule Thirteen says no dumb shooting or firing in the air is admissible in any case. That children's play is dishonorable on one side or the other and is accordingly prohibited."

"So all I have to do is aim at Eli?" Asa asked.

"Correct."

"Gurdon, help me up."

With Gurdon behind him lifting his shoulders, Asa managed to get into a sitting position. Dr. Bayard and Ruggles cleared out of his way.

Asa felt Gurdon jump as the shot sounded. He wasn't trying to hit Eli, just satisfy the rules. Apparently, the bullet had come closer than he'd intended. Eli ducked. Tappan fell to his knees.

Eli rounded on them, sputtering. "Wha-what are you doing?"

"Dueling," Asa explained weakly. "I missed. You can either come and apologize to my satisfaction, or we go a third round."

Eli was coming back all right, but from his stride and the redness of his face, it didn't appear that he was going to apologize. "Never have I seen . . . and believe me, I've seen some crazy things, but never . . . I mean, never . . . You have to be the craziest, most insane—"

"Watch it," Asa said. "Or I'll be forced to challenge you to another duel."

"Look at you! You're lying on the ground. Bleeding. Duel's over."

"Not until I have satisfaction."

"Actually, the doctor can—," Ruggles began.

Eli picked up on it immediately. "You're the surgeon," he told Dr. Bayard. "This man's wounded. Duel over."

"Actually," Dr. Bayard said, wincing, "according to the code—"

"Rule Twenty-Two," Ruggles inserted.

"—that gives the grounds upon which a surgeon can stop the duel."

"Then cite them and put an end to this nonsense," Eli demanded.

Dr. Bayard continued. "Any wound sufficient to agitate the nerves and necessarily make the hand shake must end the business for that day."

Everyone turned to Asa.

"Extend your hand, son," Dr. Bayard said.

"Help me get up," Asa told Gurdon.

Once Asa was on his feet, Gurdon took a cautious step back. Asa had to favor his right leg, but he could stand.

As calmly as he could, even though he was in tremendous pain, Asa lifted his right hand in which he still gripped the pistol. He pointed the weapon at Eli Cooper's chest and held it there.

Steady. His hand did not shake.

"It's out of my hands," Dr. Bayard ruled.

Eli and Asa locked eyes.

It was the first time Eli had looked directly at Asa today, other than to shoot at him. For a second it appeared he might back down. Then his gaze crystallized. "Tappan!" He pivoted toward his second.

The moment proved too much for Gurdon. His hands shook. He began to weep. "I can't do this . . . I can't do this . . . I can't do this . . ."

Dr. Bayard led him away.

"Ruggles, could I persuade you to—," Asa asked.

"I'm on it, sir." Ruggles's expression was one of awe, as if he were thrilled and humbled to be asked. Taking the pistol from Asa, he went to load it in front of Tappan.

Did he just call me sir? Asa thought for sure he must have heard wrong.

For the third time Eli Cooper and Asa Rush stood back to back a safe distance from the others.

Gurdon sat in Dr. Bayard's carriage, his back turned, his fingers in his ears.

"Why are you doing this?" Eli hissed.

A hundred replies flashed in Asa's head. He couldn't pick one out of so many, so he said nothing.

"One!"

"Two!"

"Three!"

Asa's wound was pulling him to the right. He corrected it.

"Four!"

"Five!"

A wave of nausea swept over him. It frightened him.

"Six!"

He couldn't pass out now. That would be the worst thing that could happen. All of this would be for nothing.

"Seven!"

"Eight!"

Asa swallowed hard. The nausea passed for the moment. He felt another wave building.

"Nine!"

Lord . . .

No other words came. Asa hoped the one was sufficient.

"Ten!"

Asa stopped. Of the three turns, this one was the slowest. More like a hobble than a turn. As before, Eli's pistol was aimed at him.

Just like Asa had planned.

He stood there, his arms at his sides, daring Eli to fire.

Eli Cooper was a statue. An armed statue that could spit deadly fire at any second.

Need help? Asa thought. *How about this . . . ?*

With one arm mirroring the other, he lifted them from his sides until they were perpendicular to the ground.

His pistol clattered to the ground.

With blood on both hands and blood on his side, Asa waited on Eli Cooper.

He didn't have to wait long.

"You think I won't do it?" The barrel of Eli's pistol was shaking.

Asa stood motionless.

"I know what you're doing! You think I don't know? I'm not Amos Henderson! Do you hear me? I'm not Amos Henderson!"

Asa didn't move.

Eli was coming toward him now, pistol raised, his face contorted. "Stop it! Stop it! Put your arms down or I'll shoot. As God is my witness, I'll shoot!"

Another wave of nausea swept over Asa, and he nearly faltered. Steadying himself with a ragged breath, he managed to keep his arms up.

Out of the corner of his eye, Asa could see Dr. Bayard, Tappan, and Ruggles running toward them.

Eli shoved the pistol in Asa's chest, nearly knocking him over. Asa stood his ground.

"It's not going to work," Eli hissed at him. "I know what you're doing, and it's not going to work."

"Then you'll just have to shoot me."

"You think I won't?" Eli shoved the pistol hard against Asa's chest, as if he were trying to force the bullet inside Asa's body without pulling the trigger.

"Ever since we met, you've wanted to kill me." Asa's chin was held high. "So go ahead. Do it. Pull the trigger. Kill me."

"Don't tempt me! I'll do it! I'll do it!" Eli's eyes were wild.

"It's the only way you'll get rid of me. Otherwise, I'll keep coming after you. Every time you turn around, I'll be there. Every time you round a corner, I'll be there. Every day you wake up, you'll have to live with the fact of knowing that I'm praying for you, speaking well of you, pulling for you, wanting God's best for you. I'll be closer to you than your conscience."

"Leave me alone!"

"You can knock me down, and I'll get back up and bless you. You can pummel me senseless, and upon recovering my senses, my first rational thought will be a prayer for you. The more you hate me, the more I'll love you. So go ahead and do it. Kill me. It's the only way you're going to stop me."

Eli was trembling now, trembling so hard he couldn't hold the pistol. He clutched the front of Asa's shirt with both hands.

"What do you want from me?" Eli bellowed.

Thank you, Lord. Finally the right question.

But before Asa could answer, Eli let loose with an animal cry that echoed over the town and shoved Asa so hard it lifted him off his feet.

The frozen ground proved to be a hard landing. Lights flashed in Asa's eyes as his head hit. For an instant he must have blacked out, or at least he thought he did. But it was only for an instant.

From his back he saw Eli jumping onto his horse and galloping away. Tappan followed him, leaving Ruggles and Dr. Bayard to check on Asa.

"You know," Ruggles said, "according to the rules—"

Dr. Bayard shot the tutor a glance that silenced him.

Asa hardly noticed. He was watching Eli flee.

"There goes one stubborn man."

CHAPTER 32

Sunday dawned, and Asa had lived to see it.

The previous morning, after Eli rode off leaving Asa on his back on the dueling field, Dr. Bayard tended to his injury, removing the bullet (which hurt far more than getting shot) and dressing the wound.

Erwin Ruggles, who had proved to be a better second in the field than Gurdon, assisted Asa into Dr. Bayard's carriage. Since the carriage sat only two, Ruggles walked Gurdon back to the campus. Both had proved to be good seconds in their own ways. Asa owed them.

The balance of Saturday, Asa spent in his room in bed. Doctor's orders. Gurdon didn't show up until after midnight, and then he was drunk and fell asleep on his bed fully clothed.

Otherwise, the day passed quietly. Asa winced a lot and contemplated how fortunate he was to be alive. He replayed the scene at the top of East Rock in his head a hundred times. He wondered if he'd reached Eli. For now all he could do was wait and see how Eli reacted the next time he saw him. That would tell, wouldn't it? If everything was back to normal, this whole thing was a colossal waste of time.

The silence of the dormitory, not unusual for Saturday since most of the fellows wanted to be anywhere but on campus, suggested that the duel had gone largely unnoticed. Good news, that. The fewer who knew about it, the better Asa's chances of not getting expelled.

Today, Sunday, Asa felt strong enough to attend church services. As always, Dr. Dwight amazed him by breathing life into a sermon Asa had already heard in the president's office.

"What about him?" the disciple Peter asked Jesus, curious about what the future held for his fellow disciple John.

"What is it to you?" Jesus replied. "You follow me."

Dr. Dwight expounded: "We enter upon the duties and struggles of our coming life—and the call from the Master is, 'Follow Me.' We know not the end, but it will be the end of service to Him here, and the opening of something higher and better than on earth."

As before, the comment elicited an "Amen" from Asa, who was grateful *his* end hadn't come the day before.

At every opportunity he looked around the chapel, hoping to see Eli. There was no sign of him.

On Monday, Asa knew his college career at Yale had come to an end when he was summoned to Dr. Dwight's office.

He knocked softly on the president's door.

"Enter," Dwight said from the other side.

Asa stepped into the room that had become so familiar to him. The books lining the shelves. The massive wooden desk that reflected the man who sat behind it—large, powerful, busy, but organized. To his right was the small desk in which Asa spent hours taking dictation, writing down paragraph after paragraph of thoughts that had influenced his thinking and inspired his soul.

At that moment, the pain from the wound in his side gave way to a superior pang of regret that he would never sit in that chair and take dictation from Dr. Dwight again.

Dwight looked up. "Ah, Asa. Take a seat."

Two large stuffed chairs, angled slightly toward each other, were to Asa's left. He sat in one. After removing a small stack of books from the other, Dr. Dwight sat in it.

Although it was still early morning, Dwight's eyes were red and tired. He rubbed them, a gesture that had become endearing to Asa. He would always remember Dr. Dwight pacing, dictating, and rubbing his eyes.

"How is your side?" he asked.

Dwight had a way of getting to the point. Four words told Asa that Dwight knew everything about the duel. Not only that, he led with his concern for Asa, not—

"I thought you were smarter than that," or,

"How could you do something so foolish?" or,

"You let me down. I trusted you, and you let me down."

Dwight had every right to say any one of those things or all of them. Instead, he said, "How is your side?"

Asa's eyes filled with emotion. "It hurts, but the doctor says it'll heal."

Dwight nodded. "A rather dramatic demonstration, wouldn't you say?"

"Aya," Asa said softly.

"Have you seen Eli?"

"Not since the duel, sir."

Again Dwight nodded. "You realize I have no choice in the matter. I have to expel both of you. The school cannot condone its students shooting at one another."

"No, sir."

So there it was. The boy inside Asa had envisioned some kind of miracle taking place at this point. Dr. Dwight saying he'd spoken to the board of directors, and since Asa had never been in any trouble before now . . .

Dwight stood.

Asa got to his feet.

The president extended his hand. It really was good-bye.

Dwight's larger hand wrapped around Asa's and pulled him close. Dwight then placed his free hand on top of Asa's head and began to pray.

"Almighty God, I count it a privilege to stand before You clasping the hand of my brother, Asa Rush, a man with the courage of a lion and the determination of a crusader; a man who would risk everything to reach a rebellious soul and claim him for the kingdom. I do not know another man who would love so greatly and go to such lengths as he did. I am humbled to know him and pray that I might serve You with the same courage and unwavering faith. Amen."

Dwight's grip tightened, as though he didn't want to let go. Asa opened his eyes. The first thing he saw were the tears on Dwight's cheeks. They'd fallen from eyes that looked down on him in admiration.

"Thank you," Asa said.

"May God bless you according to your faithfulness," Dwight replied.

Asa turned to leave. He didn't know one could feel so good about being expelled from college.

When he reached the door, Dr. Dwight called to him. "I spoke to Eli earlier."

"Oh?"

"Your plan worked. You reached him."

CHAPTER 33

It probably shouldn't have surprised him, but the whole campus knew that he and Eli had been expelled the instant Asa stepped out of President Dwight's office.

Of the fifty or so comments fired at him between the president's office and the dormitory, none of them expressed regret over his being expelled. They wanted to hear about the duel and were disappointed—some were outright hostile—when he wouldn't tell them.

The door to his room was open when he got there. Gurdon sat Indian-style on his bed, with a half-dozen fellows surrounding him. Asa's entrance interrupted his story between shot numbers one and two. Gurdon was basking in his role as eyewitness to a duel, seemingly oblivious that it could get him expelled too.

Asa couldn't help but wonder what his roommate's plans were when he came to describing what had happened after the second shot. Didn't he have his back turned in the carriage for the third shot?

"Hey, Asa!" Gurdon said happily.

Gurdon's audience turned to Asa, wanting the same thing from him all the others wanted.

"Sorry." Asa waved them off. "Gurdon tells it so much better than I do."

"There's a message for you." Gurdon pointed to Asa's bed.

It was a single sheet folded over once.

Asa opened it.

Meet me in the chapel.

Eli

Folding the message over, Asa turned to face a new round of requests for him to tell the tale of his duel with Eli Cooper.

He waded through them and others who were gathering in the hallway outside the door and made his way to the chapel.

There was something about empty cathedrals and chapels that always made Asa feel as though they were holy ground. Maybe it was the vaulted ceilings, the religious furniture, the silence, or a combination of all three. But fill them with people, and he just didn't have the same feeling of awe he had when they were empty. It made him wish everyone could have his own private cathedral. People might pray more often.

The sound of the door closing echoed when he stepped in. A solitary figure knelt on the steps in front. Even though the figure was hunched over and could only be seen from the back, Asa still recognized Eli.

Eli gave no indication he'd heard anyone arrive.

Asa walked up the aisle between the rows of pews. He didn't call out. That wouldn't be right . . . not in a chapel. Not to a man who appeared to be praying.

Reaching the front of the chapel, Asa folded his hands and waited for Eli to finish praying.

A couple of minutes passed.

Then five.

Asa cleared his throat softly.

Eli didn't stir, so Asa waited a few more minutes. It was just the two of them. No one else came in or out. Surely Eli had heard him enter or clear his throat. What was he doing? He had sent for Asa, not the other way around.

Finally, rather than waste any more time, Asa decided to join him. Might as well spend the time praying.

He knelt on the steps beside Eli. Leaning forward on another step, he folded his hands, bowed his head, and closed his eyes.

"I don't know what to say," Eli said.

Asa looked over at him. "To me or to God?"

Eli kept his head bowed. When he spoke, he didn't look at Asa. "I don't understand. I did everything to drive you away, to hurt you, to humiliate you."

"Aya. And you did a good job of it too."

"At East Rock I wanted to kill you. I'm not just saying that. I have never in my life wanted to kill another man. But I wanted to kill you."

"I know."

"And you know what really sticks in my craw?"

"What's that?"

"I knew exactly what you were doing up there." Eli's voice quivered. "And still it worked. I let you get to me."

"It wasn't me who got to you."

Eli sniffed. "I know."

"Well, that's a relief," Asa said glibly. "I'd hate to have let you shoot me, and then you get the wrong idea."

Eli chuckled. He turned around and sat on the step, propping himself up with his arms. "Back in Kentucky, when I first heard about Amos Henderson, I thought he was such a simpleton to fall for your theatrics. When I saw you pulling the same kind of stunt on me, it infuriated me to think that you'd believe I was that simple headed."

Asa started to mirror Eli's sitting position. But when he placed his arms back, his wound complained loudly. So he sat forward instead.

"How bad is it?" Eli asked.

"It'll heal."

"In time to take the next fellow up to East Rock?"

Asa laughed. "Let's hope the next fellow isn't as stubborn as you."

For a time they sat in silence, which was fine by Asa. In fact, it was perfect. Sitting next to Eli Cooper, feeling no fear, no animosity. He could sit like this for hours and not grow tired of it.

"Dr. Dwight was helpful," Eli said. "I spent the better part of yesterday afternoon with him."

Asa nodded.

"If you're thinking I'm the one who told him about the duel," Eli added quickly, "he already knew. I don't know how he knew, but he did."

"The man's president of Yale College. He knows everything."

"Did he talk to you?"

"Called me to his office this morning."

"So you're . . ."

"Expelled? Aya. I like to think of it as seeking gainful employment." Eli hung his head. "It's my fault."

"Aya. But what's new?"

"You're not going to let me off the hook, are you?"

Asa shrugged. "The century's young. What are your plans? Will you stay here or go back to Kentucky?"

Eli shrugged. "I'll probably try to find work on the docks. I have some connections there."

"Annabelle?"

For a split second the old Eli flashed in his eyes, but only for a second. "You're wrong about Annabelle."

Asa grinned. Hadn't he sung that same tune?

"I was thinking more of Captain Byrd," Eli said. "Now that I got myself kicked out of school, I'll probably have to find a way to pay the man back."

Something twisted in Asa's gut, uncomfortably close to his wound. "Let me ask you something. When was the last time you saw Captain Byrd?"

Eli Cooper and Asa Rush stood shoulder to shoulder in the dark in Captain Byrd's bedroom. Moonlight spilled through the window, illuminating the bed. Stretched out in front of them, just as he had been during Asa's previous accidental visit, was the dead captain.

"Couldn't you have just told me he was dead?" Eli whispered.

"I had to let you shoot me just to get your attention before."

"Point taken."

Eli seemed in no hurry to leave. Asa understood. It takes time to accept the truth that you've been living your life based on a lie.

On the way to the mansion, Eli had informed Asa that all he had seen of his benefactor was paperwork—a letter informing him that his impressive first year at Yale had not gone unnoticed and that the captain wished to reward him by sponsoring his second year. Given the advanced state of the captain's decomposition, it was obvious now that the paperwork had been forged.

The agreement stipulated monthly reports be delivered personally to the captain. However, every time Eli came to present himself, he was informed that the captain was ill or away on business. He had entrusted his first report to Martha, at which time he had caught a distant glimpse of Annabelle.

"I know the feeling." Asa sighed.

He hadn't meant to say it aloud. It just popped out. He hastened to say, "So you'd seen her before that day in the park?"

"From a distance."

Eli went on to explain that from then on Annabelle took his reports. Not only didn't he question the fact that the captain was never available, he welcomed it. What was not to prefer? He'd much rather be swinging Annabelle in the garden than standing in front of some crusty, old captain giving an account of his academic performance. The money arrived as scheduled, and he had a monthly session with a beautiful woman. What was there to question?

Now at the dead man's bedside, Asa said, "She set up the whole thing."

"Annabelle doesn't have anything to do with it," Eli spat.

"Think about it! She targeted you last year and forged the letter by which she arranged to see you monthly. To do what? Besides playing hide-and-seek, what has she been talking to you about?"

From the way Eli set his jaw, Asa knew he'd hit the mark.

"I won't believe Annabelle is in on this until I talk to her," Eli said.

Asa gave an exasperated grunt. "Answer me this. What sort of woman keeps her dead father in an upstairs bedroom and leads others to believe he's still alive?"

"You don't know everything. There are things going on in this house over which Annabelle has no control."

"What kind of things?"

"They call themselves the Illuminati, and they meet regularly downstairs."

"All right." Asa's mind was racing. Two questions took the lead. "What is their purpose, and how do you know this?"

Asa knew he wasn't going to like the answer to the first question. With a name like the Illuminati, it was highly unlikely they were a civic-minded benevolence society.

The groan of a hallway floorboard interrupted them.

Both men gave a start. Their eyes darted to the door, expecting it to open any second.

When it didn't, Eli said, "Let's continue this conversation at the Minuteman Tavern."

"Good idea," Asa said. "You first."

They'd come up the stairs through the back kitchen door separately. That way, if one of them got caught, the other might slip away. It would be far easier to explain away one of them in the house uninvited. Both of them defied rational explanation.

Asa watched as Eli slipped out the door. After giving him sufficient time to get out the door and to the road, Asa opened the bedroom door a crack. He peered down the upstairs hallway. Clear. He stepped out of the room, careful to close the door silently behind him.

Voices filtered down the hallway. At the far end a door stood partially open. He thought he'd heard Annabelle giggle, but just then Martha's voice was dominant. From the tone and cadence, it sounded as though she was reading.

"Executions are necessary to appease the people of Paris—an indispensable sacrifice. 'The voice of the people equals the voice of God' is the truest and most republican adage I know."

"Well said!" Annabelle cooed. "The voice of the people equals the voice of God. I like that."

A paper rattled. Asa stepped closer. He bit his lower lip in frustration. He wished Eli were here so he could hear this for himself.

"Listen to this," Martha said. "It's an eyewitness account of Louis XVI's execution: 'I saw people pass by arm in arm, laughing, chatting familiarly as though they were at a party.'"

Annabelle squealed. There was a time when that sound had made Asa's heart shiver with delight.

He saw movement through the crack and pulled back. His heart hammered, urging him to leave.

Then he caught a glimpse of Annabelle. All she did was move into view, pause, and reach up to undo her hair. Even from the back, it was enough. Asa stood paralyzed. Despite what he knew of her, her beauty still had power to overwhelm him.

"We're so close," she cried. "So close, Martha! Just think—it will be you and me, arm in arm, strolling, laughing as though we were at a party when the nation celebrates the death of Mr. John Adams!"

Annabelle's words doused Asa like cold water, breaking any hold her beauty had on him. He could hear Martha clapping.

"And then, on the same day, the assassination of Monsieur Thomas Jefferson! Oh Martha! What a day that will be!"

Asa was so dumbstruck, he couldn't move.

"The people will rise," Martha proclaimed. "The Federalists will blame the Jeffersonians."

"The Jeffersonians will blame the Federalists," Annabelle echoed.

"And we will teach the French a lesson or two on how to orchestrate a reign of terror."

"I only wish Father had lived to see this day."

Asa had heard enough. He turned to leave.

"Do you think our boy is ready?" Martha asked.

Asa stopped. Martha's words hooked him and reeled him back.

"Eli? He will do us proud. The smoke rising from New Haven will be the signal of a new order. Cells in Washington, Philadelphia, and Boston will follow our lead—you'll see."

"If Robespierre taught the world anything," Martha said, "he taught us that virtue is created through terror. And Marat too. There were never too many executions. He was always calling for more. Blood is the grease of revolutions, Annabelle. Never forget that."

"Tell me again what it was like."

Annabelle disappeared from Asa's view. He heard a bed creak. Martha took the tone of a mother telling a bedtime story.

"It was September 1792. The call went out from Danton. 'Arm yourselves! Search every house! Drag all those who are enemies of the people into the streets and kill them!' And so we did. I remember Andre—did I tell you about Andre? He was such a delicious distraction that summer—leaped onto a coach filled with priests, thrusting and slicing with his rapier. Some of the people looking on appeared shocked. 'So this frightens you, does it?' he called. 'You must get used to the sight of death!' I'd never thought of Andre as a prophet before then, but over the next five days we slaughtered over twelve hundred people. We stopped only to eat and drink."

Asa had heard enough. He backed quietly away.

"I remember one *septembriseur*—that's what we called ourselves—slicing open the chest of a noble . . ."

Asa turned to go down the stairs and ran headlong into an old woman. She stumbled backward, and Asa had to grab her by the shoulders to keep her from falling.

Terror filled her eyes. She screamed as loud as her tired old lungs would let her.

Martha and Annabelle charged out of the bedroom.

"Asa! What are you doing here?" Annabelle screamed.

Heavy boots pounded up the stairs. The person who emerged wasn't anyone Asa had wanted to see anytime soon—a scraggly Jacob Benson clutching his serrated hunting knife.

Asa forced a grin. "Your letter . . . you begged me to come visit you again, Annabelle. Well . . . here I am."

CHAPTER 34

❧◦◦◦◦◦◦❧

Eli Cooper sat alone at a table in the Minuteman Tavern watching the door. He clung to a half-empty mug, though he hadn't taken a drink for at least ten minutes.

It was over an hour since he'd left Asa standing beside the dead Captain Byrd. It was an image that kept haunting Eli—not so much for its gruesomeness, but for what it meant.

It meant that Annabelle had been deceiving him. In itself that revelation didn't surprise him. She wasn't the first woman to put on airs while courting, nor would she be the last. It was all part of the courting game, was it not?

But if Asa was right about her, her deception went far beyond the normal pale of courting. Eli's mind played image after image of his involvement with her, attempting to see motive behind her flirtations—which, by the way, were incredibly effective. Even now just the remembrance of them aroused amorous emotions and clouded his reasoning.

The door to the tavern opened. Eli looked up, hoping it was Asa. Three men he didn't recognize stumbled in, laughing and slapping each other on the back. They called to Tinker about rooms for the night.

The door slammed shut. Still no Asa.

Eli pulled out his pocket watch and placed it on the table before him. With each tick of the second hand, Eli's concern grew. He'd give Asa ten more minutes.

Taking a swallow from the mug, Eli made a face. Tinker must have drawn his drink from the bottom of some barrel. Eli set the mug down next to the watch.

The second hand ticked and ticked ominously.

Shoving himself away from the table, Eli grabbed his watch and headed out the door.

As usual, Martha opened the door. She didn't look pleased to see him. But then, Martha never looked pleased to see him.

"My apologies for the late hour," Eli said. "But it's important that I see Captain Byrd."

From the Minuteman Tavern, Eli had gone to Connecticut Hall and checked Asa's old dormitory room. His roommate—Eli didn't know his name but recognized him as Asa's second during the duel—had already spread his things out, taking over Asa's part of the room. He said he hadn't seen Asa.

From there, Eli backtracked to the Byrd mansion, hoping to run into Asa along the way. Having reached the mansion, he concocted what he thought was a reasonable story to get in. What he would do once he was in, he didn't know.

"Eli Cooper, is that you?" Annabelle's voice announced her. She came up behind Martha, looking worried. "What has brought you out at this hour? Is something wrong?"

"I feel horrible disturbing you like this," Eli said, "but I need to speak to Captain Byrd. Is he available?"

Annabelle and Martha switched places. Annabelle placed a hand on Eli's arm. "You look absolutely frightful!" she said to him. "Come in." As she was pulling Eli into the house, she said to Martha, "Be a dear and get us some libations."

Eli allowed himself to be tugged into the sitting room and down onto a sofa. Annabelle sat beside him, taking his hand in hers. Even in a housecoat she looked like a goddess.

"I hope he hasn't already gone to bed," Eli said.

"Father? I'm so sorry, Eli, but you just missed him. He rode out to Boston just a short time ago. I wish you'd come earlier. I know he would have loved to speak with you personally—tomorrow being the big day and all."

Eli hung his head and tried to appear disappointed.

Smiling, Annabelle cupped her hand to his cheek. "I think it's adorable you're nervous. But Father wouldn't have chosen you if he didn't have every confidence that you were the perfect man for the job. And I know you'll do just wonderfully."

Eli forced a smile but kept his head down. Every time he looked at her, he seemed to lose all reasoning power.

And right now his mind was racing with thoughts of Asa. Where was he? Had he been discovered in the upstairs bedroom? He couldn't imagine two women overpowering him and forcing him to stay against his will. But then, they could have had help, couldn't they? Or was Asa still upstairs for reasons of his own? How to find out?

Mixed in with these questions of Eli's were thoughts of his role tomorrow—the boardroom in which he was introduced to the Illuminati was just down the hallway. The memory of his appearance before them and their proposal was the stuff of dreams. To be given a chance to alter the course of a nation's history was heady stuff, and Annabelle's behavior afterward when she learned he'd agreed would fuel his dreams for a lifetime.

At the time he'd thought that one of the men in the boardroom was Captain Byrd. Now he knew that was impossible.

"Really, Eli, you'll do fine," Annabelle said. "Everything is going exactly according to plan."

Martha reentered the room carrying a tray of bottles and glasses. Annabelle's inappropriate touching drew her attention. She scowled but didn't say anything.

Eli stood. "I should be going."

He tried hard to come up with a way to bring up Asa's name but came up empty. It wasn't something the old Eli would do.

"Martha, tell him everything will go according to plan tomorrow," Annabelle said.

"The guillotine and scaffold are erected and in place. You will speak from the scaffold."

"Dramatic, isn't it?" Annabelle squealed. "Using the scaffold as a speaker's platform was Martha's idea."

"We have roughly two dozen dockworkers salted into the crowd to urge you on as you speak," Martha explained. "They've been going tavern to tavern, pub to pub, since election day, stirring up mischief. Mr. Benson trained them well. New Haven is a powder keg, and you're the spark."

Annabelle clapped her hands. "Father has been dreaming of this day ever since Citizen Genet spoke in Philadelphia! To hear him tell it, Genet's effect on the crowd was electrifying."

"They nearly dragged President Washington into the streets and hanged him that night," Martha chimed in wistfully.

It was the first time Eli had ever seen the woman show any real signs of life. Given the subject of discussion, it was eerie.

He made his way to the door, still trying to think of a way to inquire about Asa. Reaching the hallway, he glanced toward the interior of the house. He didn't expect to see anything, but right now he was grasping at anything.

"Are you terribly disappointed you didn't get to see Father?" Annabelle asked, coming up behind him.

"He's a busy man," Eli replied. He opened the door.

Annabelle closed it with him still inside. She had an impish glint in her eye. Rising up on her toes, she kissed him on the mouth. "Couldn't let the neighbors see that," she said wickedly. "They'd talk."

When the door closed behind him, Eli made his way back to the tavern, hoping to find an apologetic Asa Rush waiting for him. If Asa wasn't there, he didn't know what he would do.

A stew of thoughts and emotions swirled inside his head. What to do about Annabelle? She'd looked at him with those hypnotically romantic eyes of hers and lied to his face about her father. Why? Why didn't she trust him with the truth?

And then there was tomorrow.

Tomorrow he was scheduled to start an insurrection that would, if successful, culminate in a second American revolution.

The gag in Asa's mouth was tight, making it hard to swallow. Ropes tied his feet to the end of the bed and his hands to the headboard. While his feet were uncomfortably bound together, his pants prevented the ropes from biting into his legs. Not so with his wrists. The rough hemp chewed on him with every movement. He tried to lie still, but with his hands stretched over his head, he found it hard to breathe. His wrists paid the price for each time he squirmed to catch a breath.

Stretched out like this made the wound in his side throb. But he couldn't complain. It could be worse.

He looked at the dead man lying next to him.

Asa's capture, as it turned out, was precipitated by Annabelle's carelessness. From what he was able to piece together, for reasons unknown to him, Annabelle locked her mother in a room at night. Asa had seen the woman only once before, seated in the garden on the day he walked in on Eli swinging Annabelle. And tonight she wandered out of her room at a most unfortunate time.

He remembered thinking the instant the woman screamed that he was in trouble. But when Jacob Benson bounded up the stairs with his knife, trouble turned to danger.

Benson tied him to the bed with Martha's supervision. The woman was very good at giving directions. And Benson proved unusually adept at knots for an academic who had an unhealthy interest in all things related to the French Revolution.

A piece to this bizarre puzzle fell into place the moment the tying was done. Benson stepped back. Martha snuggled against him under his arm. And then—this is the piece of the puzzle Asa wished he could get out of his mind—they kissed . . .

The bedroom door opened, breaking Asa's reverie. Annabelle strolled in, closing the door behind her.

"Father would never forgive me if I didn't say good night to him," she cooed.

She tiptoed playfully over to Asa's side of the bed, bent over him, and untied his gag. It took her a minute to untie the knot, and during that time her arm brushed his nose and mouth. She smelled wonderful.

"There!" she said, standing back. "You're not going to holler and scream, are you? Martha would be very cross with me if she knew I was in here with you."

Asa worked his mouth and tongue. It was so dry and stiff, he didn't know if he could utter a respectable scream even if he wanted to.

"Didn't you feel absolutely wicked sneaking into my house like that, Asa? It's really quite flattering, you know. And I can't help but wonder what you would have done had you made it all the way to my bedroom undetected." She leaned forward. "What were you going to do to me?"

Asa was in no mood for Annabelle's games. "Why are you keeping your father's death a secret? And why go to such lengths to keep him here? Why not bury him and pretend he's alive?"

Annabelle looked at him with disappointment in her eyes. "I'd miss him! Besides when I tell people that I'll discuss something with father, I can say it convincingly."

Her tone was matter of fact, as though her actions were perfectly reasonable.

"You're taking all the fun out of this," she pouted.

She waited—for him to apologize, to try to make it up to her, to beg her forgiveness. That's what he used to do whenever she put on her pouting face. When she saw he wasn't playing, her face drained of flirtatiousness and the tone of her voice became cold and hard.

"You really have come in quite handy, Asa Rush. When I recognized you in the park, I instantly saw in you a chance to get information regarding Abigail

Adams that might prove useful. I recalled the pompous way your sister had bragged about her being a family friend. Silly little fool. The Adamses think they're royalty. The only kind of feelings Abigail Adams could possibly have for someone of Maggy's social status would be akin to feelings she might have for a servant or a domesticated animal. Ah, but that will soon change, won't it?"

The woman standing over him bore no resemblance to the Annabelle Byrd who had bewitched him. Her eyes were cold, the lines of her face hard. As though some bitter spinster were wearing Annabelle's dress.

"And you were a naughty boy to ruin the kidnapping attempt. Your name was abused around here for days afterward." She appeared to think back to that time. "But then," she whispered, "you redeemed yourself by making Eli Cooper deliciously jealous. You don't know this, but . . . I was seeing Mr. Cooper the same time I was entertaining you."

She jumped back and held a hand over her mouth, playful. She was Annabelle again.

Asa chose not to tell her he knew. Given the fact that he was stretched out, it seemed best not to do anything to rile her.

"Ooooooo, he was jealous! Which, of course, made him try all the more to get into my good graces, which is exactly what I wanted. Does it hurt knowing that I never felt anything for you? Of course it does. You can bury a romantic dream a hundred times, and it'll still find a way to claw its way out of a grave, won't it?"

Asa was pretty sure his was in the ground for good this time.

She turned curious. "So why did you stop coming to see me? That is a puzzlement, isn't it? It's not that I really needed you any longer, but I thought it best to keep you around a little longer just in case for some inexplicable reason Eli began to lose interest." She crinkled her nose. "I shouldn't have worried, should I? When the two of you showed up side by side in the park, I knew that the gods had blessed me. Do you realize how easy you made it for me?"

"Glad to oblige," Asa said flatly.

Annabelle frowned and clucked her tongue. "Sarcasm, Mr. Rush?

How unbecoming of you." She brightened. "Can I tell you what the future holds for us? I'm dying to tell someone, and well, seeing that you're not going anywhere anytime soon . . ."

She threaded his gag between her fingers and began pacing. Every time her back was turned, Asa worked the ropes. All it seemed to get him were deeper cuts on his wrists.

She turned suddenly. Asa ceased his effort. So certain was he that she'd caught him, he even ceased breathing. However, she wasn't looking at him. She was looking over him. To her father.

"It's all right if I tell him, isn't it, Father? No need to keep secrets from him now that he's going to help us with our little plan."

An act for his sake? Or was she mad? Asa couldn't tell. Before, he'd thought she was just an incredible actress. But now . . . There was an element of realism that went beyond show.

Her gaze fell on him. "You don't know this, Asa dear, but tomorrow is the dawn of a new day in America. My father, rest his soul, saw this day coming from nearly a decade away. And I didn't have the heart to put him into the ground until he could see it."

"You're a considerate daughter," Asa muttered.

Annabelle didn't appear to hear him. "All across the nation, in every major city, men of vision have formed secret societies, waiting, waiting for a signal to rise up and reclaim the nation for the people. We will tear down the royalist republic that has been ruthlessly erected against the people's will. A true democracy will be built on the ashes of Washington and Adams."

"Haven't you heard?" Asa said. "Your man Jefferson was elected president."

Annabelle scoffed. "Jefferson has betrayed his own kind. His early support of the French Revolution proved to be a sham. It appears our Mr. Jefferson has forgotten what it's like to be a revolutionary."

"Blood, blood, and more blood," Asa said.

Annabelle reacted as though he had struck her. She stood over him and slapped him hard enough to make his ears ring. "Blood is the seed of democracy. Tomorrow you will see that I am right. And you, Asa Rush, will figure prominently into the history of a new order. For over a year I have been grooming Eli Cooper to sound the cry of the people. I selected him. Recruited him. Inspired him. And tomorrow all my hard work will yield dividends."

"Your work? Or the work of the Illuminati?"

The mention of the Illuminati had its desired effect.

"How do you know about the Illuminati?" she asked.

Asa just stared at her.

A second later any concern she had was shrugged off. "It doesn't matter. Those old fools don't have the nerve to embrace true revolution. A little rhetoric, killing a departing president. Do they truly think that's enough? Ah, but killing Jefferson! And on his inauguration! Now that is a stroke bold enough to start a revolution. Both Federalists and Jeffersonians will take to the streets."

"It'll be anarchy," Asa said.

Annabelle squealed. "Yes, it will, won't it? Everyone equal. And from that, a true democracy."

Asa was putting it together. "Jacob Benson."

Annabelle smiled. "Rode out tonight for Washington. Just one of Jefferson's many admirers arriving to congratulate him on his first—and last—day in office." She moved closer to him, stretching the cloth gag with her hands. "Get a good night's sleep, Asa. For tomorrow you will represent the Federalist cause to the good people of New Haven."

She bent over to gag his mouth again, then appeared to have a thought. Instead of the gag, she placed her lips on his. After kissing him she slid her cheek against his cheek and whispered in his ear, "How many times have you imagined lying in bed and kissing me?"

Not risking an answer, she quickly gagged him, tighter than it had been before, bid her father good night, and left Asa to contemplate the last hours of his life with a dead man.

CHAPTER 35

Eli awoke the next morning at the Minuteman Tavern with two things on his mind. Asa Rush and insurrection.

The day of the uprising finally arrived. For weeks Eli had thought of little else, with the possible exception of the duel. At the time, he viewed the duel as little more than an annoying pothole on the road to his destiny. Asa Rush changed all that when he stood with arms outstretched and openly invited death. It was a shot to Eli's heart. Asa couldn't have killed Eli any more dead had he put a pistol to his chest and pulled the trigger.

With Eli's rebirth came a new destiny with an old schedule attached to it. One in which he was supposed to rally a thousand longshoremen to revolution.

He threw back the threadbare covers to see a pair of bare feet in his face. Sitting up, he hoped they were Asa's.

A heavily bearded man in his midfifties lay with his head back and his mouth open. Tinker really packed them in at night. And from the smell of the bedding, he didn't wash it often. Eli never thought he'd see the day when he missed the dormitory.

He glanced around the room at the mounds of sleeping humanity and didn't see Asa. From Tinker he learned that Asa had never come back to the tavern.

"Asa, where are you?" Eli moaned with equal parts of frustration and concern.

He cleaned himself up. There was only one person in town, besides Asa Rush, he knew he could trust. Only going to him would be hard.

"It's Eli Cooper, sir."

"Certainly I have time. Show him in."

Dr. Dwight's secretary held the door open. Eli was no more than two feet inside the president's office when Dwight caught his hand in a viselike grip.

"I hope I'm not disturbing you, sir," Eli said. "But it's a matter of utmost importance, and I didn't know where else to turn."

"Just tell me what I can do to help." Dwight's face reflected concern as he showed Eli to a chair.

"A couple of things, really. I need your advice and your help."

"Go on."

"It's just that, well, I'm involved in some things that . . ." Eli hung his head.

"These things—holdovers from your old life?"

"Yes, sir. I'm afraid you're going to be disappointed with me."

"Not possible, son. There is a BC and an AD in every Christian's life. Before Christ and anno Domini, living in the Lord's favor. The work of Christ on the cross effectively dealt with all our shortcomings before salvation. No exceptions. If our Savior buried the guilt of that sin, who am I to dredge it up?"

Eli smiled gratefully. He'd always thought Dr. Dwight was the pompous, righteous type. He'd been wrong.

"Tell me what's troubling you, son."

"First off—I don't know where Asa is . . ."

That afternoon, when Eli arrived at the docks, more than a thousand men had already gathered. He had to give it to Jacob Benson. The guy knew how to promote a revolution. Men of all sizes and shapes milled about, gripping an assortment of clubs and sticks, looking for any excuse to hit something. Some had knives and pistols shoved into their belts . . . and who knew what else concealed under their clothing.

Overhead the skies were dark and threatening, muting the already black-streaked wood of the waterfront docks.

Ale lubricated the mob's minds and tongues. Stacks of kegs were tapped at various locations, dispensing liquid disorder.

The centerpiece of the scene was a guillotine, elevated above the crowd on a scaffold. Its twin beams stretched to the sky. Its blade was raised, poised for the kill.

On the scaffold a slick-looking man with a prominent mustache addressed the crowd with a familiar harangue about how the Federalists were secretly working to establish an English-type monarchy in America. The content sounded like a resurrected preelection speech, but it still struck a contentious chord with the crowd.

The mood of the men was dark and menacing, like storm clouds on the horizon. Ripples of discontent sounded like thunder. All they needed now was a flash of lightning to start a fire that would spread quickly throughout the town.

Eli was to be the lightning.

He pushed his way toward the scaffold. The closer he got, the larger the death machine loomed. Two rough men with clubs in their belts and arms folded defiantly blocked his passage onto the platform. He gave them his name. They didn't appear impressed, but they parted to let him up the stairs.

The speaker glanced over, saw Eli, and gave a slight nod. His job now was to hand the crowd over to Eli.

Standing on the edge of the platform, a few feet distant from the imported French guillotine, Eli Cooper had never felt more alone and unsure of himself than he did now. Gone was his cocky attitude, his eagerness to jump into the fray. The fray was now stretched out in front of him like an angry ocean, and if he wasn't careful, it would swallow him up as surely as it had swallowed Jonah.

What would they do to him when they found out he wasn't the same man they'd enlisted to do this job? And they were going to find out. Would they turn on him? Would his blood be the first to christen the shiny blade hovering overhead?

The mob roared in response to the speaker who described Adams and Hamilton reclining comfortably in their lavish homes as innocent women and children attended their every need, and as they sent their men into the countryside to round up ten virgins each for their pleasure.

The speaker then elicited vindicated shouts and huzzahs as he portrayed George Washington's last breath. "The old man opens his eyes to eternity, expecting to see a million angels welcome him into heaven. But when he opens his eyes, what does he see? A wrinkled, black-toothed hag—Satan's mistress—who seizes him by the scruff of the neck and drags him down into a room of fire and brimstone. She tells the pompous old fool that she has interceded with Satan on his behalf and for the first millennium of eternity, he will be her personal slave, and after that he'll be taken to hell!"

The mob erupted with cheers.

"And today, citizens, we will send Adams and Hamilton and all their kind to hell to join him!"

The response was deafening.

Drowned out by the noise, the speaker used the time to glory in his handiwork.

Eli joined him in scanning the crowd. He was hoping to spot Asa.

During his search he saw several familiar faces. Tappan was in the crowd. Eli expected he would be. Any opportunity to hit something or someone, and Tappan would be there. He also spotted the *Code Duello*–quoting tutor. Ruggles, wasn't it? Hard to forget a man who had such an irritating attention to detail. Also in the crowd was Asa's roommate and second at the duel. Eli couldn't remember his name, but his heart skipped with hope. Perhaps Asa would be standing beside him.

Eli's heart failed. Asa was nowhere to be seen.

At the edges of the crowd, seated in carriages, observing, were men wearing expensive clothing and grim expressions. Eli recognized a few of them from his meeting with the Illuminati. Naturally, they were interested in watching their plan unfold, yet cautious enough to keep a distance and a ready escape. Eli half expected to see Annabelle and Martha in one of the carriages, though they had told him they would be relying on runners to keep them informed of events.

He remembered Annabelle explaining to him why she wouldn't be present for his moment of glory. Since she'd appeared to be on the verge of tears, he consoled her. Thinking back on it, Eli knew that was what she'd really wanted.

The noise of the crowd died down.

"I give you the lady of the hour!"

The speaker stepped aside, giving Madame Guillotine center stage.

While the mob burst into a frenzy of cheers and toasts to the guillotine, Eli felt someone bump him from behind. He stepped aside to let a man pass.

Broad shouldered, with close-cropped hair, the man had to shout in Eli's ear to be heard. "At your signal!"

Their eyes met. Then the man donned a black executioner's hood and took his place next to the guillotine.

Fear's icy fingers clutched Eli's heart as he realized that he hadn't been told everything.

During his meeting with the Illuminati, he'd been given a signal. At the climax of his speech, he was to shout, "Citizens of America, arise!" At the signal, local toughs, recruited by Jacob Benson, would initiate the mayhem and destruction. If Eli had done his job inciting the crowd, they would take it from there.

Only now it appeared his signal would not only unleash a political revolt, but mass killing as well. What a fool he'd been! The Illuminati told him that the people needed a symbol. The guillotine provided that. But Eli didn't think they would ever press it into service.

His mind was racing at his own foolishness. What did he expect? Something along the lines of the Boston Tea Party, perhaps. Destruction of property. A march on Washington. If there was resistance, there could be shooting. And deaths. But wholesale slaughter?

How smug he'd been, sitting in a classroom defending a bloody revolution that took place an ocean away. Now that the blood was about to be spilled at his feet, it took on a different perspective.

The speaker was shouting again. "And what kind of party would it be if we invited such a beautiful lady to our shores without providing her dancing partners?"

A cheer went up.

"*Federalist* dancing partners!"

A louder cheer.

"One Federalist from every state in the Union!"

Up the steps, onto the scaffold, a line of men was marched, their hands tied behind their backs. Eli looked at each as they passed. Some were resigned to their fate. They eyed him stoically, or in anger. Others were scared. Their eyes bulged. They cried. Their chins shook. They begged him for mercy. Others couldn't keep their gaze off the basket at the base of the blade.

The crowd was shouting. There were so many voices at once that it was difficult, at first, to make out what they were saying.

Finally, one voice spoke for them all. "There are only fifteen! You said one for each state of the Union!"

The speaker appeared surprised. He made a pretense of counting the victims. It was obviously a show. The crowd didn't seem to mind. A little levity before the killing seemed to agree with them.

"Well," the speaker said, his hands on his hips, "that won't do, will it? What kind of symbolic gesture would it be if we were missing a state?"

He looked at the line of condemned men. "I see the problem. We don't have a representative from the good state of Connecticut! Any volunteers?"

Uneasiness crept up Eli's spine.

The mob was thirsty for blood. They could smell it. He could see it in their eyes. Spill some, and there was no telling where it would stop. But then that's what the Illuminati had in mind after all, wasn't it?

Eli glanced at the carriages. Grinning faces of wealthy men stared back at him.

The speaker turned to him. "Would you care to volunteer?"

Eli took a step backward.

A hand gripped his arm.

"No?" The speaker answered for him. "Ah! No matter. Here's number sixteen."

The hand pulled Eli out of the way so that the sixteenth victim could be led onto the stage.

One of Eli's problems had been solved. He no longer had to search for Asa.

To the cheers of the revolutionary crowd, Asa was led to the front of the line of those awaiting execution.

CHAPTER 36

Eli couldn't move. Couldn't breathe. Nor could he take his eyes off Asa as he ascended the scaffold steps.

The mob surrounding the guillotine undulated restlessly with cries for his head.

Asa saw him. They exchanged a glance. It was the briefest of glances, for Asa's guard shoved him from behind.

Asa stumbled on the last step and nearly fell. When he caught his balance, the guillotine captured his gaze. Eli watched Asa's eyes climb the beams to the blade.

Eli wanted to read some kind of message in the instant of their silent exchange. A direction perhaps. An encouragement. But the moment was too brief. That, or if there was a signal, Eli's stunned mind was incapable of recognizing it.

The speaker grabbed Asa by the arm and presented him to the crowd. "An historic personage this," he proclaimed. "For this is the man who by his blood will launch the second American revolution!"

Asa opened his mouth, but the roar of the crowd drowned out his words. The guards pulled him roughly aside and forced him onto his belly before the guillotine. The yoke was lowered, securing his neck in place.

From Eli's position on the scaffold, he lost sight of Asa's head.

The speaker walked past Eli, his mustache framing a self-satisfied smirk that said, "Let's see if you can top that!"

Then Eli was at center stage, unaware of how he got there. Before him was a riotous mob, eager to be fed and then set loose on the town. Behind him, his head in a guillotine, was the most courageous man Eli knew. The man who had loved him and kept coming after him despite every mean act Eli could think of to drive him away.

The crowd cried for the executioner to release the blade. He stepped into place, his hand on the release rope, and awaited Eli's signal.

The next few moments would determine if Asa lived or died. His fate was in Eli's hands. That realization, and a rush of blood, quickened Eli to action. He alone could save Asa.

A plan formulated in his mind.

He stepped forward with confidence and thrust his fist into the air. "Citizens!"

The crowd roared.

Eli grinned. He could do this. "A little rebellion now and then is a good thing!"

The crowd went wild. Jefferson's quote always worked.

Eli followed with another one. "In the words of president-elect, Thomas Jefferson, 'The tree of liberty must be refreshed from time to time with the blood of patriots and tyrants!'"

A chant of "Liberty! Liberty! Liberty!" was punctuated with upthrust clubs and weapons.

"Lofty thoughts, these," Eli shouted. "Mr. Jefferson speaks of the sacred tree of liberty. And when he speaks of nurturing it, he speaks of violence, blood, and manure. I ask you: how can anything sacred be born out of violence, blood, and manure?"

Uncertainty blanketed the crowd. They gazed up at Eli, as though waiting for the punch line to a joke.

"Has the French Revolution taught us nothing? Revolution is a hungry beast that feeds on blood. Its appetite is insatiable. Like any beast, the more it eats, the larger it grows, until it is so large it turns on the very people who fed it!

"Jean-Paul Marat fed the beast, and it turned on him. A scientist and physician, Marat called for more and more executions until the beast came for him in his bath."

The mob stilled. Eli took that as a good sign. He pressed on.

"Robespierre fed the beast, and it turned on him! List after list was made, and the beast was unleashed on them. When there were no names left on one list, another was made, until one day Robespierre's name was added to the list, and the beast consumed him.

"Do you want to see the beast? To look into his eyes? Turn and look at the man standing next to you. Go ahead, do it! You see it, don't you? Once the beast starts feeding, there's no stopping him. If you don't go after your neighbor, your neighbor will come after you."

The mob was milling about like lost sheep.

Eli knew what to do next. Give them direction.

"Mr. Jefferson, you speak of violence and blood and manure, but liberty will not be found in this unholy trilogy. You say a little rebellion now and then is a good thing. I say a little revival now and then is a good thing!

"What our nation needs is less rebellion and more revival! Less blood, and more contrition! Less manure and more worship!"

Eli stood tall on the platform. He'd done his best. He knew he'd reached them. Their weapons were lowered. The fight had gone out of them.

Then, from the back of the crowd, someone shouted, "Pull the cord! Off with his head!"

To Eli's horror the beast roared back to life. Weapons danced once again in the air. Rage molded men's faces. A wave of shouts erupted from among them, like wisps of wind, with each pass growing louder until it reached gale force.

Staring into the refreshed face of the beast, Eli realized his error. There was no reasoning with a monster.

It was loud.

Thirsty.

And it was fixated on Asa.

The force of the shouts backed Eli up. He looked over at Asa and could see only the top of his friend's head. From beneath the black hood the executioner's eyes were fixed on Eli.

Standing on the far side of the platform, where Eli had stood a short time ago, the speaker with the mustache was clapping furiously. "Masterful! Masterful!" he shouted, as if Eli had goaded the beast to fury pitch on purpose.

Eli's heart failed within him. He didn't understand what had gone wrong. This is what he was good at. He should have been able to turn the crowd away, but he'd failed. And Asa would die for his failure.

"I'm sorry," Eli said, knowing that Asa couldn't hear him. "You deserve a better friend than me. I only wish I could trade places with you. For I would. As God is my witness, I would willingly take your place."

That's when it came to him. Just like that, it came to him. Eli knew how to save Asa. If he couldn't reason with the beast, he had to slay it.

East Rock held the key. Eli Cooper had died at East Rock. And dead men no longer fear death.

To the astonishment of all, Eli leaped onto the guillotine, straddling the yoke that cradled Asa Rush's head, and placing his body between the blade and his friend.

The mob gasped as one man. Surprised, the executioner let loose the rope and took a step back, lest he accidentally release the blade on Eli.

The momentary silence gave Eli the opening he needed. "Do you know what this is? You recognize it, don't you?"

He gave them a moment to think, but not too long. Meanwhile, he reached over and grabbed the release rope. Now he really had their attention.

"This"—with his free hand he indicated the space between the two wooden beams—"is death's door. And they"—he pointed to the men bound and waiting their turn at the guillotine—"They stand in line waiting to go through it."

Smiles broke out among the crowd. they were beginning to like this act.

"And they will! If not today, then tomorrow, or the next day, for they shall surely die. Do you see how frightened they are? Look at them! And look at the line they form. Why, it stretches past them, to Mister Speaker there, and the two mean-looking men at the steps, and down past them, and winds around and around . . ." Eli's pointing finger passed back and forth over the crowd.

"Every single one of you is lined up in front of death's door, and it will have you! Yes, yes, you are a great and powerful beast whose name is Violence. But there is a greater beast than you! Its name is Death. And it will have you. No matter where you go, it will hunt you down, and it will have you.

"Turn a corner, and it'll be there. Take a journey, and it will stalk you. Everywhere you go, there it will be, waiting . . . waiting . . . waiting to devour you. On the street . . . at your hearth . . . in your bed . . . it will have you. It will have you and your brothers and your wives and your children and your children's children. For it is an insatiable beast, and it will come for you. It will bind your hands, and it will lead you to death's door, and—"

At this point, Eli's heart stilled. Everything depended upon this next moment.

His life.

Asa's life.

The destiny of the men looking on.

". . . it . . ."

He leaped from beneath the blade.

". . . will . . ."

With one hand he lifted the yoke. With the other, he pulled the rope.

". . . have you!"

He pulled Asa from beneath the blade.

There was a *whoosh*, a flash of silver, and a heart-stopping *thud* as the blade buried itself in wood.

At the sound of the blade, the crowd hushed.

"There is only one person who can save you! One man who stands in the gap between death's blade and you!"

Eli spied a knife on the executioner's belt. He grabbed it and held it high.

"Only one man who can set you free! He is Jesus, the Son of God, the only man to conquer death! Citizens of America, repent!"

Eli slit the ropes on Asa's wrists.

The instant he did, the Spirit fell.

CHAPTER 37

The New Haven docks looked like a natural disaster had hit it. Neither Asa nor Eli had ever seen anything like it, not even at Cane Ridge, where the Kentucky revival took place. It was as though the Spirit had arisen from behind them like an ocean wave and crashed down upon them, sweeping men's legs from under them.

Everywhere they looked, men were on their faces or their knees crying out to God to save them. Scattered among them on the ground were weapons of every kind, useless in the battle at hand.

Even on the scaffold, men were weeping and praying. The first speaker sobbed loudly, the line of bound victims wept and prayed, and even the executioner was on his knees.

Asa and Eli alone were still standing.

"Not bad for a first sermon," Asa said.

Most of the carriages occupying the members of the Illuminati were gone. One remained. Two men sat in it, their heads buried in their hands.

The executioner clawed at Eli's pants. Desperate eyes peered up at him. "What must I do to be saved?"

Eli put a comforting hand on the man's shoulder. He started to say something, then stopped. Standing next to a French guillotine gave him an idea.

The line to the guillotine stretched down the scaffold steps, along the wharf, and doubled back again. Asa pulled the blade up, and Eli released it.

Whoosh. Thud!

One by one the men came to the guillotine and knelt, confessing their sins. Eli prayed over them. The man then bowed his head and placed a hand on the side of the guillotine.

Eli released the blade.

The guillotine shuddered.

Whoosh. Thud!

"Having died to yourself, you are alive to Christ. Rise, my brother."

Mournful men knelt. Cheerful men rose and shook Eli's hand or hugged him as Asa reset the blade.

Among those who knelt on the scaffold were Tappan, Ruggles, and Gurdon. Eli greeted each of them warmly, for they had witnessed his death and resurrection at East Rock.

"I have a mission for the three of you." After giving them directions to the Byrd mansion on Crown Street, he said, "Simply report to them what you have seen and heard here."

From the grins on their faces, Eli concluded he couldn't have picked three more eager missionaries. "Wait!" He called them back. "You can go together, but deliver your reports separately. Space them out. Say, four or five minutes apart. It'll make more of an impact that way."

When he saw the gleam he felt in his own eye appear in their eyes, he knew they understood.

Slaying the revolutionary beast in New Haven took time. After a couple of hours Asa's arms grew tired, and someone had to take over for him. Eli gave no sign of tiring, which was good because word had spread throughout the town. People came in great numbers to the docks to see for themselves if the stories circulating in town were true.

Asa never learned who started it, but the men who gave their lives to Christ and touched the guillotine were calling themselves Citizen Christians. And as the initial Citizen Christians moved among the townspeople, the line to the guillotine grew even longer.

Recognizable faces from Yale College began appearing. Among them was Dr. Dwight. When he caught the eye of both Asa and Eli, he clasped his hands and raised them over his head in the sign of a champion. Then he began ordering the students who came with him to assist as needed.

Soon groups of men and women formed around open Bibles. There was instruction, and prayers and voices lifted up in song.

"Look who's here," Asa said.

Eli turned in the direction Asa was pointing.

At a safe distance stood a carriage. Inside were two women. Annabelle and Martha. They didn't look happy.

"Let's give them something to remember us by." Asa stood beside Eli Cooper, putting his arm around him.

Eli put his arm around Asa.

They smiled and waved at Annabelle Byrd.

The carriage was too far distant for them to hear what was said in it. Maybe Asa imagined it, but he thought for sure that he heard a recognizable screech.

The carriage bolted and was soon gone.

Asa gave a start. "President Adams! In all the excitement, I forgot. We have to warn—"

Eli stopped him. "Already done. I spoke with Dr. Dwight about it this morning. He sent word to Washington to warn Mr. Adams."

"And Jefferson?"

"What about Jefferson?"

"Jacob Benson is on his way to Washington right now. They plan on assassinating Jefferson during the inauguration."

Eli shook his head in disbelief. "That was never the Illuminati's plan."

"It's Annabelle's plan. Assassinate both Adams and Jefferson on the same day. Both sides will accuse the other. What better fuel to throw on a fledgling revolution?"

"The plan was never to assassinate Adams. Just to make sure he vacated the White House."

Asa gave him a look. "And I thought I was the naive one."

"How can one woman be so evil?"

"Two women. Martha has been tutoring her. Apparently she's a veteran of some rather nasty business in France."

"You tried to warn me about Annabelle. I wouldn't listen."

"Maggy warned me, and I wouldn't listen."

"Maggy warned you?" Eli said. "How dumb can you be not to listen to her? Your sister knows what she's talking about."

This wasn't the time to get into that, so Asa let it pass. "We need to send word to Washington."

"No," Eli replied.

"No?"

"We need to *go* to Washington." When Asa started to object, Eli explained. "Who better than us? If we send word, all they'll have is a description. We can recognize Benson instantly."

"And when we do, then what?"

"We'll think of something along the way. Let's go."

A voice came from behind them. "Where are we going?"

It was Ruggles. Tappan and Gurdon were with him, still aglow in having accomplished their first missionary task.

"Jacob Benson is going to assassinate Jefferson. We have to stop him," Asa explained.

"Great! Let's go!" Ruggles said.

Tappan nodded. "Count me in!"

"Me too," added Gurdon.

Already Eli was shaking his head. "We don't know how Benson is going to react if he sees us. It'll be best if just Asa and I go."

"Suit yourself," Ruggles said.

Asa furrowed his brow. Ruggles had given up too easily.

The tutor turned to Tappan and Gurdon. "I've been thinking of riding to Washington to see the Jefferson inauguration. Want to come along?"

Both Tappan and Gurdon agreed enthusiastically.

Ruggles turned to Eli. "Guess what? Tappan, Gurdon, and I are planning on going to see Jefferson's inauguration. We heard you and Asa are headed that way too. How about if we travel together?"

Eli laughed and threw up his hands. "I know when I'm outmatched."

"And don't you forget it," Ruggles said good-naturedly.

CHAPTER 38

After four days on the road, they were still two days out of Washington and Eli worried that they weren't going to make it on time. The weather conspired against them. A late winter storm of wind-driven sleet pelted them mercilessly all the way through New York and New Jersey.

At the moment, they were stuck north of Baltimore, holed up in a tavern at Middle River, their day's journey cut short by the storm.

Just sitting here—knowing that Benson was already in position to kill Jefferson and knowing they could stop him if they could reach Washington in time—was driving Eli mad. Depression curled up like a faithful dog at his side and settled in for the night.

He thought of his Old Testament namesake. Hadn't the prophet Elijah experienced much the same feeling following the trial by fire atop Mount Carmel? The great man of God had gone a day's journey into the wilderness, sat under a broom tree, and prayed that he might die.

Eli chuckled. Of all the possible traits he might share with his namesake, did it have to be depression?

"Could be worse," he muttered to himself. "Could be outside in the snow. Could be traveling alone."

He propped his feet closer to the flames and felt the warmth of the fire through the soles of his boots. A short distance away, laughter distracted him. He didn't have to hear what was said. Just seeing Asa and

Ruggles and Gurdon and Tappan huddled together was enough to make him smile.

They'd shared a lot together in a short time. The duel at East Rock. The riot turned revival on the docks of New Haven. And now a mission to save the president-elect of the United States. Eli had had friends before, but he'd never felt the way about anyone as he felt toward this band of Christian brothers. He'd do anything for them. And he felt confident they would do anything for him.

What an unlikely group they were.

He looked at them with pride. Ruggles, Gurdon, and Tappan were shoulder to shoulder on the far side of a long wooden dining table. Ruggles and Gurdon, both with pen in hand, were hunched over, applying their skills for the good of the group. At the end of the table, Tappan and Asa sat opposite each other.

The topic of discussion was the same as it had been on the road, when the wind wasn't snatching the words from their lips. Given the momentous events at the docks, what would God have them do now?

God had kindled a fire inside each of them. An eternal fire that burned but would never burn up. The kind that had sent Moses from the wilderness back to Egypt on a mission.

They felt compelled to do something of import. To the man, they were ready to go, to head back to Egypt and then on to the Promised Land. All they needed now was directions.

Ruggles, Tappan, and Gurdon came to identical conclusions. For them, the path of obedience did not lead back to school. It was a fact that amused Eli, since he and Asa were the ones who had been expelled and they wanted to go back. The other three, however, were feeling a call to the wilderness, the western frontier. So many people were heading west and were facing all kinds of difficulties and dangers. They would need God if they were to survive.

It was the plan to head west that had set Erwin Ruggles to work. He was now busily drawing up a set of guidelines for them, anticipating that other men would want to join them. "The early church fathers drafted confessions of faith," he told them. "I want people to know what we stand for. I'm putting into writing—"

"Reverend Ruggles's Rules for Frontier Preachers," Gurdon had quipped.

"Go ahead. Laugh if you will. But you'll see . . ."

There was no offense given or taken. In fact, since East Rock, Gurdon and Ruggles had developed into fast friends—much to everyone's surprise. You hardly ever saw one without the other. Even now they sat on the same bench.

Eli took a sip of hot cider. It warmed his insides all the way down and made him feel better.

Gurdon worked next to his friend with equal intensity, only his pen didn't touch paper. His canvas was the back of Tappan's hand.

It seemed Gurdon had artistic talent, and he was quite good. Two nights ago, at a tavern, he had passed the time fashioning a symbol to commemorate their experience at New Haven. He had inked it on the back of his hand. An impermanent tattoo. The symbol was composed of two parts: a stylized guillotine with a cross superimposed over it. The moment Ruggles had seen it, he'd wanted one. So had everyone. Eli had one. So did Asa. Tonight it was Tappan's turn.

He sat passively, his left hand outstretched, as Gurdon worked on him. Tappan's right hand cradled his chin as he listened to Asa read from the Bible.

Of all the conversions at the docks, Tappan had been the biggest surprise. The change in him was instantaneous and astounding. He wasn't the same man. About the only remnant of the old Tappan was his depth of passion. God had redirected it. The man had an insatiable craving for the Bible. The fervor that had once been directed at abusing underclassmen during trimmings was channeled into a thirst for the Scriptures.

Even now, an open Bible between them, he hung on Asa's every word. And for his part, Asa was always available, always willing to share what he knew.

Watching the two of them face to face like that brought a lump of emotion to Eli's throat.

They had been so cruel to Asa, yet look at him now—teaching, laughing, encouraging the very man who once took delight in hurting him.

Asa was the common denominator among them. They were all here because he had refused to give up on them.

"On me," Eli said softly.

Gurdon said something that set them all to laughing. Eli hadn't heard what he said. It didn't matter. Whatever it was couldn't bring him any greater joy than watching them interact with one another.

Ever since they had set out from New Haven, moments like these brought tears to Eli's eyes. He couldn't imagine that ever changing.

March 4, 1801. Inauguration Day. Washington D.C.
Jacob Benson shifted from foot to foot impatiently as he hid in the midst of a crowd of well-wishers outside Conrad and McMunn's boarding-house. They waited for President-elect Thomas Jefferson to make an appearance. The procession to the site of the inauguration would start here.

The activity surrounding the boardinghouse resembled a beehive. Everybody was doing something. Nobody knew what the other was doing. It was perfect for Benson's purposes.

The boardinghouse itself was an unimpressive structure—a trait it shared with its surroundings. Farmyards and recently cleared forests stretched across open rolling land. Close by, numerous small craft dotted the surface of the blue Potomac.

Benson's attention was fixed on the boardinghouse. Word had it that, despite his recent election to the highest office in the land, Jefferson persisted in dining here at the common table with a handful of congressmen and their wives.

Today, following a swearing-in ceremony, he would move up the road to the president's house, which was as yet unfinished. The entire area was under construction. The inauguration ceremony would be held in the chamber of the Senate wing of the Capitol Building, a little more than a quarter of a mile distant from the boardinghouse, because it was the only completed structure.

The fact that this was the first inauguration to be held in Washington worked to Benson's favor. Nobody knew what to expect, or who. His plan was simple. Smile a lot. Just be one of Jefferson's many enthusiastic supporters. Jefferson was a man of the people. At some point or other he would make himself accessible. And when he did, Jacob Benson would be there to greet him with a pointed exchange that would cut right to the heart of the matter.

Benson grinned at his own cleverness. It was a gift.

All the signs were favorable for a successful assassination. The sky was overcast, but it wasn't raining or snowing. It was cold enough that no one would question a coat heavy enough to conceal an eight-inch blade, and clear enough that Jefferson would be accessible to the crowds.

Benson began humming a little French Revolutionary ditty Martha had taught him about a nobleman's head falling from a guillotine scaffold and being kicked by peasant children too poor to own a ball.

Having already walked the route of the procession—without a crutch, but not without a limp—Benson had selected two locations that would give him access to Jefferson. Here, at the boardinghouse, before he climbed into his carriage, and when he ascended the steps into the Capitol Building.

He wondered if Jefferson realized what a favor he was doing him. When word had first reached America of the revolution in France, like all true Americans, Jefferson had endorsed it enthusiastically. More recently, Jefferson had been less enthusiastic about the French Revolution. Politics and age had ruined him. He no longer had a fire in his gut. Killing for a cause was the mark of a true patriot. And now, by his death,

Jefferson would once again set the country ablaze and fulfill his destiny as a great revolutionary.

"You're welcome, Mr. Jefferson," Benson said.

"Pardon? Did you say something?" A man standing nearby turned and peered over the top of his glasses at Benson.

Benson didn't acknowledge him. He only moved closer to the front of the boardinghouse.

Should I tell him? Benson pondered. *He'd want to know, wouldn't he? To realize with his dying thought what he was dying for? Maybe something like, "Mr. Jefferson, your pen started the first American revolution, and your blood will start the second."*

Benson smiled. He liked that. It was poetic. Jefferson would like that. It was a little long, though. Benson wondered if he should shorten it.

At that moment the door to Conrad and McMunn's opened. There was a pause, then tumultuous cheers. Thomas Jefferson emerged to greet his destiny. It was eleven o'clock.

Benson's eyes narrowed, focused on the task at hand. It was time to make history. He took in every detail . . .

Jefferson was wearing a plain suit. A plain suit for a common man. His hair was not powdered in the pompous style of the Federalists. He wore no sword strapped to his waist, choosing instead to keep pageantry to a minimum. How unlike his predecessors, who demanded pomp and ceremony.

Benson eased his way closer to Jefferson. The president-elect appeared nervous, or was he just impatient? He looked about, waiting for someone to give him directions. There was no sign of a coach.

A delay.

"Perfect," Benson said under his breath.

Jefferson acknowledged those closest to him. He shook hands. Exchanged greetings and quips.

Benson moved closer. No one stopped him. He slipped into an informal line of well-wishers that was making its way toward Jefferson. This was going to be easier than Benson had anticipated. No doubt history books would list the late arrival of Jefferson's coach as one of the factors that contributed to his death.

Benson was two men away from Jefferson. Like everyone else around him, he kept bright, admiring eyes on the president, regarding him as some kind of god. Just one of thousands of Thomas Jefferson's admirers—that's what Benson needed to be right now.

Behind a forced smile he practiced his line. "Mr. President, your pen started the first revolution . . ."

Only one man separated him from Jefferson.

Benson extended his right hand in anticipation of shaking Jefferson's hand. He would grip it firmly. Pull Jefferson toward him. Benson's left hand would do the deed.

Slip it in.

Pull it out.

Turn as if nothing unusual happened.

And disappear into the crowd.

While riding to Washington, Benson had mulled over the possibility of leaving his knife in Jefferson's gut. It made for a more lasting image. But then he decided against it. He wanted a souvenir of the day.

He inched closer. His left hand reached under his coat and found the knife. He told himself to keep smiling.

The man in front of him was making a nuisance of himself, reminding Jefferson of when they had met in New York. Jefferson obviously didn't remember. The man didn't notice. He went on as though he and Jefferson were longtime friends.

Step aside . . . step aside, Benson muttered in his head.

A commotion pulled Jefferson's attention away. A militia unit arrived and was getting into formation for the procession. Jefferson was being hailed.

Excusing himself, Jefferson turned away.

No! Benson raged.

He was so close. Too close to let the opportunity pass. He could still get Jefferson from behind.

Benson stepped forward at the same time the New Yorker turned around. The two men collided.

The New Yorker became angry. "Hey now! Can't you see I'm walking here?"

The moment passed. Jefferson was out of reach.

"I'm talking to you!" the New Yorker persisted. "If you were any sort of a gentleman, you'd offer me an apology."

Benson was tempted to offer him something a little more substantial than an apology. Mightily tempted. However, the life of this little man was nothing compared to what was at stake. He wasn't worth the risk.

Ignoring him, Benson walked away.

The New Yorker pelted him in the back with a variety of off-color oaths.

Benson made his way along the procession route and once again caught sight of Jefferson. With the militia in the lead, the president-elect followed on foot. There would be no carriage.

Benson was impressed. In Philadelphia, President George Washington was never seen on the street except in an elegant carriage pulled by the finest horses. Jefferson walked down an unpaved street, sidestepping mudholes from yesterday's rainstorm.

Skirting the backside of the group of well-wishers lining the street, Benson ran ahead to get a place on the Capitol steps. He knew just the spot. In fact, this would work out even better than the boardinghouse. With all the jostling and shoving, he could make it appear that he'd been pushed into Jefferson's path. Before anyone knew otherwise, Jefferson would be dead.

Benson vaulted the wooden barnyard fence that surrounded the Capitol Building and sprinted up the gentle slope to the summit. At the base of the steps, he turned to chart the procession's progress. He'd arrived in plenty of time. From this vantage point he could see not only the procession route but also the president's house to the west. Jefferson would not survive long enough to live in it.

Well-wishers and supporters packed the steps. Benson weaseled his way among them until he reached a point that would suit his purposes perfectly. Now all he had to do was wait. Slipping his left hand inside his coat, he readied the knife.

Two people stood in front of him. Murmuring his apologies to a woman standing beside him, he inched closer to her so that when the time came, he could slip between them. He didn't want a repeat performance of the New Yorker kind with someone getting in his way.

The cheers of the crowd grew louder. Jefferson was approaching.

Benson wished Martha could be here to witness this. Not so much Annabelle. She was too flighty for his taste . . . though her father's money and position had proved useful. Martha had controlled her masterfully.

He wondered what Martha was doing right now. By now the revolution in New Haven was proceeding nicely, and she was probably standing at the foot of Madame Guillotine, cheering lustily with each fall of the blade.

The crowd jostled him off balance, bringing his attention back to the present. This was Benson's moment in history. He would tell his grandchildren about this day. Mr. Jefferson didn't know it yet, but in just a few seconds he was going to complete what he'd started in 1776.

Jefferson reached the foot of the Capitol steps. His gaze forward, he began the ascent.

There was more jostling, but Benson held his place. This was perfect. It was a wonder no one had been pushed into the procession yet. Jefferson was three steps away.

Benson turned sideways, aiming his shoulder between the two men in front of him. His left hand gripped and regripped his knife until it was comfortable.

He readied his historic line.

American history and Jacob Benson's lifeline were about to cross.

He leaned forward, starting his fall.

A hand grabbed his arm to steady him.

Benson silently cursed whoever it was who thought he was being a guardian angel by saving him. He tried to yank free his arm.

The grip held.

He looked at the hand holding his arm and saw what looked like a cross superimposed over a guillotine.

Another hand found his left arm. Then another. And another.

"Greetings Citizen," Eli Cooper said to him.

President-elect Thomas Jefferson passed almost within an arm's reach.

"Eli! You don't know what you're doing!" Benson seethed.

Eli didn't appear to share his concern. "We just wanted to give you a report of how things went in New Haven."

"Better than expected," Asa Rush said from his other side. "Wouldn't you say, Eli?"

"Definitely. Much better."

Tappan agreed. So did Erwin Ruggles.

The four of them pulled Benson out of the crowd, two men on each arm. Running toward them was another of Benson's former students. With him were half a dozen militiamen.

Behind them the cheering continued as Jefferson disappeared into the Senate chamber, where the inaugural events were scheduled to begin.

In appreciation for thwarting an assassination attempt on President-elect Jefferson, the boys from Yale were handed over to an official, who escorted them into the rear upper gallery of the Senate chamber. The gallery was packed, and they had to stand with their backs to the wall, but they didn't mind. Even though the chamber was warm and stuffy from all the bodies.

Below them sat the members of both the Senate and the House of Representatives. The introductions were over, and Jefferson was delivering his inauguration speech.

Eli found it hard to believe he was here. For as long as he could remember, he had heard about and read about Thomas Jefferson. And now to see him. To hear him.

The man behind the podium appeared so human. At first that bothered Eli. But upon reflection it made him admire the man even more. And not only Jefferson, but *all* the men who had assembled at Carpenter's Hall and drafted the Declaration of Independence. They weren't just a story.

For an instant, Eli even felt a warm kinship to John Adams. But the moment passed.

His voice softer than Eli had imagined it, Jefferson offered assurances to members of the Federalist party of his cooperation and hope that they could put the vitriol of the recent campaign behind them. That they might unite in common efforts for the common good.

Then he outlined his expectations for his term in office, insisting that there was no need to further strengthen the national government. His wish was for less government.

Lastly, he explained that his electoral victory was a triumph for America and all nations.

"It is," Eli whispered to Asa, who was standing beside him. "A bloodless revolution. The first of its kind. We're witnessing history."

Jefferson's speech took less than thirty minutes. After the applause died down, Chief Justice John Marshall administered the oath of office.

It was official. Thomas Jefferson was president of the United States.

One of the last little tidbits the boys from Yale heard about Jefferson before heading back to Connecticut was that following the swearing-in ceremony, he returned to Conrad and McMunn's boardinghouse for dinner with the other boarders.

CHAPTER 39

"Expelled for dueling!"

Maggy Rush lowered the letter in disbelief. She stared open-mouthed at her brother.

"I told you a letter from Dr. Dwight wouldn't help," Eli said, then immediately regretted it when he saw the look in Maggy's eyes. Coming to Asa's defense was a mistake.

Maggy turned on him. "And you! I don't even know where to begin with you. You're worse than he is!"

The two men sat opposite each other at the table with a half-eaten pan of biscuits between them. Eli munched contentedly on one. He'd ridden all the way to Greenfield to see Maggy's face, and even though it was presently crimson with anger, the ride had been worth it.

At first Asa's plan had been to inform Maggy by letter that he'd been expelled. He'd actually written it.

But Eli talked him out of sending it. "There are two kinds of news," he explained. "Letter news. And face-to-face news. The things we've been through? Face-to-face news, without question."

That's when he offered to go along, for support. Only after they had New Haven at their backs did Asa tell him about the letter from Dr. Dwight. Eli didn't think it would help. But then, he didn't think it would hurt either.

However, he could be wrong.

Asa jumped out of his seat. "Look here," he pleaded. "Did you read this part?"

It took him a minute to find the part to which he was referring. When he did, he read it out loud: "'I never expelled two finer students.' There. Dr. Dwight's own words." He stepped back, awaiting her response.

Maggy gave the impression of being persuaded. "High praise. High praise, indeed. In fact, it's right up there with a magistrate's proclaiming, 'I never executed two finer convicts.'"

Eli chuckled. "She's got you there." He took another bite of biscuit.

"Well, what about here?" Asa said. "The part where he tells us to make application for enrollment in the fall. I quote: 'I will do my utmost to persuade the board of directors to reinstate them to this college.' Well? What about that?"

Maggy's hands dropped to her sides in exasperation. "Dueling, Asa? *Dueling?* You could have killed each other!"

Asa took his seat. "You just don't understand. I thought it was a good idea. Well, maybe not at East Rock . . . on the day of the duel . . . and when I was lying on the ground . . . bleeding . . . looking up at the sky . . . but it turned out well, didn't it? God used it for good."

"You gotta give him that," Eli said. "It did turn out well."

When Maggy rounded on him for a second time, Eli made a mental note to keep his mouth shut.

"It turned out well?" Maggy screamed. "That's your defense? It turned out well? And yes, God may have been able to bring good out of it, but imagine what He could have done if He had two obedient servants to work with rather than two pigheaded stooges!"

Eli munched his biscuit. *She had a point.*

For a while no one said anything.

Maggy's anger finally seemed to deflate. She eyed Eli. "Did you really stand between a guillotine blade and my brother?"

Eli looked up at her cautiously. "If I admit to that, are you going to scream at me?"

Tears came to Maggy's eyes. She went to Eli and put her arms around him, pressing her forehead against the side of his head.

"Thank you," she whispered. "Thank you." Stepping back, she took a deep breath to compose herself. "Now, if the two of you will wash up, I'll put some supper on the table."

Over a dinner of baked chicken, yams, onions, gravy, and bread, Eli and Asa learned the details of President Adams's departure from Washington on the day of Jefferson's inauguration. Maggy filled them in with information communicated to her by Abigail Adams.

"After receiving Dr. Dwight's warning," Maggy explained, "the president's advisors saw to it that he was spirited out of Washington by coach at four o'clock that morning."

"So then, in effect," Eli said, "between the time he left and the time of Jefferson's swearing-in, we didn't have an acting president for eight hours."

"All I know is that Abigail is glad to have her husband at home again," Maggy replied. "The two of them have spent most of their married lives apart." Swallowing a bit of yam, she added an aside. "That said, Mrs. Adams has confided in me that, at times—when he gets in one of his cantankerous moods—she wants to ship him back to Washington."

Eli studied Asa, who sat across the table. He looked like he was ready to fall asleep. Eli felt the tug of slumber himself. It had been a long day's ride into Greenfield.

Maggy, on the other hand, was primed and ready for an evening of conversation. "And speaking of cantankerous, what happened to Annabelle Byrd?"

"Flew the coop," Eli quipped, eliciting a groan from Asa.

"When we got back to New Haven, she was gone," Asa said. "The authorities found her mother locked up and babbling in an upstairs bedroom and her father dead on the bed, where Annabelle had left him. But there was no sign of Annabelle or Martha."

"Where do you think they went?" Maggy asked her brother.

"It's hard to speculate. She no longer has access to her father's holdings, so all she's left with is what she was able to cart off. She can't go far."

"And the Illuminati can't help her," Eli added. "The authorities found a list of names. Annabelle probably kept it as some sort of insurance to protect herself. Anyway, they're on the run too. If the authorities catch up with them, they'll be charged with treason against the United States and conspiracy to assassinate the president."

"Well, I'd be lying if I said I felt sorry for her," Maggy said. "She's getting exactly what she deserves."

"You never did like her," Asa complained. "You just didn't know her like we did. Actually, she was a lot of fun to be with."

"Never had so much fun in my life," Eli agreed.

Maggy threw a yam at him.

While Asa chopped wood, Eli helped Maggy with the dishes. She washed. He dried.

It was Maggy who had assigned the chores after dinner. Asa accepted his assignment willingly. He closed the door behind him with a half-grin on his face.

"What are your plans?" Maggy asked.

Eli finished drying a cup, set it aside, and reached for another one. "I'll probably go back to Kentucky to see my folks. I have some apologizing to do."

"I'm sure they'll be glad to see you. Are you going to tell them about how you almost killed my brother in a duel?"

Eli cringed. "I may leave that part out."

Maggy smiled. "What then?"

Eli stared vacantly at the wall, as though he could read the future by it. "I may come back here for the summer. Get a job. Something to tide me over until school starts again. What do you think of that?"

"Of what?"

"My spending the summer here."

Maggy's attention was on the dishes. "Greenfield's as good a place as any, I suppose."

"It's just something Asa said, that's all."

Maggy glanced at him askance. She saw through the setup but asked anyway. "What did Asa say?"

Eli grinned. "He told me you said there might be hope for me."

"Oh, that. You must have misunderstood. I told him I didn't think there was any hope for you."

EPILOGUE

In the fall of 1801 Eli Cooper and Asa Rush were reinstated to Yale College. Four years later, Asa Rush graduated with honors. He went on to become a tutor and, later, a professor of philosophy at Yale.

Erwin Ruggles, Rufus Tappan, and Sam Gurdon followed their call to the frontier. They formed a band of itinerant preachers that soon grew to two dozen men preaching the Word of God to the far reaches of the western territory, a mission that expanded greatly when President Thomas Jefferson secured the Louisiana Purchase from France. Calling themselves the Band of Citizen Preachers, they wore identifying silver necklaces of a cross superimposed over a guillotine.

Under Dr. Timothy Dwight's leadership, Yale College became Yale University. His powerful presence and imposing intellect equipped students with the necessary leadership skills America needed at the beginning of a new century. While Dwight was proud of all his accomplishments at Yale, the one he spoke most fondly of was the students' spreading the campus revival beyond the campus boundaries.

Among the greatest of these students was Reverend Eli Cooper. A dynamic and popular preacher, Cooper became best known for sparking the great foreign-missionary movement of the nineteenth century.

He and his wife, Maggy, had one child, Daniel.

Iſt ſedmych y mey zyetliwoſci.

In cœlo et clariſsimam ſolem nigra nubes par

AUTHORS' NOTES

To tell this story, we departed from a strict chronology of events in order to portray what it was like to live during the last decade of the eighteenth century. To do this, we telescoped an entire decade into roughly a year. The actual events from which we drew were spread over a period stretching from 1793 to 1802. For example, if we were to use the same approach to portray the 1960s, we might include such things as Vietnam, rock-and-roll, the assassinations of Kennedy and King, and the birth of the Jesus Movement compacted into twelve months.

Historical events places, and persons that appear in the book include:

- *Yale College*: The life on campus during this time period, including textbooks, course of instruction, discipline (trimmings), the facilities and surrounding area, such as East Rock, which was and still is a popular recreational getaway.

- *Dr. Timothy Dwight and the Yale revival*: The Yale Revival is a matter of record, as is Dwight's battle against the popular teachings of French philosophers. We have done our best to describe the man, his personality, and his tremendous influence on the students. His sermons, from which we drew directly, can still be read and enjoyed today.

- *Kentucky revivals*: Popularly known as the Cane Ridge revivals. Events portrayed in this story are drawn from eyewitness accounts.

- *The French Revolution*: Citizen Genet, his popular reception, the secret societies he left in his wake, and the riot outside President Washington's Philadelphia residence; Americans calling each other "Citizen"; Jean-Paul Marat; Robespierre; the Reign of Terror, and the shipment of guillotines to America. All these are historical.

- *The election of 1800*: the vitriol of the election that drove a wedge between John Adams and Thomas Jefferson, once good friends; Alexander Hamilton's letter criticizing his own president and dooming Adams's chances of reelection; Burr's irascible personality and political tactics; the electoral tie; and the account of Jefferson's inauguration day. The animosity between the Federalists and Democrat-Republicans (called Jeffersonians in the text so as not to confuse modern readers) cannot be overstated. The fear that Federalists would not relinquish power and that the new White House would have to be taken by force was real. To characterize the election as a bloodless revolution is not an understatement.

- *Duels and the Code Duello*: While outlawed by most states and preached against from pulpits, they remained a popular way of settling disputes. The most famous was the duel fought a few years after the scope of this book by Alexander Hamilton and Aaron Burr.

- *Secret societies and the Illuminati*: popular during this time period and a valid threat to national order, especially during the height of the French Revolution.

AUTHORS' NOTES

Fictional events and persons that appear in the book include:

- *Asa Rush and Eli Cooper*: Their rivalry allows us to explore the colliding worlds of revival and revolution. Asa's innovative forms of witnessing are products of the authors' imaginations and are not recommended as models for personal witnessing. We recommend sticking with the Four Spiritual Laws.

- *Annabelle Byrd, Captain Byrd, Martha, and Jacob Benson*: Though they moved in a real world and handled real-world things (such as the novel *Tristram Shandy*), these personages are fictional and are not intended to represent any real or historical persons.

- *The boys from Yale*: Sam Gurdon, Erwin Ruggles, and Rufus Tappan; their conversion; their itinerant society and its symbol are not historical but are meant to inspire historical acts of Christian brotherhood.

- *The revival at the New Haven docks*: While dramatic and symbolic, this revival is fictional; it pales compared to the miraculous conversions that take place every day when Christians take their faith, their personal witness, and the power of the Holy Spirit seriously.

Ysłat se drużyną y mey zyerkbwossi.

In ... et clarissimam ... solem nigra nubes ...

Ysłat se drużyną y mey zyerkbwossi.

In ... et clarissimam ... solem nigra nubes ...

Agunt

READ THE SNEAK PREVIEW

OF THE EXCITING FOURTH BOOK

IN THE

GREAT AWAKENINGS SERIES

FURY

1825-1826

BY

BILL BRIGHT & JACK CAVANAUGH

Egregiis viri domini Nicolai Cocinii [illegible]
[illegible] collegii [illegible] [illegible] [illegible] [illegible]
Andreae [illegible] et [illegible] [illegible] [illegible]
Omnibus [illegible] [illegible] [illegible] [illegible]
[illegible]
[illegible]
[illegible] y mey zyczliwosci.
In coelo et clarissimum solem nigra nubes pa

Egregiis viri domini Nicolai Cocinii [illegible]
[illegible] collegii [illegible] [illegible] [illegible] [illegible]
Andreae [illegible] et [illegible] [illegible] [illegible]
Omnibus [illegible] [illegible] [illegible] [illegible]
[illegible]
[illegible]
[illegible] y mey zyczliwosci.
In coelo et clarissimum solem nigra nubes pa

Agunt

[illegible]

CHAPTER 1

Once again his best friend had betrayed him.

Sixteen-year-old Daniel Cooper sat sulking atop a wooden barrel behind Gregg's Casket Shop, hunched against the winter night. A shaft of moonlight sliced the blind alley into two halves. Daniel sat in the dark half, in a dark mood.

He wanted only two things in life: to play his music and to be left alone. Was that asking too much? Yet every time he played, someone showed up, drawn to the music like flies to honey.

"Why can't they just leave me alone?"

He stared at Judas, his black bass recorder. He used to call the woodwind his Faithful Friend because it understood him. It never judged him. And it always reflected his mood. Lately, however, he'd renamed it Judas for obvious reasons.

Even so, it was a sweet betrayal. If a soul could sing, Daniel's soul would be mistaken for a recorder—a lone, haunting voice that did not belong to this world. Most people he knew preferred a lively fiddle or a foot-stomping banjo. Not Daniel. When he played the recorder, his very being vibrated with matching pitch.

The instrument was silent now. So was the street, which wasn't surprising at this late hour.

"Dare we try again, old friend?"

He lifted the mouthpiece to his lips.

Closed his eyes.

And played.

The alley came alive with music, a mournful tune that wafted from wall to wall to wall, surrounding him, penetrating him. Daniel's soul sighed with pleasure.

He'd played less than a minute when a discordant animal noise slashed the melody. Frowning, Daniel lowered the recorder and listened.

The night lay under silent stars.

Daniel was certain he'd heard something. Possibly a complaining cat. He cocked an ear in the direction of the street. Whatever it was, it was gone.

Once again the recorder touched his lower lip, but before it uttered a sound, the noise repeated itself.

A painful, moaning sound. A wounded cry.

There was a scuffle on the cobblestones, then another moan.

Daniel's heart seized. This time it didn't sound like an animal.

Just then a man stumbled into the mouth of the alley and collapsed. He whimpered. Tried to get up. Collapsed again.

Startled, Daniel's first impulse was to flee. Brick walls on three sides blocked his escape.

The man in the alley lie facedown, his breathing ragged and labored. He obviously needed help, though Daniel was at a loss as to what to do.

Setting the recorder aside, he slid off the barrel.

Two cautious steps and he pulled back, stopped short by an unseen voice. High-pitched, it sounded like a child playing a game. Only it wasn't a child. And if this was a game, Daniel didn't want to play.

"Come out, come out! Where are you?"

The man on the ground heard the voice. It stirred him to life. Whimpering, the man's hands clutched at the icy cobblestones. He dragged himself deeper into the alley.

"Come out, come out!" sang the voice.

Daniel reversed his direction and dove behind a stack of barrels. Then, scrambling to the balls of his feet, he crouched, ready to explode out of the alley like a ball shot from a cannon.

It was at that moment that Daniel realized he'd left his recorder sitting in plain sight atop the barrel. He rose up to reach it, then stopped.

At the mouth of the alley, the voice had taken shape. A silhouette stood against the streaking moonlight.

Broad-rimmed hat.

Shoulder-length hair.

Knee-length travel coat.

And in the man's right hand—a knife large enough to gut a bear.

"Asa, he's gone."

Camilla stood in the doorway of the study, one hand worrying the other.

"Did you look in the—"

"I think I scared him off." Her voice quivered as she spoke. Her eyes, normally a portrait of compassion, revealed a tender soul that was as attractive to Asa Rush now as it had been two decades ago when he first fell in love with her.

"When I went to slop the hogs," she continued, "I thought I heard somebody behind the barn. I stopped and listened. Then I heard music. Oh Asa, he has such talent."

Asa slammed shut his book. Chair legs scraped against the floor. He reached for his coat and hat and cane. "A man can't support a family playing a pipe. Where did you see him last?"

"Running into the forest. When he finished his song, I clapped. Then, when I went to tell him how beautiful it was, all I saw was his back disappearing into the woods."

She stepped aside. His cane striking the floor with force, Asa strode past her.

"Don't wait up," he said.

"Go easy on him, Asa. It's been hard on him."

"It's been almost a year. Long enough for him to know we have rules in this house. Long enough to know I expect him to obey them."

"There you are!"

The silhouette at the mouth of the alley held his arms wide. The tone of his voice was playful, but the blade in his hand was deadly serious.

From his hiding place in the back of the alley, Daniel could hear the hunted man, but not see him.

"No . . . no . . . please, no," he pleaded. "I haven't told anyone, I swear."

The hunter threw the man's words back at him in a singsong voice. "I won't tell . . . I won't tell . . . Please don't hurt me!" Then the tone of his voice changed. Hard. Menacing. "You know, I believe you," the hunter said. "Honestly, I do. But do you know why? I'll tell you. I believe you because it's hard for a man to tell anyone anything when he has no tongue. Harder still when he has no heartbeat."

The hunted man's whimpers turned to grunts. From the scratching sounds and the way the barrels shook, Daniel feared the man was trying to claw his way up them. The stack shuddered and threatened to topple. Daniel braced them from his side.

There was a scuffle. Then a scream bounced off the same walls that, moments earlier, had provided sweet acoustics for his recorder.

The stack of barrels gave an earthquake rattle. Daniel looked up just as one of the barrels tipped over the edge toward him. He ducked. It hit him on the back with force, flattening him. He winced and bit back a yelp of pain as his head slammed against the cobblestones, the side of his face resting in a slushy patch of melting snow.

When he opened his eyes, to his horror, his head stuck out from behind the last barrel. He could see the length of the alley . . . and be seen . . . if he didn't scoot back.

At that instant a mirror image of his fall occurred on the other side of the barrel. The hunted man's head hit the ground, his face toward Daniel. He was dirty, bloodied, eyes scrunched in pain. Then he opened them.

Both men's faces lit with recognition.

"Braxton!" Daniel mouthed.

He knew it was a mistake the moment he said the name, because his bloodied mirror image began to say his name in reply. "Da—"

Braxton never got a chance to finish. A hand grabbed him by the hair and lifted his head. A flash of silver crossed his neck.

Braxton's head hit the ground a second time. This time, however, nothing reflected in his eyes. The light in them had gone out.

Daniel began to shiver with fear. He bit back a whimpering sound. If the killer heard him . . . .or if he moved, so would the barrel on top of him and, for all he knew, he could set off an avalanche of barrels.

All he could do was to lie still.

Not make a sound.

Not breathe.

And stare into the lifeless eyes of Horace Braxton.

Daniel's heart jumped at the sound of whistling. But whistling was good, wasn't it? If the killer had spotted him, he wouldn't be whistling, would he? He'd be killing. Whistling was good.

Then it stopped.

Braxton's head moved away from Daniel. Was dragged away.

The back of the killer came into view. He pulled Braxton by one arm, then dropped it. Braxton's lifeless arm hit the ground with a fleshy *thud*.

The killer straddled the body. He searched Braxton's pockets. Then, when he grabbed Braxton's shirt to roll him over, the killer's head crossed into the moonlight. His hair fell to one side, revealing a tattoo of a coiled snake on the back of his neck.

From the street came the sound of an approaching carriage. The killer crouched. His knife, looking eager for more blood, poised for action.

The carriage stopped at the end of the alley.

"There you are," said a voice that was familiar to Daniel.

The killer relaxed.

The man in the carriage climbed down and entered the alley on foot. "Did you find—" A cry of revulsion cut short his sentence. "Why didn't you warn me? You know I can't stand the sight of—"

Retching sounds echoed in the alley.

Daniel watched as the man slipped on an icy patch, catching himself on the side of his carriage. Hunched over, he steadied himself with a hand on the wheel. It took him several minutes to recover.

Meanwhile, the killer finished his business with Braxton. Heaving the dead man onto his shoulder, he strolled toward the carriage as casually as a sailor would carry a bag aboard ship.

"The deed is done; payment is due," said the killer.

Averting his eyes and steadying himself all the way around the carriage, the man climbed into the seat. "Just get rid of that thing. Come to the shop tomorrow. I'll have your money."

With his free hand, the killer touched his hat to signal farewell.

ABOUT THE AUTHORS

Bill Bright passed away in 2003, but his enduring legacy continues. He was heavily involved in the development of this series with his team from Bright Media and Jack Cavanaugh.

Known worldwide for his love of Jesus Christ and dedication to sharing the message of God's grace in everything he did, Bill Bright founded Campus Crusade for Christ International. From a small beginning in 1951, the organization he began had, in 2002, more than 25,000 full-time staff and over 553,000 trained volunteer staff in 196 countries in areas representing 99.6 percent of the world's population. What began as a campus ministry now covers almost every segment of society, with more than seventy special ministries and projects that reach out to students, inner cities, governments, prisons, families, the military, executives, musicians, athletes, and many others.

Each ministry is designed to help fulfill the Great Commission, Christ's command to carry the gospel to the entire world. The film *Jesus*, which Bright conceived and funded through Campus Crusade for Christ, is the most widely viewed film ever produced. It has been translated into more than 730 languages and viewed by more than 4.5 billion people in 234 countries, with 300 additional languages currently being translated. More than 148 million people have indicated making salvation decisions for Christ after viewing it live. Additional tens of millions are believed to have made similar decisions through television and radio versions of the *Jesus* film.

Dr. Bright held six honorary doctorate degrees: a Doctor of Laws from the Jeonbug National University of Korea, a Doctor of Divinity from John Brown University, a Doctor of Letters from Houghton University, a Doctor of Divinity from the Los Angeles Bible College and Seminary, a Doctor of Divinity from Montreat-Anderson College, and a Doctor of Laws from Pepperdine University. In 1971 he was named outstanding alumnus of his alma mater, Northeastern State University. He was listed in Who's Who in Religion and Who's Who in Community Service (England) and received numerous other recognitions. In 1973 Dr. Bright received a special award from Religious Heritage of America for his work with youth, and in 1982 received the Golden Angel Award as International Churchman of the Year.

Together with his wife, Vonette, he received the Jubilate Christian Achievement Award, 1982–1983, for outstanding leadership and dedication in furthering the gospel through the work of Campus Crusade and the Great Commission Prayer Crusade. In addition to having many other responsibilities, Bright served as chairman of the Year of the Bible Foundation, and he also chaired the National Committee for the National Year of the Bible in 1983, with President Ronald Reagan serving as honorary chairman. When Bright was named the 1996 recipient of the one-million-dollar Templeton Prize for Progress in Religion, he dedicated all of the proceeds of the award toward training Christians internationally in the spiritual benefits of fasting and prayer, and for the fulfillment of the Great Commission. Bright was also inducted into the Oklahoma Hall of Fame in November 1996.

In the last two years of his life, Bright received the first Lifetime

Achievement Award from his alma mater, Northeastern State University. He was also a corecipient, with his wife, of the Lifetime Inspiration Award from Religious Heritage of America Foundation. In addition, he received the Lifetime Achievement Award from both the National Association of Evangelicals and the Evangelical Christian Publishers Association, which also bestowed on him the Chairman's Award. He was inducted into the National Religious Broadcasters Hall of Fame in 2002. Dr. Bright authored more than one hundred books and booklets, as well as thousands of articles and pamphlets that have been distributed by the millions in most major languages.

Bill Bright celebrated being married to Vonette Zachary Bright for fifty-four years. They have two married sons, Zac and Brad, who are both actively involved in ministry today, and four grandchildren.

Jack Cavanaugh is an award-winning, full-time author who has published sixteen books to date, mostly historical fiction. His eight-volume American Family Portrait series spans the history of our nation from the arrival of the Puritans to the Vietnam War. He has also written novels about South Africa, the English versions of the Bible, and German Christians who resisted Hitler. He has published with Victor/Chariot-Victor, Moody, Zondervan, Bethany House, and Fleming H. Revell. His books have been translated into six languages.

The Puritans was a Gold Medallion finalist in 1995. It received the San Diego Book Award for Best Historical in 1994, and the Best Book of the Year Award in 1995 by the San Diego Christian Writers' Guild.

The Patriots won the San Diego Christian Writers' Guild Best Fiction award in 1996.

Glimpses of Truth was a Christy Award finalist in International Fiction in 2000.

While Mortals Sleep won the Christy Award for International Fiction in 2002; the Gold Medal in *ForeWord* magazine's Book of the Year contest in 2001; and the Excellence in Media's Silver Angel Award in 2002.

His Watchful Eye was a Christy Award winner in International Fiction in 2003.

Beyond the Sacred Page was a Christy Award finalist in Historical Fiction in 2004.

Jack has been writing full-time since 1993. A student of the novel for nearly a quarter of a century, he takes his craft seriously, continuing to study and teach at Christian writers' conferences. He is the former pastor of three Southern Baptist churches in San Diego county. He draws upon his theological background for the spiritual elements of his books. Jack has three grown children. He and his wife live in Southern California.

Look for the rest of

THE GREAT AWAKENINGS SERIES

In this suspenseful series, award-winning authors Bill Bright and Jack Cavanaugh explore the electrifying era of the Great Awakenings—one of the most controversial periods of American religious history.

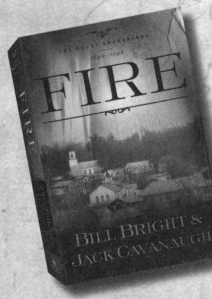

FIRE (1740–1741)

The scars of a long-ago fire haunt Josiah Rush as he dares to face his past and return home. But a deadly evil has infected the colony he once loved. Can he help the townspeople overcome this unseen enemy when he's still mistrusted for his old life?

PROOF (1857–1858)

Harrison Shaw, an aspiring young attorney, finds himself in the courtroom battle of his life—fighting against the father of the woman he loves and in defense of the Holy Spirit. But he soon finds that the Holy Spirit can defend Himself!

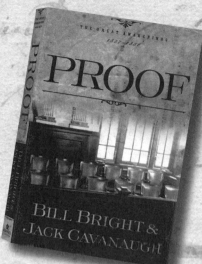

And Coming Soon . . .

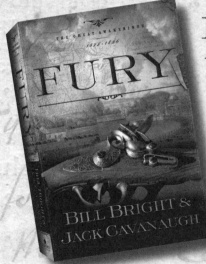

FURY (1825–1826)

Asa Rush inherits the fire of his grandfather, Josiah Rush, as he tracks his runaway nephew to Rome, New York, who has fled to escape a murderer. Unexpectedly, they all encounter a new kind of fire as they are set ablaze by the fiery sermons of Charles Finney.

"The Great Awakenings series will have readers waiting with Left Behind–like anticipation for the next episode."
—*Christian Music Planet* magazine

Enjoyment Guarantee

If you are not totally satisfied with this book, simply return it to us along with your receipt, a statement of what you didn't like about the book, and your name and address within 60 days of purchase to Howard Publishing, 3117 North 7th Street, West Monroe, LA 71291-2227, and we will gladly reimburse you for the cost of the book.